WIDOW
WOMAN

By the same author

In the Tildy series:

SARA FRASER

WIDOW WOMAN

WARNER BOOKS

A *Warner* Book

First published in Great Britain in 1991
by Macdonald
Published in 1991 by Futura
This edition published by Warner in 1994
Reprinted 1997

Printed in England by Clays Ltd, St Ives plc

ISBN 0 7515 0897 7

Warner Books
A Division of
Little, Brown and Company (UK)
Brettenham House
Lancaster Place
London WC2E 7EN

Introduction

England in 1830 was racked by turmoil. New machinery was driving men and women from their employment, and hunger and hardship stalked the land. Driven beyond endurance the needle workers of Redditch Town attempted to halt the inexorable march of progress, and violently challenged the forces of law and order.

Tildy Crawford was caught up in those bloody events, and this is the story of her part in them.

Chapter One

Studley Parish, Warwickshire
March 1828

The wind blustered from the east rattling the leafless branches of the hedgerows and cutting mercilessly through the threadbare clothing of the small gang of women and children gathering stones from the furrows of the ploughed field. Tildy Crawford straightened from her bending posture and kneaded the aching muscles along her spine with hands that were numbed with cold, then bent once more to lift the heavy stone-filled wooden bucket and carry it across the frozen ground to the horse and cart standing by the gate that led out into the lane.

The elderly carter, muffled in an ancient watchcoat and huddling against the vehicle in a vain effort to shield himself from the wind, grinned toothlessly as the young woman tipped her load over the tailgate, the stones cascading with a clatter upon the thick layer already covering the floor of the cart.

'‘Tis a hard way to earn your bread, arn't it, Tildy?’

She smiled ruefully. 'I'll not dispute that, Billy.'

His rheumed, red-rimmed eyes regarded her appreciatively. Even now with her body swathed in shapeless wrappings of sacking, a battered bonnet covering her glossy dark-brown hair, and her face chapped and reddened by the biting wind, Tildy Crawford was a beautiful woman.

A sudden harder gust of wind brought tears to both their eyes and the old man swung his arms and brought them thumping against his body.

1

'Bugger me, it fair chills your bloody innards, doon't it?'

Tildy nodded agreement, then qualified. 'It does, Billy, but at least it's keeping the mud away. Better frost than mud when you're picking stones.'

The man cackled with laughter. 'Gi'en the choice, I'd sooner ha' neither.'

Two small children came towards the cart carrying a half-filled bucket between them. A pang of pity struck through Tildy as she saw their hands blued with cold and their runny-nosed, pinched faces prematurely aged by want and hardship.

'What's this then? That arn't a bloody full 'un, is it?' The old man scolded the children, and Tildy was quick to intervene.

'For shame, leave the poor mites be. That bucket's too heavy for them to be mauling about if it's filled. Here, let me have it.' She took the bucket from them and upended its contents into the cart.

'Youm too sarft wi' these bloody kids,' the old man grumbled. 'You'd oughter know be now that iffen you gives 'um an inch, then they'll try and take a bloody mile.'

Tildy smiled at the children as she handed the bucket back to them. She patted their solemn faces and told them, 'Ne'er mind, lovies, it'll soon be time to go home.' Sudden anger coursed through her as she dwelt on the sparse rags covering their stick-thin bodies, and their bare dirty rickety legs, and to hide that anger from them she forced a smile. 'Off you go now, lovies. Don't stand about or you'll be catching your deaths of cold.'

Silently they obeyed her, dragging their broken clogs across the iron hard furrows as they returned to their harsh toil.

'Youm too sarft wi' 'um,' the carter scoffed, and she turned on him heatedly.

'It's a crying shame that tiny kids like those, little more than babes, should have to slave like this. They should be in school learning their lessons, not out here in the fields

2

labouring like brute beasts.'

The old man's toothless jaw gaped in surprise at this display of temper. Then recovering himself he answered jeeringly, 'Youm talking sarft now, girl. I was working in the fields when I was half their bleeding age, and it never done me no harm. If it was good enough for me, then I'm bloody sure it's good enough for them little buggers.' His jaw worked up and down as a fresh idea dawned on him.

'Besides, what's the good in bloody book larning for the likes o' them? Book larning is for the gentry, not for us to moither our yeds wi'. I arn't never had any book larning, and I arn't a bit the wuss for it neither. Book larning wun't help a man to use his scythe, or drive a cart, 'ull it? What good can book larning do for the likes of us, answer me that?' Without awaiting reply he answered his own question. 'No bloody good at all, girl, and you well knows it. It 'ud only serve to gi' folks ideas above their station. It's like the parson says, girl, God gives us all our stations, and we mun be content wi' 'um. And if a book-larned man like a parson says that, why then, it's got to be the God's truth, arn't it?'

Realising the futility of further argument Tildy only nodded resignedly. 'If you say so, Billy.' And taking her bucket in hand she went back to her work.

She bent low once more, her numbed fingers lifting the stones from the cold embrace of the earth as sleet flurried against her hunched body, the white flakes clinging to the rough sacking and alighting on the unprotected skin of face and neck to melt and add chill wetness to her myriad other discomforts. Nearby, the two children she had aided whimpered softly as the raw sores on their claw-like hands scraped painfully against the ground.

The flurries of sleet thickened and now larger firmer flakes swirled down and Tildy straightened and gazed up at the darkly lowering skies and saw that the air was thick with white swirls. She glanced around her at the lumpish figures scattered about the field, and shouted loudly, 'That's it. Bring what you've got to the cart.'

The women and children hastened to obey her, their bodies made stiff and clumsy by the cold and their feet stumbling across the iron-hard ridges of the furrows.

The old carter scowled doubtfully. 'Be you finishing work already?'

'Of course we are,' Tildy told him. 'I'm not forcing kids to work in a snowstorm.'

'The master wun't like this, not one little bit he wun't.'

'Then he'll just have to lump it, won't he,' Tildy replied tartly.

'But he wanted two more loads afore nightfall at least,' the old man argued mulishly. 'He wun't take it kindly, you skiving off like this. He wun't take it kindly at all.'

Tildy bit back the hot retort that sprang to her lips and instead said reasonably, 'Look Billy, this snow is falling thicker by the minute, and some of these women and kids have got to travel more than four miles to get home.'

A nervous quaver entered the old man's voice. 'But what am I agoing to tell him when he wants to know why the work arn't done?'

Tildy recognised his fear of his master and softened towards him. 'You can tell him that I called a halt because of the snowstorm. And tell him weather permitting we'll make up the loads tomorrow.'

By now all the buckets had been emptied into the cart and Tildy turned to the small huddle of women and children. 'Get off home with you now, before the snow lies too thick. We'll meet at the Barley Mow at crack of light tomorrow.'

Spirits lightened by this early reprieve from their gruelling labours, the group hurried through the gate and into the lane and away towards their homes. Left alone with the old carter Tildy offered, 'Look Billy, if you're feared of what your master will say to you, then if you like I'll come back to the farm now and explain to him why we've finished early.'

The old man gratefully hastened to accept her offer. ''Ull you do that, Tildy?'

She sighed heavily, thinking of the miles she had yet to trudge to her own home, then nodded. 'I will, Billy. Come now, let's be off shall we, before we're snowed in here.'

Mitchell the farmer was not at home when Tildy and old Billy reached the isolated farmhouse, but his wife, plump bodied and motherly, listened to Tildy's explanation of why the contracted number of cartloads had not been filled, and was quick to agree with the younger woman.

'O' course youm right to let your gang get away home now it's snowing so hard, Mrs Crawford. Doon't you pay no mind to what this silly old bugger says about my husband being angered by that. He's a fair-minded man.' The woman's eyes studied Tildy curiously, and after a momentary pause, she asked. ''Ull you take a sup o' tay afore you get's off, Mrs Crawford?' She saw demurral in the younger woman's expression, and hastened to add, 'Only there's summat I wants to ask you, and it'll not take more nor a minute.' She turned to the carter. 'You get to your work, Billy. 'Tis private between me and this young 'ooman.'

The old man shambled away across the farmyard, and Mrs Mitchell invited Tildy into her large warm kitchen. She waved to a chair at the side of the roaring fire in the great inglenook.

'Set yourself down theer, my duck, and get a bit o' goodness from that fire.'

Gratefully Tildy seated herself and held out her hands towards the leaping flames, feeling their heat bathing over her face and seeping through her damp cold clothing.

The dish of tea was steaming and Tildy sipped it, relishing its spicy fragrance. Mrs Mitchell seated herself on a chair facing Tildy's and leaned forwards causing her fat stomach and breasts to bulge hugely against the clean white apron that she wore. Beneath her floppy white mobcap the woman's face wore a curiously diffident expression, as she asked tentatively:

'Is it true that you lives wi' that old witch-'ooman,

Esther Smith, over at Mappleborough Green?'

Tildy was instantly defensive. 'Yes, it's true, I live with Esther Smith. But she's no witch.'

Mrs Mitchell was quick to placate her. 'No, Mrs Crawford, don't you take my words wrongly, for I mean no offence to the old soul. I suppose what I really want to know is if it's true that she can see the future, like folks says she can?'

Recognising that the other woman was driven by genuine curiosity and sensing that there was no harm in her, Tildy pondered for a moment, then told her: 'Well, Mrs Mitchell, although Esther's not a witch, yet she does seem to have some sort of powers in her at times. She's told me certain things which came to pass.'

Tildy had deliberately re-asserted that Esther Smith was not a witch, because she knew from personal experience that there were many people in the district who, dogged by superstition, believed that the old woman was truly a black witch, and as such was in league with the Devil.

''Ud she read the future for me, do you think?' the fat woman questioned.

Tildy smiled, having suspected that this question would come. 'Well, Mrs Mitchell, Esther's not well these days, so she hasn't been doing a deal of such conjuring lately.' She saw disappointment in the other woman's features, and added, 'But I'll ask her for you, if you want. Perhaps when she's feeling a bit better she'll do it for you.'

Mrs Mitchell was profuse in her thanks and Tildy took her leave and went back into the snowy cold to make her way home. The snow was already settling to blanket the earth and Tildy lifted a layer of the sacking from around her shoulders over her bonnet so that it formed a rough cowl around her head and sheltered her face from the tumbling flakes. The tumbledown cottage that she shared with her small son, Davy, and her friend, Esther Smith, was situated on the fringes of the wild heathland known as the Mappleborough Green, some three miles to the west of the farmhouse as the crow flew, but Tildy was reluctant to take the shorter cross country route to it in such heavy snowfall, so decided to stick to the cart lanes although it added another mile or so to the distance she must travel.

Her route traversed many small hills and the lanes were deeply rutted and potholed, but the snow cushioned the ground beneath her heavy iron-shod man's boots and at twenty-seven years of age her body was strong and lithe so in little more than an hour she breasted the final slope that lay between her and the heathland.

It was dusk when she walked up to the low-built cottage to be greeted by the barking of the two dogs that served both as pets and guardians, for the times were hard and lawless and two women living without men in this isolated spot needed added protection. The low door of the building swung open shedding the rosy glow of fire-light and silhouetted by that glow a small slender figure came running eagerly to meet her.

'Mam! Mam! Come quick! We'se got company. Nanny Esther's kin's come to see us!'

Tildy's heart welled with love as she lifted her son and hugged him, then kissed his rosy cheek while he struggled to be free. Aged seven and a half years, Davy Crawford considered he was now too grown up to be cuddled like a baby, particularly when company was in the near vicinity.

'Put me down, Mam. Put me down,' he demanded.

'Why should I?' she teased.

'Because I'm big now. I'm not a babby any longer.' His face was very serious beneath his mop of black curls.

Reluctantly Tildy released her son from her embrace and he scampered back into the cottage exclaiming excitedly, 'Mam's come, Nanny Esther. Mam's here!'

The whitewashed room was warm and fragrant with the smells of burning wood and dried herbs and from the iron pot slung above the hearth the bubbling scent of rabbit stew brought Tildy to acute awareness of how hungry she was.

'Here's Tildy, Daniel. Didn't I tell you her was a bonny

wench?' Old Esther's cracked voice held as much pride and affection as if Tildy had been born of her own loins, and indeed the old woman did look upon the younger as her daughter, and loved her very dearly.

The man rose from the rough-cut bench before the hearth and turned to disclose features that were hard-etched, and deeply bronzed by suns far savager than those to be found in England. His light blue eyes widened admiringly as Tildy removed the cowl-like sacking and battered bonnet from her glossy, neat-braided hair and smiled at him in welcome, disclosing her small white even teeth.

'This is Daniel Lambert, Tildy, me sister's youngest boy. Just come back from foreign parts, so he has.'

'You're very welcome here, Mr Lambert.' Tildy held out her hand and he took it in his own calloused palm and shook it warmly.

'Please, call me Daniel, and I shall call you Tildy, for I'm sure that we're well met, and shall prove to be good friends to each other.'

He was tall and strong-bodied, his shoulders and chest broad and thick beneath his red shirt and sailor-like reefer jacket, and he exuded a clean masculine smell of well-washed flesh and linen and tobacco. Tildy thought him very attractive physically, even though his sun-bleached light brown hair was thinning and two of his lower front teeth were broken. She judged him to be about thirty years old, but could detect no family resemblance in his features to the diminutive, withered features of old Esther.

The old woman rose from her own chair and busied herself at the hearth, ladling out the savoury stew into wooden bowls. She really did resemble the witches of fantasy, clad in rusty black, with bright piercing black eyes, a toothless jaw almost meeting her long hooked nose, her wrinkled skin as dark as a gypsy, and her grey and black hair hanging in long oily tendrils about her head and shawled shoulders.

'Come now, set yerselves down and ate some vittles. You can talk all you wants arter you'se got this across your chests.'

Thankfully Tildy seated herself at the fireside and spooned the hot stew into her mouth, savouring its delicious pungency and feeling its goodness replenishing the strength she had expended during her long hard day in the fields. As her body's needs were slowly assuaged she became increasingly aware of Daniel Lambert's covert scrutiny of her face and body, but this did not cause her any unease. Tildy was well accustomed to the admiring stares that many men directed upon her and accepted without vanity the fact that many men considered her to be beautiful.

The simple meal was washed down with glasses of tart-tasting homebrewed cider and, replete, Tildy gathered the utensils and put them by the outer door to be washed later in the small stream that ran close by the cottage. She returned to her seat on the wooden chair facing opposite to old Esther's and Davy came to sit on the floor before her and lean back against her legs. She gently stroked his curly head while Daniel Lambert produced a short-stemmed clay pipe from his pocket and filled its bowl from a small leather tobacco pouch. Clouds of strong-scented smoke wreathed around the man's shortcut hair as he used a twig from the fire to light his pipe, and Tildy suddenly realised that at this particular moment of her life, seated in this warm room, her loved ones beside her, she was experiencing a rare moment of perfect contentment.

As Daniel Lambert stretched forward to return the glowing twig to the fire the sleeve of his coat and shirt was drawn back and Tildy noticed tattooing upon his muscular forearm.

'Are you a sailor, Mr Lambert?' she asked curiously.

He mock frowned. 'My name is Daniel to you.' Then he smiled and shook his head. 'No, Tildy, I'm no sailor, for all that I've sailed many and many a thousand miles.'

He glanced briefly at his aunt and winked reassuringly, then said quietly, 'It's no secret, Tildy, as far as I'm concerned anyway. I'm not a sailor, I'm a returned transport.'

Tildy took a sharp intake of breath and sudden apprehension flooded through her as if her subconscious mind had a presentiment of what he would say next.

He coughed as if nervous and his light-blue eyes mirrored uncertainty. Hesitantly he began. 'I've that to tell you, Tildy, that may come as a great shock. Perhaps it might be better left unsaid until a little later.' His eyes flickered meaningfully downwards at little Davy. The child was half-asleep, made drowsy by food and warmth, and had not appeared to have noticed this interchange between his elders or taken any cognisance of Daniel Lambert's words.

Tildy experienced a peculiar sensation of an increasing constriction within her chest and as her apprehension strengthened it seemed that the air became increasingly difficult to breathe. Old Esther recognised the younger woman's burgeoning turmoil and, with a strength that belied her appearance of bodily fragility, gathered the drowsy child up into her arms and disregarding his sleepy protests carried him through to the bedroom, the only other room in the one-storeyed cottage.

'You goo to sleep now, my precious.' Her cracked voice came muffled through the partition wall. 'You close your eyes because there's some lovely dreams coming to you. You'll be seeing fairies this night, old Nanny Esther knows that for a fact. The fairies be awaiting to come and visit you in your dreams. They'se told me so. So you close your eyes now, my precious, and sleep.'

The shadows wavered across the while walls as the flames leapt and fell and Daniel Lambert leaned forwards so that his elbows rested on his thighs and his bronzed face was ruddied by firelight. He kept his gaze fixed on the burning wood and his strong hands toyed with the clay pipe as he told Tildy in a low voice, "Tis a hell of a coincidence, you living here wi' my old auntie, Tildy. When she told me who you were and all about you I couldn't believe my ears, and that's a fact.

'Like I told you, I'm a returned transport. I've bin out

in Australia for ten years. Got sentenced to seven years transportation back in 'eighteen. I'd got taken by Squire Littleton's keepers in the castle woods over the Studley wi' a few prime birds under me coat-tails.' He grinned mirthlessly. 'Littleton was real happy to have me committed to the assizes, I'll take my oath on that. He reckoned I'd been the scourge of his coverts for a deal too long. Anyway, off I went to Botany Bay, and being a rebellious bugger who could ne'er learn to keep his mouth shut, I very soon found meself on Norfolk Island. It lies about a thousand miles east of Australia and some four hundred miles from New Zealand. I believe that Lord Bathurst ordered Governor Brisbane to prepare "A place of ultimate terror for the incorrigibles of the system".'

He paused, and his hard-etched features momentarily became a mask of savage bitterness. 'It's that all right.' He spat the words. 'It truly is.'

He fell silent, and the silence lengthened until Tildy stirred uneasily and at this Daniel Lambert smiled directly at her and said apologetically, 'Forgive me, Tildy, I was remembering things that I'd sooner forget.'

His smile metamorphosed into solemnity. 'Your husband, Tom Crawford, came out to Norfolk Island in the summer of 'twenty-six, Tildy, it seems he'd been bonded out to a merchant in Sydney as a manservant, and he made a bit too free wi' the cove's wife. The merchant was a big friend of the Governor's, and so Tom Crawford ended up in the chain gang wi' the rest of us.

'We always used to enquire for them who came from our own part o' the world, and so I got talking wi' your husband a few times. I was always greedy for news of home you see. I won't say that me and him were friends, because to speak frankly he wasn't the type o' man that I cared for, but we used to talk about these parts, and he often spoke about you.'

Again his narrative halted for a few moments, and he smiled grimly. 'Tom Crawford didn't lie when he said how pretty you are, Tildy. But after hearing what Aunt

Esther has to say about you and the way you've had to struggle, and then meeting you myself, well, I know now that he lied about a lot of other things. Anyway, you're free of him, Tildy.'

'Free?' Her voice was tremulous, and Daniel Lambert's hand reached out and covered her nervously entwined fingers as if to comfort her, and told her softly, 'Tom Crawford died on Norfolk Island, Tildy. I was one of those who dug his grave and helped lower him into it. You've been a widow woman for more than two years.'

Concern showed in his eyes as he saw the sudden pallor of her face.

'Are you all right, Tildy? I'm sorry to have told you so blunt, but there's no easy way to give such tidings.'

She shook her head. 'I'm all right, it's only that this has come as a shock to me.' She drew several long deep breaths, her eyes downcast, then looked directly at the man.

'How did he die?'

Lambert shrugged his broad shoulders. 'There was a fight, Tildy. Tom Crawford was stabbed. He died quick and suffered little. The sort o' death that all on us there prayed for at one time or another. It's a living hell, Norfolk Island is, and a convict's life is held very cheap. Men kill without compunction there, because for some the hangman's rope is counted as a blessed release.' He suddenly shook his head as if to drive the memories from his mind and apologised. 'Forgive me for bringing such grievous news to you. I'd no wish to cause you grief and distress.'

The initial shock of the news was rapidly passing and although her face was still pale the young woman's voice was steady as she said quietly, 'I'll not lie and play the hypocrite, Daniel. I hated Tom Crawford while he lived, so I won't pretend to feel any grief for his death. My only sorrow is for my little Davy, to have had for father a man who showed him no love or care. I dread the day when I must tell him how Tom Crawford came to his death, and why he was out in Botany Bay to begin with. Davy may well feel shamed.'

'Then don't tell the boy,' Daniel Lambert urged, but Tildy shook her head sadly.

'If I could be certain that no other would ever tell him, then I'd keep it a secret to my grave. But you know as well as I do that there are always those who take delight in carrying such tales. No, when I judge the time is right, then I'll tell him myself. It's best he should hear the story from my lips.' She grimaced bleakly. 'If Tom Crawford had been transported for poaching it wouldn't be shame, not in these times. But he was transported for mean, vicious crimes.'

'Then let it be later rather than sooner when the boy is told, Tildy.'

She nodded agreement, and Daniel Lambert removed his hand from hers as old Esther came back into the room and announced, 'The babby's sleeping like a little angel, bless him.'

Her bright bird-like eyes flashed a silent question at Daniel Lambert and he nodded slightly, causing the old woman's head to bob in satisfaction. She perched on her chair and briefly studied Tildy's features as the young woman gazed into the fire. She then caught Daniel Lambert's eyes and with a jerk of her head indicated that he should leave.

The man nodded, and got to his feet. 'I must be getting back to Redditch, Aunt.'

Tildy looked up at him. 'We can make a bed of sorts up for you before the fire here, Daniel.'

'That's very kind of you, but I've already paid for a bed at the Unicorn Inn over in Redditch there.' He paused and regarded Tildy speculatively for a couple of seconds, then asked, 'But can I call on you again, Tildy, and talk with you?'

'It's your aunt's house, Daniel, I cannot forbid you it.' Her tone was deliberately neutral and he had sensitivity enough not to press her for another answer.

After Esther Smith had seen him out of the door she came to stand at Tildy's side and gently squeezed the young woman's shapely shoulder.

'I'm away to bed, Tildy. You set here awhiles and try to get used to the fact that youm a free 'ooman again. You can think better when youm by yourself.'

Tildy smiled briefly at her, then stared into the fire once more, and the old woman left her. Tildy felt curiously dazed, her mind blank, and she gazed unseeingly before her as the flames lowered and the wood cracked and settled and dulled; her head drooped in exhaustion and sleep imperceptibly stole over her.

Tildy awoke with a slight start, cold and stiff from her inadvertent sojourn on the hard wooden chair. The fire was dead ashes and the room was very dark. She grimaced and rose to fumble her way to the outer door.

Outside the air was still and the sky black with cloud, but the thick snow imparted a faint luminosity and Tildy could see her white pluming breath before her face. The clean icy air cleared the fug of sleep from her brain and she swung her arms and moved briskly around to warm the stiffness from her body.

Random thoughts entered and left her mind, memories of her violent, loveless marriage. Her lips twisted bitterly as she remembered how Tom Crawford had raped her, and how she had been forced into marrying him back in 1820 because that rape had left her pregnant with little Davy.

'Stop tormenting yourself with such memories,' she told herself angrily. 'You're free of that devil now. Free!' A sudden exultation flooded through her, and she lifted her arms high and wide and laughed aloud into the silent night. 'Free! I'm free, at last! I'm free!'

Chapter Two

The ancient half-timbered coaching inn known as the Barley Mow stood in the centre of Studley village where the roads from Redditch and from Crabbs Cross joined the turnpike road that ran north to the City of Birmingham, and south through Alcester village to Stratford Town.

As the day dawned on a snow-mantled landscape Tildy met the small gang of women and children outside the arched entrance to the Barley Mow's stableyard. Despite the early hour the inn was already awake and bustling with preparations to greet the travellers that the morning would bring to its doors and from its kitchens the appetizing smells of baking bread and frying bacon wafted on the still air to torment the hungry women and children clustered around Tildy, whose own mouth watered freely as she smelled the cooking.

'Right, are we all here then?' Tildy counted heads, then asked a shivering gaunt-bodied woman, 'Where's your daughter, Moll?'

'I'se had to leave her at home, Tildy. Her was coughing and wheezing all bloody night through. Her arn't fit to do a tap this day.'

Tildy nodded understandingly. 'It's best to leave her indoors then, Moll,' and as she looked at the pathetic faces of the other children in the gang thought pityingly, 'I wish all of these poor mites could be left indoors in weather like this.'

Her thoughts turned to her own child, Davy, and fiercely she vowed to herself, 'I'll never bring Davy out to work, not while I've strength enough to lift a hand. I'll get him educated somehow so that he'll never have to labour like a slave just to earn a crust, like these poor souls must do.'

'Come on then, let's get off to Mitchell's,' she said aloud and led her shabby, ragged group away from the inn.

'Does you reckon Mitchell 'ull have work for us this day, Tildy?' the gaunt-featured Moll asked anxiously. 'Only I arn't got a penny piece in the house.' She gestured with one grimy hand at the thick snow through which they crunched. 'We arn't agoing to be able to pick bloody stones wi' this lot hanging about, am we?'

Tildy reluctantly agreed. 'No, that's a fact, Moll. But we'll see if he's got anything else we can do. There was wind last night, and maybe his lane's drifted up. We might find work shovelling it clear. And if not that, there's bound to be something or other for us to do.'

Despite her outward show of confidence, inwardly Tildy doubted that they would be able to find work at Mitchell's farm that day, and she wished fervently for a sudden thaw to melt the snow from the earth, then smiled wryly at her own foolishness. 'Rather than wish for a miracle like that, I'd do better to wish for a pot of gold; there's as much chance of one coming as the other, after all.'

'No, my wench, I've naught for you today, not while this snow's about.' Mitchell's broad red face was regretful, because he was a kind-hearted man who had a genuine sympathy for these wretched women and children standing so forlornly in the snow outside his yard door.

He smiled kindly, 'I'll pay you for what you'se done up to yesterday, and then when this lot's melted you can come back and do a bit more stone picking for me if you wants.'

'Thank you for that, Master Mitchell. I'm very grateful for it.' There was no hidden irony in Tildy's words. She knew that small farmers like Mitchell were also having a

16

hard struggle to make ends meet in these years of bad harvests and trade recessions and was grateful to him for having found some sort of employment for them during these last few days.

'Just hold on here for a minute, 'ull you, my duck,' the man requested, and went back inside his farmhouse. When he reappeared he was carrying in his hands a dish piled with cold boiled potatoes. 'Here you be. Share these among you.'

Eager hands stretched out and in seconds the dish was empty and mouths chewed voraciously. The farmer shook his head in a gesture of compassion, then shrugged and, handing coins to Tildy, asked, 'won't the parish gi' you anything, my duck?'

Tildy shrugged. 'I think some of the women get a few shillings allowed them, but that's not sufficient to care for their children properly, and some of the poor creatures have husbands who drink the parish allowance away in the beershops.' A flash of anger caused her to add, 'There's none of them would be looking for work in this weather unless it was really necessary, would they?'

'How about you, my duck? Does you get aught from the parish?'

Tildy shook her head sharply and not wishing to continue this conversation thanked Mitchell for the potatoes and money he had given them and led her followers away. The man stood watching as they went, his eyes intent upon the figure of Tildy Crawford. She moved gracefully despite her heavy boots and makeshift sack coverings and the man pursed his lips thoughtfully.

'What's a clane pretty cratur like you doing wi' that bloody lot, I wonder? There must be many a man who'd be only too willing to look arter you.' He grinned with self-mockery. 'Including me, if truth be told.'

Once away from the farm Tildy gathered the others around her and shared the coins out. Each woman, including herself, received exactly the same amount, and each child exactly half that sum. She sighed as she looked at the pathetically few coins left in her hand. Ten pence, and for that she had laboured from dawn until dusk, in hail, sleet, and biting winds for the last three days.

'Ah well,' she told herself resignedly. 'Ten pence is better than no pence. At least we'll all eat tomorrow.' Her eyes fell upon one small frail-appearing woman whose worn face bore scars and bruises inflicted by brutal beatings. 'And mayhap it'll save you from being hammered this night by that animal you're wed to, Irene. You can give him his beer money now. That might persuade him to let you alone for once.'

Having herself been married to a wife-battering drunkard, Tildy's heart bled for those tragic defenceless women who were in that same plight and bitterly resented the fact that in her world married women were considered to be merely the chattels of their husbands, and this was enshrined in the law of the land.

'What now, Tildy?' Moll, the gaunt-faced woman sought to know. 'Wheer can we try for work now?'

'I'm trying to think where myself,' Tildy acknowledged ruefully and glanced up at the cloud-heavy sky. 'I wonder if it's going to snow again.'

She was uncomfortably aware that all the others were also waiting for her leadership in this search for work and experienced a sudden exasperation that she should be in this position. 'I've worries enough of my own without having to look out for these as well.' Then her eyes fell upon the face of one of the children, and seeing the trust with which he regarded her a sense of shame swept over her at her own reactions to their need. 'They're desperate, God help them. But where can I take them now? Who is there who has any work to give us?'

Chapter Three

Redditch, Parish of Tardebigge, Worcestershire

Daniel Lambert tilted the pot high and drained the last of the ale, then gusting a sigh of satisfaction set down the empty pot on the table in front of him and signalled the tapster to refill it. Lambert had breakfasted well on beefsteaks and fresh eggs and new baked bread, and now, happily replete, he leaned back in the wooden armchair and stretched his booted feet towards the blazing fire while his fingers filled a new long-stemmed clay pipe with tobacco. Clouds of strong smelling smoke wreathed his head as he contentedly puffed his pipe and took sips from his refilled pot. The tap-room of the Unicorn was quiet, only he and the old tapster present, but he knew that as the morning passed it would begin to fill, the day being Saturday when the market was held in the town. For now he was happy to sit here quietly digesting his breakfast and reflecting on the dramatic changes his life had undergone during the past year.

Thomas Mence, landlord of the Unicorn Inn came into the taproom and exchanged a few words with his employee who was lounging behind the high narrow serving counter which stood at one end of the long narrow room. His small eyes set close together in his plump florid face stared hard at the man seated before the fire halfway down the room and he frowned slightly as faint recognition tugged at his memory.

'Is that the one who come yesterday night?' he asked the tapster.

The man nodded disinterestedly. 'Ahr, gaffer, that's

him. I put him in number three. He paid for three nights in advance.'

'What's his name?' Mence asked.

'He ne'er said.'

Mence's eyes remained fixed on the sun-bronzed profile and the naggingly elusive sense of recognition persisted irritatingly.

'Does he sound like a local?'

'Ahr, gaffer. But there's times he doon't.'

'What sort of an answer is that, you old fool?' Mence hissed.

The tapster shrugged. 'Whatever sort you wants to mek on it, gaffer. Sometimes he sounds local, and sometimes he doon't. That's all I can tell you. Especially seeing as how he arn't spoke above a few words to me.'

Thomas Mence was cursed with an excessive nosiness, particularly about people who stayed beneath his roof and he knew that he would have no peace of mind until he had found out all he possibly could about this mysterious newcomer. He prided himself on his local knowledge of people and places and had indeed until only a few months past acted in the capacity of postmaster for Redditch town. Now, unable to resist the impulse, he went to the fireplace and spoke to the stranger.

'Good day to you, sir. I trust everything's bin to your satisfaction. I'm Thomas Mence, proprietor of this establishment.'

The man grinned up at him. 'I know you, Tommy Mence. Known you since we were lads together.'

Thomas Mence's plump jaw gaped and quivered. 'Well bless me! It's you, arn't it! God strewth! I thought you was long dead!' His head shook rapidly from side to side. 'Well bless me! Does you know, I stood there looking at you and I thought I knew you. But you'se changed a deal, Daniel. You'se changed a great deal.'

Lambert smiled sardonically. 'Ten years such as I've spent will change any man, Tommy.'

Mence's expression became uncertain as remembrance

came fully. 'Yes, you was transported, warn't you? Must be near ten years since.'

'That's right,' Lambert agreed pleasantly. 'The pitcher went to the well once too often, didn't it? But in my case I haven't been broken. I'm back again as good as new.'

The innkeeper nodded agreement. 'Well, you certainly looks to be in good health, Daniel. There's no denying that.' He patted his own rotund belly. 'Mind you, we'em all getting older, arn't we?'

Now that his curiosity had been satisfied Thomas Mence began to wonder if his upstanding reputation in the district would permit him to be seen in friendly conversation with a man who was, after all, a returned convict and as such to be considered as something of a desperado and an unsavoury acquaintance for a successful man of business and pillar of the community such as himself.

As if sensing the other's burgeoning unease, Daniel Lambert terminated the conversation abruptly. 'It's been pleasant meeting you again, Tommy,' he said quietly and rose to his feet. 'And now I must bid you farewell for a time. I've errands to attend to.'

When he had gone Thomas Mence told the tapster, 'That's Daniel Lambert, that is. He was a wild bugger, I'll tell you. Got himself bloody well transported in the death. And now he's back again, just like a bad penny turning up. God strewth! Life's a queer thing, arn't it?'

A flight of worn stone steps led down into the courtyard from the taproom and as Daniel Lambert descended he pulled his wide brimmed hat low down over his eyes and turned up the collar of his reefer jacket against the chill breeze.

The Unicorn Inn stood on the top of the steep western slope that levelled onto the plateau which was the centre of Redditch Town. That plateau was bounded to the north by another sharp falling hillside. To the east the land fell away more gently but to the south were sharply rising slopes which narrowed abruptly into the long turnpiked ridgeway known as Mount Pleasant. A large triangular open green was bounded by varied rows and singled buildings on its three sides, and on the southwestern edge of the base of the triangular green stood the single storeyed Chapel of Saint Stephen, with its cupola and gothic window arches.

Daniel Lambert halted at the central crossroads opposite the chapel and let remembrance invade him. A lump came to his throat as he visualized the small boy walking with slate and satchel towards the school of Henry James which lay in Evesham Street that led southwards from the crossroads. A little later tears glistened in his eyes as he stood above the simple stone that marked his parents' final resting place in the chapel graveyard and remembered how that same small boy had stood by that same grave and sobbed with a breaking heart as the mother he loved above all else in his young life was lowered into the cold dank clay.

'How different my life would have been if you had lived, Mam,' Lambert thought sadly. 'But at least you were spared from the bitter shame of having a convict for a son. My poor Dad had to live with that.'

Remorse cut deep within his being. His mother and father had been God-fearing, respectable beings who would have died before knowingly breaking any of the Ten Commandments. Daniel Lambert had been the only child born to them who had lived beyond the third year. The small flat slab next to his parents' gravestone covered the remains of four of his siblings, none of whom had survived infancy.

He remained at the grave for almost an hour, oblivious to the curious looks and comments of passers-by on the other side of the railings that surrounded the chapel and its grounds, immersed totally in his memories. Slowly his initial pain and sadness lifted and he was able to smile fondly as he finally whispered, 'I don't know if you can somehow see or hear me, Mam and Dad. But I want you to know that I've always kept you in my heart, no matter where I've been, or what was happening to me. I'll try now to make you proud of me. I'll try to restore the name that I disgraced in the eyes of this town, I swear it.'

When he finally left the graveside he saw that on the southern side of the chapel green the market was now in full swing. A long line of canvas-covered stalls had been erected and traders' hoarse voices bawled their wares to the thronging crowds of early-shopping, white-aproned housewives, smock-clad country people and the varied loungers and hangers on and curiosity seekers that a mart always attracted.

There were sellers of pots and pans, crockery and earthenware, old clothes and new clothes and bolts of cloth, buttons and thread and hanks of wool, eggs, cheeses, butter, meat and bacon, sausages and black puddings, roasted chestnuts and baked potatoes, ginger snaps, toffees and humbugs, candles and oil lamps, pills and panaceas, coffee and tea and sassafras, gimcracks and geegaws of all descriptions, their vendors' chaffering and shouting mingling with the plaintive grunting, cackling, bleating, mooing of the live fowls, pigs, sheep and cows and horseflesh down at the eastern end of the line, where the square-towered, castellated, two-storeyed lock-up, the town jail, glowered in grim warning to potential wrong-doers.

As he passed through the crowds Daniel Lambert regarded the grey-stone lock-up with some interest. Having been built only four years before, it was new to him, as were several other of the buildings around the green. He grinned inwardly, a spark of mischief in his eyes. 'I don't doubt that if it had been here when I was a youngster then I'd have made its intimate acquaintance.'

The road branched at the lock-up, the right-hand fork being called Red Lion Street after the name of the public house which stood on it, the other fork being Alcester Street, which led on past the fetid, green-scummed water of the Big Pool and down through the outlying district of Bredon where it forked once more towards Beoley or Studley villages.

Daniel Lambert went along Alcester Street and left the bustle of the market behind him. His destination which lay midway between Bredon and the Big Pool was the great Fountain Needle Mill owned by Henry Milward, one of the foremost needle masters in the Redditch district; a district which held the distinction of being the world centre for the manufacture and distribution of needles, the production of which commodity engaged the services of the vast majority of the population of the town and its environs.

Daniel Lambert smiled again as he remembered once meeting an aborigine in far off Australia who wore a long sail-needle pushed lengthways through the gristle of his nose as prized adornment. 'I'll wager old Henry wouldn't take kindly to the idea of a black savage treating one of his precious needles as a geegaw.'

The massive wooden gates in the front wall of the tall structure were open and at the left hand side of the mill a horse plodded round and round hauling the huge horizontal gin wheel above its drooping head in endless circles to power the mill's machinery. As Daniel Lambert entered the gloomy archway he could hear the clattering and rumbling of pulley wheels and the clinking and ringing of metal on metal issuing from the workshops that rose in multi-windowed stories around the mill's courtyard.

'And who the bloody hell be you?' The challenge came from a portly figure wearing a black tophat and a fur-collared black greatcoat that reached down to his booted ankles, who was standing just inside the courtyard.

Daniel Lambert lifted his broad brimmed hat from his head. 'It's Daniel Lambert, Mr Milward.'

Unlike Thomas Mence, the needle master evinced no sign of shock or surprise at Lambert's uninvited appearance. Instead he only said gruffly, 'I had an idea you'd be showing your face here sooner or later.' He jerked his head. 'Come on into the office.'

He led the way into a gloomy room around the corner

of the entrance which was furnished with a roll-top desk, two or three high stools and big, glass-fronted cases of needle samples attached to the grimy walls. Breathing stertorously Milward produced a large bunch of keys and unlocked the front of the desk, then fumbled within its pigeon-holed interior and eventually pulled out a bunch of rusty keys, a slender roll of parchments tied with a ribbon and a small well-filled leather pouch which thumped metallically when he dropped it onto the desk top together with the parchments and keys. He stared with open hostility at his companion.

'I'se guarded these for your feyther's sake, young man. Just as it was for his sake I wrote to the office of the Governor o' New South Wales and requested that you be notified of your feyther's illness and death five years since. And for the same reason I forwarded you money from your feyther's estate arter you'd bin released from your bondage.'

'I'm truly grateful to you for having done all these things, Mr Milward,' Daniel Lambert told him sincerely, but the older man held up one gloved hand to cut him short.

'I want no thanks from you, Lambert. I did all those things solely because your feyther was among my oldest and dearest friends. You broke his heart wi' your wickedness and I believe that the shame of having a convict for a son helped to bring on his death.'

A spasm of pain flashed across Daniel Lambert's features, but he instantly mastered his emotions and met Milward's angry glare with steady eyes.

'I loved my father dearly, Mr Milward, and have paid a heavy price for whatever I have done.'

'Humph!' The other man only snorted disgustedly and pointed at the articles on the desk. 'Take these and goo, Lambert. I doon't want to have anything else whatsoever to do wi' you. Youm a bad lot, my bucko! A thorough bad lot!'

Knowing that nothing he could say would alter

Milward's opinion, Daniel merely pocketed the parchments, keys and the pouch of money and went from the mill.

Fish Hill was the name given to the road that plunged steeply downwards from the northern edge of Redditch Green to cross the broad valley of the River Arrow and on towards the city of Birmingham some fourteen miles distant from the town. As Daniel Lambert walked down the steep hill unbidden memories of his youth again thrust themselves into his mind and visual images of people and happenings came and went in rapid succession. His heart thumped heavily and his breathing quickened as he sighted the tall gabled house towards the bottom of the slope, set well back from the roadway, its front garden a wilderness of untamed weeds and overgrown shrubbery.

A high fence of rusted iron railings topped with balled-spikes surrounded the house and grounds and an ornately patterned wrought iron gate led into the roadway. Daniel Lambert stood at that padlocked gate with its rusted bell-pull dangling to one side and for long moments gazed along the unkempt pathway at the boarded windows and the weathered paintwork of the house, contrasting the sad neglected appearance of his home to what it had been when he last walked out from its front door.

On sudden impulse he clutched the thin chain of the bell-pull and tugged hard upon it. From the interior of the deserted house he heard the faint janglings of the bell and the sadness of loss entered his very soul and tears threatened to spill from his eyes.

With blurred vision he fumbled to open the rusted padlock with one of the keys Henry Milward had given him and was forced to exert his full strength before the tumblers moved in the lock and the hasp gave way. At the front door he again halted, curiously loth to open that door and enter, fearful of the emptiness he would find within. An emptiness that in his dreams of home he had never permitted himself to discover, for in those dreams the door would always open to disclose the smiling face of his father, arms outstretched in joyous welcome and forgiveness.

Tears now fell freely down Daniel Lambert's cheeks as he inserted the long key and turned it, then slowly pushed the door open, nerves rasping as the rusted hinges squealed in protest. The air was heavy with damp, musty decay and his footsteps rang hollowly as he slowly walked along the passageway, halting at each door and opening it to peer into the dark room peopled only with the ghostly shapes of sheet-covered furnishings. He went up the stairs to the room that had been his parents'. It too was in darkness, only chinks of daylight showing through the warped planking of the boarded windows. The great fourposted bed still dominated the room, but had been stripped of sheets and blankets. Only the bare mattress and bolster were left on it. Daniel Lambert felt that his heart was breaking afresh as he looked down on the bed where his mother had died and, from what he understood, his father also.

'Forgive me,' he whispered brokenly. 'Please forgive me.' Slowly he slumped down onto his knees and leaned forward so that his head rested against the mattress; his grief whelmed over him and his tearing sobs shuddered through his body.

Chapter Four

It was full darkness before Tildy returned home, and she was hungry, weary and depressed as she slowly trudged across the heath towards the cottage. After Mitchell had turned the gang away that morning, she and several of the other women and children had walked many weary miles from farm to farm seeking work, and at each one they had been turned away. Some of those rejections had been kindly, the farmer seemingly genuinely regretful that he could offer them nothing. Other rejections had been brutal and they had been driven off with curses, and at the last farm the tenant had threatened to set his dogs on them, the savagely snarling beasts causing the children and the more timid of the women to flee in terror away from the farmhouse.

As she neared the cottage Tildy tried to compose herself into a more cheerful mood, not wishing her own depression to affect her son and old Esther.

'Mam, look what Zeke's give me. Look at these.' Davy excitedly ran to show his mother half a dozen bright new fish hooks.

The smile on her son's face instantly lightened Tildy's depression and she made a great show of admiring his new treasures.

'Let your Mam get through the door afore you starts werritin' her,' old Esther scolded fondly, and told the man sitting by the fire, 'Hitch up your arse a bit, Zeke, and let my wench set hersen down.'

'How bist, Tildy?' Zeke Pickering, shaggy-haired and as swarthy complexioned as any of his gypsy ancestors, moved his chair so that the young woman could come and sit by the fireside.

28

'I'm very well, thank you, Zeke. And you?' Tildy smiled warmly at the tall, lean-bodied middle-aged man.

'Ne'er better, Tildy,' he grinned at her. 'But I could ha' done wi'out this bloody snow.'

'Couldn't we all,' Tildy agreed fervently, and she removed her bonnet and discarded her protective outer layers of sacking.

'Zeke's said he'll take me with him tonight to the river and show me how to set these hooks,' Davy announced, and begged eagerly, 'Can I goo with him, Mam? Can I?'

Seeing the dawning doubt in her expression, the child redoubled his pleas. 'Ohh, let me goo, Mam. Let me goo wi' Zeke. You promised me I could goo with him.'

Tildy hesitated uncertainly. Zeke Pickering lived with his gypsy woman in an old tented shack half a mile distant across the heath and during the four and a half years she had lived in this cottage with old Esther he had proven a good friend to the two women and to little Davy. He could best be described as a very likeable rogue, and a thorn in the sides of the local landowners, whose game he poached and whose goods he purloined, and they would have dearly loved to lay him by the heels. But Zeke Pickering was as cunning and bold as a fox and despite the concerted efforts of landowners, gamekeepers and the constables to stop his depredations he continued to roam freely and poach their game with apparently miraculous impunity. One of the reasons for that impunity was the fact that many tenant farmers hated the savage and iniquitous game laws, by means of which the landowning classes prevented a poor man from killing a wild hare or bird to feed his hungry family purely to protect their own sport of hunting these same creatures. The damage done to the crops of the tenant farmers by the protected birds and animals ensured that those farmers would in many cases secretly applaud the poacher who was brave enough to cock a snook at the landowner, and turn a blind eye to the presence of the poacher in their fields and coverts, particularly when a plump rabbit or tender young pheasant might be left on their doorstep early in the morning.

Now, understanding the reason for the young woman's hesitance, Zeke Pickering grinned and reassured Tildy, 'There's naught for you to get moithered about, my duck, I arn't agoing to poach this night. I'm going to set the lines down by the Paper Mill theer. Matthew Mills told me this morn that iffen I'd gi' him half the catch I could use his stretch o' water.'

Conscious of young Davy's beseeching eyes, Tildy weakened. 'All right then, he can go with you, just this once mind.'

Davy crowed with delight and hurried to put on his coat and thick stockings and clogs.

'Wait a bit, young snapper,' old Esther intervened. 'You arn't agoing nowhere 'til you'se had summat to ate. And you'll not take a few mouthfuls o' blackbird pie amiss, 'ull you, Zeke?'

'I'd walk from here to Banbury Cross and back for a mouthful o' your blackbird pie, Esther,' the man chuckled.

Later, when Zeke and little Davy had gone off to lay their lines, old Esther told Tildy, 'Zeke's bin atelling me a bit o' disturbing tidings. He says he was down at Studley this morn at the Marlborough Arms, and theer was talk down theer that Robert Knight, him who lives at the Priory Manor, is agoing to enclose the heathland here. Greedy robbin' bastard that he is!'

Dismayed alarm struck into Tildy as she heard this news. 'Enclosure? Here?'

The old woman's bright black eyes glittered in the firelight. 'Ahr, enclosure it's to be, by the telling on it. From what Zeke heard there's bin a bill passed already in the bloody parleyament down in London theer.'

'Perhaps it's just talk, Esther. Perhaps it's not true.' Tildy desperately sought to discount this news as unfounded rumour. 'After all it's not three years since that Robert Knight enclosed the Studley Common, is it? He took it all from the Marlborough Arms to Node Hill. Surely that should have been enough to satisfy him.'

'I dunno that it is just talk, Tildy. I scried the omens arter he told me, and all the signs was theer, right enough. Signs o' troubles acoming on us.'

Anxiety caused Tildy to snap impatiently. 'Don't talk to me of omens and signs, Esther. I want to know exactly what was said at the Marlborough Arms.'

The old woman reacted huffily. 'I'se already told you, arn't I.'

Tildy realised that she was badgering the other woman unfairly, and said quietly, 'I'm sorry I spoke sharply, Esther. It's just that this news is very upsetting for me.'

'It's upsetting for me as well, my wench.' The old woman was not to be so easily mollified. 'I'se dwelt here for a good many years. How d'you think I feel, being told that my home might be knocked down about me ears, just so that some greedy gentry pig can line his pockets wi' more money stolen from the poor?'

Concern and pity caused Tildy to lean forward and take the old woman's hand between her own. 'Try not to let it upset you too much, Esther. We don't know for certain that it's true about this enclosure coming. It might well be only idle gossip. And if the worst comes to the worst, and it is true, then at least we'll still be together. No matter what happens we can care for each other, can't we?'

Esther Smith's cracked old voice was tremulous. 'Youm a young 'ooman, Tildy, and a pretty cratur. You'll find some man to care for you and gi' you a home now that youm a widow-'ooman and free to wed again. I doon't want to tie you to me. I'm getting too old to be any use to man nor beast. It arn't right to tie you wi' me. It arn't fair to you.'

'Don't you dare say such things to me, Esther.' Tildy was genuinely annoyed. 'I care for you as if we were blood-kin and Davy loves you with all his heart. You'll go where we go and I'll never let you leave my side.' She softened when she saw the lined features crumple tearfully and she moved so that she could hug the old woman to her, cradling the tiny worn figure to her own full breasts as if she held a child in her arms. 'I love you, Esther, and Davy loves you,' she crooned softly. 'We'll stay together always, no matter what happens, I'll always care for you. Don't cry now. Please don't cry...'

Chapter Five

The cold spell persisted, and more snow fell during the next three days, making it impossible for Tildy to find work in the fields. In one sense she welcomed the brief respite. For more than four years she had laboured as a casual fieldhand around the district, for the first year in a labour gang of pauper women and children rented out to a contractor by the Tardebigge Parish Select Vestry, in an effort by that body to cut the cost of their poor relief bills. The contractor had eventually quarrelled with the vestry and the gangs had been disbanded. Tildy had then continued to work on her own account, at times with other women and children, at times alone. To her own surprise she had found that the other women looked upon her as their leader, a tribute to her personality that Tildy found unwelcome, considering with justification that she faced difficulties enough in bringing up her son alone and, now that old Esther's health was failing, in caring for her also. She could not however find it in her heart to refuse those others who sought her aid in finding work and settling prices for their labour with whoever employed them. But this unlooked for respite from the constant importuning of others was a definite recompense for the loss of income she was now undergoing. If this weather continued, however, then very quickly that loss of income could prove disastrous.

Tildy could not apply for poor relief in the Parish of Studley, because she had no legal right of settlement in this parish. Her legal settlement was over the boundary in the Tardebigge Parish, because she had been born close by Redditch town, and her son had been born in the Tardebigge Parish poorhouse, which meant that Davy also had no rights here in Studley Parish. If she was to apply locally for relief, then the parish authorities would merely drive her over the boundary back into Tardebigge.

Her problems now weighed on her mind as she stood at the wooden tub set on trestles outside the cottage door, washing the coarse linen sheets from little Davy's bed. The morning sky was clear and pale blue, but the sunlight had little warmth and the breeze was chill on her wet arms. One problem loomed menacingly above all others. The rumour of the forthcoming enclosure of the heath. She had talked with Zeke Pickering about what he had heard, and from what he had told her, it appeared that the rumour had a strong basis in fact. Tildy had grown up in an era of enclosures and, like all of her class, she bitterly resented what to her was a form of legalised robbery of the people's rights. During the past decades countless acres of common land had been taken into the private ownership of the rich and powerful. The reason given for these take-overs had been that the new landowners would improve the land and bring it under cultivation, and so increase the agricultural wealth of the country.

Tildy grimaced contemptuously. It had certainly increased the wealth of those who had stolen the common land. But it had made paupers out of tens of thousands of country people, who had used the commons to pasture a cow or feed a pig or flock of fowls, who had been able to build a place to live in on that land, and create gardens to grow vegetables to feed their families, to collect kindling for their bake-ovens and dig peat and turf for their hearth. Once the common land had been enclosed, the people had nowhere to graze any animals, or grow any produce, or build any shelter, or collect any firing.

She angrily pummelled the wet linen. 'All enclosure does for us is to take away any little bit of independence we might possess. It just reduces us to being serfs once more, as we were in times past. What gives men like

Knight the right to steal the land in this way? What gives them the right?'

Lifting the sheet from the tub she wrung the water from it and pegged it out on the line to dry. She looked at the other articles of clothing waving in the breeze and drew satisfaction from their cleanliness. Then, hands on hips, she stared out across the heathland towards the town of Redditch spread upon its hillsides some three miles distant.

She had lived and worked in Redditch and had some good friends there. But living as she had in the poorer quarters of the town her child's health had begun to suffer. Two thirds of the children born in the fetid slum streets of Redditch died before their fifth birthdays, and many of those who survived that carnage were sickly, runted creatures, whose lives were always shadowed by ill health.

So, for Davy's sake, she had come to live out here on the heath and she had never regretted that decision. At seven years old he was tall and strong, ruddy-cheeked and lithe-limbed, a child of the clean aired woods and fields in which he spent nearly all his waking hours.

'God forbid that I should ever have to take him back into the town to live.' Tildy dreaded that prospect.

She lifted the heavy tub and carried it some yards from the cottage to where a long, slightly sloping run of smooth ice had been formed as a slide. Carefully she poured the water onto the worn patches in the ice, knowing that once the sun had set the night's frost would harden the surface. One of Davy's greatest pleasures was sliding down this ice-run and Tildy herself joined him in that sport at times. Engrossed in the task she did not at first notice the horseman approaching across the heath, until he came near enough for her to hear the muffled thudding of hoof-beats upon the snowy ground.

It was Daniel Lambert, but now his reefer jacket had been replaced by a fine blue riding coat with gilt buttons and his rough tarpaulin trousers and tarred boots by buckskin riding breeches and Spanish leather kneeboots. His white linen and pale cravat emphasised the mahogany tan of his features and the military-style peaked forage cap he wore at a rakish angle on his head gave him the air of a dashing cavalryman. He reined in his snorting horse next to Tildy and saluted her with a flourish of his riding crop.

'I bid you good morning, Tildy. 'Tis a wonderfully crisp day, is it not?' His face was animated with his sense of pleasure. 'By God, I used to dream of days such as this when I was sweltering out there in Botany Bay.'

Her surprise at the fine horse and clothing showed clearly and he laughed aloud. 'You look shocked, Tildy.'

Embarrassed at her own ill manners, she flustered. 'It's only that I'm surprised to see you here, Mr Lambert.'

He mock-scowled. 'Haven't I told you that my name is Daniel? Pray don't address me as Mr Lambert. You make me feel like some unwelcome stranger.'

His light blue eyes regarded her admiringly. 'By God, Tildy, you're even prettier than I remembered.'

She frowned slightly, conscious of her sacking apron and shabby black gown and her untidily piled hair, strands of which hung down around her cheeks and neck.

'Now don't take my compliment amiss, Tildy.' He smiled easily. 'For I mean no harm by it. It is only an honest opinion that I give.'

For some reason unaccountable to herself Tildy felt awkward and ill at ease. 'Do you seek your aunt?' she asked somewhat stiffly.

'Is she here?' His mood sobered, as if he were affected by her manner.

'She's indoors, sitting by the fire. She's not feeling too well this morn.' Tildy nodded towards the cottage. 'But go you on in, she'll be pleased to see you, I'm sure.'

The man's eyes studied her gravely for some moments and then he replied quietly, 'I could wish that you yourself had been more pleased to see me, Tildy.'

Tildy felt a blush rising from her throat and was furious with herself for reacting to this man in this unaccountable

36

manner. Forcing herself to meet his eyes levelly, she told him, 'I don't know you well enough yet to be either pleased or displeased at seeing you. Only time will bring an answer to that question.'

His white teeth showed in a brief grin. 'Well, Tildy, if there's one thing I've a deal of at this moment, it's time. So I shall endeavour to spend it in such a manner that before too much of it has elapsed, you shall be pleased to see me when I visit you and my aunt.'

He dismounted and led his horse to a nearby shrub to tether it to a leafless branch, then turned back to Tildy.

'Will you join Aunt Esther and myself inside, Tildy?'

'Later perhaps; I've got to go and bring Davy back home now.'

A shadow of disappointment crossed his face, but he only nodded and went inside the cottage.

Tildy walked slowly across the heath towards the tented shack of Zeke Pickering. It was only since she had lost her work on the farms that she had come to realise how much time her son actually spent with the man and, although she knew that Pickering could be trusted with the boy, still she was beginning to have misgivings about some of the things Davy was learning from him.

'By the Christ, I'm becoming a hypocrite,' she mentally chided herself. 'Of course Davy is learning the arts of poaching from Zeke, but doesn't every boy in these parts learn such things from someone or other?' She smiled ruefully. 'At least he's being taught by a master of the craft.' Then a shaft of worry caused her to frown. 'But suppose some day or night without my knowledge Zeke takes him on one of his expeditions? What would happen to Davy if the keepers took them? His age wouldn't save him from jail, would it? There's many a child his age been sent to the Bridewell for pilfering a few potatoes, never mind taking game.'

Davy's lack of formal education had also caused Tildy many a sleepless night. She tried to teach him how to read and write, but she was unhappily aware of her own lack of schooling, and the fact that despite her efforts over the years to gain knowledge, she still possessed only the scantiest store of that commodity.

She came in sight of the tented shack and what she saw added to her disquiet. Zeke owned a couple of half-broken young horses, and Davy was mounted bare-back on one of these, galloping round and round the shack, whooping with delight. Tildy came to a standstill and stared with mingled pride and trepidation at her son. As she watched Zeke came from the shack and shouted something and Davy brought the horse to a halt. Man and boy stood close and Tildy's breath caught sharply in her throat.

Despite the snow and cold Davy had cast aside his clogs and stockings and his legs and feet were bare. His jacket also had been thrown down and, dressed only in his shirt and breeches, his face flushed and his tangle of black curls wild about his face, he looked like a gypsy boy.

'I swear if some stranger saw him and Zeke together now, then he would swear that they're father and son.'

A pang of jealousy struck Tildy as she recognised the obvious affinity between the man and boy and she disliked herself for feeling that emotion.

'Jesus, I'm becoming a sour bitch, these days. I ought to be thankful that Davy's got a kind-hearted man like Zeke to befriend him and show interest in him. The poor little soul would have no friends but me and old Esther otherwise. And only Esther most of the time with me being away at work all the hours God sends.'

As she walked on Zeke lifted Davy down from the horse and sent it running with a sharp slap on its steaming flank. Davy spotted his mother and came whooping to meet her.

'Did you see me, Mam? Did you see me riding Zeke's horse? Did you?'

She bent and hugged him quickly, smothering the impulse to lift him and crush him to her breasts, knowing that this would only embarrass him.

'Hello, Zeke. Has Davy been a good lad?'

The man chuckled fondly, and ruffled the child's black

curls. 'Ahr, o' course he has. My mate Davy's allus a gennulman in his manners. Come on inside and see what he caught on his new hooks. I'se already claned and gutted 'um for you.'

In the gloomy interior of the shack, which was half-tent, half wattle and daub, Zeke Pickering's gypsy woman crouched above a smoky fire. A full blood Romany, she wore her long oiled black hair in plaits coiled about her head and had huge gold rings in her ears. Her skin was dark brown and her eyes as black as ebony and her clothing was garishly coloured. In the years Tildy had known her, she had never heard the woman speak. Now she only smiled and nodded in greeting, then turned her attention to the iron pot suspended on its tripod above the fire, in which a greasy mess bubbled and steamed and despite its unsavoury look, smelled deliciously appetizing.

Zeke lifted a rag-wrapped bundle and opened it to disclose four good sized fish, silver grey in colour with long dorsal fins.

'Theer now, thems prime graylings, them am. They'll make good ateing, they 'ull.'

'Many thanks to you,' Tildy told him, but he waved her words aside.

'Theer's no thanks due to me, Missus. Thank your Davy instead. 'Twas his line they was cotched on.'

The child's face glowed with pride and Tildy's love for him brought a lump to her throat.

'Then I'll say thank you, Davy,' she told him.

'Shall we eat them today, Mam?'

She nodded assent. 'Now say goodbye to Zeke and Mrs Pickering and we'll go and bake these fish for our dinner.'

On the walk back Davy chattered continuously and Tildy was content to listen to his stories, suppressing any twinges of jealousy she felt as she heard the name Zeke constantly recurring.

The eastern border of the heathland was a range of low wooded hills where in the warm months the three of them – Tildy, Davy and old Esther – spent many hours searching for mushrooms, berries, nuts and herbs, and collecting fallen branches and dead wood for their fires. This woodland was owned by Sir Francis Goodricke of Studley Castle but, since it was on the fringes of his vast estate, the gamekeepers and foresters did not visit as often as they might have done, and over the years had normally turned a blind eye when on rare occasions they had encountered the oddly assorted trio roaming through the trees.

Tildy could not repress a regretful sigh as she thought about how much she would miss this beautiful stretch of countryside if the enclosure took place and she should be driven away from here. She had found peace here and although her life had been hard, still there had always been something to eat and sweet water to drink and clean air to breathe. She dreaded the prospect of having to make a home once more in the fetid alleys of Redditch town, and having to work in one or other of the needle mills, spending her days in dirt and noise and stench.

'What's the matter, Mam? Why do you look so sad?' Davy wanted to know. 'Are you angered wi' me? Are you, Mam?'

She smiled lovingly down at his solemn face. 'Angered with you? Of course I'm not. How could I be angry with a boy who's brought me such fine fish to eat?'

'Then why did you look so sad just now?' Davy persisted.

She chuckled wryly. 'Because I had a touch of the toothache,' she told him.

'Shall you have it pulled out then, Mam. Shall that man who wears all the teeth around his neck pull yourn out for you, as well? Will he put your teeth on a string around his neck? Will he, Mam?'

She laughed with delight at his innocence and, catching him up, smothered his excited face with kisses, while he howled and struggled to get free.

She let him down, and took his hand. 'Come on, let's go to the woods and find some faggots for the back oven.'

'I'll race you,' he cried, and scampered towards the treeline and laughing like a young carefree girl Tildy lifted her long skirts to her knees and gave chase.

A couple of hours later, happy and flushed with exertion, Tildy and Davy bore their loads of deadwood back to the cottage.

Old Esther was alone and while Tildy filled and fired the oven set into one side of the inglenook, her friend told her what Daniel Lambert had been doing since his last visit to them.

'He's opened his house down the Fish Hill, but he reckons it's in sore state and he's looking for a woman to clean and keep house for him. He asked if I thought you might be interested in the work. He said he'd pay well.' She paused expectantly and Tildy frowned doubtfully.

'I don't know, Esther. That would depend on the terms he offered.'

'Oh he'd pay all right,' the other woman assured. 'His Dad left him well provided for, you know. Our Daniel's not short of a few bob.'

Tildy did not reply to this. Her doubts did not concern wages, but rather what might come about if she spent time in close proximity to the man. She had worked as a housekeeper to a bachelor before and he had become besotted with her and wanted to make her his mistress, despite the fact that he had known she had then had a husband.

'Daniel said he saw my son at Studley.' The old woman scowled fiercely. 'Our William is still the same bad wicked bugger he's allus bin, according to what Daniel told me of him. He was in the Barley Mow, drunk as a Lord, offering to fight all and sundry agen. Daniel said that be the looks on him, the "rot" has took hold. I shouldn't say it, but I 'ull. It'll be a blessing for that poor wench he's married to when the bloody "rot" puts the bugger in his grave. He serves her terrible, so he does. The same as he served me and his old Dad afore I showed the sod the door.'

Tildy once more made no reply. Old Esther's only

living child, her son, William, was a needle pointer. The pointers dry-ground the needles produced in the district and earned very high wages because the work that they did took a murderous toll of their health, bringing the vast majority of them to early graves. Only the most reckless and uncaring young men dared to take up the pointing trade and they were notorious for their brawling and drinking. Because, knowing that they were doomed to survive for only scant years, they gave no thought to the morrow and would fight like savage beasts with no fear of consequences. People both feared them for their savagery and admired them for their careless courage. The 'pointers rot' which killed them was caused by the constant breathing in of the fine dust of stone and steel created during the grinding process. This dust eventually so clogged and lacerated the lungs of the pointers that after scant years they could hardly breathe and constantly coughed up blood and at last drowned in that blood.

'Daniel's gone back to Redditch. He was real disappointed when you ne'er come back to have a talk.' Old Esther grinned slyly, disclosing her toothless gums. 'I reckon he's very taken wi' you, Tildy, is our Daniel. Fairly smitten, I reckon he is. About ready to tek a wife to himself, I'd say he was.'

Tildy returned the grin. 'Now don't try marrying me off to your nephew, Esther. I've had one husband and he put me off the idea of ever having another. I don't want to go through hell and high water twice in my life.'

The old woman cackled lasciviously. 'Ahr, maybe you was unlucky wi' that 'un, my duck. But iffen you was to find a good man, who treated you lovesomely, then just think o' the pleasurin' you'd get from him. It arn't natural to goo through life wi'out having a man inside you at times. By Christ, when I was your age I needed it hard and often, I'll tell no lie.'

Tildy could not help flushing with embarrassment. Although she was a woman of considerable fastidiousness, and could never be promiscuous, yet she was forced to admit to herself that during the last few years there had been many nights when she had lain in her bed hungering for the feel of a man's hard body against her own, and desperately needing the aching void within her to be filled with a man's loving. Her celibacy was self-imposed and at times she derided herself for that imposition. But despite her body's needs and hungers she could never overcome her own innate sense of morality, and the times that she had made love with men could be counted on the fingers of one hand. In her marriage she had never known love-making, just brutally enforced congress which could only be termed rape.

Now she sighed and said quietly, 'Maybe someday I'll meet the man that is right for me and I'll get wed again, Esther. But for now, I'm happy enough as I am.'

She took a shallow baking tin from its wall peg and readied the fish for cooking, greasing their silver scales with salt-butter, and seasoning them with a pinch of coarse salt. As she worked she thought once more about the threatened enclosure of the heath and what it would mean for them. Although she had known hardship and poverty here, at least she had been spared the worst ravages of hunger and cold.

Old Esther was wise in the lore of edible wild plants and creatures and she had taught Tildy well, so that between them they had always garnered sufficient food for the table and, by the standards of their class, had eaten well enough. In the past, during the times Tildy had been forced to eke out a living in the town, she had known virtual starvation all too often. Thankfully her beloved Davy had never known such. 'But if we're forced from here, then he might come to know what an empty belly really means.' The unbidden thought sent a shiver of fearful dread through Tildy's body and a visual image of the ill-nourished, shivering, rickety-legged children of the labour gang etched itself sharply in her mind. 'No! I'll not let that happen to you, Davy. No matter what I must do to prevent it. No matter what...'

Chapter Six

The cold snap lasted for two more days and then the winds shifted to the southwest bringing warmer currents of air and constant downpours of rain. Now there was a fresh demand for fieldhands as the snow disappeared and the farmers readied their land for the planting of early potatoes and Tildy and her gang followed the harrows picking the white roots of couch grass and twitch weed from the soaking ground, and once more gathered the seemingly ever-increasing crops of stones.

Tildy hated this wet weather. The skin of her hands became softened and split by constant immersion in water and mud. Footwear also became a problem, because the cracked leather uppers of her boots let in water and fungoid infections attacked her feet causing her to hobble at times with the pain. But Tildy had no money with which to buy stout waterproof footwear.

At home also the wet weather brought problems. The ancient thatch of the roof leaked and no matter how assiduously the hearth fire was tended the interior was always damp and musty smelling. As was their clothing and bedding. The all pervading dampness brought on old Esther's rheumaticky aches and pains and she was confined to the bed she shared with Tildy, since any attempt to rise caused her dreadful agonies. Tildy herself developed a racking cough and suffered a continuous feverishness, but dared not give in to her bodily afflictions and stay at home, since to do so would reduce her to an absolute penury.

Paradoxically, little Davy appeared to thrive throughout this wet chill weather and he was a tremendous help to the two women, taking upon himself the task of caring for old Esther during Tildy's absences at her work. He also gathered wood for the fire and cleaned the cottage and scoured the heath and woodland for anything edible, setting snares for rabbits and birdlime for sparrows, starlings and blackbirds. Although Tildy worried greatly about his hunting, fearing that he would fall foul of the law, yet she could not bring herself to forbid him from activities which not only gave him his greatest sense of achievement, but also brought much needed food to their cooking pot. She had, however, banned one particular method of catching the birds which she considered too cruel, even though it might mean empty stomachs for themselves. This was the baiting of hooked fishing lines, which the birds would swallow and then tear their own innards to shreds on, as they fluttered frantically to escape. Childlike, little Davy had not understood why this method was unacceptable to catch birds by, yet perfectly acceptable to catch fish and Tildy could find no logical explanation to give him, but hooking birds remained banned nevertheless.

Today the rain had not fallen, although the sky was grey with low clouds blanketing the earth. The wind gusted fitfully across the broad, flat field but it had lost its cutting edge and although chill it caused no shivers amongst the men and women busily setting potatoes along the straight drills left by the plough.

Robert Knight reined in his mount and sat easily in the saddle overlooking the hedgerow, his eyes roaming across the toiling figures. Although to a casual observer the activity within the field might seem haphazard, yet to the perceptive eye it was a scene of almost military precision. Midway along the field a plough team cut single drills through the saturated earth. Paralleling the plough a laden manure cart moved slowly along the opened drills with a man dragging heaps of the rotted manure from the cart at precisely spaced intervals. A woman followed close behind the man. With her long-handled, triple-pronged dung-graip she divided the heaps into three smaller heaps in adjoining drills and in each drill a woman with a short-handled dung-graip spread the manure evenly along the bottom of the drill, then lightly trampled it down. Behind these latter trio followed two further lines of three women each. They carried big round willow baskets filled with the potato sets for planting. Their right hands moved rapidly from basket to earth to basket to earth. Nearer to where Robert Knight watched, a second plough team followed the planters, closing the drills over the potato sets once more, creating long neat ridges.

Knight reached inside his thick warm coat and took his watch from its fob pocket. He flicked open the gold casing and glanced at the ornate face, then frowned slightly as he replaced the watch and looked once again at the rearmost plough team. He turned his horse's head and spurred it along the hedgerow until he reached the field gate, then entered the field and trotted easily along its edge until he came abreast of the second plough team.

'You there!' His strong voice carried easily, and the ploughman swung round to see who had shouted. Upon sighting the top-hatted horseman the man instantly whipped off his own battered billycock hat.

'Yes, Marster, what does you want?'

'Quicken your damned pace, man. Else come nightfall you won't have covered the sets.'

'Very good, Marster.' The man answered submissively, and cried up his twinned team. 'Hup now! Hup now, blast ye! Hup now!'

The bowed heads of the horses lifted slightly and their hooves, massive with clumped mud, rose and fell more quickly. Satisfied, Robert Knight wheeled his mount and trotted from the field. At the rear of the manure cart, Tildy Crawford momentarily leaned on her long-handled dung-graip and peered at the retreating horseman, her eyes screwed against the gusting wind.

'Is that Robert Knight?' she asked the man who was dragging the manure from the rear of the cart.

'Yes, that's the barstard,' the man grunted morosely, without looking at her.

Tildy smiled bleakly. 'You don't sound as if you like him much.'

'I 'ates the sight and sound of him,' the man growled. 'And so does nearly every other manjack in Studley village. Barstard robbed us of our bit 'o commonland not three years since, didn't he?'

'He's taking Mappleborough Common next, isn't he?' Tildy sought confirmation.

The man now stopped his work and turned to look at her. His unshaven face was thin, his coat torn and threadbare and his shirt greasy with dirt. 'So they say,' he confirmed, then stated, 'Youm living in Machboro Common, anna you, wi' the old witch-'ooman?'

Tildy nodded slowly.

The man grinned wolfishly. 'Well then, pretty-'un, you tell old Esther Smith to conjure summat agen that barstard afore he pulls the house down around your ears. He did it to four families up agen Node Hill. Did it when the bloody frost was hard on the ground as well. He's a 'ateful barstard.'

'Why do you work for him then, if you hate him so much?' Tildy was genuinely curious.

The man's narrow shoulders shrugged in resigned helplessness. 'I'se got a wife and childer to feed, my wench. And work anna easy to find these days. Needs must when the Devil drives. Even when his name is Robert Knight.' His blackened teeth showed in a fleeting grin. 'Better I should ha' said, 'specially when his name's Robert Knight.'

They fell to work again and as Tildy lifted the stinking lumps of manure with the bent prongs of her tool she pondered anxiously on what the near future might bring. She knew that old Esther and her husband had come to the wild heathland as squatters and had claimed their right to live there by the age-old tradition of erecting a rough shelter with a stone hearth on which a fire was lit within twenty-four hours and its smoke rising up a roughly constructed chimney stack. Tildy's lips twisted angrily. Although this traditional belief was trusted in by those who squatted, it had yet to save any common-dwelling poor people from being evicted from their homes whenever any rich and powerful man decided he wanted to enclose the land they dwelt on.

A fit of coughing racked her chest, forcing her to cease working until it had passed, and bringing tears to her eyes. She moaned slightly at the pain of her sore throat and drew breath cautiously, afraid that the intake of fresh air would bring on a further fit of coughing. Then from her apron pocket beneath her rough sacking overskirt she drew a small stone bottle and removing its cork took a sip of the horseradish syrup it contained, one of old Esther's homemade remedies for bronchial infections.

The hours of gruelling labour slowly passed and then it was dusk, and with relieved sighs the gang women straightened their aching backs and prepared to trudge homewards. The field they were working in lay some two miles south of Studley Village near the hamlet of Spernall and Tildy now faced a journey of some four miles to her cottage. A distance that normally she would have made light of, but today – ill and feverish – that distance loomed fearsomely before her. So when the cart driver she had been working with offered her a ride on his vehicle as far as Studley village, she accepted gratefully.

The man had been gloomily taciturn during the day, but now he became more cheerful and almost garrulous and despite feeling unwell, Tildy listened with great interest as he told her about his employer, Robert Knight.

'The barstard anna bin here for more nor a few years, you know, my wench. Army man, that's what he were afore he come to the village. He bought the priory fust. You knows wheer that is don't you? Just across the turnpike road from the Barley Mow.'

Tildy knew the house. A fine old Tudor building standing a few hundred yards east of the inn, parts of it dating back to the original priory of the Order of the Knights Templars to which it had belonged centuries past.

'Then, arter a bit Knight started to buy up any piece o' land that come on the market. He's got parcels o' fields all round these parts now. And o' course, he's took Studley Common as well. They do say as how he's got connections wi' nobility. He's got a lot o' money, that's for sure.'

'What sort of connection with nobility?' Tildy wanted to know.

The man winked broadly. 'The usual kind, my wench. They do say that he's the barstard son of some great lord down in Lunnon theer.' The man winked again. 'But I'se heard talk that his dad could even ha' bin royalty. Arter all, when old George were still only the Prince Regent, the bugger babbied a powerful lot o' wenches, didn't he? So it could well be true that Knight's another of his bye-blows.'

Tildy could accept that possibility quite easily. The sons of royalty and nobility were notoriously promiscuous, and the present King, George the Fourth, had been notably debauched in his youth and early manhood.

'You'd ne'er come across Knight afore today then.' It was statement rather than question.

Tildy shook her head. 'No. It was Master Gittins who engaged us for this day's work.'

'Marster Gittins, is it!' The driver spat in disgust. 'Marster Gittins, bailiff, that's what he calls hisself now. I knew the bugger when he was just Snotty Gittins, and his old 'ooman took in bloody washing for the neighbours. That's the trouble see, my wench. When bloody Johnny Newcomes comes into the village and buys out the old gentry, then they doon't know their arses from their elbows. And they gives good jobs to lazy, useless barstards like Billy Gittins. He anna done a decent day's work in his bloody life, that barstard anna. And now he calls hisself a bailiff! God strewth! I doon't know what this bloody world's acoming to, I swear I doon't.'

Tildy's cough suddenly erupted once more and left her

feeling so sore and spent that she was content to remain silent for the remainder of their journey and merely listen to the driver's fulminations about the world in general and his own resentment of those more fortunate than himself in particular. While the cart lurched onwards towards Studley Village, two horsemen were moving slowly side by side across the Mappleborough Green.

Zeke Pickering saw them as he came out of the woodland and quickly stooped and hid the dead hare he carried beneath some bracken, together with some brass-wired snares. Then walked steadily onwards across their line of travel.

Robert Knight pointed with his riding crop. 'Who is that man? Do you know him, Gittins?'

His companion stared for a moment then nodded. 'That I do, sir. His name's Pickering. He's a real wrong 'un, so he is. Lives wi' a gyppo 'ooman over on the Beoley side o' the heath. He's a squatter.'

Knight made no reply, but only spurred his horse into a canter and Gittins, being a very poor horseman, grimaced in dismay as he was forced to follow suit. Zeke Pickering grinned to himself as he recognised the oncoming men, the lean-bodied, aquiline-featured Robert Knight and the stubby, flabby-faced Billy Gittins, but did not alter his pace or line as he heard Knight's shout.

'You there, hold fast, damn you!'

Robert Knight vented an angry curse as the walking man ignored him and kicked his mount to a gallop which quickly brought him across the other's path. The horse's hooves slithered across the wet ground as Knight viciously reined it to a halt and it whickered nervously and stamped and plunged for an instant, but with a consummate mastery Knight steadied the highly strung beast and then challenged the walking man.

'What the hell are you doing on my land?'

Zeke Pickering affected an air of surprise. 'Your land, your Honour? I thought this was common land.' He snatched off his battered wide-brimmed hat, and bobbed his head respectfully. ''Tis allus bin common land to my knowledge, your Honour. Beggin' your pardon for suggestin' such a thing, but mayhap you'se made a mistake, your Honour?'

Gittins came up with them, his body jogging clumsily in the saddle and his pot belly bouncing up and down. Zeke Pickering turned to him and exclaimed as if in pleased surprise.

'Well now, here's Marster Gittins come. How bist, Marster Gittins?'

Knight's thin lips were a hard compressed line and his hazel flecked eyes hot with anger as he recognised the mocking contempt that lay behind Zeke Pickering's outward show of humble submissiveness.

'I've met men like you before, you scum,' he thought furiously. 'Well you'll soon learn not to come the old soldier with me.' Aloud, he snapped curtly, 'I'm awaiting your answer, my man.'

Zeke scratched his shaggy head and looked bemused. 'Answer, your Honour? Beggin' your pardon, your Honour, but what answer is it youm meaning?'

Knight was itching to slash down with his riding crop, to thrash this insolent ruffian until he screamed for mercy, but forced himself to remain outwardly calm and controlled, reminding himself that he was no longer an army officer and that this was not a soldier whom he could have flogged for the mere suggestion of insolence in his manner, that this man before him was a civilian, and as such held certain rights under the law. But his eyes were murderous, as he repeated in clipped tones, 'I want to know what you are doing on my land? Let me remind you that I can have you taken up by the constables for trespass if I so wish.'

Billy Gittins decided that he must support his employer. 'Mr Knight could have you taken up and charged for trespass, Pickering. So you keep a civil tongue in your yed, and give answer.'

For a brief instant Pickering's contempt showed through as he heard the flabby man's blusterings. Then the veil of humble submissiveness came down once more and he screwed his hat in his hands and bowed his head.

'I don't mean any offence, your Honour. Truly I thought this was common land. I was just taking a breath of air afore I ates me supper. That's all, your Honour.'

Knight frowned and he appeared to ponder his course of action while his eyes moved up and down Zeke Pickering's tall figure, then locked onto the wide-skirted corduroy coat the man wore.

'Gittins, search him,' he ordered curtly.

The bailiff clumsily dismounted and moved forwards, then halted as Zeke Pickering scowled threateningly at him. 'I reckon he'll turn nasty, Mr Knight, sir,' he flustered nervously.

Pickering laughed mockingly and opened his coat wide. 'Search away, Marster Gittins, I've naught to hide.'

'Blast your eyes, Gittins, do as I bid you,' Knight shouted in temper, and timidly the bailiff stepped up to Pickering and made a hurried search of his body, then with obvious relief stepped smartly backwards.

'There's nothing there, sir.'

'Now hear me, my man.' Knight leaned forwards across his horse's head and pointed his riding crop at Zeke Pickering's face. 'This common is being enclosed by me. Fencing will be erected. If I catch you on this side of that fencing, then I'll have you taken before the magistrate. You live in that shack at the Beoley end of this land, do you not. You had better be gone from there by this time tomorrow.' With that he wheeled his mount and used spurs and crop to drive the beast into a gallop.

Gittins stared after his master with dismay and then looked at Zeke Pickering with obvious fear, but the other man only chuckled scornfully. 'You'd best get arter him right quick, Billy Gittins. There's strange things can happen to a man like yourself out alone on this heath arter nightfall.'

The bailiff struggled to raise his fat body into the saddle and went clumsily bouncing away, with the laughter of Zeke Pickering floating after him.

Chapter Seven

'So, what do you think, Zeke? When will the fences be erected?' Tildy sat facing the man across the hearth, their faces ruddy in the firelight.

He shrugged and spread his hands. 'That's hard to say, my duck. The bugger told me to get off the common tomorrow. So he might plan on pulling my shack down then. But he ne'er mentioned this place at all.'

Tildy frowned worriedly and desperately snatched at straws. 'Perhaps he might not bother with this place. It lies on the edge of the common, after all.'

'So does my shack, Tildy,' Zeke pointed out quietly.

'Dear God, what'll happen to us?' Tildy's fears were more for little Davy and old Esther, both asleep at this late hour, the old woman's snores sounding through the wood partition that divided the cottage.

Her companion grunted sympathetically, and offered, 'Look Tildy, me and my 'ooman can easy find somewhere else to pitch our tent. You lot can always bunk in wi' us.'

'I take your offer very kindly, Zeke,' she told him. 'But that wouldn't serve. Esther's too old and frail now to stand living rough.'

She left unspoken the fact that she didn't want Davy to live like a gypsy. In her dreams she envisaged a future for him that would be superior to the life he lived now.

''Ud her son tek her in?' Even as he asked the question, Zeke dismissed that idea. 'Forget I said that, Tildy. That bugger's no use to hisself, let alone his old mam.' He paused for a moment. 'How about her nephew, the convict? He's got the house his dad left him, arn't he? And he's fond o' the old 'ooman arn't he?'

'He might agree to take her in, but then, who's to care for her while she's poorly like she is now?' Tildy, not knowing Daniel Lambert well, was doubtful. 'It's like people say, Zeke, fish and company both begin to stink after three days. He's still a young man and he might not take kindly to having the responsibility of a sick woman to look after.'

The man grinned and winked knowingly at her. 'I doon't doubt but that he'd be only too pleased to have a pretty 'ooman like you living in the house and caring for his auntie.'

Tildy was honest enough to admit that that thought had occurred to herself also but, fiercely independent as she was, the prospect of being dependent on a man she hardly knew for roof and board caused her strong misgivings. She voiced this to Zeke Pickering.

He did not reply for some time, only stared into the flickering flames as if deep in thought. Then he suggested: 'Look Tildy, I knows you well enough to spake me mind. Now I knows how bloody-minded you can be and how you likes your freedom. But you anna getting any younger, be you? Youm a pretty wench and there's many a man in these parts who'd be only too willing to wed you. You'se told me many's the time that you'd like to see your boy eddicated and be brought up to be a gennulman. Well that's never gooing to come to pass while youm working in the bloody fields, is it? Schooling costs money and youm ne'er going to have sufficient to pay for it the way youm living. My advice to you is to start thinking about finding yourself a man who'se got sufficient to keep you well fed and well shod, and to pay for your boy's schooling.'

He held up his hand as if to ward off any angry retort she might make. 'I'm spaking as a friend, Tildy. A friend both to you, and to your lad. I thinks the world o' Davy, and I'd raise him as my own son if you'd gi' him to me. But then, he'd become a bloody didikai like I am, and you doon't want that for him, does you. But the way youm agoing on that's all he's agoing to end up as anyway.

'Mind you, having said that, I'll tell you true that I likes my life and I want no other. I'm free as any bird, I am, and that's the way I always wants it to be. But if you wants summat more for your boy, then you'd best think on what I'se said to you, because like it or lump it, the only way youm agoing to get them things you wants for Davy, is to get enough money to buy 'um wi'. And the only way youm agoing to get that money, is to find a man who can give it to you.'

He stopped speaking and sat staring at her keenly.

Tildy also remained silent. His words had cut deeply and now she battled inwardly to come to terms with them. Logically she knew that what he said was the truth. Emotionally, everything in her being rejected that truth.

'I'd be acting the whore if I wed a man just for what he could do for me and Davy. Just for what he could give us in the way of money and possessions.' Her thoughts focused on the dichotomy. 'But do I not owe it to Davy to do whatever is best for him? If I can wed a man who can give him his education, who can give him security, who can give him a respectable station in life, then is it not my duty to do so? Am I being selfish and a bad mother if I continue in my present solitary way of life? God knows I dearly wish at times that I could rest from struggling to support us both. That I did have someone who I could turn to when I'm feeling ill, or depressed and weary of my life. But how could I be wife to a man that I did not love? How could I share his bed, and bear his children? I've known that sort of marriage before, but all it brought me was misery and left me full of hatred and contempt.'

Unconsciously she shook her head. 'No! I can't do it. I can't ever bring myself to wed a man that I don't love.'

Then, mercifully, her own roguish sense of humour came to her rescue, and her lips curved in a self-mocking smile. 'Jesus Christ! Here I am worrying myself to death about something that doesn't even exist. Who is badgering me to wed him? Chance might be a fine thing.'

'Well? What say you, Tildy? What do you think?'

Zeke Pickering's voice brought her back to awareness and she blinked dazedly as she came out of the deep reverie she had fallen into.

'What do you think o' what I said, Tildy? About finding a man who could gi' you and Davy what you need.'

Tildy smiled mischievously at his serious features. 'I'm giving thought to it, Zeke. I'm giving thought.'

A little later, when he had gone, Tildy once more considered possible courses of action against the dangers that threatened.

'What if I go to see Robert Knight, and offer to pay him rent for the cottage? After all, we're nearly off the common and in the woodland here. He could run his fence around us without losing more than a few square yards of land. Or if he wants to cultivate the land, then he could plough right up to our door if necessary. We'd just have to give up our bit o' garden, and keep the chickens penned small.'

The more she considered this idea, the more appealing it became to her and by the time she went to join old Esther in bed, she had committed herself to approaching Robert Knight the very next day.

Chapter Eight

Daniel Lambert's father had been a needle maker who apart from sub-contracting work from the principal needle masters of the district, also did some business as a factor on his own account. By his hard work and shrewd dealings he had eventually accrued some considerable degree of wealth and standing in the town.

Daniel himself had been brought up to the trade, but had been too wild and reckless as a youth to be able to stand the long dull hours of tedium involved in the manufacture of needles. The Napoleonic Wars were raging and Daniel lusted for adventure and excitement. Still only a boy in years he had run away from his fond father and comfortable home and had enlisted as a soldier. On the bloody battlefields of the Spanish Peninsula, Southern France and Belgium the boy had become a man and when, after Waterloo, Sergeant Daniel Lambert had taken his discharge and returned to his hometown, he wanted only to live in peace for the remainder of his days. But, after scant months, the life of tedious respectability and industry began to weigh heavily on his spirits and the old cravings for excitement and adventure reasserted themselves.

There were other young men like himself in the district, who had served in the war and now found it very hard to readjust to civilian life. Having little in common with those who had stayed at home throughout the war, Daniel sought the company of his fellow war veterans, bonded with them through shared experience, and spent more and more of his leisure hours drinking, gambling, brawling and poaching with the wilder elements among them. His father, church-going and sober-living, grieved privately over his son's conduct and constantly remonstrated with the young man over his wildness. But, although Daniel dearly loved his father and did genuinely try to be more like the dutiful, God-fearing son the elder Lambert wanted, his inner devils refused to be exorcised and, seemingly inevitably, Daniel Lambert's course had led him to the prison hulks and transportation.

Now, back once more in his hometown, Daniel Lambert found himself in a curious state of mind. He was lonely, yet had no desire to mix in company for its own sake. When he had returned from the war he had felt something of an alien amongst the local people. This sense of alienation had returned to envelop him now with doubled force. He was a stranger amid these familiar surroundings and when he walked the streets and environs of this hilly town the faces that he recognised were only distant echoes from the past. Men and women would glance casually at him as he passed them and then stare after him, frowning slightly as remembrance struggled to emerge from the recesses of their minds.

There were many buildings that were new to him and new faces and accents, for while he had been away there had been influxes of migrants from other countries: needle makers themselves, whose trading outlets had been lost to them as the thrusting needle masters of Redditch continually expanded their markets and drove their competitors from other areas out of business, forcing those competitors to move here to the district that was now the world centre of the needle industry, where they could attempt to work in concert with the Redditch Masters and thus survive.

Yet despite this sense of alienation, this feeling that he was a stranger among strangers, Daniel Lambert was content to be back. His roots were deep buried in this landscape and he loved its red brick buildings, its profusion of woods and meadows, its hills and valleys, streams and pools, and the ancient sunken trackways that traversed it, upon which men had walked since time immemorial. Lamberts had dwelt here for centuries and now Daniel Lambert was determined to dwell here also for the rest of his days.

The house had lost its forlorn deserted air. Daniel had scrubbed and cleaned, warmed and aired its rooms, keeping coal fires burning constantly in every fireplace to drive out the smell of damp mustiness and although the rains persisted the wood and fabrics within the house dried and Daniel bought scented resins from the apothecary which he burned so that their fragrances sweetened the interiors of the rooms.

Tonight he sat before the fire in the living room, reading by the light of a candle, puffing on his pipe and occasionally sipping from the pewter tankard of ale that stood on the small table at his elbow. Outside in the darkness the wind moaned and raindrops pattered against the window panes. Daniel finished the chapter and closed the book, then sat with the leather bound volume on his knee, relishing the peace and comfort, comparing his present situation with the nights he had known on Norfolk Island. Nights locked into fetid cells crammed with the stinking bodies of men who vented every bestial instinct that they possessed on those weaker than themselves.

Daniel shook his head to drive away the fearful memories, but still they persisted and visual images crowded into his mind. His fingers moved without conscious volition to touch the long thin scar that ran down the left hand side of his muscular neck.

He had not known the youth's name. The lad had only arrived on the island that day and had been put in the cell before the return of the gangs from their back-breaking labours. Daniel could see again the terror on the youth's face as the human beasts dragged him from the corner he cowered in. Hear his screams as brutal hands tore the rough clothing from his slender body and held him powerless while lust-crazed men fought to be first to violate him. Unable to bear the piteous shrieks of agony and horror Daniel had fought like a madman to save the youth from being raped and the scar was the legacy of that hopeless fight. The sharp blade, wielded by one of the youth's attackers, missed his jugular vein by the merest fraction. It was a miracle that he had escaped with his life that night. By some stroke of fortune the guards had for once intervened to quieten the uproar in the cell and Daniel could hear again the thunderous hammerings on the doors as the guards burst them inwards.

Abruptly he was jolted from his reveries. The hammering was not only in his memories, but was happening now and the front door of his house was shaking under the blows. Taking his candle he went along the passageway to the front of the house, shouting as he did so. 'Who is it? Who's there?'

'It's the night patrol, Master,' a voice shouted. ''Ull you open the door?'

As it swung ajar the wind blew out Daniel's candle, but the men outside were carrying lanterns and Daniel saw that they were four in number, dressed against the weather in caped greatcoats, hats pulled down low on their heads. Each one was armed with the crowned stave of a constable.

The wind drove rain into the hallway, and Daniel invited them in. 'Please to step inside, gentlemen, and let me shut this wet out.'

With the door closed he turned and faced them. 'What can I do for you, gentlemen?'

The biggest of the men lifted his lantern so that the beam fell across Daniel's features, causing him to blink hard and shield his eyes against the light.

'Lower your light, man,' he snapped curtly. 'You have me dazzled with it.'

The big man made no move to comply, instead he questioned challengingly. 'Has you bin here indoors all this night?'

Daniel had a hot temper, but his life had taught him how to keep it under a rigid control. So although the other

61

man's manner and tone was aggressively offensive he answered calmly, 'Yes, I've been here since fall of dusk.'

Another man shone his lantern beam at Daniel's slippered feet. 'Wheer's your boots?'

Now Daniel's resentment rose sharply. 'What business is that of yours?'

'Just answer the question, Lambert,' the big man ordered.

'I'll answer nothing until you take that light out of my eyes and tell me your business here,' Daniel snapped.

'Crows like a dunghill cock, doon't he,' one of the men growled.

'I can do more than crow, my bucko, as you'll find out if you don't mend your manners. Let me remind you that you are beneath my roof,' Daniel warned.

'Now let's all calm down, shall us.' The shortest of the four spoke for the first time and his tone was calm and authoritative as he addressed Daniel.

'I'll tell you our business here, Master Lambert, but mayhap it might be better if we went into your living room. This passage is a trifle crowded, arn't it?'

'Very well, pass on through the door there,' Daniel acquiesced.

Once they were all in the room, Daniel lit more candles so that he could see his visitors clearly.

The short man removed his broad-brimmed hat disclosing his balding head and bushy side-whiskers. He looked to be about thirty years old and a chord of recognition struck Daniel.

'You're Jonas Crow, arn't you, son of Jonas Crow who is the scourer?'

'That's right,' the man acknowledged. 'I see that your time out in Botany Bay arn't destroyed your memory, Daniel Lambert.'

Daniel stared hard at the other three men and one by one their names came to him. William Merry, red-faced and jowly, Richard Wyers, a narrow head balanced on a scrawny neck, James Lewis, big and bulky. They were all members of needle making families, whose fathers were factors and masters in varying sizes of business, as he remembered. Aloud, he questioned: 'What's all this about then? What do you want with me?'

'There's been a robbery this night, Lambert. From William Gould's warehouse. Nigh on two hundred thousand needles taken as near as Master Gould can tell, and some French shillings as well.'

'So, how does that concern me?' Daniel challenged.

'They was seen coming back over Gould's wall, and shouted after. They dropped some o' the needles, but made away wi' the rest on 'um, and came down in this direction,' Crow told him. 'We found these outside your front gate.'

The man extended his open palm, disclosing some needles.

'Can you explain how they got theer, Lambert?'

Daniel shrugged. 'I suppose the thieves dropped them in their haste.'

James Lewis interrupted, 'Did they drop this in haste as well, Lambert?' He thrust a small paper-wrapped parcel of needles in front of Daniel's eyes. 'This was under the bushes in your front garden.'

Again Daniel could only shrug. 'I don't know how that came to be under the bushes. I've not been out of the house since fall of dusk.'

He saw the disbelief and suspicion in the faces before him, and protested hotly. 'I'm speaking the truth. I haven't left the house this night at all. I give you my word on that.'

'Your word doon't carry a lot o' weight in this town, Lambert,' the big man growled. 'A bloody convict's word arn't got no value.'

Daniel's anger surged and his fists clenched as he gritted out, 'You'd be well advised to watch your mouth, Lewis. It could get you into serious trouble.'

'Could it now,' the big man sneered, and his headed stave began to rise. 'And who from, might I ask?'

'From me!' Daniel was ready to teach this surly

intruder a lesson he would not soon forget.

'That's enough o' that, from both of you.' Jonas Crow stepped between the two antagonists. 'You wait outside, James Lewis.'

The big man scowled and Crow's voice hardened. 'Do as I bid.'

After a few moments the big man lowered his stave and turned away, threatening Daniel Lambert as he did so.

'You and me has got a score to settle between us, Lambert.'

'I'll not forget it, don't you fret,' Daniel retorted.

When the big man had gone, Jonas Crow said warningly, 'You ought not anger that one you know, Lambert. He's got a bad temper, and he's quick to strike a blow.' Daniel made no answer. He had survived too many savage, life-threatening encounters to feel afraid of meeting any man in one to one battle.

'Now then,' Crow went on. 'What about that packet o' needles? How could that have come by wheer we found it?'

'How the hell should I know?' Daniel's patience had been tried to its limits. 'I've told you repeatedly that I've not left this house since fall of dusk.'

'Why are you getting so aereated?' Crow asked, with a suggestion of jeering baiting in his manner. 'We'em only here on lawful business, asking you to answer a few simple questions. And we am acting in our rightful capacities, because we'em all deputised as constables o' this parish, being the night patrol.'

Daniel expelled a noisy gust of impatience. 'Listen, Crow. Don't talk to me as if I'm some thick-skulled chaw-bacon. You're here because I'm a returned transport. An ex-convict. Because of that fact you think that I've had something to do with this robbery tonight.' He paused and drew a deep breath, then continued more calmly. 'All right! I can accept that suspicion might well fall on me. But let me just remind you, that I was transported for poaching. Not for robbery. I've never stolen anything from any man, woman or child in my life. I've taken game, yes, I freely admit that. But are there many men living in this town who haven't snared a rabbit or knocked down a bird on somebody else's land at some time or other in their lives? Are there? Give me your opinion on that?'

The other man was forced to acknowledge the point. 'No, I doon't suppose there is more nor a few who arn't done such.'

'Good!' Daniel nodded in satisfaction. 'So at least you've accepted that being a poacher is not the same as being a thief. Now to avoid any further harrassment, I'm prepared to let you search this house and the garden from top to bottom if you so wish. I know nothing about this robbery you speak of and I've nothing to hide here. I'll remain in this room while you make your search. Will that satisfy you?'

Crow nodded. 'That's fair enough. Master Merry, you take upstairs, Master Wyers goo and tell Lewis to search the garden, then you take this floor and the cellar. I'll stay and keep you company, Lambert.'

When they were alone Jonas Crow's manner became more friendly and he apologised. 'I'm sorry if we come a bit high-handed wi' you Lambert, but we'em all feeling a bit aggravated by this robbery having took place whiles we was the duty night patrol. It's like the buggers who done it was cocking a snoot at us, arn't it.'

Daniel Lambert, deciding there was nothing to be gained by further overt resentment of this invasion of his privacy, relaxed his manner also.

'Night patrol? That's a new thing for Redditch, isn't it?'

'We bin forced to bring it in, Lambert.' The other man puffed out his cheeks and coughed noisily. 'Damn and blast this bloody cold o' mine. I can't shift the bugger.'

Heeding the hint, Daniel invited, 'Take a can of hot ale, Master Crow. That might ease it a little.'

'Well that's uncommon civil of you, Master Lambert. I'd certainly appreciate a drop.'

Daniel filled another pewter tankard from the small keg

on the table, then heated a poker in the fire and plunged its red hot tip into the ale, causing the liquid to hiss and seethe and bubble.

Crow seated himself in the other wooden armchair at Daniel's invitation and smacked his lips noisily as he drank.

'You were saying about the night patrol?' Daniel prompted.

'Yes, the select vestry brought it in about the beginning o' November last. There's been a whole lot o' robberies committed this wintertime. Not only o' needles, but livestock and foodstuffs and household goods as well. We think's it's an organised gang. Folks calls 'um the "Rippling Boys". But we arn't bin able to lay any on 'um by the heels. They'm cunning buggers and that's a fact.'

'Have you no suspects?' Daniel's curiosity was fully aroused.

'Oh ahr, we got plenty o' suspects, Master Lambert. But suspecting summat, and proving it, am two very different kettles o' fish. We'em fairly sure that they'm locals. Any foreigner wouldn't have the knowledge to carry out such a lot o' successful robberies and, besides, any foreigner is too easily noted in this parish.' He shook his head. 'No, they arn't foreigners, that's for sure. They'm locals all right.'

The two men lapsed into silence and on the floor above his head Daniel could hear the clumping boots of the man searching the upper floor. Then the sound of the front door being slammed open and James Lewis's excited shouts banished the silence.

The big man came into the living room and Wyers and Merry crowded after him.

'What about these then, Lambert?' In his hands he carried more packets of paper-wrapped needles.

Jonas Crow jumped to his feet. 'Wheer did you find them, Master Lewis?'

'In that shed out the back o' the house theer. Under a pile o' coals.' Lewis' teeth were yellow in the candlelight as he grinned in savage triumph. 'You took us for bloody mawkins, didn't you Lambert? Thought you was a fly cove, didn't you? Well your bloody Botany Bay tricks doon't cut no bloody ice here, my buck!'

Daniel Lambert had also got to his feet and now he hotly denied any knowledge of the needles being in the coal shed, but even as he did so his heart sank at the expressions of disbelief on the faces of the men about him.

Jonas Crow's broad features were hard set. 'I'm agoing to have to arrest you, Lambert, and bring you up afore the magistrate for examination. You'd best come along quiet for your own good.'

For a brief moment sickening despair swept over Daniel, but he realised the futility of protest. He could not fight four men armed with staves, and if he attempted to escape then that would only confirm his guilt in the minds of those present. He nodded in bitter acquiescence.

'Very well, Crow, I'll go with you. But you are grievously in error here. I am innocent of any wrongdoings.'

'That'll have to be for the magistrate to decide, Lambert.' Jonas Crow's voice held a hint of sympathy, and he advised, 'You'd best wear a warm coat, because there's no fire in the lock-up.'

'When will I see the magistrate then?' Daniel asked.

'When he sees fit to see you.' James Lewis was exultant. 'I shouldn't be in too big a hurry to meet him, my buck. Because the sooner you does, then the sooner youm agoing to be sailing for Botany Bay again.'

''Ull you hold your tongue, Master Lewis, and leave the man be,' Jonas Crow snapped angrily, and explained to Daniel, 'Reverend the Lord Aston is the justice o' the peace for this parish, Lambert, and Parson Clayton acts for his Lordship here in the town. But they'm both away from here at present, so you'll have to be kept in the lock-up until they comes back.'

Despite his anger and bitterness at what was happening to him, Daniel forced himself to think rationally. 'Will you permit me to damp down the fires and leave the house secure, Master Crow, and to bring a few items with me if I'm to be kept locked up?'

'Bugger me! Just hark to him, 'ull you! He thinks he's bleedin' royalty, doon't he? You'll take nothing from here, Lambert. Youm going to bloody jail, not to a bawdy-house.'

James Lewis's jeering voice almost caused Daniel's self-control to snap and his body momentarily shuddered as he fought down his rampaging lust to close the big man's loud mouth with his fists.

Jonas Crow was a fair-minded man, and lacked the instincts of the bully. He also found James Lewis offensive, and now he told the man sharply, 'I'm in charge o' this patrol, Lewis, it's me who says what 'ull be done.'

When the big man started to bluster, Crow angrily cut him short. 'If you wants to argue the toss wi' me, then I'll put that in my report as well, Lewis. And we'll see what the magistrate has to say about it. Youm in bad odour wi' him already, arn't you? So if I was you I'd just keep quiet and do what youm told, wi'out further dispute.'

The big man subsided morosely, and Crow ordered him, 'Now get you off to Cashmore's house, and get the keys o' the lock-up from him. Tell him that we'se taken a prisoner, but there's no need for him to come out at this ungodly hour. We'll do what's needful and return the keys to him when we'se done wi' 'um.'

Once the big man had stamped from the room, Jonas Crow told Daniel, 'All right then, Master Lambert, let's get this house secured and your things collected together, shall us?'

Chapter Nine

The skies were weeping mournfully and Tildy's mood was as grey as the morning as she squelched through the puddles of the long straight entrance drive towards the big half-timbered house known as the priory.

She tugged the bell-pull at the side of the massive iron-studded front door and heard the janglings of the bell echoing through the house. It took several minutes and repeated tuggings on the bell-pull before the door was creaked open and a diminutive boy stared up at her.

Tildy smiled down at him. 'I want to see Mr Knight, lovey. Is he in?'

The door closed once more as the small boy disappeared behind its dark panels. Tildy sighed and drew her shawl more closely around her head against the drizzling rain, which had already begun to soak through her outer layers of sacking overskirts.

After a while the door reopened, and this time a young woman neatly dressed in a dark gown, and dazzlingly white apron and mobcap stared questioningly at Tildy.

'If you please, ma'am, I'd like to have a word with Mr Knight,' Tildy told her.

The young woman's face mirrored her doubt as her eyes moved up and down Tildy's body and Tildy felt constrained to explain apologetically, 'I've got to go to my work, that's why I've come at such an early hour and I'm dressed this way. But it's very important that I see Mr Knight. Is he at home?'

The mobcapped head bobbed in confirmation.

'Can I see him then?' Tildy sought to know.

The mobcapped head shook in negation.

Tildy was beginning to wonder if this young woman was dumb, but had no other recourse than to persist.

'Listen, ma'am, I know it's very early in the day to be calling on the gentleman, but it really is most urgent that I speak with him now. I have to go on to my work, you see, but my business with him won't wait until later in the day anyway.'

The white mobcap and apron moved back into the shadowed hallway and the door closed yet again. Tildy shook her head in mystification, and didn't know whether she wanted to laugh or to cry at such strange behaviour. In a fit of exasperation she grabbed the bellpull and tugged hard and long. The bell was still jangling when the door reopened and this time an elderly man wearing a dark suit and white neck-stock and cravat stood in the entrance.

Tildy released the bellpull and as the jangling echoes died away wearily repeated, 'I'm sorry to be calling so early in the day, Master, but it's very urgent that I speak with Mr Robert Knight.'

The elderly man stared superciliously at her bedraggled figure. 'My master?' he challenged. 'You wants to hold speech wi' my master?'

'Yes,' Tildy confirmed hopefully.

The man's manner displayed a contemptuous puzzlement. 'What could a tinker-'ooman want wi' Mr Knight, might I wonder?'

His attitude stung Tildy's fiery spirit. 'That is a personal matter between him and me,' she retorted sharply.

The man snorted in dismissal. 'Get you gone from here, young 'ooman. My master doon't hold speech wi' your sort about personal matters.'

He made as if to close the door, but Tildy stepped quickly forward and pushed her hand against the panelling to prevent his doing so. Desperation caused her to plead. 'Listen, I'm sorry if I've caused you any upset by coming here so early in the day, but it really is important

70

that I speak with Mr Knight. I must see him!'

The old man cursed pettishly and shoved hard against the door, but his decrepit body was no match for Tildy's work-toughened strength, and after some futile struggling he was forced to lean panting against the doorjamb and abandon his attempt to shut her out.

'If you don't get off from here, I'll have the constable to you, you tinker bitch!' he gasped breathlessly.

'Please Master, I'm not a tinker, nor a bitch either.' Tildy knew that she could not allow her indignation at his insult to overcome her. Her need was too great. 'All I ask of you is to let me speak with Mr Knight. I wouldn't be here if it wasn't a matter of great importance. I must speak with him.'

The old man made another attempt to slam the door in Tildy's face and again they struggled as she fought to prevent him.

'What is happening here, Smith? Who is this woman?'

Robert Knight Esquire came down the hallway, bareheaded and wearing a long dressing gown with a fur collar, the silent mobcapped woman hovering anxiously behind him.

'If you please, sir, this saucy bitch is insisting that she holds speech wi' you,' the old man panted. 'She's forced the door agen me, so she has. I'se told her to get away from here, sir, but the saucy bitch wun't tek no for answer.'

Knight jerked his close-cropped greying head in dismissal and the old man backed into the house, glaring furiously at Tildy as he did so and muttering abuse beneath his breath. Knight's aquiline features were impassive as his cold eyes measured Tildy and when he spoke his tone was clipped and equally cold.

'Well, what do you want of me?'

Flustered by his unexpected appearance, and embarrassed that he should have caught her scuffling like a true tinker-woman with his servant, Tildy flushed hotly, and at first had difficulty in finding words. Then she drew a deep breath and steadied herself. She stood proudly erect and found with a slight shock of surprise that her eyes were on a level with his. For some unaccountable reason she had thought him to be taller than he actually was. All at once she felt perfectly calm, and was able to explain clearly and concisely the purpose of her visit.

He listened without interruption, but his face betrayed no reaction, only an emotionless impassivity.

Tildy finished and waited silently for his answer.

'So, young woman, you propose to rent your cottage and the land it stands on from my estate?'

Still she could read nothing in his face or eyes.

'Yes, sir. If it pleases you to permit it,' she confirmed.

He nodded curtly. 'I will give thought to the matter. Now get you gone from my door, if you please.'

Tildy stood facing the closed door, perplexed and uncertain. Her hand lifted once towards the bellpull, but she let it fall, fearing that if she pestered the man for anything other than his bare statement that he would give thought to her proposal, then she would destroy any chance at all of saving her home. Despondently she squelched back towards the turnpike road, struggling mentally to find hope that he would agree to rent her the cottage.

'He didn't reject the idea, did he?' she told herself repeatedly. 'He said that he'd think about it, didn't he?'

The continual repetition of his words to her gradually brought about a kindling of hope and by the time she had reached the farm where she was working that day, Tildy had managed to convince herself that all would be well and that she would continue to live with Davy and old Esther on the Mappleborough Green.

The farm she was working on that day was within a mile of her cottage, it lay just to the north of Mappleborough hamlet, and was known by the name of its tenant, Claybrook. The tenant, old David Claybrook, was reputed to be the oldest man who was still working in the four adjoining parishes of Tardebigge, Ipsley, Studley and

Beoley, and at the age of ninety he still walked to the parish church at Studley on every Sabbath day and joined his fellow bell-ringers in pealing out the call to prayer.

The gang was again setting potatoes in a field next to the crossroads where a public house, the Greyhound, stood with its profusion of ancient crooked gables and red-tiled, moss-grown roof.

Sitting in the kitchen of the Greyhound in front of the glowing cooking-fire, Billy Gittins emptied his pot of ale in a series of long gulps, then belched loudly and wiped the froth from his loose lips with the back of his hand.

'Master Stockley?' Gittins shouted. 'More ale here.'

Gilbert Stockley, Landlord of the Greyhound, came from the bar with another foaming pot and handed it to the bailiff.

'Any sign o' my men coming yet?' Gittins wanted to know, and the big-bellied landlord shook his head.

Gittins sighed morosely. 'Shouldn't wonder if the buggers doon't come at all. Can't say as I'd blame 'um. It arn't a job that I relishes meself, I'll tell you, Master Stockley.'

The landlord's broad pink features frowned resentfully. 'It arn't a job any honest man could relish, is it, Master Gittins? Fencing in land wheer our forefathers has bin free to wander and do what they would since the time of Adam and Eve. I'se had to rent land from old David Claybrook to run me own livestock and geese on now our last bit o' common's being enclosed. That master o' yourn is a prize barstard, so he is. And I'll tell him so to his bloody face iffen he ever steps across my threshold.'

Gittins stared doubtfully at the other man. 'You'd be taking a risk doing such a thing as that, 'udden't you, Master Stockley?'

The landlord snorted his disparagement of that statement. 'I'm a freeholder, I am, Master Gittins, and I arn't beholden to any man for the roof over me head, or the right to earn me bit o' bread. No bugger pays my wages so Robert Knight arn't nothing to me, and I doon't give a toss for the bugger, gentry though he may be.'

'I wish I had your independence, Master Stockley,' Gittins said glumly. 'But I arn't, and that's all there is to it. I must just do what he bids me to do and hold my peace about it.'

'What's going to be done about old Esther Smith's cottage?' Stockley asked. ''Ull you run your fence round it?'—

Gittins shook his head. 'That's the wust part o' the business, Master Stockley. I got me orders this very morn from Mr Knight to pull it down.'

'Pull it down?' Stockley was openly shocked. 'When?'

'This very day. That's the fust thing I bin tasked wi' doing. Pull the old witch's cottage down, and Zeke Pickering's shack as well.'

'But old Esther has got that young 'ooman and her kiddy living theer with her. What's to become o' the three on 'um?' The landlord shook his head pityingly. 'It's a cruel shame, so it is. A cruel shame.'

'They'll have to shelter in the poor 'us wun't they, if they can't find anybody to take 'um in.' Gittins suddenly grinned lewdly. 'Mind you, Master Stockley, I 'udden't mind taking the young 'ooman in meself, but my missus 'ud bloody well kill me iffen I was to suggest such a thing.'

The landlord chuckled hoarsely. 'That counts for both on us, Master Gittins, or I'd be offering that young 'un a share o' my bed and board this very instant.'

Loud voices sounded from the bar and Stockley's wife came to tell him, 'The constable's come from Studley, Gilbert, and he's got some rough looking chaps wi' him. You'd best come and serve 'um, because they'm only giving me a lot o' sauce.'

'They'll be the chaps I'm expecting.' Billy Gittins puffed out his cheeks and rose importantly. 'I'll soon put a stop to their sauciness, Mrs Stockley, doon't you fret.'

There were half a dozen men in the bar, five were ragged, unshaven roughs, and Gittins recognised some of them. The dregs of Studley Parish. The sixth man was standing apart from the others, a long thick staff topped with a carved wooden crown held like a pike in his large strong hands. This was William Shayler, constable of Studley Parish. His caped greatcoat increased his burly bulk, and his rugged features glowered dourly from beneath his low-crowned tophat as he regarded the noisy group clamouring for beer.

'Good day to you, Master Shaylet,' Gittings greeted respectfully, and the constable acknowledged him bleakly.

'Is it, Master Gittins? I reckon you'd best not let this rabble stay here too long or they'll be too bloody drunk to work and then it won't be a good day for you, will it?'

'Is Mister Knight coming, did he say, Master Shayler?' the bailiff queried.

'He said naught to me about his intentions.' The constable appeared to be in a very sour mood. 'I don't doubt that it 'ull be the same here as it was at Node Hill. We'll have to do his dirty work and he'll stay well out on it.'

'You know that I'se got to pull down Esther Smith's cottage and the Pickerings' shack, doon't you, Master Shayler?' Gittins queried tentatively.

The other man nodded slowly, and scowled. 'Your employer told me not an hour since. And I told him that I thought it was a sin to destroy an old woman's home. If I warn't the constable o' this parish, and bound by the law, then I'd have naught to do wi' this day's work.' He sighed heavily. 'I'll tell you straight, Billy Gittins, Node Hill was one o' the worst days o' my life and I reckon this 'ull be another 'un just like it.'

''Ull you take a drink o' summat, Master Shayler?' the bailiff invited.

'No.' The constable shook his head. 'Mr Knight asked me to tell you that you're to fetch the horses for the job from Claybrook Farm. I'm surprised that a good Christian man like David Claybrook 'ud lend anything towards this day's work. But then, the old fool is well on into his second dotage, arn't he, and him and Knight are as thick as two thieves, being fellow church members.' He smiled acidly. 'Makes me glad I'm of the Wesleyan persuasion meself.'

The bailiff stood uncertainly, desperately needing another drink, but too nervous of the other man's scathing regard to display his craving. Shayler saved him any further sufferings.

'Well, Master Gittins, you know where you can find the horses you need. I'm going to go on ahead to see old Esther and do what I can for her. You can do the Pickerings' shack first. It's no more than a bloody tent anyways and Zeke's more than likely shifted already.' The hard eyes briefly scanned the men at the bar and he warned, 'You'd best keep these worthless scuts in good order, Master Gittins. Because if they overstep the mark while they're doing this job, then I'll be breaking a few heads, and I'll also know where else to lay the blame.'

Leaving Billy Gittins uneasily digesting his warning Shayler went off on his errand of mercy.

Tildy was following the cart, dividing the large heaps of manure into three smaller heaps. The ploughed ground was soggy with rain and her boots had become huge balls of clayey mud which as the day wore on demanded an ever increasing muscular effort to wrench free from the sucking embrace of the earth. The man pulling the heaps from the cart was a young labourer from Studley village and when he saw the group of men entering the field he drew Tildy's attention to them.

'Look at this lot acoming, Tildy. What's they adoing here wi' the old man, I wonder?'

Tildy shaded her eyes against the driving rain and stared at the oncomers. The bent, but still remarkably spry figure of old David Claybrook, was at the head of the group in company with Billy Gittins, and the labourer with her grunted, 'I knows them buggers, Tildy. Bloody worthless wasters, all on 'um. They'm surely not come here to work wi' us.'

Old Claybrook's wavering shout sounded and the ploughman opening the drills halted his team and went to speak with the farmer, then hurried back to his plough and unhitched his pair of horses from the lead chains. The farmer waved to the second ploughman who was closing the drills behind the women planting the sets to do the same as his fellow.

The young cart man screwed up his face in puzzlement.

'What the bloody hell's agoing on here? What's they taking the teams away for?'

He called to the young boy at the cart horse's head to stand fast, then laid down his dung-graip and hurried across the furrows to talk with his employer himself. As the two teams of horses were led from the field the cart man came back towards Tildy, his youthful face troubled.

'What's the matter?' Tildy asked, and experienced a sudden strange chill of apprehension.

'You'd best get on home straight away, Tildy,' the young man told her. 'Them buggers be agoing to use them hosses to pull down old Esther's cottage.'

Tildy gasped with shock and horror. 'No! No, they can't be. I spoke with Mr Knight this morning and he told me they wouldn't do such.' Her thoughts were a confused jumble and her reluctance to accept what was happening caused her to remember more what she wished had occurred rather than what actually had passed between her and Robert Knight.

'You spoke wi' Robert Knight this morn, Tildy?' the cart man questioned.

She nodded distractedly, her eyes fixed on the two teams of horses and the men with them, now crossing the turnpike ride and beginning to trek across the heathland.

'I asked him to let me rent the cottage from him and he told me he'd give it thought.' Her voice rose on a note of strained indignation. 'He told me he'd give it thought. He told me that.'

'Well, that arn't the same as telling you he 'udden't

knock the place down, is it Tildy?' the young man pointed out reasonably.

Tildy ignored him and, with heart thudding painfully and her breath rasping in her throat, she ran across the field towards the turnpike road.

When she reached the cottage she found old Esther sitting in her chair rocking her body backwards and forwards, whimpering piteously, while little Davy vainly attempted to comfort her.

He flung himself into Tildy's arms, and in tearful distress told her, 'The man came and spoke with Nanny Esther, Mam, and then he went away again, and Nanny Esther just keeps on doing this and won't answer me. What did he do to make her like this, Mam? What did the man do?'

Tildy's own distress and anger battled for dominance over her, but she knew that to give way to either emotion would not aid her at this moment. She hugged the child and soothed him.

'Now don't you fret, darling, your Mam's here now. Everything will be all right.'

'But why is Nanny Esther crying, Mam? Why is she?'

Tildy's heart wept within her as she looked down at his woebegone little face, and she swallowed hard. Holding him away from her breasts so that he could see her face, she said quietly, 'Now you must listen to me very carefully, Davy, and you must be very brave and make me very proud of you. Everything will be all right, that I promise you, and Nanny Esther will soon stop crying and be happy again. But before that can happen, then you and I have got to be very brave, and not shed any tears. Can you do that for me?'

He stared solemnly at her, then nodded slowly. 'Yes, Mam, I can be very brave.'

'I know you can, honey.' She forced herself to smile cheerfully. 'Well, I think that the man told Nanny Esther that we must leave this place and go somewhere else to live.'

Alarm showed in his eyes. 'Leave here, Mam? Leave the dogs, and Zeke?'

She nodded, but tried to smile and reassure him. 'Oh I'm sure we can take the dogs with us, honey, and we shan't be going very far away from Zeke, so you'll still be able to see him, and go out with him.'

The child cheered up a little as he heard this, then asked, 'Why can't Zeke and Zeke's woman come with us, Mam?'

'Because I haven't decided where we shall go yet, honey. Mayhap Zeke will come with us. I just don't know.' She drew a long breath. 'Now, honey, I want you to help me get ready to move.' She smiled confidently. 'We're going to have a great adventure, aren't we? Finding a new place to live and seeing all manner of new things. It's exciting, isn't it?'

For a few moments he pondered on this, then to Tildy's heartfelt relief, he suddenly grinned happily, and exclaimed excitedly, 'Yes, Mam. Can I goo and tell the dogs that we're moving? Can I tell them we're going on an adventure?'

'Of course you can.' Tildy chuckled fondly, and her heart lifted as she realised that so long as she had this child safe and sound by her side then what did anything else really matter? 'Go and tell them now then.'

She released him and as he scampered away smiled lovingly after him. Then she looked at old Esther and her smile faltered and died.

'Esther?' She went to the old woman's side and knelt in front of her, taking the gnarled, twisted hands in her own. 'Esther, I know that you're upset, but you mustn't give in to it this way,' she urged gently.

The old woman's features were a mask of misery. 'What 'ull become o' me now, Tildy? I'll have to goo into the poor 'us, wun't I?'

'No, you shall not go there!' Tildy told her forcefully. 'I'll not let them take you into the poorhouse. You shall go with me and Davy.'

'But I'll just be a burden to you, Tildy. I'm all crippled up wi' the rheumatics. It's all I can do to move about, let alone work.'

'Don't you worry about that.' Tildy tried to sound confident. 'Everything will be all right in the end, just trust me.'

For a moment it seemed that old Esther was comforted, then her eyes flickered wildly about the room and she wailed plaintively. 'I doon't want to leave here, Tildy. I'd sooner be dead than leave me home.'

'We'll find another home,' Tildy promised desperately. 'We'll be happy there, you'll see.'

She leaned forward and put her arms about the old woman's frail body, trying to soothe her. 'It's not where we live that's important, Esther. It's who we live with that counts. And as long as we three can stay together, then we shall be happy enough.'

Slowly the racking sobs of the other woman eased and despite the pain of kneeling so awkwardly on the hard floor, Tildy remained in that same position while the minutes passed, knowing that at this time old Esther needed her warm embrace more than anything else in the world.

'Mam! Mam!' Davy came bursting back into the cottage. 'Mam, theer's some men coming and horses!'

Gently Tildy disengaged herself from old Esther and went to the door to look out across the heath. Coming towards the cottage, led by the mounted Billy Gittins, were the wrecking crew. One man had a long chain wrapped around his upper body like a bandolier. The others carried long iron crowbars and sledgehammers, and bringing up the rear were the two teams of plough-horses.

The rain was falling steadily and for the first time Tildy thought of the bedding and household implements and the few sticks of furniture within the cottage.

'Everything will be ruined by this wet.' Dismayed, Tildy could not think clearly and was still standing in the doorway, vainly trying to formulate her thoughts when the gang arrived at the cottage.

Billy Gittins rode his horse right up to the doorway and from under his coat produced a cylinder of thick paper which he held out towards Tildy, and blustered hectoringly, 'This here's a copy o' the Notice of Enclosure for this land, young 'ooman. Youm trespassing here, and youm breaking the law by being here. So I'm telling you to clear off, right now, and take the old 'ooman and the kid wi' you.'

Tildy looked up into his flabby jowled face with acute dislike and found that her mind was clearing fast.

'I went to see Mr Knight this morn, and he told me that he would give thought to renting this cottage to me. So until he gives me his answer, then I don't see that we are trespassing here.'

'It's Mr Knight who's gi' me the orders to evict you now, my wench,' Gittins informed her pompously.

Tildy could hear the sobs of old Esther coming from inside the cottage, and the heart-rending sounds kindled her stubborn fighting spirit.

'Well, Master Gittins, I think it only just that Mr Knight himself serves that Notice of Enclosure on me, and tells me to my face that he wants me gone from here.'

'Mr Knight's a gentleman, not a notice server,' Gittins told her petulantly. 'Who does you think you am, young 'ooman, to demand that he must come and tell you hisself? Youm acting above your bloody station, arn't you?'

'My station has got naught to do with it.' Tildy's fiery temper was rising fast. 'Esther Smith has lived here for forty years or longer and I don't think anyone has got the right to throw her out of her home.'

Behind the bailiff the half-drunken crew, ripe for any mischief and enjoying the bailiff's discomfiture, applauded Tildy jeeringly.

'That's it, my duck, you tell him!'

'Get bloody Knight down here, my wench!'

'Yeah, you sort the bugger out, girl!'

At heart Billy Gittins was not a vicious man and he truly did not relish what he was now having to do. But he was a weak man, and timid, and he went in mortal fear of his employer, and in mortal fear also of losing his present position. He heard the jeers of the crew and dreaded what tales of his own weakness in this present situation might get back to the ears of Robert Knight. Driven by this dread he became a bawling bully.

'Get out of here now, you bloody slut. And take the brat and the old cow wi' you!'

He hurled the rolled enclosure notice at Tildy, and it struck her in the eye, causing her to cry out in shock and lift her hand to her face. Little Davy had been standing at Tildy's side throughout the heated exchange and although frightened by the towering, shouting man, when he heard his mother cry out, the child was transfused by a blinding fury, and he darted forwards.

'You let my mam alone. You let my mam alone.'

Gittin's mount, alarmed by the sudden apparition of this tiny noisy creature beneath its muzzle, started and bucked, and the bailiff lost his stirrup and balance and fell from the saddle, his body thumping heavily onto the soggy ground.

A howl of raucous jeering laughter erupted from the wrecking crew and they cheered vociferously.

'Good on you, little 'un!'

'Ten to one on the nipper.'

'Fust blood to the kid!'

Winded by the impact, Billy Gittins rolled over and wheezing for breath stayed on hands and knees for some seconds, the rain beating down on his bowed head, his hat crushed flat into the mud by the hooves of his horse.

Tildy grabbed little Davy and thrust him back into the cottage. 'Stay there!' she shouted and, fearful at what he had caused to happen, the child obeyed her.

Gittins clambered groaningly to his feet, and his flabby face was purple with rage as he glared murderously at Tildy.

'You fuckin' cow!' he panted out. 'You fuckin' bastard cow!' He swung on the laughing men behind him. 'You and you,' he pointed to two of them. 'Get in theer and fetch this fuckin' bitch out on it, and that fuckin' kid and the old witch as well. The rest on you get the horses chained up and pull this fuckin' pigsty down.'

When they were slow to move, he screamed, 'Do it now, or I'll be telling Mister Knight that you refused to do the business, and then it 'ull goo hard wi' the lot on you. Do it now!'

The most drunken of the men laughed and spat on his hands. 'I'll tek the young 'un out on it. I fancies a feel of her tits.'

His words introduced a fresh and frightening element and a couple of the other men now stared at Tildy with a rapidly burgeoning lust.

'I'll help you tek her out, Cully,' one of them grinned lewdly. 'Her tits am big enough for both on us to share, by the looks on 'um.'

Sudden sexual dread overlayed Tildy's anger, and her mouth dried as the two men began to move towards her, mouthing lewd invitations.

'Come here to me, sweet thing, let's see what you'se got atween your legs. Come on and give us a feel.'

She thought of Davy and old Esther and knew that these men in their present drink-clouded mood were a terrible threat to both of them and capable of committing any outrage, and she summoned all her courage and readied herself to fight and if necessary to die in defence of her son and her friend.

The men came on, arms outstretched, hands reaching greedily, mouths loose and wet-lipped as they savoured what was to come. Then, abruptly, they jolted to a halt and shocked alarm replaced gloating lust on their bestial faces.

'Get you behind me, Tildy.' Old Esther hobbled through the doorway, the ancient blunderbuss pointing unwaveringly at the transfixed men. 'This is loaded and

83

iffen any one o' you so much as takes a single step onnards, I'll blow you to kingdom come.'

'Her's bluffing! The old cow's bluffing!' Billy Gittins blustered. 'Get it off her.'

Old Esther's cackling laughter rang out insanely and her black eyes glittered ferociously. 'Bluffing, d'you say? Bluffing am I? Then step you up Billy Gittins and you try a taste o' this in your belly. Come on, man!' Her cracking voice rose into a high-pitched shriek. 'Come on, Gittins, call me bluff. Call it!' She hobbled forwards, gun aimed and the men fell back before her and Billy Gittins blanched and fell back quicker than all.

One of the men raised his arms and waved them in a gesture of rebuttal. 'Fuck this for a game o' sodgers. I didn't engage for this job to get me bleedin' tripes blown out by a fuckin' mad 'ooman. I'm off.' Suiting action to words he turned on his heels and scurried away. The others seemed powerless to move, and the two parties stood facing each other in the rain, locked in impasse.

Tildy lost all track of time, aware only of the hissing of heavy breathing and the pattering of the rain upon the ground. To one side of her, little Davy clutched her skirt, and at her other side old Esther stood like a graven statue, her hair a wild frieze about her withered face, only her black eyes moving, darting ferociously from man to man.

'Esther, put that bloody gun up!' It was William Shayler, tramping hurriedly towards them. 'Don't any of you others make a move until I gets to you.'

His breath came short and heavy as he reached them and he confronted Billy Gittins furiously. 'What in hell's name 'as you bin about here, Gittins? Didn't I warn you that I'd break bloody heads iffen these scums stepped over the mark?'

Gittins indignantly drew attention to his muddied clothes and crushed hat. 'Now hold hard, Will Shayler, I bin nigh on killed here. Look at the state I'm in. 'Tis not us who stepped over the mark, but this bloody lot.' He pointed at the two women and child. 'They caused me horse to throw me and then that bloody black witch theer come threatening to blow us to pieces with that soddin' blunderbuss. It's them that's stepped over the mark, not us. I wants 'um charged, both on 'um.'

'Charged with what?' the constable demanded.

'Charged with trying to murder me,' Gittins flustered.

'Doon't talk so sarft, man,' Shayler snapped curtly, and walked up to old Esther. 'I'll take this for the present, Esther.' Calmly he lifted the gun from her unresisting hands, and casually checked its priming pan. Then he chuckled contemptuously at the bailiff. ''Tis not even primed, you great fool.'

The constable knew Tildy and had a lot of respect for her. Now he grimaced sympathetically. 'It's a bad business this, Tildy Crawford. I'm really sorry to see you in this plight.'

'Is there any way you can stop these men from pulling our home down, Master Shayler?' Tildy asked.

Regretfully he shook his head. 'No, my wench, there's naught I can do. They'm acting within the law. But you doon't have to be without a roof over your head this night. I can get you all admitted to the poor'us.'

'No! Never! I'd sooner die out here than goo into the bloody poor'us!' Old Esther was emphatic and Tildy, with memories of her own sojourn in the Tardebigge poorhouse, was in agreement with her.

'Youm talking daft, Esther,' the constable snapped curtly, and addressed Tildy. 'Doon't you think that you'd all be better off in the poor'us, than wandering abroad in weather like this, looking for shelter?'

'I'm grateful for your offer, Master Shayler,' Tildy told him quietly. 'But I think the same as Esther. I wore the pauper badge once, I'm not going to have my child wearing it. Not even for a day.'

'Come over here for a minute.' Shayler jerked his head at Tildy, and together they walked out of earshot of the others.

'Now listen well, Tildy Crawford.' The constable spoke

in a hoarse whisper. 'I can tell you now that theer's nobody in this parish who'ull give old Esther shelter beneath their roof. They'm too feared to because her's known as a black witch. You and your kiddy 'ud find it easy to get took in, I'm sure, but you'll needs be on your own. Nobody 'ull take old Esther in. I reckon it 'ud be good sense for you to leave her to her own devices and do what's best for your kiddy. He's too young to be wandering abroad and sleeping in ditches. You think on it now.'

Tildy didn't need to think. She had no intention of abandoning old Esther, no matter how difficult it might make things for herself and Davy, and she told the man so.

'All right then, my wench. If that's how you wants it to be,' Shayler accepted.

As they went to rejoin the others Tildy asked, 'What's become of Zeke Pickering? Are they going to knock his place down this day?'

'That's what they intended, but Zeke had already gone. No doubt him and his gyppo 'ooman 'ull have got their tent pitched somewhere snug by now.'

Despite her own troubles, Tildy was relieved to hear that her son's friend had avoided a confrontation with the wrecking crew.

'Now then, Will Shayler.' Billy Gittins was displaying irascible impatience. 'I must get on wi' the business. So can you do your lawful duty and keep these women out on our way?'

Shayler frowned sullenly. 'I'se got no choice in the matter, has I, Gittins? Iffen I had, then I'd not lift a bloody finger to help in this.' He beckoned to the two ploughmen standing apart with their horses. 'You lads can come and gi' me a hand to help these poor souls get their belongings out of the cottage. I doon't trust these other buggers not to steal whatever they can.'

When one of the roughs snarled his resentment at these words, Shayler scowled fiercely. 'Doon't you show your bloody teeth to me, Morris, or you'll be feeling the weight o' my staff across your head. I knows you too well, my lad. You bin a bloody thief ever since you was breeched.'

The ploughmen and constable began to help Tildy and little Davy to fetch out the contents of the cottage, and after a few moments old Esther, now displaying a dour stoicism, hobbled to join them.

It did not take long to empty the building because the women possessed little. Tildy felt tears stinging her eyes as she regarded the rain soaking the pathetic jumble of crude furniture and bedding, cooking utensils and storage pots placed some twenty yards from the cottage.

There was little stone used in the construction of the cottage, it was mainly thick mud walls and timber supports, and the men smashed holes in the walls with crowbars and sledgehammers then passed the long thick chain through those holes and secured its ends to the two teams of horses.

'Hup, hup, hup! Gerron now. Gerron theer! Hup, hup, hup!' The ploughmen urged on the teams and the massive muscles writhed and bunched beneath the muddy steaming hides as the beasts took the strain and heaved with all their mighty strength.

'Hup, hup, hup! Gerron! Gerron theer! Hup, hup, hup!'

The walls buckled and toppled and the thatched roof crashed down upon the dusty debris.

Tildy knuckled the tears from her eyes with one hand and put her other arm around old Esther's frail shoulders to comfort her. But the old woman was curiously calm, seemingly detached from what was happening to her home, and she remained dry-eyed.

The men swarmed over the wreckage smashing down with their crowbars and sledgehammers to complete the destruction.

By Tildy's side little Davy watched with wide eyes, his hands clutching the leashes of the two dogs who danced about barking wildly with excitement.

Their work finished, the wrecking crew walked away, callously laughing and joking. The two ploughmen were silent and shamefaced as they glanced at the forlorn figures of the women and child and one of them mumbled apologies before he led his team off.

Billy Gittins fumbled with his crushed and muddied hat, then crammed it on his head and remounted his horse.

'It warn't any wish on my part to do this, so 'tis no use you alaying the blame at my door. I had to do what my master bade me,' he flustered guiltily, and would not meet Tildy's eyes as he went from the scene.

William Shayler came to stand in front of the bedraggled group. 'Listen to me now, you can't stand out here in this weather. Come on into the village wi' me now and let me get you admitted to the poor'us.'

'I'se told you already, Will Shayler, that I'd sooner be dead than enter that place.' It was old Esther who answered him.

Paradoxically the destruction of her home had appeared to infuse her with new strength and resolve.

'We'll be all right, wun't us, Tildy?'

In the face of the old woman's courage Tildy felt ashamed at her own momentary display of weakness in giving way to tears as she had and she forced herself to smile confidently.

'That's right, Esther, we'll come through this.'

The constable's hard face was troubled as he stared at them.

'Where will you goo?' he wanted to know. 'And what about these things?' He pointed at their possessions. By now the bedding was completely saturated and the pouring rain showed no signs of easing. 'If you leaves 'um here unguarded then the chances are that they'll all be pinched afore nightfall. You can bet that them buggers who'se just left 'ull come back poking around when they thinks that the coast is clear.'

Again it was old Esther who gave him answer. 'I shall

stay here wi' Davy and the dogs and watch over our things. Tildy can goo to Redditch and see if my nephew, Daniel, can give us shelter until we finds a place of our own to live in agen.'

William Shayler mulled over this for some seconds, then queried, 'But what if your nephew won't take you in, Esther? What 'ull you do then?'

Amazingly, the old woman chuckled and told him with a mischievous glint in her black eyes. 'Then I'll just have to conjure summat up for us, wun't I, Will Shayler? Arter all, 'tis well known that I'm a black witch, arn't it?'

The man grinned in acknowledgement of her courage, and nodded.

'Very well then, Esther. If that's what you intends. I'll goo across and see if old David Claybrook can gi' the loan of a tarpaulin sheet, so that we can cover your things agen this rain. You and the kiddy can shelter under it as well, can't you, while this young 'ooman goes to Redditch. I'll be as quick as I can.'

With that he walked off towards Claybrook Farm.

'What does you think to my idea then, Tildy? About asking my nephew to give us houseroom until we can find our own place?'

Tildy smiled wryly. 'I think that beggars can't be choosers, Esther. And I'll be very grateful if he does agree to shelter us. But it must be on the clear understanding that we pay our way.'

The old woman nodded acquiescence and, satisfied, Tildy kissed her and Davy goodbye and set out towards Redditch town.

As she trudged along the rutted muddy lanes waves of despair threatened to engulf her. It seemed that she was destined to trouble, no matter what she did, or how hard she tried to live a life of normality. She experienced a terrible sense of weariness.

'Will I ever know peace?' she wondered miserably. 'Will life ever get better for me?'

Then, as she sank into the deepest pit of despondency a

strange sense that someone was walking at her side caused her to look sharply about her. She came to an abrupt halt, standing perfectly still in the muddy lane, with the rain driving against her face. Then she almost cried in fright as she felt the distinct pressure of a hand upon her shoulder. She turned, although knowing that no one was there, yet still she felt that hand. But all at once her fright disappeared and, from being a frightening, unseen presence, the pressure upon her shoulder became a comforting, strengthening reassurance that she was not alone and friendless in this world. The pressure lifted and disappeared as mysteriously as it had come and Tildy remained motionless, trying to make some sense out of what she had just experienced.

Eventually she walked slowly onwards, but now, instead of despair, she felt a burgeoning of new strength and the hope that all would eventually be well was reborn within her.

Chapter Ten

The windows were shuttered and no smoke rose from the chimneys of the house. Tildy knew instinctively that she would find no one there, yet still pulled at the bellrope on the side of the outer gate. She was soaked through to the skin, and could feel the squelching of water in her boots, while her saturated shawl was a clammy cowl about her head and shoulders. Again she pulled the bellrope, mocking herself as she did so because she knew that no one would come in answer to the summons, but for some unaccountable reason unable to resist the impulse.

'Who be you seeking, young 'ooman?'

Tildy swung about.

The voice had come from a woman standing in the door of one of the terraced cottages facing Daniel Lambert's house on the opposite side of the roadway.

'I'm looking for Master Lambert. I was told that this was his house.'

She crossed the road to go to the other woman.

'Do you know where I might find him?'

The woman stared curiously at Tildy.

'Be you kin to him?' she asked.

'No, I'm not kin myself. But I've come on behalf of his aunt.'

'Who might she be then?'

'Widow Smith.'

'Which Smith is that? Only there's a few Widow Smiths around these parts arn't there?'

'It's the Widow Smith over at Mappleborough.' By now Tildy's patience with this prying was beginning to wear thin. 'Look, ma'am, I mean no offence, but I've no time to waste. Do you know where I can find Daniel Lambert?'

'He's in the lock-up, my wench,' the woman told her, then went into her house and closed the door.

For a moment or two Tildy stood digesting this shock news, wondering what Daniel Lambert had done that warranted him being put in the lock-up.

'Well, there's only one sure way to find that out, my girl,' she told herself. 'You'd best get up there now and ask him yourself.'

She went first to the home of Joseph Cashmore, the Tardebigge Parish constable, which stood a little distance back from its neighbours in Evesham Street, the road running south from the central crossroads on the green. The burly, taciturn man evinced surprised recognition when he saw who the caller was.

'It's Tildy Crawford, arn't it?' He glanced out over her shoulder into the street. 'It's bad weather to be out in, my duck. You'd best step inside and state your business.'

Tildy was grateful to gain a brief respite from the driving rain and breathed a sigh of pleasure as the warmth of the room enfolded her. The big man gestured in invitation. 'Step up to the fire, girl, and thaw yourself out a bit.'

Tildy obeyed and stood as close to the fire as possible, so that the steam began to rise from her sacking overskirt.

'It must be nigh on two years since we last met, Tildy Crawford. Last time I heard you was living wi' the old witch-'ooman at Mappleborough. Still theer wi' your nipper, am you?'

She nodded, and then very quickly explained what had happened that day and her purpose in coming to see him now. He heard her out in silence, pursing his lips reflectively and frowning on occasion. When she had done, he told her with some sympathy, 'By Christ, my wench, you certainly has your fair share o' troubles, doon't you?'

She smiled wryly. 'Others have worse troubles, Master Cashmore. Mine haven't killed me yet, and these present ones won't either.'

'That's the spirit, girl.' There was a warmth of admiration in his eyes. 'Never say die!'

He raised his voice and shouted, 'Wife? Bring me things here. I'm going out.'

A mouselike little woman came hurrying from the back kitchen carrying a huge caped greatcoat, a long crowned staff of office and a tricorn hat. She fussed about her husband as he donned the hat and coat.

''Ull you be long away d'you think, Mr Cashmore? 'Ull you be wanting your dinner at your usual time? Shall I put the mate in to goo on cooking?'

'I shall be as long away as needful, Wife. So give over werritin' me, 'ull you?' he told her sternly, and taking up a huge bunch of keys from the dresser he nodded to Tildy. 'Come on then, my wench. We'll goo and visit wi' Master Lambert.'

As they walked to the crossroads and then turned eastwards down the marketplace towards the lock-up, Cashmore explained to Tildy why Daniel Lambert was in the jail.

'But I can't believe that Daniel Lambert would be stupid enough to steal needles when he's only just returned from Botany Bay!' Tildy shook her head. 'Besides, from what old Esther tells me, he has no need to steal anything. His father left him well provided for.'

'Well, strictly atween ourselves, girl, I shares your opinion.' Cashmore frowned unhappily. 'But there's a deal o' prejudice agen Daniel Lambert in this town. As there 'ud be agen any returned transport, in all fairness.

'I'se known the chap since we was all kids, and I'se always liked him well enough. He arn't what you 'ud call a wicked bugger, even though he was sent to Botany Bay. He was only took up for poaching, like a lot of other chaps round these parts. But he's always bin a wild sort o' cove, and there's them whom feared on him because o' that wildness.'

Tildy stared at the squat castellated tower which was the lock-up, with its massive iron-studded door and the arrow slits which admitted air and scant light to the ground floor cell.

'Daniel Lambert must be feeling very depressed being shut away in such a place,' she remarked.

Cashmore's heavy features creased into a bleak grin. 'Oh he arn't too depressed, my wench. He's allowed to buy whatever vittles or drink he wants and have his pipe and bacca. He's got his own bedding as well because, really speaking he arn't bin charged wi' anything yet, he's only being held for examination by Parson Clayton. Strictly atween ourselves I reckon the parson 'ull let him goo. I don't think he'll commit Lambert to the Worcester Bridewell for sessions trial. The evidence agen him arn't strong enough for the grand jury to find a true bill agen him. No, once the parson's come back and examined him, I reckon Lambert 'ull be as free as a bird in double quick time.'

By now they were almost at the lock-up and to her amazement Tildy could hear the sounds of singing coming from the arrow slits.

The constable chuckled grimly. 'Theer now, didn't I tell you that Daniel Lambert warn't feeling too depressed? Just hark to the bugger. He's as merry as a cricket, by the sound on it.'

The two of them stood and listened for a while to the tuneful voice and the catchy melody.

'Cut yer name across me backbone,
Stretch me skin across a drummm,
Iron me up to Pinchgut Island
From todaaaay, till kingdom come!

I will eat your Norfolk dumpling
Like a juicy Spanish plummmm,
Even dance the Newgate hornpipe,
If you'll onleeeey give me rummmmm!'

As the song ended another voice applauded noisily.

'That's prime that is Danny! That's bloody prime!

That's a real convict song, that 'un is!'

Joseph Cashmore selected a large key from his huge bunch and inserted it into the ornate lock of the great door. Tildy stepped after him into a sort of antechamber from which a flight of stone steps led up to the second storey of the building. In the inner wall almost directly opposite the great door was another door, with a small lattice grille set into it. The constable bent and peered through the grille and, apparently satisfied with what he saw, unlocked this door also and pushed it open.

'Here's a visitor come to speak with you, Lambert. And you mind your manners, Tom Chance, because it's a young 'ooman, and a decent 'un as well.'

Tildy peeped around the constable's bulk into the gloomy cell. There was a straw mattress on one side of it and a heap of bedding on the other. Daniel Lambert was sitting on the bedding and sprawled on the straw mattress facing him was a young, shaggy-haired, unshaven man, wearing a shabby coat, torn breeches and a grease-thick shirt. On the stone-flagged floor between the two men were strewn the remnants of a substantial meal and several bottles, some empty, others as yet still corked. The dank air was thick with the fug of tobacco smoke and heavy with the mingled smells of rum, food and unwashed flesh.

Daniel Lambert rose unsteadily to his feet and Tildy saw that in contrast to his companion he looked freshly shaven and clean. His thinning hair was tidily brushed and his linen white and starched. He screwed up his eyes and peered at Tildy through the gloom, then his eyes widened with surprise and he came forward exclaiming, 'What brings you here, Tildy?' His eyes were bleary and his words slurred, but with a visible effort he tried to sober himself. 'Has anything happened to my aunt?'

Once again Tildy related the events of the day, and as she did so Daniel Lambert scowled and muttered angrily beneath his breath, then apologised.

'I'm sorry you should find me in such a condition,

Tildy. But I wasn't expecting visitors. But don't worry, although I'm a trifle drunk, I know well enough what I'm doing.'

He fumbled in his coat pocket and produced a small bunch of keys which he proffered to her. 'Take these and open up my house. You shall all move in there. You'll find coals and candles in plenty. I'm using the main bedroom above the front hallway, but you may choose any of the other rooms that you please to sleep in.'

He waved aside her thanks, then lifted up one forefinger and swayed slightly. 'Hold hard. You'll needs to have your belongings fetched here as well.' He took coins from his pocket and despite her protests forced them into Tildy's hand. 'Take this and hire a cart. Don't argue the toss, woman, if it upsets you so to take my money, then you can regard it as a loan.'

He turned to the constable. 'Will you see to it that she's not cheated over the cart hire, Master Cashmore?'

The other man nodded. 'I'll do that, Lambert.' He turned to Tildy. 'I've other business to attend to as well, my wench, so you'll ha' to make your goodbyes now. You can come again tomorrow and visit Master Lambert.'

Again she thanked Daniel Lambert, then the doors were relocked and she was out in the rain once more.

In the cell Thomas Chance grinned salaciously at Lambert, who was still standing, staring musingly at the locked door.

'You lucky bastard, Danny. I wish I'd got a piece o' meat like that awaiting back at home for me.'

Daniel Lambert turned slowly and stared warningly at the other man. 'Have a care what you say, Cully. I don't think of her as a piece o' meat.'

'Now doon't you get uppitty wi' me, Danny Boy.' Chance's brown teeth remained bared in the grin. 'I'm just wondering iffen you knows anything about that pretty bird.'

'I know enough,' Lambert snapped curtly. 'Now just let it drop.'

Chance ignored the warning. 'I knowed of her years back. When her man come and snatched her babby from her. She had him took up afore the beaks and he got whipped at the cart's end, all the way through the bloody town. She's a regular tartar, that 'un is. I reckon Tom Crawford must have asked hisself manys the time iffen fuckin' her was worth all the trouble it landed him in.'

Anger brought a hissing note to Daniel Lambert's voice. 'I've told you to drop it, Chance. I won't tell you again.'

Drink always made Tom Chance aggressive and he carried the reputation of being an eager brawler who had won many street and tavern battles. His present incarceration stemmed from one such conflict, in which he had rammed a broken bottle into the face of his unfortunate opponent. Confident that he could easily master his cellmate, who was several years older than himself, the young man got to his feet, clutching a half-filled bottle in his right hand as if it were a bludgeon. Then deliberately he provoked.

'Mind you, Danny Boy, Tom Crawford allus reckoned her was a bloody awful shag. That's why I never bothered to fuck her meself when her was hawking her cunt around the pubs.'

He stood poised and ready for any move his prospective victim might make against him, trusting confidently in his own speed of reaction to counter that move with his own devastating attack. He licked his lips in hungry anticipation of releasing the clamouring violence within him.

Daniel Lambert realised that Chance was determined to force a fight upon him and knew also that if he turned away and refused to fight, then the other man would simply launch into an assault. Schooled in the manifold savageries of war and penal servitude, he coolly weighed the situation, his eyes noting the position of potential weapons and the stance and balance of his prospective opponent. Abruptly he assumed a semi-crouching, almost cringing posture and spread both hands out in appeal as he whined nervously.

'I thought me and you was become good mates, Tom. I don't know why you're taking this attitude with me. I don't want any trouble with you. Haven't I been good to you? I've shared my food and drink with you haven't I?'

Tom Chance's confidence burgeoned into an absolute surety of easy victory in the face of this display of cowardly submission and momentarily he was offguard as his tensed muscles relaxed and he sought in his mind for foul taunts and insults to heap on Lambert's head, before he battered his cringing body into bloody pulp. Daniel Lambert had anticipated that momentary relaxation and he struck now with the speed and deadliness of a cobra, pivoting his body on his bent left leg and spearing his right foot forwards with crushing impact against Chance's kneecap. The younger man's leg crumpled under him, bringing him to the floor, and he screamed as the blinding agony of breaking bone was coupled with the further agonies of Lambert's riding boot smashing down upon the hand that still clutched the bottle, crushing fingers and lacerating flesh against the razorlike shards of glass.

Breathing hard, Daniel Lambert stood over his fallen opponent, ready to kick him senseless should he show any signs of continuing the fight. But the other man only writhed and sobbed and screamed with pain, and Lambert's ravening combat fury left him as quickly as it had risen and he stooped and dragged the shrieking man away from the broken glass in case he should cause himself further damage as his body rolled and twisted on the floor.

Daniel Lambert went to the arrow slit and began to shout through it in hopes of attracting the attention of any passers-by. Eventually a man came to the outer wall, and Daniel requested, 'Fetch a surgeon here straight away, will you please. Here, this is for your trouble.' He handed a shilling coin through the slender aperture. 'There'll be another of those for you when you bring the surgeon.'

The man hurried off and Daniel seated himself on his bedding and lifting a bottle to his lips took a long swallow of the fiery spirit it contained, then sat staring stonily at the sobbing Thomas Chance.

When Tildy finally got back to the wrecked cottage with the hired horse and cart she found that Zeke Pickering was sheltering under the tarpaulin sheet with old Esther and little Davy.

'I'se come over to see if youm all right, Tildy,' he told her, 'and to let you know that iffen you needs shelter then me and my 'ooman has pitched our tent down by Ipsley Alders. We can all squeeze in together if needful.'

To Davy's obvious disappointment, she shook her head. 'Thank you all the same, Zeke. But we're going to move in with Esther's nephew at Redditch for a time. It's better for Esther that she's in a house, with her rheumaticks being so bad just lately.'

The man's swarthy features looked downcast. 'I'll miss you lot,' he said quietly, and ruffled Davy's curls. ''Specially my little mate here.'

'We're not going so far away that Davy can't come and visit with you, Zeke.' Tildy could see clearly that both the man and the boy were upset at their imminent parting and on impulse she offered, 'Listen, how about if Davy comes and stays with you now for a day or two until I get things settled in Redditch?'

Davy crowed with delight and Zeke Pickering grinned happily.

'That's the ticket, Tildy. You leave my mate wi' me until you gets sorted.'

He helped them load the cart with their belongings and took the tarpaulin sheet to return it to Claybrook Farm. They parted at the crossroads by the Greyhound Inn and Tildy was unable to completely suppress her pangs of jealousy as she watched her son go happily off hand in hand with the tall, shabby figure of Zeke Pickering.

Old Esther's black eyes fixed on Tildy's expressive features and read what was in them. 'Youm doing the right thing, my duck,' she told her young friend approvingly. 'They'm good for each other, them two am. You'll find that by not tying Davy to your apron strings, then you'll bind him all the more securely to you.'

'I know you're right in what you say, Esther,' Tildy answered pensively. 'But I still find it a hard thing to do.'

The hired driver stared meaningfully at the Greyhound Inn. ''Tis a fair old walk to Redditch in this bloody weather, Missus. A man 'ud travel easier iffen he had a drop o' summat to give him strength.'

'You'll get summat when we'em at Redditch and all unloaded,' old Esther scolded. 'So let's have no nonsense from you, my buck, because you'll get naught afore then.'

Sulkily the man led his horse onwards, with Tildy and old Esther walking behind the cart tail, and so they continued until, weary and bedraggled, they reached their destination.

Chapter Eleven

John Clayton, curate to Reverend the Lord Aston, vicar of Tardebigge Parish, was noteworthy for both his ugly face and his remarkably muscular physique. He was fortunate in that his ugliness was such that it became paradoxically attractive to look upon and his native intelligence and shrewdness of character were of a high order. Reverend the Lord Aston was the resident justice of the peace in the Parish of Tardebigge, but during his frequent absences from the parish then John Clayton acted as his deputy in that respect.

Now the young parson sat at his roll-top desk in the candlelit study of his house, which was near the top of the Fish Hill, and considered what he had just heard from Joseph Cashmore, standing to his side. Clayton steepled his forefingers in front of his brawny chest and bent his close-cropped, unpowdered head as he pondered.

'The man Chance claims that Daniel Lambert assaulted him without cause, you say, Master Cashmore?'

'That's so, parson, but knowing Chance like I does, and having some knowledge of Lambert as well, 'tis my opinion that Tom Chance was more nor likely the one who started the trouble. Lambert says that Chance was determined to force a fight on him and knowing what the young bugger is like when he's took drink, then I'm inclined to believe the truth of Lambert's statement.' The constable realised his slip of the tongue, and muttered, 'Beg pardon for swearing like that, parson.'

Clayton dismissed the offence with a jerk of his chin. 'No matter, Master Cashmore.' Briefly his teeth nibbled at his full lower lip. 'Concerning the other matter, of the theft of the needles from Master Gould's warehouse, what think you to that?'

The constable shrugged his meaty shoulders. 'I think the evidence agen Lambert is a bit weak to have him committed to sessions, Parson Clayton. I doon't think that the grand jury 'ud find a true bill agen him.'

Clayton nodded thoughtfully. 'I find myself in agreement with you there, Master Cashmore, having read the statements made by the night patrol. Anyone might have hidden the needles under the coals in the outhouse without the occupant of the dwelling house hearing them. Particularly on such a stormy night. And as Jonas Crow admits himself, there was no wet clothing found in the house which might indicate that Lambert had been abroad that night.'

He lapsed into silence and Cashmore stolidly waited. After a while Clayton stirred himself and took a paper from his desk which he scanned by the light of the candle.

He grimaced wryly. 'Judging from Doctor Taylor's report, it seems that Tom Chance caught a tiger by the tail when he forced a fight upon Lambert. Broken kneecap, broken fingers, broken handbones, lacerations of the hand and fingers also.'

'It bears out Lambert's story though, doon't it, parson?' Cashmore observed. 'That Chance was holding a bottle which he meant to use.'

Clayton came to his decision and slapped the top of his desk in emphasis. 'Lambert will have to be released. The allegation of the theft of needles cannot be sustained and he must be given the benefit of doubt in the matter of assaulting Thomas Chance. I'm of the belief that he is speaking the truth when he claims that he acted in self-defence.'

''Ull you be wanting to have words with Lambert yourself, parson?' Cashmore wanted to know. 'I can bring him to you if you require me to.'

The other man considered this for a moment, then

grinned and nodded. 'I think that I might have words with Lambert, Master Cashmore. I'm curious to meet a fellow who can cause such upset. But there's no need to bring him here, I shall come up to the lock-up with you.'

'He arn't in the lock-up, Parson Clayton.' Cashmore's normal stolid taciturnity was overlayed with a suspicion of diffidence which was foreign to his nature. 'I couldn't keep 'um both in the same cell arter what had passed. So I had to move Lambert.'

'Where is he now then?'

'He's in the old cell, parson. The coal-hole under the free school.'

'Those are hard quarters, Master Cashmore.' Clayton's grin held a hint of boyish mischief. 'I'll wager he's not known harder, even out in Botany Bay.'

For three nights and three days Daniel Lambert, heavily manacled, had shivered the hours away in the almost pitch blackness of the coal-hole. Joseph Cashmore or one of his assistant constables came twice a day to bring him bread, cheese and water, and a bucket in which he could perform his natural functions. He still wore his own clothing, but his only other covering against the freezing cold of the cellar was a single threadbare blanket. He slept on top of the heaped coals, the scant floor space not covered by coals being an inch deep in filthy water.

Daniel did not allow himself to indulge in fruitless anger and recrimination for his present plight. His long years as a convict had taught him the futility of such a course. It had also taught him the art of stoical endurance and patiently he waited for this present period of grim incarceration to come to its end, concentrating his thoughts on matters far removed from his filthy surroundings.

Joseph Cashmore had told him that Tildy Crawford had tried to gain access to him, but Cashmore had turned her away. The constable had explained why.

'Tom Chance has got a lot o' mates in this district, whom just as mad and bad when in drink as he is. They'll be looking for revenge for what you'se done to their mate, Lambert, and iffen they got to know that you and Tildy Crawford was friends, then they might well try and harm her. So until this business is all settled, then it's best that she keeps well away from you. But she's asked me to tell you that her and the old 'ooman are moved into your house and that they'm taking good care on it for you.'

Public opinion was also one of the main reasons that Daniel was undergoing such privations.

'I can't let you live comfortable arter what's happened,' Cashmore informed him. 'Because wi' feeling agen you running so high, iffen you was to be sitting comfortable in the lock-up, then God only knows what might happen. One time, afore I become constable, a gang broke a prisoner out o' the cell and nigh on killed him, because they thought he was having too easy a time on it.'

Personally, Daniel Lambert felt that he would have preferred to take his chances and remained in the comparative comfort of the lock-up, but he realised that Cashmore believed he was acting with the best motives for his prisoner's safety, and so forebore to argue the matter.

The entrance to the coal-hole was by a doubled trapdoor fashioned from stout planking which opened up to give access to the flight of brick steps leading down into the cellar. Daniel, immersed in reveries of other times, heard the sounds of the padlock being removed and the iron locking bars dragged aside from the trapdoor. He blinked in the darkness, trying to estimate how long it had been since his last visitation by his keepers.

The heavy shuttering crashed open and a beam of lantern light shone upon the narrow steps. The booted feet of Joseph Cashmore came into Daniel's view and then the bulk of the man blocked out the starlit night sky and the beam flashed into Daniel's face.

'Got some good news for you, Lambert.' The constable's hoarse tone was friendly. 'Youm to be released.

Come on over here and I'll take them fetters off you.'

Daniel let the blanket fall from his shoulders and clanked stiffly across the watery space of flooring to the foot of the steps. The constable retreated up the steps and Daniel followed. Gratefully he filled his lungs with the cold sweetness of fresh air and stared in the darkness at the second man standing facing him.

Released of his fetters Daniel rubbed the sore bands of flesh at his wrists and ankles, but said nothing. He merely waited, poised and watchful for any treachery. This present period of imprisonment had brought back to him in full measure all the wary distrust of the hardened convict for his fellow men.

'This here's Parson Clayton, Lambert,' the constable informed him. ''Tis the parson you can thank for your release.'

A brief mirthless smile curved Daniel Lambert's lips. 'Doesn't the fact that I'm innocent of this theft have aught to do with it then, Cashmore?' Then he bowed briefly towards the cleric. 'Nevertheless, I do give you my thanks, sir. These present lodgings are not really to my taste.'

Clayton lifted his own lantern so that he could see the ex-convict's features.

In the pale beam the other man's features were grimy with coaldust and heavily stubbled, the eyes dark-shadowed with deep etched lines of weariness patterned about them. At first glance it was the face of a desperate character, but Clayton detected a quality in the hard set features that he found at variance with the popular conception of what a hardened villain should look like.

'I trust that you fully appreciate why you came under suspicion, Lambert. In the circumstances it was only natural that the night patrol should put you under arrest.' There was no suggestion of apology in Clayton's tone. He was a product of his time and class and the idea of apologising to an ex-convict would never even occur to him. Indeed, in the eyes of his peers, even this exchange would be considered a very gracious concession to a social inferior.

'However, I have decided that there is not sufficient evidence against you to carry this matter of the theft of the needles any further. In the case of the assault on Thomas Chance, the constable has informed me that he believes your account of the incident and I am prepared to accept that you acted in self-defence. Therefore no charge will be brought against you concerning that. But I must tell you, Lambert, that as a returned transport, you must tread a very careful path in this parish. Obviously you have a sorry reputation here. Therefore it behoves you to so conduct yourself in the future that there will be no need for any re-occurrence of arrest.'

Although the cleric's pomposity aroused a burning resentment within Daniel Lambert, he knew that the other man held the power to do virtually whatever he wished in this parish, and that any overt display of his, Daniel Lambert's, resentment could easily result in his re-arrest on the spot. He swallowed hard, and asked curtly, 'May I go now? I need to cleanse the filth of this hole from me.'

Clayton nodded. 'Yes, Lambert, you may go.'

'Then I'll bid you both a good night.' Daniel walked away.

Clayton stared after him, conflicting emotions coursing through his mind. 'Do you know, Master Cashmore, I am very uncertain about that fellow,' he remarked.

'In what way, sir?' The constable sought clarification.

Clayton's broad shoulders rose and fell helplessly. 'I don't really know myself, Master Cashmore. But there is something about him that makes me uneasy. He reminds me somewhat of a powder keg, primed to explode.'

The heavy features of the constable grinned sourly. 'I should think that arter ten years in Botany Bay even the dullest powder keg 'ull have learnt that when it explodes it blows itself to kingdom come. I should think meself that Daniel Lambert has got more sense than that. Surely he's damaged hisself enough for one lifetime? I can't really see him deliberately courting any more trouble.'

'We shall see, Master Cashmore. We shall see,' Clayton murmured.

Chapter Twelve

The kitchen was warm and snug, and Tildy reluctantly left the fireside in answer to the summons of the bell. At the outer gate Daniel Lambert watched her slender figure approaching and his heartbeat quickened. When she reached him she smiled in warm welcome. 'They've let you go, Daniel. I'm so pleased.'

She unlocked the gate and led him towards the house. 'Are you hungry? I've got a pot of stew and dumplings on the fire. I came every day to see you at the lock-up, but Cashmore always sent me away. But he hinted that you'd soon be set free again. Your aunt's well. We've not disturbed any of your things and I've kept your bed aired ready for when you came back. Would you like something hot to drink? We've coffee, and there's a pinch of tea as well, if you'd prefer that.' She felt embarrassed at her own loquacity and was angry at herself for becoming so flustered at seeing him that she babbled to hide her feelings. 'Dear God,' she told herself angrily, 'will you stop chattering like some idiot maid. You're a woman full grown, not a silly girl.'

In the hallway he told her, 'First I must bathe and change my clothes, Tildy. I'm not fit to mix in company until I do so.'

'I'll go and heat water for you,' she offered immediately, but he shook his head.

'No, Tildy. You're not my servant. I shall look to myself.'

'But it's no trouble for me,' she insisted. 'Look, come

and sit in the kitchen and talk with your aunt, while I see to the copper and prepare your bath.'

He smiled and accepted. 'Very well then, and thank you.'

Tildy was glad to get away from him, so that she could compose herself. While she laid and lit the fire under the big copper in the wash-house and drew water from the pump in the scullery, she marvelled at her reaction to Daniel Lambert's homecoming.

'I'm behaving for all the world as if he were my lover,' she realised with a frisson of disquiet, and tried to force herself to think rationally. 'There's no reason for behaving this way. All right, I admit that I find him physically attractive, but I've met and talked with other men who were handsomer than he is without behaving like some moon-struck maid. What is it about Daniel Lambert that affects me so powerfully? I can't possibly be in love with him. I hardly know the man. I'm going to stop being such an idiot.'

Despite this resolve, she could not keep from thoughts of him, and to her own dismay when she had filled the tin hip bath and put towels in the wash-house she found herself visualising how his tall muscular body would look, glistening wetly in the light from the two candles she had arranged on the wash-house windowsill.

'Are you gone mad?' she furiously demanded of herself. 'Are you really so shameless? These are the thoughts of a whore, not a respectable woman who has a son to bring up.'

She went to the kitchen to tell him that his bath was ready and to her mortification felt herself blushing hotly when he smiled at her and gently teased, 'By God, but my fortune's changed for the better, Tildy. Not even the Pharaoh of Egypt could have boasted of having a hand-maiden as beautiful as you, that I'll swear to.'

Old Esther's sharp eyes had missed nothing and, when the two women were alone, she chuckled and observed,

'My nephew has a powerful effect on you, doon't he, my duck?'

'Don't talk so silly, Esther,' Tildy snapped shortly, but her blush deepened and the other woman cackled with laughter.

'Now doon't be vexed wi' me, Tildy. I'm only spaking the truth, arter all. And 'tis only natural that a healthy young 'ooman like you be, should feel a bit warm and aereated when her meets a man she fancies.'

'I swear you're in your dotage, Esther, talking such nonsense,' Tildy snapped irritably, but then could not help meeting the old woman's sly grin and giggling at her own foolishness.

'Well, supposing I do find him attractive?' she admitted. 'Where's the harm in that?'

'No harm at all, my duck.' The old woman's black eyes danced in her withered face. ''Specially as our Daniel's powerful struck wi' you as well.' She rubbed her clawed hands together. 'I'd love to see you two make a match on it, Tildy. I really 'ud.'

'Now that is silly talk, Esther,' Tildy reprimanded. 'And you'll please me best if you speak no more of such things.'

The old woman held her peace, but at intervals Tildy was aware of the bright black eyes sneaking sly glances at her and the toothless mouth curving in a knowing smile.

Later, when Daniel had bathed and shaved and changed his clothing, he sat by the fireside in the kitchen and devoured a bowl of stew and hunks of fresh bread that Tildy had baked that morning, washing it down with draughts of ale. Afterwards, replete and satisfied, he smoked his pipe and talked with the women. At one moment he suddenly realised that he was enjoying a sense of perfect contentment and sighed wistfully at the knowledge that such moments were all too rare in life.

With gentle probings Tildy drew from him many stories of his past life and she marvelled at his accounts of strange lands and stranger happenings. She felt that she could have sat and listened all through the night but, as the big old grandfather clock chimed out the hours of early morning, she reluctantly rose to her feet.

'I must go to my bed. I have work to go to in a few hours.'

'What work is that, Tildy?' There was a note of surprise in the man's voice.

'We're finishing the potato setting for Master Claybrook,' Tildy told him.

'But I thought that you were looking after this house now?' Lambert's surprise was now obvious. 'Surely you're not going to go on working in the fields, now that you're living here?'

Tildy's proud independence caused her to react more sharply than she cared to. 'Oh but I am going to go on working, Master Lambert. I'm very grateful that you should have given us shelter, but I thought it was on the understanding that we paid our way. I've no wish to be dependent on you.'

She saw the concern and dawning hurt in his eyes and could have bitten out her tongue for replying so sharply.

'Look, I'm sorry for answering so sharp. I didn't mean to sound so shrewish. But ... but ...' Her voice trailed away, as she sought vainly for words to explain how she really felt.

There was an uncomfortable silence, which persisted until old Esther spoke out scornfully. 'God strewth! You'm a real pair o' bloody mawkins, arn't you!' She pointed her clawed fingers at Tildy. 'You set yoursen down for a minute, my girl. And both on you pay heed to me.' Her black eyes darted at each of their faces in rapid succession. 'Now let's stop mekkin' difficulties wheer there arn't none.' Again she ordered Tildy, 'I'se told you to set yourself down for a minute, arn't I, girl?'

Tildy dutifully reseated herself and, satisfied, old Esther went on:

'Now Nephew, the fust thing you has to understand, is that me and Tildy am real independent and contrary craturs. So I'll tell you my mind and then we can see iffen we'em all able to be suited ...' She spoke at length and then invited their replies, and the exchange went on for some considerable time, until finally matters were arranged to mutual satisfaction.

Between them, Tildy and old Esther would look after the household, in return for their own and little Davy's full bed and board. Tildy would also continue working outside the house, because she wanted now to have Davy schooled and this she insisted on paying for herself, as well as buying all personal necessaries for him and herself also. Old Esther also insisted that she be allowed to continue her arts as a 'cunning woman', so that she could earn some money for herself.

Daniel Lambert's sense of fair play was somewhat troubled still and he made one final effort to persuade them both to give up any outside work.

'Listen, you will be working as my housekeepers. Doing my washing, my cooking, my cleaning. Surely that's work enough for you both, looking after this house? I've money enough for all our needs, so there is really no necessity for either of you to go out to work, or to conjure spells to earn money. I can give you money when you want it.'

'No, Daniel,' Tildy again refused, gently but very firmly. 'If we are to live here as a family, then it must be as a family of equals, not as master and dependents. As Esther has already explained to you, we've been independent for a long time now and we've grown used to that. If we all fulfill our parts of this bargain, then we can dwell very happily together.'

With a good grace, the man finally surrendered. Having these women here with him this night had made him realise just how lonely his own life was and he would have done almost anything rather than see them leave. Particularly Tildy.

'Very well, ladies, so be it. It's a bargain, so let's shake on it.' With a grin he held out his strong hand and the two women smiled also and clasped his outstretched fingers in their own.

Chapter Thirteen

Before many days had passed Tildy realised that if the arrangement she had made with Daniel Lambert was to be successful, then she would have to find some other means of earning money than field-work. The now extended distances she had to travel meant that she left the house long before break of day and returned to it correspondingly later at night. The main burden of tending to the household fell upon old Esther, who did her best and made no complaints, but Tildy knew that the old woman's increasing bodily infirmities were taking a heavy toll of her failing strength and that the work was too much for her. Davy was now living with them and appeared to be settling in his new environment, but because of Tildy's long hours of absence the child was forced to spend his days helping old Esther, instead of starting school, as Tildy wanted so desperately for him to do.

Daniel Lambert knew that Tildy was troubled by the situation, but by now he also knew just how fiercely proud the young woman could be and so he made no attempt to persuade her to give up the field-work, realising that she would resent any such interference on his part. He had tried to help old Esther with some of the heavier house-work, but she also had demonstrated her own fierce pride and had soundly berated him for doing so, demanding to know if he thought that she was a useless invalid and driving him away from her work. With rueful good humour he accepted that these two stubborn women would only ever go their own ways and that he would not be able to change them. That apart, Daniel Lambert was very happy to share his house with this readymade family, and more than content to have Tildy Crawford beneath his roof, for by now he knew that he was in love with her and was hopeful that someday she would reciprocate that emotion.

It was Easter Sunday, the sixth day of April, and Daniel Lambert rose from his bed as the dawn was breaking and stared out of his window. He smiled in satisfaction when he saw that only a smattering of cloud hung almost motionless in the paling skies and hastened to dress himself before hurrying along the corridor to hammer loudly on the women's bedroom door.

'Aunt Esther, Tildy, come rouse yourselves and wake Davy up. Have you forgotten what day it is? Come now, stir yourselves.'

From the hallway below the voice of his aunt shouted peevishly, 'We'se all bin up an hour since, you lazy bugger. Come you on down and get your breakfast. Tildy's just putting it out.'

He clattered down the stairs and along the stone-flagged passage into the kitchen. A cheerful fire burned in the inglenook grate and set out on the white-scrubbed table were a dish of boiled eggs, fresh bread and salt butter, and a steaming pot of tea. Tildy hummed happily to herself as she fired the oven in preparation for the leg of lamb on which they would feast later that day. At the table behind her Daniel Lambert, old Esther and little Davy were sitting contentedly, digesting their breakfast. Tildy closed the oven door and seated herself on the wooden bench across the table from Daniel Lambert. Despite the earliness of the hour the chimes of the chapel bells sounded faintly and Daniel Lambert's eyes were fond as he gently teased.

'Now Tildy, you should be up at the chapel praying for my soul, instead of sitting here taking your ease.'

She smiled mischievously. 'Now why should I wear out my knees praying for a hopeless sinner like you, Daniel? Especially when all the chapels you go to so often have handles on their prayerbooks.'

'Well said, my duck!' old Esther crowed, then asked her nephew, 'Which chapel was you at so late last night, our Daniel? Was it the Crown or the Unicorn, or the White Hart up at Headless Cross theer?'

He grinned good humouredly. 'It was none of them, Auntie. To tell truth I hardly touched a drop last night. I was down at Bredon, talking to Brandon Whittle. He's offered me to go into business with him.'

He spoke directly to Tildy. 'Do you know Brandon Whittle, Tildy?'

She shook her glossy, neat-braided head.

'Brandon's a needle maker, and a good one,' he informed her. 'He used to work with my dad, and since I've been away he's set himself up as a factor and master in a small way.'

'And will you go into business with him, our Daniel?' old Esther queried.

The man pursed his lips. 'I'm giving thought to it. I'll needs find something to earn my bread by. I've money enough at present, but it'll not last forever. But to be honest, I always found the needle trade very tedious to work at.'

'You allus found any steady work tedious, our Daniel,' old Esther scolded. 'That's why you went for a soldier, warn't it? Couldn't rest content until you was wearing a red coat wi' all them other bloody ne'er-do-wells and scapegraces.'

Daniel winked at Tildy, and teased the older woman. 'Now Auntie, you didn't call me scapegrace and ne'er-do-well when I was keeping Napoleon Bonaparte from coming over to Mappleborough and having his wicked way with you.' He shook his head in mock indignation. 'Oh no! I was a hero then to you, wasn't I? It would serve you right if old Nappy's ghost came back to haunt you, and this time I'd just stand by and refuse to save you from him.'

'Phsswhaww!' the old woman snorted scornfully. 'I

116

'udden't need you nor twenty like you to save me from a ghost, my bucko! I wish old Nappy 'ud come back, I'd soon conjure such a spell agen him that he'd bloody quick run scrawkin' back to wheer he come from.'

Tildy laughed at their banter, but Davy's eyes were huge and he asked, 'Can you do that, Nanny Esther? Can you put a spell on a ghost?'

The old woman's clawed hand lovingly stroked the child's cheek. 'O' course I can, my lovey. That's why none on 'un 'ull ever come near to any on us. They'm too feared to.'

'Oh Esther, don't fill his head with such fancies,' Tildy remonstrated gently, but Davy protested. 'No Mam, let Nanny Esther tell me. I like her stories.'

'I know you do,' Tildy told him. 'But then you get feared by them when it's dark and time for your bed, don't you?'

'I don't, Mam!' he protested stoutly. 'I'm not feared of anything and when I'm big I'm going to be a soldier like Uncle Daniel was.'

'And a very fine soldier you'll make too, my brave little fighting cock!' Daniel Lambert grinned and ruffled the mop of black curls. 'And now, let's you and me go out and feed and water Saturn before we go down to the Abbey Meadows. You shall have a ride on him when we get back and then you'll be a true cavalryman, like your Sergeant Hawk.'

Sergeant Hawk was Davy's most treasured possession, a large wooden soldier dressed and mustachioed like a bold hussar. The child beamed with delight, and Daniel Lambert went out hand in hand with him. 'Theer now,' old Esther remarked fondly. 'They'se took to each other real well, them two has. Daniel 'ud make a wonderful father for the boy.'

Tildy was aware of the black eyes staring meaningfully at her face and she could not restrain an exclamation of impatience. 'Esther, give over do! Some day, God willing, Daniel will be finding a young maid and fathering children of his own. I get tired of you trying to matchmake between me and him.'

'Our Daniel has already found the maid he wants to wed wi', and you knows that well, my wench. He'd marry you today iffen you'd but gi' him the least encouragement.' The old woman was not at all deterred by Tildy's show of impatience. 'Come now, girl, you canna tell me that you doon't like the lad well enough.'

'Of course I like him well enough,' Tildy admitted. 'But liking isn't loving.'

'And how long does loving last?' the other woman demanded forcefully. 'Loving is just for moon-struck maids. Liking is what makes happy marriages, my wench. Liking, not bloody loving!'

Tildy rose from the table and went out into the scullery taking the dirty dishes with her. At the slate washing trough she worked the handle of the small pump, bringing the cold clear water gouting. She gazed unseeingly out of the barred scullery window, her mind filled with old Esther's final words.

'Liking makes happy marriages. Liking, not loving. Yet what is liking if it's not a form of loving? I know that Daniel thinks himself to be in love with me, and I like him a lot. He's kind and he's intelligent. I find him physically attractive.' Her cheeks burned as she remembered her dream of the previous night, in which she and Daniel had been nothing if not loving. A dream from which she had awoken with embarrassment and confusion and more than a little self-disgusted that she could even in a dream have behaved so shamelessly.

In an effort to drive these disquieting thoughts and memories from her mind she busied herself in washing the dishes, but try though she might the memories and thoughts persisted.

When the four of them left the house and walked northwards down towards the Abbey Meadows other people were also heading in the same direction.

'Where are we going Uncle Daniel?' Davy's face was rosy with excitement. 'And where are all the people going?'

Daniel Lambert smiled down at the child. 'We're going to the Abbey Meadows, as I told you yesterday we would. And all these people are going to the same place.'

The groups walking down the long hill were a cross section of the town's population. Needlemakers in the white aprons and square brown-paper hats of their calling, their womenfolk shawl-wrapped and mobcapped. Young women, dressed in all their finery of frilled and feathered bonnets, flirting demure or bold eyes at the dandified young blood and colourful swallowtailed coats and tight-fitting pantaloons and stovepipe tophats. Respectable, staid artisans and tradespeople, paunches bulging against their sober frockcoats, their faces solemn and dignified beneath their belltoppers and billycocked hats, their voluminously cloaked wives decorously walking behind their lords and masters, leading their flocks of offspring, scrubbed and starched and polished in honour of the day. And interspersed with all these came elements from the rougher quarter of the town. Needle pointers in red shirts and sleeveless leather jerkins, bleary-eyed and brawl-scarred from the previous night's carousing, navvies in their weekend fineries of velveteens and garish neck-cloths, and the wild haired, gypsylike slumwomen, bedraggled and bangled and as tough-looking as their menfolk.

'Tell me again, Uncle Daniel. What are we going to see?' Davy begged eagerly, and the man chuckled. 'Have you forgotten so soon what I told you yesterday?'

The child's features screwed up in concentration. 'I can remember some of it,' he offered at length.

Daniel Lambert chuckled again and fondly ruffled the boy's black curls. 'Never mind. I'll tell you again. We're going down to the Abbey Meadows because it's Easter Day and on this day's morning the sun dances.' He sang quietly to the boy:

'But Oh! She dances such a way,
No sun upon an Easter Day
Is half so fine a sight ...'

'Will it really dance for us, Uncle Daniel? Will the sun dance?' Davy pestered and Daniel Lambert smiled down at the child.

'Of course it will. You just wait and see. It dances like a Merry Andrew.'

The steep fall of the Fish Hill became a gentler gradient which stretched arrow-straight to the Pigeon Bridge which marked the northern boundary of the town. The bridge crossed the stream from which the town had anciently derived its name, Rubeo Fosetto, the Red Ditch, so called because of the reddish colouring given to the water by the iron oxides it sucked from the soil it cut through. At the Pigeon Bridge the procession of people turned eastwards and traversed the few hundred yards along the stream's northern bank which brought them onto the Abbey Meadows, the site of the once mighty Cistercian Abbey of Bordesley. Now there were only mysterious mounds and hummocks beneath the green turf of the meadows, sheep grazing where once monks had walked their cloisters.

The crowd spread out across the meadows, becoming curiously subdued and muted. Some seated themselves on the close-cropped grasses, others stood in solemn congregation, even the children were silent and still. Every eye stared fixedly at the rising sun, transformed into a hazy shimmering globe of fire by a misted cloud drifting across its face.

Tildy stood as silently intent as everyone around her. She did not question why she had come to this ancient site to see the sun dance. Ever since she could remember the local people had come here on Easter Day morning, and waited as they were doing now. There were those who mocked the watchers, calling them self-deluding superstitious fools, but those mockers were a minority in the district and none would dare to come to this meadow and mock on this day.

Suddenly a man shouted and pointed up at the sun. 'Theer it goes! It's started the dance!'

A ripple of excitement passed through the silent watchers and then others shouted and pointed and clapped their hands joyfully. People smiled and slapped each others' backs as if in congratulation of some victory. A wave of cheering erupted and the children, infected by the excitement of their elders, began to prance about wildly. An emotion inexplicable to herself overwhelmed Tildy and her eyes filled with tears. Through blurred sight she saw the sun moving in graceful stately pavan and she clapped her hands as a wild exultation filled her and lifted Davy in her arms and started to dance with him, singing out in her joy. All over the meadow fifes and fiddles were produced and small drums struck up a rhythmic beat, as couples paired and rings were formed and men and women stepped off in the ancient patterns of the country dances. The meadows became a swirling maelstrom of sound and movement and for a brief period age and youth, wealth and poverty, sickness and health, knowledge and ignorance, hope and despair, love and hatred ceased to divide, and all were fused in one embracing unity.

Tildy moved in the dance with a sensuous grace, her shawl falling back to her shoulders, her long glossy hair forming a soft cloud of darkness about her glowing face, her lustrous eyes shining with delight, and her beauty caused Daniel Lambert's senses to reel and when they faced as partners, their hands clasped as they whirled round and round, his love for her overcame him and he pulled her body against his own and hungrily kissed her mouth.

The kiss lasted only a fleeting instant and then the pattern of the dance parted them. Facing another man Tildy dipped and curtsied, stepped forward, back and forward, clasped the stranger's hands and whirled anew

121

and her mind grappled with the knowledge that she had tasted Daniel Lambert's mouth and hungered to taste it once more. Again they met and their hands clasped, but this time no kiss passed between them, only an unspoken message from their eyes which both understood. In that brief exchange a silent question was asked and an answer given and, standing watching them, old Esther's black eyes sparkled as intuitively she sensed what had come to fruition between these two people that she loved.

There was no pre-arranged time for the dancing to come to an end. But as if by instinct after barely an hour had elapsed the crowds were now leaving the Abbey Meadows in high-spirited, laughing, chattering groups. Tildy walked in silence by old Esther's side and ahead of her Daniel Lambert carried little Davy on his shoulders. The wild sense of joyous exultation that Tildy had experienced at the dancing had subsided now and to replace it had come a quieter happiness. She knew, despite the flashes of doubtful uncertainty that momentarily assailed her, that she and Daniel Lambert were going to become lovers, perhaps even man and wife. She marvelled inwardly at this sudden metamorphosis and tried to recall the exact moment that this new and strange certitude had entered her mind.

'It wasn't when he kissed me, but afterwards. When next time he partnered me. I looked at him then, and I just knew somehow ...'

'Eh? What's that youm saying, my duck?' Old Esther stared at her curiously and Tildy blushed as she realised that she had unconsciously voiced her thoughts aloud.

'Nothing, Esther. I said nothing,' she flustered, and the old woman cackled with laughter and nudged her with a sharp bony elbow.

'I reckon that I might soon be sleeping by mesen agen, judging by the way you and our Daniel was alooking at each other.'

Tildy's blush deepened. 'I don't know what you mean, Esther. I think you must be near to your dotage, some of the nonsense you come out with.'

Embarrassment caused Tildy to speak more sharply than she cared to, but the old woman only cackled anew with laughter and after a couple of seconds Tildy's own laughter bubbled out and she linked arms fondly with the old woman. 'There's times I think you really are a witch, Esther. You seem to be able to read what's in my mind.'

'It warn't no witchcraft, my duck. Anybody with an eye to see could tell that you and our Daniel was agoing to be paired sooner nor later. Mrs Daniel Lambert. It's got a fine ring to it, Tildy.'

Tildy silently repeated that title, almost as if tasting its feel and savour upon her tongue.

'Mrs Daniel Lambert ... Mrs Daniel Lambert ... Mrs Daniel Lambert ... Yes,' she decided happily. 'It does sound just fine, doesn't it?'

Aloud, she objected. 'Daniel hasn't yet asked me to be his wife, Esther.'

The shrewd black eyes twinkled. 'Oh but he's going to, my duck. He's agoing to. That's as sure as God made little apples, that is.'

Chapter Fourteen

Although it was the Sabbath day the three members of the managing committee of the Redditch night patrol had come to the house of the Right Honourable and Reverend Walter Hutchinson, Lord Aston, vicar of Tardebigge Parish and justice of the peace of the county of Worcestershire. The meeting had been summoned by Lord Aston and the sole subject on the agenda was the failure of the night patrol to curb the depredations of the 'Rippling Boys'.

In the opulently furnished drawing room of the vicarage the four men sat around a highly polished mahogany table on slender framed, brocaded chairs which appeared too delicately fashioned to bear their weights. The heavy sallow features of Lord Aston bore the permanent scowl of the martyr to an acute dyspepsia, an affliction which owed more to his own inveterate gluttony than to any visitation of God. Fifty years of age, Aston always appeared in public in the black full-skirted coat, knee breeches and stockings of his vocation and he wore the white clerical short-queued tie-wig on his shiny pink bald pate. It was this wig that he now scratched beneath with his stubby fingers as he scanned the latest report of the night patrol which lay on the table before him. Finishing that report, he removed the gold-rimmed pince-nez from his bulbous nose and scowled at the other men.

'This is a sad state of affairs, gentlemen. Houses robbed, warehouses broken into, sheep and cattle stolen, and not a single one of the miscreants yet laid by the heels. What the Devil is the night patrol about? Are you sending the blind and deaf out to protect our property?'

His audience exchanged frowns. They were all men of standing in the district, every one a needle master, and in the case of William Hemming, a considerable landowner of ancient lineage, and they were not pleased to be spoken to in such a manner by any cleric, titled though he might be.

Thomas Holyoake and William Boulton imperceptibly nodded at Hemming, and he spoke for the three of them. 'No my lord, we do not send out the blind and deaf.' His resentment showed clearly in his clipped curt tones. 'The patrol is drawn from respectable householders, and all are active-bodied, intelligent men.'

'Well they ain't active and intelligent enough to catch a thief, so it seems, Mister Hemming.' The cleric stressed the 'Mister', as if to emphasise the difference in rank between himself and the committee members.

'We have our suspicions as to the identities of the culprits, my lord.' Hemming's lean features framed by dark sidewhiskers were suffused with the dull flush of suppressed anger.

'Suspicions, Mister Hemming?' Aston's tone was jeering. 'Suspicions? What may I enquire is the use of suspicions if there ain't the proof the law requires?'

Hemming made no reply and Lord Aston replaced his pince-nez and once more scanned the report before him. His stubby forefinger traced the lines of writing and halted at a name.

'This man, Lambert?' he demanded. 'The returned transport? Why wasn't he brought before me for examination?'

Hemming's anger momentarily broke from its chains. 'Dammee, it's clearly stated in the report why he wasn't brought before you, my lord. Your own curate, John Clayton, had him released due to lack of any firm evidence against him.'

Aston looked up sharply at the other man and, as if realising that he was provoking the needle master too much, modulated his voice and said in a mollifying tone,

'I wasn't implying that you had erred in this matter, Mister Hemming. But I regard the present criminal activities in the parish as being of the utmost danger to the maintenance of public order. If these so-called "Rippling Boys" are permitted to continue their outrages with impunity, then who can tell what may be the final outcome? The labouring masses are seething with unrest throughout the kingdom, gentlemen. Any sign on our part of weakness or uncertainty, or inability to find and punish transgressors against the law could well prove as a signal to the revolutionaries among our people to unleash bloody rebellion upon us.'

Boulton and Holyoake glanced at each other with sly smiles. Reverend the Lord Aston's belief that the masses only waited their opportunity to unleash fire, rapine and slaughter throughout the realm was very well known.

William Hemming himself had to struggle to retain his air of gravity. 'I'm sure you are right, my lord,' he said in a voice so obviously strained that the cleric frowned doubtfully at him.

The needle master coughed to ease the constriction in his throat, and then asked, 'Do you have any suggestions as to how we can deal with these "Rippling Boys", my lord?'

The cleric stared over Hemming's head, pursed his thick lips reflectively, puffing out audible wheezing breaths as if the process of thought was a physical effort.

The other men waited, staring at the ceiling, exchanging fleeting glances of wry amusement, tapping fingers upon the polished mahogany, fiddling with watch chains. The time passed with an excruciating slowness and William Boulton's eyelids actually closed and he dozed fitfully.

In Bredon the large red-brick chapel of the Wesleyan Methodists was filled for this Easter morning service, the eager congregation gathered to greet their newly appointed circuit minister, the Reverend Thomas

Fletcher, a young man whose soulful eyes and long flowing blond locks caused tremulous flutterings in the breasts of the young women, and not a few of the matrons, when he mounted into the high pulpit above the seated ranks of the faithful and gazed out across his flock, his fresh youthful features contrasting so dramatically with the grim dourness of the deacons seated in their high pews facing the congregation in the body of the chapel.

Outside the chapel two young men dressed like needle pointers shambled slowly past and the taller of them paused to listen to the rousing verses that declared for all the world to hear that on this day the Lord Christ had arisen from the tomb.

'Christ the Lord is risen today!
Vain the stone, the watch, the seal,
Christ hath burst the gates of hell:
Death in vain forbid His rise,
Christ has opened Paradise,
Watch for Him and pray!
Watch and pray!
Watch aanndd praayyy!'

The tall pointer grinned at his shaggy-haired companion. 'Just hark to that, Abel. I'll bet your Tommy wishes he could bost open the gates o' the bleedin' lock-up as easy. But all he can do right now is just watch and bleedin' pray that they'll unlock the bloody gates for him.'

Abel Chance was a slightly older mirror version of his brother, Thomas Chance, and shared with him the same propensity for violence. Now his face twisted viciously and he grabbed his tall companion by the throat with his left hand and balled his right fist in readiness to hit.

'That anna funny, you bastard!'

'No Abel, doon't.' The lanky John Hancox blanched with fear and he patted the other's muscular shoulders with both hands as if soothing a savage beast. 'I meant naught by what I said, Abel! I meant no harm by it. Honest I didn't!'

For several seconds the pair remained locked in a motionless tableau, then Abel Chance bared his yellow teeth in a savage grin and with a snort of contempt pushed the other man so that he reeled backwards.

Chance remained where he stood for a few seconds, listening to the hymn singing, his head nodding unconsciously in time to its cadences, then he looked up and down the deserted street. Its rows of terraced cottages were still and silent, and the large house adjoining the chapel likewise. Chance's low brow furrowed in thought and he jerked his head at Hancox to come closer. Still nervous of possible violence from his unpredictable companion the taller man approached cautiously, ready to flee if any danger threatened.

Abel Chance grinned and spoke in a conspiratorial whisper. 'The bleedin' street's as empty as my fuckin' pockets be, Johnno. Everybody's either in the chapel or gone to see the sun dancing down at the Abbey Meadows.' His shaggy head nodded towards the large house adjoining the chapel. 'That's the Turners' place, Johnno. I'se often thought that there'd be good pickings to be got from them. The bastards spends all their time bothering God in the fuckin' chapel theer. They'm as tight as ducks' arseholes, all the soddin' boiling on 'um. And today there'll be all the bloody preachers and their wives' stuff in theer as well. The preachers allus stays wi' the Turners when the Methodys am having a big meeting like they am today.'

John Hancox's grimy, lantern-jawed features were a study of temptation battling with fear. 'But it's broad daylight, Abel. We'll be seen.'

'Doon't be so bleedin' lily-livered,' Abel Chance snarled. 'Does you want me to tell the lads that youm a gutless cunt?'

Hancox swallowed hard, his face working with his conflicting emotions. Then, screwing his courage up, he blurted, 'All right, Abel. I'm wi' you.'

'Abel Chance grinned wolfishly. 'That's better, Johnno. That's more like my mate, that is. Cummon now, we'll goo round the back and knock to see if theer's anybody inside. If theer is, then we just asks for a drink o' water.'

There was no answer to their knocking, and Chance tried the back door to find it locked. 'Fuckin' Methody pisspots!' he joked roughly. 'They only ever puts their bleedin' trust in God, doon't they? They doon't trust anybody else enough even to leave the bloody door unlocked for a few minutes.'

He went into a small outhouse and returned almost instantly with a spear-bladed spade. He inserted the blade into the crack between jamb and door and levered hard. The door sprang open with a loud splintering cracking and John Hancox jumped fearfully.

'Somebody might have heard us!' he whispered through dry lips.

Chance hefted the spade in his hands and hissed menacingly, 'Iffen you doon't stop shittin' your breeks, I'll fit this fucker over your yed. Now come on, let's do the business.'

They ransacked the rooms with a speedy efficiency that betokened much practice, taking only whatever money they found and articles which they could conceal about their persons.

'That's it then, Abel, let's get off out on here.' John Hancox was pale with strain, and his hands were visibly shaking with nervous tension.

'Just a minute.' Abel Chance in contrast to his companion appeared elated with excitement, displaying no trace of apprehension. He went into the kitchen and swept the great white-scrubbed table clear of its contents, bringing pots and earthenware, jugs of milk, and plates of cold victuals smashing onto the stone flags of the floor. Then he scooped soot from the cooking fire's chimney and using the puddles of spilled milk to wet it scrawled in big

129

black wavering letters across the white expanse of the table top, the words, 'Watch and Pray!'

For a few moments he stood staring down at his handiwork, laughing uproariously, then led his frightened accomplice out of the splintered back door. The street was still silent and empty, only the muted chorus of voices chanting the responses to prayer sounding from the chapel. Whistling jauntily Abel Chance thrust his soiled hands into his breeches pockets and sauntered away, with John Hancox trailing apprehensively at his heels.

In the drawing room of the Tardebigge vicarage, Reverend the Lord Aston suddenly slapped the palms of both hands resoundingly on the polished mahogany, causing William Boulton to awake with a startled snort and blink dazedly about him. 'The present length of time that the patrol does duty is from midnight until five o'clock of the morning, is it not, Gentlemen?' Aston sought confirmation.

'That is so, my lord,' Hemming agreed.

'Very well then, gentlemen, as from this night, the hours of duty must be extended to give longer protection. I think that the patrol should commence at eleven o'clock, and end at six o'clock. We shall also post notices of reward for any information leading to the capture and conviction of these "Rippling Boys", the reward monies to be drawn from the parish chest. Also we must all of us exhort our people to be ever vigilant, and to ask Our Lord in our prayers to aid us in catching these evildoers.' The cleric's heavy sallow features became almost animated as he declaimed sonorously, 'That shall be our war cry, gentlemen, "Watch and Pray! ... Watch and Pray!"'

'Watch and Pray! I likes that Abel, I really does like that. Watch and Pray! Yes, that's a prime 'un, that is.' The speaker was tall, and spare-framed with slightly stooping shoulders, clad in sombre brown swallow-tailed coat and knee breeches with black stockings and a tall black stove-pipe hat perched on his greying hatchet-featured head.

'Ahrr, I thought you'd get a laugh outta that, Master Crowther,' Abel Chance preened himself.

Jonas Crowther stood in company with Abel Chance and John Hancox at the serving hatch of the bar-parlour of the White Hart Inn at Headless Cross, the hamlet where the long rising ridgeway named Mount Pleasant split into its separate spurs, a mile and a quarter from Redditch Town Green.

A fourth man came into the small room and Crowther greeted him.

'You'm come at the right time, Ben. Hark to what Abel's been adoing.' He nodded to Chance who proceeded to tell the newcomer about his exploit of that morning.

The newcomer, Ben Fairfax, was a stocky, tough-looking man, and the son-in-law of Jonas Crowther and like the older man favoured sombre coat and breeches and a tall stovepipe hat. His tobacco stained teeth bared in a fleeting grin when Chance's story ended and he grunted appreciatively.

'Well now, Abel, has you got anything that I might be interested in?' Crowther wanted to know, and when the young man nodded assent, he grinned in satisfaction, showing long porcelain false teeth. 'Right then, Abel, we'd best step into the kitchen. We wun't be disturbed theer.'

Crowther hammered on the serving hatch. 'Nail? Can I have a word? Am you theer, Nail?'

Nail Styler the innkeeper, was an ex-needle pointer and local prizefighter, who had had the sense to leave his deadly trade before the pointer's rot had gripped him in its murderous embrace. Now his shaven flat-nosed head poked through the hatch.

'What's your need, Jonas?'

'I needs your kitchen for a bit o' private business, Nail. It'll not take more nor a minute or two.'

Styler grinned and nodded. 'You knows the way,

Jonas. Tell my missus I sent you through.'

'Bring us a sup o' beer, Nail,' Ben Fairfax ordered, and when it arrived he drank deeply from the pewter tankard, his hard eyes scrutinising John Hancox's uneasy manner over the tankard's rim. Lowering the tankard, Fairfax belched with satisfaction, and then asked, 'What's up wi' you, Johnno, you anna looking very pleased wi' yourself, considering you'se had a nice tickle this morning?'

Hancox's dirty fingernails rooted nervously among the thick stubble of his unshaven lantern jaw.

'Come on, Johnno, what's ailing you?' Fairfax urged, and reluctantly the other man told him.

'I anna happy about what went off this morn, Master Fairfax. I doon't like doing a job in broad daylight. Anybody could ha' sin us and for all I knows, somebody might ha' done and be telling the constable about it right this minute.'

As he finished speaking the other two men returned, both looking well satisfied. Abel Chance called to Nail Styler to bring more drinks. The conversation turned to Thomas Chance, who was still lying on his sick bed in the lock-up.

'They tell me that your kid took a terrible pasting from that Lambert cove.' Jonas Crowther's eyes gleamed spitefully as he baited Abel Chance. 'I always thought your kid was a real tough pug, Abel. But from all accounts it seems that Lambert leathered him real easy, doon't it?'

Chance's face crimsoned and he cursed loud and long. Crowther's eyes gleamed with satisfaction at the response his words had provoked. He was a man who although taking care never to fight physically himself, took great pleasure in stirring others to do so.

'I should think you'll not risk tackling Lambert yoursen, 'ull you, Abel? From the sounds on it he'd do for you as well. He's a real tasty 'un wi' his fists, so they tell me.'

'I anna scared o' bloody Daniel Lambert,' Chance asserted blusteringly. 'And afore he's ate too many more dinners he's agoing to find that out for hisself, or my name anna Abel Chance. I'll trim his fuckin' lamps for him some day soon, you see if I wun't.'

Jonas Crowther grinned inwardly, but when he spoke appeared to be very serious. 'I'd like to be theer when you does that, Abel. You'll let me know exactly when it's to be, won't you?'

Abel Chance glared suspiciously at the older man, suspecting that he was being mocked by him. But Jonas Crowther stared blandly back at him with an expression of innocent interest, and after a second or two Abel Chance nodded. 'Doon't you worry, Master Crowther. I'll let you know when it's to be. And then you'll be able to come and see me give that bastard his lumps.'

He gulped down the remainder of his drink and said brusquely, 'I'm off, Master Crowther. Come on Johnno.' He nodded farewell to the two men and with his reluctant satellite trailing behind him like a whipped dog, left the room.

Ben Fairfax immediately tackled Jonas Crowther. 'Youm taking a bit of a risk, arn't you, Jonas? Buying stuff that that young bugger only took this morning, in full bloody daylight.'

For a while the older man made no reply, only stared quizzically at his son-in-law. Then he smiled bleakly and asked rhetorically, 'How long has I bin the kingpin o' the Rippling Boys, Ben?' He answered his own question. 'Quite a few years now, arn't it? And I arn't bin laid by the heels yet, has I?' He paused and sipped his ale, visibly savouring its taste, then went on. 'I'se got me own reasons for talking wi' that bloody mawkin this day.'

'It needs to be a good reason then, Jonas, because if he was spotted, and if the traps does take him up, then you can bet your bottom pound he'll bloody soon blab about who he sold to.'

For the first time the older man showed a flash of anger. 'God blast your eyes, Ben, does you take me for a bloody mawkin, or summat similar? I anna took the stuff from him. I'se only agreed a price. I'll only take delivery when I'm sure he's in the clear.'

Ben Fairfax sighed with relief, and grinned shame-facedly. 'I'm sorry, Jonas. I should ha' known.'

'Yes, you should ha' known, you thick-skulled chaw-bacon,' Crowther jeered, and laughed sneeringly at his companion's discomfiture. Then he sobered and leaned forwards conspiratorially. 'Now listen well, Ben, because youm the fust and only one that I'se told this to, or that I'm going to tell. I'm dealing wi' Abel Chance because I'se got a score to settle wi' Daniel Lambert and I might find a use for the Chance brothers in doing that.' His mouth twisted viciously. 'Only Abel doon't know that. And Daniel Lambert doon't know neither what the score is.'

Ben Fairfax frowned in puzzlement. 'How can Lambert not know what the score is?'

'Because it was his Dad's doing,' Crowther informed. 'It was through his fuckin' Dad, Henry Lambert, that my son John, and my daughter, Mary got topped down in London theer. It ne'er come out at the trial who had laid information agen 'um for coining, but I knew who'd done it. I knew it was that mealy-mouthed, chapel-going bastard, Henry Lambert. I knew it was him, because our John had passed off a few shams on him just afore he went down to London.

'I swore then that I'd get even one day. But the bugger died afore I had opportunity. When he died I cursed my bad luck. But then, when I heard a few weeks since that Daniel Lambert, his son, had come back from Botany Bay, I could ha' cried wi' joy, because I was getting the chance to take the revenge on the Lamberts that I thought I'd never have.'

'But why should you want revenge on Daniel Lambert? How could he have any anything to do wi' John and Mary getting topped? He was transported years afore that happened.'

'I didn't say he'd had anything to do wi' it, did I?' Crowther scowled. 'But that doon't matter, does it? He's

Henry Lambert's only son, arn't he? He's got that bastard's blood in his veins. Henry Lambert 'ull be screaming in his grave to know that I'se got his son sent back to Botany Bay agen.'

Ben Fairfax stared troubledly at the older man, made uneasy by the almost insane glare in the deep-sunk eyes. He was not a stupid man and he could think quickly and shrewdly. Now understanding of a matter that had puzzled him slowly dawned.

'That job the lads did at Gould's warehouse,' he whispered hoarsely. 'It was you who told Joe Wright to put some packets o' needles in Lambert's coal shed, warn't it?'

Crowther nodded, grinning delightedly, and pointed his long forefinger with its black nail at his own head. 'It arn't full o' feathers in theer, Ben. It arn't bloody feathers ...'

Chapter Fifteen

The candlelit kitchen was warm and snug. At one side of the fireplace Daniel Lambert sat quietly reading, across from him Tildy and old Esther were sewing. In its corner the old grandfather clock whirred and chimed the hour of ten o'clock and old Esther put down her sewing and yawned hugely.

'I'm off to me bed,' she announced, and her black eyes twinkled at Tildy, ''Ull you be coming up soon, my duck?'

Tildy smiled at her and indicated the shirt she held in her hands. 'Just as soon as I've finished this, Esther.'

'Well, try not to wake me iffen I'm asleep. Goodnight, Nephew.'

'Good night, Aunt.' Daniel Lambert had waited impatiently ever since that morning to have an opportunity of being alone with Tildy. Now that the moment had finally arrived, he experienced a sense of nervousness and his breathing seemed to be curiously restricted, as if bonds were tightening around his chest. He kept his eyes fixed on the printed pages before him, but the sentences were only a meaningless jumble as he struggled to give voice to his feelings.

Tildy also was conscious of the palpable tension between herself and this man opposite and equally nervous as she tried to rationalise her feelings. Despite her engrained morality she accepted that Daniel Lambert's kiss had aroused strong desires within her. Desires that she had always tried to suppress, but which now had broken free and had coursed within her all through that day and evening. 'I need his loving. I need to feel his body against mine.' She blushed at her own shamelessness, but knew that at this moment in time all the forces of her repressed sexuality were clamouring for release and assuagement.

Daniel Lambert stole covert glances at the beautiful woman sitting so quietly, her glossy head bent over the shirt that her slender fingers were working on. His breathing quickened, and he tried to raise the courage to break through the invisible barrier that stood between them. But he was afraid that she might reject him and knew that such a rejection would wound him more deeply than anything else could ever do. He inwardly cursed himself for lacking the courage to speak out, but try as he might to do so, the words stuck in his throat. A sudden surge of self-directed anger caused him to cast his book onto the floor and Tildy looked up in shock at the sudden movement. The pale light of the candle mingled with the gold-red firelight touched her face, and her beauty was such that Daniel Lambert's hands trembled and a lump rose in his throat. He swallowed hard and then without conscious volition he came from his seat and knelt before her, his hands covering her slender fingers. For long, long moments he gazed at her and the love he felt for her filled his being and flowed from his eyes. When he spoke his voice was a husky whisper.

'I love you, Tildy. I love you more than my life.' He lifted her work-roughened hands to his lips and kissed them tenderly, then looked at her pleadingly. 'Wed me, Tildy. Be my wife.'

Tildy gazed at him in silence, her dark eyes lucent and hugely large in the flickering shadowed reflections of the firelight. Now that this moment had come, she was experiencing the most consummate sense of déjà vu that had ever assailed her. In her life she had known flashes of psychic intuition many, many times, but the sheer intensity of this present emotion was breathtaking and filled her with awe. She seemed poised to tear away all the veils of time and space, to penetrate and come to know all the mysteries of life and death. Her lips opened slightly and she trembled and the man felt that trembling transmitted through her fingers and feared that he had frightened her.

'Don't be feared of me, Tildy,' he begged hoarsely. 'Please don't be feared. I'd never harm you. I love you too much ever to harm you in any way.'

The strange emotion receded, leaving Tildy feeling almost dazed. She blinked and shook her head to clear her thoughts and Daniel Lambert's heart fell and distress showed clearly in his face.

He released her hands and leaned back upon his heels. 'Does that mean no, Tildy?' His voice was strained. 'Does that mean that you'll not marry me?'

Tildy stared at him uncomprehendingly for a second or two, then her lips curved and her white teeth glistened. She threw back her head and laughed in sheer happiness. Then, while Lambert still stared at her with pain in his eyes, she leaned forwards and threw her arms about his neck, and kissed him.

Pulling her head back so that she could see his puzzled face, she laughed once more, then told him fondly, 'Of course I'll marry you, you great fool.'

She wanted to shout aloud in joy. For the first time in her life she was experiencing an absolute surety that this man and she had been predestined to meet and to love, and even as she searched her mind for any lingering doubts as to the rightness of what she was now doing, she knew that no doubt was to be found.

'This was meant to be, Daniel,' she declared with the fervour of absolute conviction. 'This was meant to be.'

He grinned happily. 'We'll wed just as soon as we can, honey,' he told her. 'I'll post the banns tomorrow.'

With a shameless daring that later was to amaze her, Tildy put her lips close to his ear and whispered, 'You may post the banns tomorrow, sweetheart, but I'll be your wife tonight.'

He lifted her bodily in his arms, cradling her to his chest, and she tightened her arms around his neck and buried her face against his muscular throat, glorying in the clean scents of his flesh.

In the bedroom he laid her gently upon the massive fourposter bed and slowly undressed her, catching his breath in wonderment at the beauty of her body bathed in the silver moonlight that lanced through the windows. Tildy lay passive as his hands removed her clothing and her own desire quickened unbearably as he slipped his clothes from his body and she saw his lean hard muscularity etched in the silvery beams. Her arms stretched towards him and he came to her, and she gasped as his warm flesh met her own. Their lips touched and tasted and then his mouth searched out her body, his hands cupping and fondling her breasts, his lips sucking her thrusting nipples. Tildy moaned in exquisitely pleasurable needing as his gentle fingers caressed her thighs and belly, roaming over her rounded hips, then searching and finding and entering her womanhood. Her own hands sought and found his maleness, throbbing and large and silky-skinned. She moaned deep in her throat, her hunger now tearing at her, her need for him to fill the aching void within her an all-consuming urgency. Their mouths crushed together and her arms tightened around his hard leanness, and she cried out as he spread her willing thighs wide and entered her and her hips thrust upwards to meet his thrusts, and her world shrank to this single pulsating, thrusting, throbbing union of flesh. Harder and harder, faster and faster, gasping for breath, sobbing in ecstasy, Tildy became a being of mindless passion submerged in seas of physical sensations that she had never known before. Waves of exquisite pleasure lifted her and she cried out and clenched her thighs around his plunging hips and her excitement redoubled its intensity as she felt and heard her lover's own excitement, and then a shattering explosion of unbearable delight sent shudders through her entire body and above her Daniel vented a long drawn-out cry, his hips stilled and he sank upon her, murmuring words of love. Their lips merged in sweet gentleness and Tildy for the first time in her life knew the real tenderness

139

of loving, as they lay cradled in each others' arms.

When the dawn came with its chorusing birds, they awoke still lying in close-locked embrace and Daniel made love to her again but this time in slow gentle tender rhythms and after the final paroxysm of passion shuddered through them Tildy lay cradled in her lover's arms and experienced a sense of such contented fulfilment that she could have wept with happiness.

Old Esther was already astir in the kitchen when Tildy went downstairs and she greeted the young woman with a cackle of delighted laughter. 'I doon't need to ask how you bist this morn, my duck. Youm looking as shining as a May bride.'

Tildy blushed, and started to make a sharp reply, but forebore when she saw the genuine pleasure in the old woman's eyes. Instead, she smiled and answered, 'Truth to tell, I'm feeling like a May bride, Esther.'

'When's it to be then? The wedding?' The old woman demanded to know.

'Just as soon as the banns have been called. Daniel's going to speak with the parson today.'

Again the old woman cackled with delighted laughter. 'I'm that pleased, my duck, I can't hardly tell you how much I am. Youm agoing to have a good marriage, you two be, that I can say for certain. I cast for the spirits last night afore I went to sleep, and they told me that all 'ud be well. I'm that pleased, my duck.' Chuckling with pleasure old Esther bustled about preparing the breakfast of onion gruel and fried salt bacon. She would not hear of Tildy helping in the task, but insisted that the young woman sit by the fireside and drink a dish of coffee.

Tildy sat happily sipping the acrid drink, sweetened with coarse cane sugar, and thinking about the events of the night.

'You wun't be going to work this day, 'ull you, girl?' Old Esther stated rather than asked, and frowned when Tildy told her, 'But of course I must. It's a good job I've only got to walk down to Easemore Farm, or I'd be late getting to work this morn.'

'Our Daniel wun't be pleased to have you working in the fields, Tildy.' Old Esther frowned. 'And it anna right that you should, now that youm going to be his wife.'

'I'm not his wife yet, Esther,' Tildy pointed out firmly. 'And I don't expect Daniel to keep me and Davy even when we are wed. It's my belief that a woman should work and help her husband.'

'That's only your contrary nature, girl,' old Esther snapped. 'Your contrary independence. A wife should do whatever her man wants her to do and if that's to stay at home and keep house, then that's what she should do. And do it wi' a willin' heart as well.'

A slight shadow crossed Tildy's happiness. Her independence had been both her pride and her pleasure. But in her world, a married woman's independence was virtually non-existent. She was her husband's property and expected to surrender absolutely to his will. Aloud, she retorted, 'I'm sure Daniel won't object to me working.'

The other woman came to stand in front of her, clawed hands resting on black-swathed hips. 'That remains to be seen, my wench. The Lambert family had a bit o' standing in this town and Henry Lambert 'ud ne'er have countenanced his missus working in the bloody fields like a common labourer. I canna see our Daniel feeling any different about it neither.'

'Different about what?' Daniel Lambert came into the kitchen, dressed only in shirt and breeches, his bare feet the reason that the women had not heard him coming downstairs.

'This 'un here says she's agoing to goo on wi' working in the bloody fields, our Daniel,' old Esther informed him, her cracked voice charged with indignation. 'I'se just told her that I canna see you countenancing such. You wun't be wanting your wife working as a bloody common labourer, 'ull you?'

He grinned easily and ran his hand through his

thinning hair. 'Well now, Aunt, I'm hoping that she won't feel the need to go on working in the fields after we're wed.' His eyes dwelt lovingly on Tildy's face and his grin widened as he saw the dawning stubbornness in her expression. 'But you know as well as I do, Aunt Esther, what a stubborn, self-willed woman she is.' He spread his hands in appeal. 'So you tell me now, how do I stop her doing what she wishes?'

'You takes a stick to her, like any other husband 'ud do,' the old woman declared heatedly, and as her listeners stared at her in shocked amazement, she abruptly cackled with laughter. 'And the day you ever does that, our Daniel, 'ull be the day that I takes my old blunderbuss to you. I'll not have my Tildy treated ill by any man, nephew or no nephew.'

Daniel Lambert's face was very serious, and he stated quietly, 'I'll speak plain what's in my mind. Of course I don't want to see Tildy working in the fields any more. But, if that's what she wants to do, then I'll accept it. All I want for Tildy is her happiness.' He smiled with a hint of mischief dancing in his eyes. 'Naturally, I'd much prefer to see Davy starting his schooling, and his mam here at home to greet him when he comes back from his classes. But that's up to Tildy.'

Tildy, despite her present happiness, was troubled by her own confused and conflicting emotions. For many years she had struggled alone to bring up her son and that struggle had at times been heart-rendingly harsh. During those long years in which her courage and endurance had been tested to their limits, she had become tough-minded and self-reliant; jealous of her independence, and fiercely proud that no matter what degradations had been inflicted upon her by others, she had remained true to herself, and had always tried to so conduct herself that she could hold her head high and walk without shame. Now she was faced with the realisation that in marrying Daniel Lambert, and loving him as she did, her own independence must be sacrificed in some degree; that in certain aspects of her life she must, as a dutiful wife, override her own inclinations and do as he wished her to do. She drew a deep breath and made her decision.

'Listen, both of you. I accept what you tell me, Esther. That it isn't fitting for me to continue with my present work, once I'm wed to Daniel. So I'll finish with the field work and find something else that I can do here at home. I'll go back to the soft work. I can use the work room at the back. With me being at home then I'll be able to take my fair share of the housework as well, so Davy can start school.' She smiled at Daniel. 'Will that be all right?'

He beamed fondly at her. 'You do whatever makes you happy, my honey.'

'Esther?' Tildy stared questioningly at the other woman.

'That's better, my duck.' The withered features creased in a contented smile. 'You and me 'ull be able to keep this place spotless and Davy 'ull be able to start his schooling, instead of needing to be here and help me. I used to be a dab hand at the soft work mesen. So mayhap I'll work alongside you. I reckon we could manage our five thousand a day, couldn't us?'

'That's settled then.' Tildy smiled, and rose to her feet. 'But now I've got to go down to Easemore Farm and earn this day's pennies.'

She made no attempt to kiss Daniel farewell. Tildy was prudish enough to dislike passionate kisses and caresses between lovers in public. She believed that such displays were best exchanged in privacy, knowing as she did that many people found them embarrassing to witness. So she merely smiled and touched his shoulder as she passed and, carrying her rag-wrapped hunk of bread and cheese, set out for her work.

The early morning sky was a clean blue paleness, with only a smattering of wind-rippled clouds and the cold air was fresh and exhilarating to breathe. As she walked down the lane that led to Easemore Farm, Tildy could hear the faint echoings of the needle mills' bells calling the in-workers to their long hours of labour and she grimaced as she remembered how she too had once answered those bells and drudged in the wet stench of the lye shop for a pittance. Her thoughts turned to her old friend, Mother Readman, who owned a lodging house in the Silver Square, one of the most notorious slums of the town, where Tildy had lived for long periods. She still visited with Mother Readman on the rare occasions when she had time and now smiled happily at the thought that she would be able to see her friend more often.

'I wonder what she'll think of me getting wed again. I'll call and see her on my way back from work this night.'

The prospect gave Tildy pleasure and humming happily she dwelt on what she would say to Mother Readman when they met.

Back in the kitchen old Esther served Daniel Lambert his onion gruel and thick slice of fried salt-bacon and, while he ate, seated herself on the bench across the broad table and stared fixedly at him, until he asked:

'Why do you look at me so, Aunt?'

'You'll be seeing the parson today, Nephew?'

'That I will,' he told her enthusiastically. 'I want the banns called just as soon as they can be.'

'Youm a very lucky man, our Daniel, to be taking my Tildy for wife. I hope you'll be good to her. She's had too much grief in her life already.' The old woman's toothless jaws worked up and down and there was a hardness in her tone which caused the man to stare curiously at her.

'I don't need telling how lucky I am, Aunt. I already know that well enough.'

The toothless jaws still worked vigorously and the withered old head nodded sharply up and down, up and down. 'Then mind that you looks arter her proper and cherishes her and Davy like they should be cherished. Because it 'ull be God help you, iffen you doon't!' old Esther snapped forcefully, and Daniel Lambert laid down his knife and spoon to stare at his relative in astonished mystification.

'Jesus Christ, Auntie! What's brought this on? I love Tildy, and little Davy as well. Of course I'll be cherishing them.' He frowned suddenly. 'Why are you acting like this, Aunt Esther? Come now, tell me.'

''Tis because I'm worried, our Daniel. I'm worried about you.'

He shook his head in incomprehension and old Esther snorted impatiently.

'It anna any use you acting so bloody innocent wi' me, Nephew. You knows well what worries me. Youm a wild bugger, and you'se ne'er bin able to settle to anything steady in your life.' She held up her clawed hands to ward off any reply. 'No! Hear me out, boy, afore you spakes. I anna blaming you for the way you am. It's in your blood and theer's naught you can do about that. Our family's always had a streak o' badness in it, which strikes wheer it 'ull through the different generations. Your grandfather was a bad, wild bugger and me own son has got that streak in him, only he's got it a sight worse than you has. He's bloody evil, he is, and I'd never call you that. Youm just wild rather than bad. God only knows I'm happy that you and Tildy am to be wed. But I canna help worrying about her, for fear that you wun't be able to settle to wedded life and make a good steady husband for her. I'm feared that blood will out and arter youm used to wedded life then you'll tire on it and goo off gallivantin' and wasting agen.'

Daniel Lambert's face was very grave, and he answered quietly, 'I know what I've been in the past, Aunt Esther, and I've paid a sorry price for all that I've done. But men can change for the better, no matter what is in their blood. And I truly believe that I have changed. I tell you this now, and I tell you with all truth, that before I'd do anything to hurt Tildy, or her boy, I would put a knife through my own heart. That woman is more precious to me than my life ever has been, or ever could be. You have no need worry about what sort of a husband I'll be to Tildy. I intend to be the best husband any woman ever could wish for, Aunt Esther, because if love was gold then Tildy is even now the richest woman in creation.'

The old woman appeared to be reassured and she nodded slowly. 'I'm happy to know that, nephew, because she deserves no less.'

After he had breakfasted Daniel shaved and dressed with care. He examined himself in the full length mirror in his bedroom and was satisfied with what he saw. The well groomed gentleman, in the dark blue swallow-tail coat and fawn pantaloons strapped down over highly-polished boots, bore no resemblance to the ragged, unshaven convict of Norfolk Island. He adjusted his high black stock round his winged collar and took his white tophat and fine kid gloves from the dresser.

The manservant who answered his knocking at the door of John Clayton's house, further up the Fish Hill towards the town green, ushered him respectfully into the hallway, where he was shortly joined by John Clayton. The young curate was surprised by his caller's identity, but greeted him politely. 'Good morning to you, Master Lambert.'

'Good morning, Parson Clayton. Thank you for seeing me. I'll not detain you long.'

'Please to step inside.' Clayton pushed open his study door and invited the other man to enter.

As soon as they were seated Daniel Lambert came directly to the point for his visit. 'I wish you to call the banns, sir, for myself and my future wife.'

Clayton's pleasantly ugly features showed open surprise. 'Do you intend to wed, Master Lambert?'

Daniel grinned. 'I do sir.'

'Might I enquire the lady's name?'

'Her name is Matilda Crawford.'

Clayton's shock caused him to gape momentarily, but he instantly recovered himself, and frowned doubtfully. 'Master Lambert, to the best of my knowledge, Matilda Crawford is a married woman.'

Lambert smiled and shook his head slowly. 'No,

Parson Clayton. She is a widow. Her husband died some two years past in the Norfolk Island convict station.'

Clayton still frowned doubtfully. 'Are you certain of this, Master Lambert? I enquire because the man, Thomas Crawford, was known to me, and I also know Matilda Crawford quite well. I have heard no report of his death.'

'I am very certain that he is dead, Parson Clayton, because I was present when he was killed in a brawl,' Daniel told him calmly.

'Do you have proof of this, Master Lambert?' Clayton's ugly features were still doubtful.

Resentment burgeoned in Daniel, but he forced himself to remain calm. 'I do assure you that I am not lying about Tom Crawford's death, Parson Clayton.'

The clergyman's muscular hands locked together briefly, then separated and rested lightly on his desk top. 'I will speak plainly, Master Lambert, and you must excuse my bluntness, I mean no offence by it. If I am to read the banns for yourself and Matilda Crawford, then I will require satisfactory proof that she is indeed a widow.'

Daniel Lambert gritted his teeth, but deep down acknowledged that the cleric was only acting as he considered right. 'What will that proof entail, Parson Clayton, to be judged satisfactory?'

Clayton considered for a few moments, then said, 'I need to receive written confirmation from the office of the commandant of the Norfolk Island convict station that Thomas Crawford is dead.' He paused, and regarded his visitor with some sympathy. 'I trust that you will accept that I act only as my office behoves me to so do, Master Lambert. My advice to you is to write to the office of the commandant and request that they send to me directly the confirmation I require.' A bleak smile fleeted across his lips. 'I believe what you have told me, Lambert, but I am answerable to those above me to ensure that any sacrament I administer in this parish is acceptable in the sight of both God and man. I cannot risk being an accessory to any bigamous marriage.'

Daniel Lambert's disappointment was very obvious, but he accepted that nothing could be done about the situation, except to accede to the parson's wishes. He sighed heavily and rose to his feet.

'Very well, sir. I shall put pen to paper this very day and trust that the confirmation will not be long in coming. I bid you good day, sir.'

Clayton rose also and rang for his manservant. Before Daniel Lambert left him the young parson smiled and encouraged, 'I'm sure that matters will eventually be arranged to your satisfaction, Master Lambert, and I look forward to performing your wedding ceremony.'

'Many thanks, sir, good day to you.'

Daniel Lambert went disconsolately from the room, and alone again John Clayton thought over what had just occurred. He visualised Tildy Crawford's pretty face and lush body and being a healthy and exceptionally vigorous young man could sympathise with Lambert's obvious disappointment.

'I'd feel more than a little peeved myself, Lambert,' he grinned. 'I take my oath that I would.'

Daniel Lambert was indeed feeling more than a little peeved as he walked on up the steep hill towards the green. He mentally computed the length of time it might take to send for and receive an answer from the distant speck of land known as Norfolk Island. He knew from his own experience of the time the long voyages took, coupled with the dilatory working of the commandant's office that it might be anything from eighteen months to two years before he would get what he wanted: the official confirmation of Thomas Crawford's death.

'Goddamn and blast it!' he swore with an intense frustration. 'I just hope that Tildy will understand, and trust in me sufficiently to wait.'

He cheered up a little. 'We can still live as man and wife, even without being churched. There's thousands who do, and they don't seem a bit the worse for it.'

Yet although he was hopeful that Tildy would live with him he was still not happy about the situation, because he wanted to bind her to him legally and was secretly afraid that he might lose her some day if she remained a single woman.

At the top of the Fish Hill he stopped and stood still, undecided as to what he would now do. Then abruptly he turned eastwards and walked quickly down the long straight Easemore Lane towards the farm at its end.

Before he reached the cluster of farm buildings he could see Tildy's gang working in a field off to his right. They were setting potatoes and as he neared them Daniel Lambert frowned unhappily, not liking to see his beloved woman toiling so hard as she spread the heaps of manure with her long shafted graip. Then his frown became a smile. Even performing this menial task she moved with a lithe grace that caused him to wonder afresh at his amazing good fortune that such a beautiful creature could profess herself to be in love with him.

As he crossed the furrows she looked up and saw him, and as if alarmed by his sudden appearance she spoke to the man at the cart tail then came running, her expression anxious.

'Don't be alarmed, honey. There's nothing the matter. I just want a quick word with you, that's all,' he called out to reassure her, and she slowed to a walk.

The rest of the gang stopped work and stared curiously at this well-dressed man and aware of their scrutiny Tildy blushed slightly and when he would have kissed her in greeting, held him away with a gentle push.

'No, not here, Daniel.'

He accepted the rebuff with a good grace, understanding that any public display of affection would embarrass her.

'What brings you here? Has anything happened at home?' she asked, and Daniel Lambert could only think how beautiful her face looked, framed by the old poke bonnet, and how not even the coarse layers of sacking could disguise the glories of her body.

149

She was both fondly amused by, and impatient with, his dumb, adoring regard. 'Yes, it is me, Daniel!' she declared, half laughing.

He grinned wryly, 'I'm sorry, Honey, it's just that each time I see you I cannot believe in my own good fortune.' Then he sobered and quickly related all that had passed between himself and John Clayton. As he spoke Daniel studied her features for reaction and when he had finished waited with considerable trepidation for her to reply. To his relief she only shrugged dismissively and smiled.

'Well Daniel, I've never been much of a one for religion anyway. What does it matter if we're churched or not? After last night I couldn't feel more wedded to you than I do right now.'

In sheer joy he snatched a kiss from her and she laughed and blushed furiously as the curious watchers clapped and cheered his action. She pushed him strongly so that he almost stumbled.

'Go away, will you? I'll see you tonight.'

Grinning broadly he walked off, restraining his urge to caper about like a small boy in wild celebration and Tildy went back to her work and the eager questions of her workmates.

'Who is he, Tildy?'

'Is he your man?'

'What's his name?'

'Wheer does he come from?'

She knew that until she satisfied their curiosity she would get no peace from their questioning, and so told them simply, 'Yes, he is my man, his name is Daniel Lambert and he comes from Redditch.'

One of the ploughmen, who had strongly fancied Tildy himself and had his advances flatly repulsed by her, sneered spitefully. 'I thought you told me that you was a respectable 'ooman, Tildy Crawford. What's you doing acarrying on wi' a man when your own man is out in Botany Bay.'

Angrily she turned on him. 'I'm a widow-woman, Sam Potts. My husband died more than two years since at

150

Norfolk Island. And I'll carry on, as you call it, with whomsoever I choose to.'

The man's heavy bovine face became a deeper shade of red. 'Yes, that's easy seen, that is, Tildy Crawford and it's easy seen as well that you arn't over-fussed about who you does carry on wi'. I knows that bloke youm wi' and I knows what he is as well, for all his fine clothes.'

Tildy was aware of the avid stares surrounding her and the greed for gossip-worthy titbits of information. She drew a deep breath and steeled herself.

'Daniel Lambert, the man I'm living with as wife, has not long returned from transportation. He's an ex-convict.'

Muted exclamations of shock and satisfaction came from her listeners and Tildy's lips curved in a scornful, defiant smile and she faced the ploughman challengingly. 'Is there aught else you'd like to know, Sam Potts? But take care what you ask me, because I might have to get Daniel Lambert to bring you the answer and I doubt you'll be so bold when you face him.'

He scowled at her furiously. 'Youm crowing like a dunghill cock now, Tildy Crawford, but from what I hears you'll not be crowing for much longer. Dan Lambert might be a fighting man, but theers a deal of such in this town. He wun't be so tough arter the "Rippling Boys" get done wi' him.'

Alarm pierced Tildy's fiery temper. 'What do you mean by that? What about the "Rippling Boys"?'

Satisfied that he had scored a palpable hit, the beefy ploughman only laughed jeeringly and walked away without reply.

Now that the free show was over the gang resumed their work, and Tildy took up her graip and went back to spreading the heaps of manure. As she worked the ploughman's parting shot reverberated through her mind and her worry increased as the hours wore on. She knew of the so-called 'Rippling Boys' and knew also that apart from being thieves, they were also reputed to be involved in other more savage criminality. Gossip had it that they had even committed murder.

'But why should they want to hurt Daniel?' she asked herself, time and time again, and time and time again could only accept that she had no answer to that question. By late afternoon Tildy had decided that she would do her utmost to find an answer before she returned home that night.

'There's one person who'll know what's going on, if anybody will.' She knew. That person was her old friend, Mother Readman.

Mother Readman sat in the vast battered armchair before the inglenook fire like a queen surrounded by her ragged courtiers. When Tildy came into the long, gloomy low-ceilinged room, with its benches and trestle tables and its grease-thick walls she smiled to see the hugely fat old woman lording it over the tatterdemalion assembly of her lodging house tenants.

Mother Readman greeted her fondly and with a wave of one grimy paw cleared a space at her side for Tildy to sit. Her brown-black stubs of teeth bared in a sly grin.

'Am I to be invited to your wedding feast then, Tildy, my duck?'

Tildy had known the old woman too long to be surprised at this display of knowledge. From her battered armchair Mother Readman's tentacles reached out across the length and breadth of the needle district and very little happened that sooner or later she did not come to hear of it.

Before Tildy could reply, Mother Readman's small eyes — almost buried in puffballs of fat — winked, and she chuckled wheezily. 'Mind you, they do say that youm agoing to have to wait a fair bit afore you can get churched, my duck. It's a long way to Norfolk Island, arn't it?'

Tildy could only shake her head in admiration for the other woman's spy network.

'Is there anything at all that happens in this town without you knowing of it, Mother?' she asked smilingly.

'Precious little, my duck. Precious bloody little.' Again the fat jowls shook and quivered as the old woman's wheezy chuckles issued forth from her mountainous body, shapeless in its myriad layers of black shawls and gowns.

Tildy's voice dropped to a whisper and she placed her lips close to the mobcapped mass of frizzy grey hair so that Mother Readman would hear her clearly. Quickly she related what the ploughman had said that day and asked her friend if she knew anything concerning the matter.

The old woman pondered silently for a short while, then in her turn whispered, 'I knows that Daniel Lambert give that young bugger Tom Chance a hammering when they was in the lock-up together, Tildy. And I knows that him and his brother, Abel Chance, am reckoned to be counted among the "Rippling Boys". It could be that's the reason the "Rippling Boys" has a score to settle agen your man. I did hear that there'd been a few threats made by Abel Chance when he was drunk.' She pursed her lips thoughtfully. 'Mind you, Tildy, I was a bit puzzled about them needles being found in your man's coal shed that time. And that was afore he give young Chance his comeuppance, warn't it?' Again her lips pursed and she gave a vigorous shake of her massive head, causing her jowls to ripple and bounce from side to side. 'Nooo, my duck, it seems to me that theer's got to be some reason other than Tom Chance for that happening like it did.' She screwed her head sideways to stare at the others around the inglenook fire and with a nod beckoned a small ragged extremely dirty youth to come to her.

When he did so, Tildy almost jerked her head back, so rancid was the stench his body emitted. But Mother Readman seemed unaware of the foul smell as she whispered instructions into the matted greasy hair that covered his ear. He slipped away and Mother Readman patted Tildy's knee comfortingly.

'You get off home to your bairn ánd your man now, my duck. And gi' my regards to old Esther. Come back and see me in a couple o' days òr so. I'll most likely ha' summat to tell you then.'

'Many thanks, Mother,' Tildy said gratefully, and leaned forwards to kiss the tallowy cheek.

She left the lodging house eased in her mind. Tildy was a woman of great courage and was ready to defend her loved ones against any danger that might threaten them, no matter what the odds against her might be. The prospect of having to confront the 'Rippling Boys' was still a frightening one, but Tildy knew that it was their very anonymity that enabled the 'Rippling Boys' to strike fear into the hearts of so many. Once identified and brought out from the dark shadows they dwelt in, then the 'Rippling Boys' would become just another group of ordinary commonplace mortals who could be faced, challenged and beaten.

As she left the winding fetid alley named Silver Street, that connected the Silver Square with Red Lion street, Tildy passed under the archway adjoining the Red Lion Inn, from behind the lighted windows of which came the sounds of men laughing and singing raucously. She pulled her shawl more tightly around her head and quickened her steps. The Red Lion was a haunt of many of the needle pointers, and Tildy had no wish to meet any of that wild and violent breed when they were in their cups.

'How bist, Tildy Crawford?'

The man's greeting caused Tildy to start in shock and she swung her head to see the tall burly figure of Joseph Cashmore, the constable, standing in a deeply shadowed recess in the inn wall.

'You gave me a fright, Master Cashmore.' She smiled, relieved.

He stepped out from the recess and fell in step with her. 'I'll walk along the road wi' you a bit, Tildy Crawford. I'm glad I'se bumped into you, because I wanted a word.'

'What about, Master Cashmore?' Her curiosity was instantly aroused.

'Oh, this and that,' he said vaguely, then went on at a tangent. 'I'se always had a deal o' respect for you, Tildy Crawford. You'se always kept yourself clean and decent and stayed an honest woman.'

Sudden disquiet assailed her and caused her to reply guardedly. 'I trust I shall always do that, Master Cashmore.'

'They do say that you'se took up wi' Daniel Lambert, Tildy,' he observed with an air of casualness.

'And what if I have?' She was instantly defensive and at the same time angry with herself for being so. 'I don't think it's anybody's business but my own who I take up with.'

'No more it arn't, and youm right to say as much, my wench,' the constable agreed soothingly, and his condescending manner provoked Tildy to snap at him.

'Listen, Master Cashmore. If you've got something to say to me, then say it straight out. and don't beat around the bushes.'

'Now don't fly off the handle, girl,' he remonstrated. 'Just remember that I'm the constable o' this parish and it is my business to know what goes on in it.'

Tildy spoke in a calmer tone. 'It's no crime if I take up with Daniel Lambert, Master Cashmore. We intend to wed just as soon as we can.'

'Well, girl, that's your own business, as you said,' the man told her, and then fell silent and remained so as they walked on past the lock-up and along the side of the green towards the Fish Hill. The night was dark and there were few people abroad. The ones that they did pass stared curiously at the couple and Tildy was uncomfortably aware of that curiosity. At the top of the Fish Hill she stopped and turned to face the constable.

'Look Master Cashmore, I mean you no offence, but I'd sooner walk home by myself.' She tried to make a joke of it. 'People think that I'm under arrest, seeing you with me like this. What was it you wanted to see me about?'

'I wanted to ask if you knew wheer Daniel Lambert was yesterday morning.'

'He was with me.' Tildy could not suppress a frisson of nervousness. 'Why do you ask me that?'

'Wheer was you both at?' The man's attitude had hardened visibly and Tildy realised that she should not risk angering him by any obduracy on her part.

'We went down to the Abbey Meadows to see the sun dancing. We took my boy and old Esther Smith with us.'

'How long did you stay there?'

'Until the dancing ended. But why are you asking me these questions?'

He ignored her request. 'Did you see anybody you knew theer? Anybody who can vouchsafe that what you tell me is true?'

By now Tildy was becoming increasingly nervous and she cast about in her mind for memories of the previous morning. 'There were people there that I knew, Master Cashmore, but whether or not they saw me, I just can't tell you. Because we kept ourselves to ourselves. But me and Daniel both joined in the dancing and there must be some of those we partnered who'd remember us being there.' She paused momentarily, then beseeched, 'But why are you asking me this? What's the reason?'

His customary dour manner had now returned in full measure and there was no trace of kindness in his voice or face when he told her.

'I'm asking because there was another robbery committed yesterday morning down at Bredon, round about the time that you claims you and Daniel Lambert were in the Abbey Meadows.'

Fuelled by a righteous indignation her fiery temper rose instantly. 'Ohh that's it, is it?' she stated heatedly. 'A robbery is committed so you straight away lay the blame at Daniel's door. Well he had nothing to do with it. He was with me all morning and all afternoon and all night and old Esther can tell you that as well. It's not fair that you should try and blame him for something he's not done, Master Cashmore. It's unjust!'

He frowned harshly. 'You think it's unjust, do you, girl? Well now, hear this, and remember it. You'se chosen to take up wi' a returned transport. To share his bed and be wife to him. Well this is part o' the price you'll need to pay for doing that. The price for being the woman of an ex-convict. Because nobody believes that leopards can change their spots, girl, and for the rest of his life Daniel Lambert 'ull always be suspect when there's wrongdoings in this town. That's the way life is, my wench, so you might as well get used to the idea and learn to live wi' it. Because it arn't never agoing to be any different.'

He turned on his heel and marched away from her and Tildy could only stand and gaze unhappily after him until his bulk was swallowed up in the darkness.

She decided to say nothing about what had occurred that day to Daniel, or even to old Esther. 'There's naught to be gained by worrying either of them with it. I'll wait and see what Mother Readman finds out for me before I say anything to them.'

Having come to this decision she entered the house, and hid her worries so well that neither Daniel Lambert or old Esther had even the slightest suspicion that anything was troubling her.

Chapter Sixteen

One of Tildy's main worries during the days that followed concerned her son's possible reactions to the fact that she and Daniel Lambert were now living as man and wife. Davy slept alone in a small room next to the room that she and old Esther had shared. Since he was normally asleep when she and Daniel went to bed, and she rose before her son awoke, Tildy was not really certain if the child knew what the new situation was. One night she discussed the matter with Daniel and old Esther and decided that she would tell the child about his own father, Tom Crawford and the fact that to all intents and purposes Daniel Lambert was now in the position of being his new step-father.

The following night at Davy's bedtime she went with him into his room and seating herself on the bed drew the child close to her.

'Now I want you to listen very carefully to what I'm going to tell you, honey,' she began, and instantly his eyes sparkled with pleased anticipation and he asked eagerly, 'Is it a story, Mam? Are you going to tell me a story?'

Her love for him welled up within her bringing a lump to her throat. 'Yes, sweetheart, it's a story.'

She was forced to swallow hard because her voice sounded so choked and strained and she could not dispel the feelings of apprehension as to what his reactions might be. She drew a long deep breath, and began:

'It's a story about your Dad and me ...' Once started she found it increasingly easy to explain to the child how she and Tom Crawford had only lived together for a comparatively short time and that Tom Crawford had been sent out to the penal colonies in far distant Australia and had died there. She made no mention of Tom Crawford's ill treatment of them both, or of the specific crimes for which he had been transported, but tried only to keep her account simple and dispassionate.

The child listened raptly, his eyes huge in his solemn little face, but displayed no concern that he had lost a father whom he could not even remember. Before Tildy could broach the subject of Daniel Lambert, Davy did so himself.

'Would Daniel be my dad, Mam? If you asked him to?'

Tildy was so surprised by this that momentarily she was lost for words, and the child argued, 'Tell me, Mam? Would he?'

She smiled, and could not resist hugging his slender body. 'Would you like Daniel for your dad sweetheart?'

'Yes,' he told her. 'I like Daniel, he plays soldiers with me sometimes, and gives me rides on Saturn. If he was my dad then he could play soldiers with me all the time, couldn't he, Mam?'

Her heart lifted and she laughed in mingled relief and delight. 'I'll tell you what, honey, you get into bed now and I'll go downstairs and ask Daniel if he'll be your dad, shall I?'

'All right then,' the child answered matter of factly, and began to undress.

In the kitchen Tildy could not keep from giggling, and both Daniel and old Esther stared at her in bafflement. With an effort she controlled herself and related what Davy had said and both of them burst out laughing.

'Bless him!' old Esther kept on repeating fondly. 'Bless the innocent little soul!'

Daniel beamed with pleasure. He had grown very fond of the boy and he too had been concerned as to the child's reaction to his assumption of the real father's place. Together with Tildy he went up to Davy's room. The child lay in his narrow cot gazing up at the two adults and

Daniel perched on the edge of the mattress. He gently touched Davy's rosy cheek, and asked him, 'Can I be your dad then, Davy?'

The child grinned and nodded vigorously, and tears stung Daniel Lambert's eyes as he stroked the mop of black curls and said huskily, 'Well, that's good. Because I want you to be my son.' His breath caught in his throat, and he rose to his feet. Then he grinned at the child. 'We must do something to mark this event, Davy. After all, it's not every day that a man gains a fine son like you, is it? Now what can we do?'

He made a great show of scratching his head as if in deep thought and the child watched him with wide eyes. Then Daniel Lambert grinned and told him, 'I know what we'll do, Son. Tomorrow you and I shall go and buy a pony.'

Davy crowed with excited pleasure. 'A pony! Shall I be able to ride it?'

'But of course you'll be able to ride it.' Daniel Lambert threw back his head and roared with laughter and Davy grinned happily as the infectious sound caught him up in its rich happiness. 'It's going to be your pony, Son. Your very own pony.'

Later that night, after they had made love, Tildy lay cradled in Daniel Lambert's embrace savouring her feelings of contentment and security. She had never been happier in her entire life and this very happiness now caused a sudden shiver of fear to strike through her. She could not bring herself to fully believe that it could ever last.

'Then enjoy it while you have it,' a small voice whispered in her mind, and she sighed and snuggled closer to her man's warmth.

'What's the matter, honey, can't you sleep?' Daniel whispered fondly and Tildy smiled in the darkness.

'I'm too happy to want to sleep.'

For a while they talked in low murmurs of the day's

events, and then Daniel suggested, 'I think that after we've bought the pony, I should go and have words with Henry James about Davy going to his school. It's time that Davy began his education, isn't it? Don't you agree?'

Tildy concurred. 'Very well then. And I shall try the mills close to us and see if any of them will give me soft work.'

The 'soft work' she referred to were the stages in the manufacture of needles which were carried out by the use of hand tools. Some soft workers were employed directly by the needle masters in the mills and factories, but the major portion of this type of work was given out as a form of sub-contract. The 'soft workers' would collect packets of steel wire cut double length and dual-pointed from the mills and bring them back to their own domestic workshops to be fashioned by hand into needles. The work was tedious, long-drawn out and eye-straining, and the earnings from it uncertain. A couple of experienced 'soft workers' acting in concert could perhaps make five hundred needles per day and earn five shillings between them. But the amount of needles made were greatly dependent on the quality of the steel wire. If it was of poor quality and flawed then it would splinter under the eye-punch and become only scrap metal. Added to this were the fluctuations of the needle trade itself. When trade was bad, the needle masters would give what work they had to their own in-workers, and the out-workers were then redundant until business improved once more.

But still the majority of local people preferred their comparative freedom as out-workers before the rigid work discipline and time-keeping the in-worker was subjected to. And, when trade flourished, the out-worker with many children was in an enviable position, for even children as young as four or five years could be trained to use a guttering file, or the small punch and hammer, or to sort and wrap the needles into their paper packets.

Daniel Lambert frowned slightly. 'There's no need for

you to do anything other then keep house, you know, sweetheart. I could get you a girl to do the heavy work for you. You can live like a lady if you want.'

'No, Daniel,' Tildy protested sharply. 'I thought that we had agreed on how we shall live. We agreed that I should keep on working and earn money for myself.'

'Yes, but when we so agreed, then things were different between us,' Daniel argued. 'Now we are man and wife it's not fitting that you should have to slave at such work.'

'No Daniel, we are not yet man and wife,' she told him firmly, and all her engrained stubbornness came to the fore. 'And if you don't keep to our bargain, then we never shall become man and wife.' She suddenly softened towards him and kissed his mouth, then urged him, 'Try to understand how I feel in this matter, honey. Please try. I want to be a partner to you, a true helpmate. Not just a possession.'

Daniel Lambert did try to understand how she felt, but he was a man of his times, who had been brought up in the belief that women should always obey their men without question, and that belief was deeply bedded in his psyche. He sighed unhappily. 'I only want what is best for you, Tildy. It's because I love you so much that I don't want you to do menial work for anyone. I want you to be regarded as a lady in this town. And real ladies do not perform manual work, do they?'

Tildy grinned impishly. 'I'm no lady, Daniel.' Her hand mischievously sought his maleness and caressed it, and within moments he was erect. Her soft moist lips moved on his chest and throat and his breath sobbed and his arms tightened about her.

'Do you really want me to be a lady, sweetheart?' she teased. 'Or do you want me to be like this?'

Her own desire was by now rekindled, and she moved on top of him and guided him into her, glorying in his hungry need. Even in the thrall of his passion the realisation came to Daniel that he would never be the master of this woman, 'that he could only ever hope to be her equal partner.

'Then so be it,' he accepted. 'So be it.'

Chapter Seventeen

There were several schools of varying scholastic and social standards in Redditch Town ranging from the newly opened Boarding School of the Sons of Gentlemen, Reverend John Clayton as principal, down to the Lancastrian Free School for the Poor, taught by schoolmaster Sidney Heath, and for the very small children a scattering of dame schools.

Daniel Lambert himself had attended the school run by Mister Henry James and his wife in Evesham Street in a large room at the rear of their private house. It was to this house that Daniel came on the morning of Saturday. Henry James himself came to the door in answer to the ringing of the bell, a swarthy complexioned, middle-sized man, whose dark clothing resembled the clerical garb and whose fine white hair denoted his advancing years. His faded eyes, magnified by the bulbous lensed spectacles he wore, regarded his visitor without any sign of recognition.

'Yes sir, what can I do for you?'

The voice that Daniel had remembered as a thundering bass was now weakened by age.

'I see that you don't remember me, Mister James. My name is Daniel Lambert, I was a pupil of yours for several years.'

The old man stepped forwards from the doorway and peered closely into Daniel's face, then clucked his tongue.

''Pon my soul! You'll be Henry Lambert's son.'

'That is so, sir.'

'Yes, I remember you now, boy. You went for a soldier, didn't you?' The old man clucked his tongue again. 'And

164

then you were transported some years past, were you not?'

Daniel nodded. 'That is also correct, sir.'

Henry James swarthy features became stern. 'What do you want with me, Lambert?'

Daniel sighed inwardly. The schoolteacher and his wife had always been the type of grim, hellfire and brimstone Christians who abhorred any weak sinners who strayed from the path of the most rigid moral rectitude. But for all that, they were without any doubt the finest teachers in the district, and any child who came beneath their roof left school thoroughly endowed with the basic education they provided in their classroom. Daniel knew that if Davy was to be accepted as a pupil here, then the fees the James' asked for would be money well spent.

'I want to enrol a boy as a pupil in your school, Mr James.'

The old man frowned and his body stiffened, and for a brief instant Daniel was transported back across the years when as a small boy he had trembled before the terrible wrath of this strictest of disciplinarians.

'I remember you well now, Lambert.' Even the old man's voice seemed to have regained its thunderous bass. 'You were a jackanapes, sir. A scapegrace. A source of worry and grief to your parents. Though I thrashed you until my arm ached, you remained obdurate.'

Daniel was forced to hide a smile. He had indeed been a problem pupil.

'And yet, for all that, I never thought you to be a wicked boy.' The old man's grim features softened almost imperceptibly. 'Sadly wild and unruly, yet not evil.' He paused, then asked, 'Tell me, Lambert, have you now changed your ways? Do you intend to follow in the godly footsteps of your father and mother?'

Daniel Lambert considered the questions for a moment or two. He did not resent the harsh words and hectoring manner of Henry James. That was the old man's way, and Daniel knew that he lived up to his own harsh strictures and, whatever else he might be accused of, could never ever be termed a hypocrite, unlike so many of the other self-professed Christians in this town. Daniel had a great deal of respect for this old man and truly believed that Davy would benefit enormously by being taught by him.

'I'll not try to gull you, Mr James,' he answered quietly, 'by claiming that I shall become a chapel-goer as my father was. I hold little brief for any religion, or for many of those who continually prate of their religious beliefs. But, I do fully intend to do all that I can to restore the good name of my family in this town, a name that I am very conscious of bringing into low repute.'

'I am pleased to hear that, Lambert. Now this boy, what age is he?'

'He's seven and a half years, sir.'

'What schooling has he received?'

'None that I'm aware of.' Daniel thought for a moment. 'But his mother has taught him the rudiments of reading and writing, and he's a very intelligent child. I can personally vouch for that fact.'

'Very well,' the old man nodded brusquely. 'The terms are ten pence the week, to be paid each Monday morning. He must be provided with slate and pencil, and be respectably clothed and clean in his body. He can commence this coming Monday morn. Tell him to attend on me at half past eight o'clock. What is his name?'

'Davy. Davy Crawford.'

The old man nodded brusquely once more. 'Very well, Lambert. Good day to you.'

'Good day, sir.' Daniel left the old man staring short-sightedly after him through the thick lensed spectacles.

Evesham Street was already starting to be thronged with market-day visitors: pedlars carrying their packs, stallholders' carts lurching along, livestock being driven by smock-clad countrymen, higglers and farmwives with their baskets of eggs and butter and cheese. There were many softworkers also from the outlying districts,

166

tramping towards the needle-mills toting their heavy canvas-wrapped packages of finished needles, square brown-paper caps on their heads, rolled white aprons around their hips. By midday the pubs would be filled with out-workers, washing the thirst of their week's hard labours away with copious draughts of ale and cider, gin and rum, and the pointers and labourers from the town itself would be in those same pubs, and then the brawls would erupt as old quarrels were settled and new quarrels provoked.

Daniel sauntered southwards towards the three-storeyed single-fronted, terraced houses of the New End which led up the Front Hill. Adjoining the New End was Harbut Street, known facetiously to the locals as God's Little Acre, because its squat cottages and cramped courts were for the most part occupied by fanatical Primitive Methodists and its environs resounded constantly with their ranting prayers and bawled hymns.

Daniel smiled to himself as he passed Harbut Street, remembering the escapades of his boyhood years when he and his fellow scamps would tease the ranting preachers until they invoked the wrath of God on their heads and were forced to flee under a barrage of holy kicks and blows. A fleeting sadness touched his smile, a sadness of nostalgia for times past. But then he thought of Tildy and nostalgia fled, vanquished by the happiness of the present.

'Dan? Dan Lambert? It is you, arn't it, Dan?'

The sound of his name being shouted brought Daniel to a halt and he stopped and turned, seeking the voice.

It was a short, broad-shouldered man who wore the brown paper cap and the rolled white apron of a 'soft worker'.

'It's me, Dan. Jackey Watts. Doon't you know me?'

The man came up to Daniel, his hand held out in greeting, and Daniel suddenly grinned in glad recognition and, taking the proffered hand in both his own, shook it hard and long.

Jackey Watts had been his closest friend when they were both youths, but Daniel had not seen him for many years.

'Christ, but it's good to see you, Jackey. How long has it been since we last met?'

The other man's bluff, florid features grinned happily. 'Well now, I can tell you that nigh on exact, my old cocker. The last time you and me sin each other was on the morn o' Waterloo. I catched sight o' you when we was passing through your regiment to take up position.'

'That's right, Jackey.' Daniel's memory flew back to that fateful morning when the British Army and its allies had fronted the mighty host of Napoleon Bonaparte for the battle that was to decide the fate of Europe. 'By Christ, there's so much we have to tell each other about, Jackey.'

'Well why doon't you come on up to Boney's Island wi' me, and once I gets shut on these,' Jackey Watts indicated the heavy packets of needle lengths that he carried slung over both shoulders, 'why then we can goo and have a few jars and talk to our hearts' content.'

Daniel happily agreed to that suggestion and side by side the two men, talking excitedly, went on up the Front Hill and along the gently rising ridge of Mount Pleasant.

Boney's Island was the local nickname for the hamlet of Crabbs Cross. It lay about a mile south of Headless Cross and was one of the chain of small settlements which dotted the long elevated road of the Ridgeway on its journey southwards towards the fertile Vale of Evesham. The hamlet had gained its nickname through being the favoured venue for all types of sporting combats. Boxing matches, wrestling matches, cudgel-fights, cock-fights, dog-fights, bull- and badger-baitings, rat-killings all frequently took place there because the borderlines of two counties — Worcestershire and Warwickshire — and four parishes — Tardebigge, Ipsley, Studley and Feckenham — dissected its immediate environs. Consequently, any attempt by the magistrates of either of the counties or the constable of any of the parishes to prevent a banned sporting fixture from taking place at Boney's Island was countered with the venue for that fixture being moved a few score yards into either another county or another parish, where the magistrate or constable possessed no jurisdiction. This happy circumstance had also influenced the notorious Jonas Crowther into making the hamlet his home and he owned several properties there.

It was in one of those properties, a cottage in a tumble-down terrace known as 'Crowther's Row', that Jackey Watts lived with his numerous family. The terrace stood on the main road at the northern edges of Crabbs Cross and they sighted it as they emerged from the thick woodland which bordered the road between the two Crosses.

Jackey Watts chuckled grimly. 'Theer's my palace, Dan. Fit for a bleeding' king arn't it?'

Daniel looked at the long crescent of the terrace, and even at this distance of some thirty yards the varied stinks reached his nostrils. About two thirds of the row appeared to be in human habitation, the remaining tenements were being used as cow-byres, pig-pens, workshops, and one on the furthest end of the row as a midden-heap.

'I've seen better places to dwell in, Jackey.'

His companion cursed bitterly. 'That's got to be the truest thing you'se ever fuckin' well said, my cocker. Jonas Crowther's my landlord, the old villain. Still, it's chape to rent, Daniel, and that counts for a lot these days, and I'se got the next door for a workshop, so that saves the babbies gettin' fuckin' needles stuck in um when they crawls about the floor. The place I was in before, I had to do me work in the same room we lived in. Jesus, I spent that much o' me bleedin' time pulling needles out o' the bloody kids' arses, it was a wonder that I ever earned a penny-piece.'

Jackey Watts' wife was a sagging-bodied, prematurely aged young woman, made sour-tempered by constant chronic toothache which she treated with frequent swigs from a stone bottle of cheap gin. The single small down-stairs room of the cottage reeked of urine and feces, and she sat slumped drunkenly on a broken-backed chair before the sooted hearth on which a tiny turf fire smoked sulkily, while her multitudinous brood crawled about the earthen floor dirty and half-naked.

The man tossed her a few coins, and warned, 'That's for grub and rent, you cow. Not for fuckin' gin.'

The woman's slack mouth opened to spew out a tirade of filthy insult, which Jackey Watts silenced by a casual back-handed blow which sent her sprawling among her sadly neglected brood, who seemed indifferent to the violence between their parents.

Daniel Lambert was neither shocked nor unduly disturbed by what he witnessed. The occurrence was a commonplace one in the world he inhabited. The same squalid domestic scene could be found all across the district. Poverty, violence, drunkenness, neglect abounded throughout the poorer quarters and with the exception of the first named was frequently encountered in more prosperous households also.

Now, as he and Jackey Watts walked on into Crabbs Cross, his old friend grumbled jocularly.

'I should have had me yed looked at for getting wed wi' that useless cow. I'd sell her this minute, but nobody 'ull buy her from me. The only thing her's any good at is having soddin' kids. She births 'um as regular as a breed sow. I swear I only 'as to put me hand to her bloody cuckoo's nest and another little sod jumps out on it.'

Daniel grinned slyly. 'Perhaps she wouldn't have so many if you kept your britches buttoned, Jackey.'

His friend laughed raucously. 'What? Me do wi' out me bit o' cunt? It just arn't possible, Dan. I'd goo bleedin' mad iffen I didn't have it regular. Jesus Christ! I arn't got much pleasure in me life, our kid, doon't take me cunt from me, for fuck's sake.'

They reached a small half-timbered inn, set back from

the road in a dip of land.

'The Royal Oak,' Jackey Watts informed. 'This is wheer Jonas Crowther spends his time.' He winked knowingly. 'That's when he arn't up to summat else, if you knows what I means.'

Tildy had told Daniel Lambert about the rumours that the 'Rippling Boys' meant to even the score with him for what he had done to Thomas Chance. Mother Readman had been unable to discover any other reason than that for the rumours to have arisen. Daniel himself was not worried by this purported enmity of the 'Rippling Boys'. He was confident of his ability to meet and deal with any physical assault. But he was anxious to keep Tildy, Davy and old Esther safe from the gang, and if he could positively identify even one of their number, then he would be in a position to strike back against them if they should seek to harm him or his loved ones in any way.

'This Jonas Crowther,' he said casually. 'They do say that he's the kingpin of the "Rippling Boys".'

Jackey Watts looked alarmed. 'Shhh!' He held a finger to his lips. 'You maun't say things like that when youm up here in Boney's Point. It arn't safe.'

Daniel deliberately prodded. 'Not safe? It's common enough talk down in the town. They do say that the magistrates know that Crowther is the leader of the "Rippling Boys" and the minute that they can obtain strong enough evidence against him then they'll take him up.'

The other man scoffed at this. 'Strong enough evidence. Is that all they needs? Well they bin trying long enough to get such, arn't they? And they arn't managed to yet.' He shook his head in dismissal. 'They'll never lay Jonas Crowther by the heels, he's as artful as Old Nick.' He stared questioningly at Daniel. 'But why be you so interested in him, Dan?'

After a moment's hesitation, Daniel related the full story about his clash with Thomas Chance and the threats

171

made by the 'Rippling Boys'. His old friend looked very serious. 'Iffen I was you, Dan, I'd walk careful of a night-time. I'se got a good idea who the "Rippling Boys" am, and iffen I'm right in what I thinks, then theer's some nasty bastards among 'um.'

'Give me their names, Jackey?' Daniel requested, and the other man frowned and appeared hesitant.

'Look, Jackey, give me their names. I swear that I'll never tell anyone who I got the names from. I appreciate that it's a bit difficult for you, living up here like you do. But we're old friends, Jackey, and you know well that if our positions were reversed then I'd help you in this way. I'm not asking you to get involved yourself. All I'm asking is for names.'

'All right then. I'll tell you who I think to be "Rippling Boys." But then you and me must part company, Dan. Because I can't afford to make an enemy o' Jonas Crowther. I'se got my missus and kids to think on.'

'Fair enough.' Daniel nodded.

'Well, I reckoned Jonas Crowther to be the kingpin, and there's his son-in-law, Ben Fairfax. Then there's the Wright brothers, Will and Joe, and young Will Fowkes. They'm the main ones, I reckon. And theer's others like Richie Bint, and John Hancox, and the Chances whom sort of auxiliary troops, like we used to have wi' us in Spain. But remember, Dan, I arn't said a word to you about 'um.'

'I'll remember, and thanks, Jackey.'

His old friend nodded. 'I wish you luck, Dan. Youm agoing to need it I reckon.' And Jackey Watts walked away from him.

Daniel strolled slowly on towards the triple fork where the road split and diverged into the different parishes, and took the left hand fork which crossed the boundary into Warwickshire, leaving the ridgeway and descending sharply down the steep Slough Hill towards the village of Studley.

'I've got names, now I need to put faces to them.' He

thought out his next move. 'I think Cousin William might help me to do that.' His lips curved in a mirthless smile. 'So long as I pay him well enough.'

Chapter Eighteen

'Love me little, love me long,
Is the burden of my song.
Love that is too hot and strong
Burneth soon to waste.
Still I would not have thee cold,
Nor too backward nor too bold;
Love that lasteth till 'tis old
Fadeth not in haste.'

Tildy sang softly as on hands and knees she scrubbed
the hallway, and in the kitchen old Esther smiled as she
heard and joined in with her cracked wavering voice.

'Winter's cold or summer's heat,
Autumn's tempest on it beat;
It can never know defeat,
Never can rebel.
Such the love that I would gain,
Such the love, I tell thee plain,
Thou must give or woo in vain,
So, to thee farewell.'

The song drew to its end and the two women laugh-
ingly applauded each other. Tildy scrubbed and wiped
the last tiles of the hallway and rose to take her bucket of
dirty water back through the kitchen and out to the end of
the garden where she emptied it into the ditch. The sun
was shining and the air tasted sweet as she drew it deep
into her lungs. Then she fetched a besom broom and
started to sweep the cobbles of the small stable yard at the

rear of the house. She smiled at the memory of Davy's shiny eyed excitement when earlier that morning Daniel had brought back the dappled grey pony, its coat glossy with grooming, its brand new saddlery's leather gleaming and brasses glittering in the sunlight.

Davy had insisted on riding out to Ipsley Alders to show Zeke Pickering his beautiful present and, although loth to permit him, Tildy had suppressed her natural worries and let the child go, not able to deny him such a harmless pleasure. She reassured herself now as to his safety by deliberately recalling what a fine little horseman he was. Had she not seen him herself riding bareback on Zeke Pickering's half-wild horses?

'He'll be all right. That pony's barely half the size of Zeke's horses. And he's not riding bareback,' she told herself, but still sighed, 'but I hope he's not riding too recklessly. Even ponies can throw their riders, can't they?'

She completed the sweeping of the yard and walked round to the front of the house to do the same for the path and steps there. As she worked a disquieting sense of being observed came upon her and she lifted her head and gazed about the garden and through the iron railings. Her breath caught in her throat as she saw that two young men, unshaven and unkempt, wearing the sleeveless leather jerkin, coarse shirts and garishly coloured neckerchiefs favoured by needle pointers were lounging against the wall of the terrace of cottages opposite, staring insolently at her. As she met their eyes the shorter of the men leered and gestured lewdly with his fingers.

Tildy's fiery spirit rose in instant resentment of his insult. But some unbiddden instinct made her pause and take stock, instead of rebuking him. A sense of unease touched her and she abandoned the sweeping and went into the house. Once inside she hurried upstairs and peeped cautiously through the net curtaining of the bedroom she shared with Daniel. The two men had not moved their position and, as she watched, the shorter, shaggy-haired man drew a small bottle from beneath his jerkin and took a long swallow of its contents, before handing it to his companion.

Tildy went to the head of the stairs and called for Esther to join her at the window.

'Do you know those two, Esther?'

'No. I've ne'er seen either on 'um afore.' The old woman stared at her friend curiously. 'You seems a mite troubled by 'um my duck?'

'I am.' Tildy admitted. 'I keep on thinking about the "Rippling Boys" threatening to harm Daniel. And those two over there look rough, don't they?'

Old Esther sniffed dismissively. 'They doon't look no rougher than a good many more around this town, my duck. They'm probably just hanging about waiting for their mates. If they was intending to do summat agen our Daniel, they'd surely not try to do it in broad daylight, 'ud they? You come on downstairs now and I'll brew us up a sup o'tay.'

Tildy accepted that what the other woman said made sense and she dutifully followed her down to the kitchen. Yet even as she sipped her small bowl of tea she still could not entirely dismiss the forebodings which the men had aroused within her.

When she had drunk her tea she again went upstairs and peered through the window. The men had gone, and Tildy was then able to accept that she had been needlessly worrying herself.

'It's bound to be what Esther said. That they were only waiting for their mates.'

Relieved, she returned downstairs and prepared to go shopping, in old Esther's company. As they left the house and walked slowly up the Fish Hill, Tildy continually glanced about her, seeking sign of the two men. But she saw no one resembling them among the people travelling up and down the hill.

Although Daniel was generous with the housekeeping money, Tildy was still a careful shopper, not wishing to take any advantage of his careless generosity by spending more than was necessary on the goods they required. And so, the walking between stalls to compare prices added to the length of time the women spent shopping, and after they had completed their purchases of food and candles and soap they went to make a brief call on Mother Readman. They spent a pleasant hour chatting and then slowly made their way homewards.

Even before she unlocked the front door, Tildy experienced a sudden chill premonition that something bad had taken place in their absence. As the door swung ajar that premonition was horrifyingly confirmed and Tildy vented a soft moan of distress as she saw a jumbled wreckage of furniture in the hallway.

'Stay here, Esther,' she ordered, and quickly hurried through the house. Every room presented a similar distressing spectacle of ripped upholsteries and shattered artefacts. The home that the Lambert family had so lovingly furnished and cared for over long, long years had been savagely and thoroughly vandalised.

Old Esther was shivering visibly with the shock of discovering what had happened and Tildy put her arm comfortingly around her friend's frail shoulders. A conviction of utter certitude seized her.

'It was them who did this, Esther.' Tildy's face was white with anger. 'It was those two bastards who were hanging around outside. They did this. I know they did.'

Impelled by irresistible impulse she ran out through the front door and onto the roadway, and stood with clenched fists, her eyes wildly seeking the two men. If she had seen them then she would have hurled herself at them in her fury. She went back into the house and for some moments could only pace through the rooms, unable to either think clearly or make any decision as to what she must do next.

Gradually she calmed a little and forced her rampaging senses into a semblance of control. She went back into the kitchen and felt ashamed of her own loss of self-control when she saw that old Esther had begun to sort amongst

177

the wreckage to see if anything could be salvaged. Wordlessly she joined the old woman in that task and as she worked her anger cooled sufficiently for her to be able to begin to think rationally once more.

'Will you be all right alone here, Esther, while I go and fetch the constable?'

''O course I shall, my duck. I doon't think whoever did this is agoing to come back, does you?' the old woman assured her. And Tildy fleeted a smile of gratitude and hurried from the house.

It was almost three hours since the discovery of the vandalism, and during those hours Joseph Cashmore had gone around the neighbouring houses questioning the tenants. Now he faced Tildy and old Esther in the parlour of their home and told them bluntly, 'Nobody saw nor heard anything amiss, or so they claim.'

Tildy indicated the chaotic mess with a wave of her arm and retorted hotly, 'I can't believe that, Master Cashmore. Somebody must have heard noises. You can't break furniture and crockery in silence, can you? And those men were standing across the road there in plain view for God knows how long. Some one of the neighbours must have noticed them. These are respectable households round here, and people would be concerned for their own safety with two roughs like that hanging around. They'd be bound to take notice.'

The constable's dour features mirrored uncertainty, as if he were unsure of what he should say. Then he shrugged his thick shoulders and said curtly, 'Theer arn't no nice way to say this, Tildy Crawford, so I'm agoing to tell you blunt and plain what's bin said to me.' He paused then, and qualified, 'But doon't you goo thinking that I necessarily agrees wi' what's bin said.' Again he paused, and Tildy urged, 'You may tell me blunt and plain, Master Cashmore. I'm not feared to hear it.'

The man grinned bleakly. 'No, Tildy Crawford, I'm sure you arn't feared. You'se always had a deal too much courage perhaps for your own good. Anyway, I shares your opinion that somebody hereabouts must have seen or heard summat. But,' he shook his tricorn-hatted head ponderously, 'to my mind, the reason that nobody is saying anything is because it's happened to Daniel Lambert and I think that the respectable folks hereabouts looks upon what's happened as a falling out between fellow rogues and they've no wish to get mixed up wi' it.'

'But Esther and me and my boy live here as well, Master Cashmore. I don't think any of us can be thought of as rogues by the neighbours,' Tildy protested, and something like embarrassment came into Cashmore's expression.

'Well, Tildy Crawford, I said I'd spake blunt and plain, and so I 'ull. Old Esther here is looked upon as a black witch and a lot on 'um hereabout 'ud cross to the other side of the road if they saw her acoming towards 'um. And as for you, my wench, well, some on 'um regards you as Lambert's fancy 'ooman, as his doxy. Because youm living here with him and you arn't bin churched.'

Mingled anger and shame caused Tildy's cheeks to burn. 'We are going to be wed, just as soon as we can. 'Tis not our fault that we're not churched. Daniel went to post the banns and the parson refused him until we can obtain confirmation from Australia that my husband is dead.'

The constable held up his massive hand defensively. 'Theer's no need for you to explain anything to me about that, my wench. What you and Daniel Lambert does is your own business and I think none the worse of you if you be living here together as man and wife. Theer's many another doing such in this town, that I know. But in your case I fear that it means we arn't agoing to get any information that 'ull help us to lay the buggers who did this by their heels.'

'I'd know those two men's faces anywhere, Master Cashmore. Will you come with me and search for them?' Tildy asked.

'They could be anywhere by this time,' he objected. 'And today being mart day, I've a powerful lot to attend to. Besides, you arn't got any proof it was them who done this. Even if I went wi' you and we found 'um, theer's naught I can do except question 'um and, if they deny it, then I'd have to take their word for it, my wench. I'm sorry, but that's the way it is.'

He saw the distress and frustration on Tildy's face, and softened. 'Listen, girl, why doon't you get Daniel Lambert to offer a reward for any information as to who done this? The quickest way to get it noised abroad is for him to goo and see the crier, Jimmy Bray, he only lives down the hill theer, in one of them cottages alongside Sam Thomas's mill.'

Tildy was reluctantly forced to accept what the man told her, and she nodded wearily.

'Good! You ne'er knows but what you might get summat we can use. And now I'll needs get back up into town.'

Cashmore started to leave, then hesitated as he was passing through the door. 'Listen, girl, I'll make what enquiries I can meself as well, and if you should get anything at all in the way of information, then you come straight away and see me. I really 'ud like to help you in this, believe me when I tells you that.'

Tildy nodded. 'I believe you, Master Cashmore.' She looked down at the broken vase at her feet and sighed heavily. 'It's Daniel I feel sorry for. All the things his dad and mam treasured being destroyed like this.'

'Come now, that's enough o' that moping and whining.' Old Esther spoke sharply. 'The more o' this we can clear up, the less painful it's agoing to be for our Daniel to see.'

Both women fell to work feverishly and, with a last sympathetic shake of his head, Joseph Cashmore left them to their sad task. After they had done what they could in the downstairs rooms the two women began to clear up the bedrooms. And Tildy's anger flared once more to a white heat as she found that the vandals had even broken 'Sergeant Hawk', Davy's beloved wooden soldier.

Hours later, when the child returned home, flushed

and happy, Tildy went out to the stable to meet him and gently explained what had happened to the house. While they were in the stable Daniel Lambert returned and came to them there. To Tildy's amazement he accepted what had happened with a remarkable calmness.

'Furniture can be repaired, honey.' He hugged them both fondly. 'So long as no harm has come to you and my boy here, or to Aunt Esther, then naught else really matters.'

'They broke Sergeant Hawk.' Davy held out the toy and sadly showed Daniel the broken arms and legs and the torn fur-trimmed pelisse and busby.

Daniel smiled down at the child. 'Sergeant Hawk is not broken, Davy,' he corrected gently. 'Sergeant Hawk is wounded. Because like the brave soldier he is, he fought to defend our home.' He took the toy and examined it carefully, turning it over and over in his strong hands, then told Davy, 'You and I shall be his surgeons, son. And when he's had his bones mended and spent some time in the hospital to regain his strength, then he'll come back to his duties as strong and well as he ever was.'

The child cheered up immediately and then beamed with delight when Daniel told him, 'And of course, Sergeant Hawk will be promoted as a reward for his gallantry in this battle. I think he might well be granted a King's Battlefield Commission, and be gazetted a full Captain of Hussars. Now, let's get this pony attended to, and then we'll mayhap find that your mam has got something nice for us to eat for our suppers.'

Later that night, with Davy asleep in his bed, the three adults sat around the parlour fire and quietly discussed the day's happenings.

'I don't think that they'll try to harm any of you,' Daniel concluded. 'It's at me that they're aiming, and I'm certain that no danger threatens the boy. But it's best that we be on our guard until I can settle this matter. I had a drink with Cousin William this afternoon and he's agreed to put faces to names for me.'

'How will he do that?' Tildy wanted to know.

'There's to be a main of cocks fought tomorrow at Boney's Point,' Daniel told her. 'It's nigh on certain that the ones I'm seeking will be there. I've arranged to meet Cousin William there also.'

Fear touched Tildy. 'Won't you be putting yourself in danger to be there amongst such a company?'

'No,' he shook his close-cropped head and his light blue eyes were hard. 'If they try anything, then it's them who'll be in danger, because I'll be well armed and ready for them.' His eyes softened as they rested on Tildy's worried face. 'Don't you be fretting yourself, honey. Do you think I'd risk any foolish action, when I've you to come home to?'

Chapter Nineteen

Tildy's sleep was troubled and broken by dreams in which she searched vainly through crowds of hostile, jeering people for Daniel Lambert, calling his name and being answered by mocking catcalls. The recurring dreams so disturbed her rest that eventually she rose long before dawn and went downstairs.

By candlelight in the wash house she drew cold water from the pump and after cleaning her teeth with a powder of wood ash and salt, stripped off her shift and bathed her body. She shivered in the chill air until she was able to dry herself with rough towelling, rubbing her skin vigorously until it glowed with warmth.

Once dressed she raked out the ashes of the grate and relaid and lit a fire, then sat down by it and began to brush her long glossy hair. The rhythmic motion slowly soothed her, but still she felt uneasy about Daniel Lambert's intended visit to the cock fight at Crabbs Cross.

There sounded the slapping of bare feet upon the stone flags of the passageway, and the shadowy figure of Daniel appeared in the doorway of the kitchen.

'Are you all right, honey? Arn't you feeling well?'

She smiled at the loving concern in his voice. 'I'm fine. I couldn't sleep sound, that's all.'

He came to her, and she saw that he wore only a pair of breeches.

'You should go back to bed, Daniel. You'll catch your death of cold like that.'

He touched her cheek with his fingers and coaxed. 'Come back to bed with me, honey. Then I'll not catch any cold.'

She chuckled fondly. 'I've work to do down here.'

His teeth gleamed palely in the dim candlelight. 'I think what I've in mind is more important than any work, sweetheart.'

She laughed and kissed him lightly, to soften her refusal, then sobered suddenly. 'Do you still mean to go up to Crabb Cross today?'

He nodded.

'I'm worried,' she told him simply. 'I'll be on tenterhooks until you get back home.'

'There's no call to worry.' Again his fingers reached to stroke her cheek. 'I'll watch what I'm doing.'

'But why must you go there?' All her troubled dreams of the night flooded back to torment her. 'Something bad will happen to you. I know it will.'

He sighed with just a hint of impatience. 'Listen, honey. I need to know who these so-called "Rippling Boys" are. I've been given names. But I need faces.' He paused, and she could sense that he was uneasy about her present mood. 'There's no danger for me up there, Tildy. I shan't be above an hour with Cousin Will, and as soon as he's pointed out the men to me, then I'll come straight back here.'

'I'll go with you,' she offered, and he answered sharply, 'No! You'll wait here for me.'

'Why can't I come?' she challenged. 'You said that there's no danger.'

'Because it's better that you stay here.'

'Why is it better?' Tildy knew that she sounded shrewish. She knew that she was goading him unmercifully. But she just could not prevent herself from doing so. 'If it's as safe as you tell me, then perhaps I might enjoy a walk out. I might enjoy seeing the cock fights.'

'For Christ's sake, will you stop badgering me?' Now his impatience throbbed in his voice.

Uncontrollable impulse caused her to retort just as impatiently. 'No! I'll not stop badgering you until you give me true answer.'

'Very well then.' His exasperation burst its bonds. 'I don't want you with me just in case there might be trouble. I don't think that there will be, but to be on the safe side, I prefer to go there by myself.' He hesitated, then reached out and took her hands in his own, fondling them gently. When he spoke again there was a note of pleading in his voice. 'Please, honey, let's not quarrel over this. Stay here and wait for me as I ask you to.'

To her own mortification tears fell from her eyes and she said plaintively, 'I'm feared that something bad will happen, and that I'll lose you, Daniel. This is the first time that I've ever really loved a man and now that I've found happiness in my life I'm feared it cannot last. I'm feared that it will be taken away from me.'

He drew her to him and cradled her closely, his lips fluttering kisses upon her cheeks, her eyelids, her forehead, her mouth.

'Nothing will happen, honey, nothing,' he whispered huskily. 'Do you think I'd risk doing aught which might take me away from you? I love you more than my life, Tildy, and I want to spend my whole life with you, and go on through eternity with you at my side.'

They stayed clasped in each others' arms until the dawn light dispelled the shadows of the night. Reluctantly Daniel released her.

'I'll needs wash and dress myself, sweetheart.' He pressed a final tender kiss upon each of her cheeks in turn and she forced a smile, and joked weakly.

'If you're not back at an early hour, I'll come up to Boney's Island with old Esther's blunderbuss and drag you back here myself.'

He chuckled with real relief that she had apparently accepted his refusal to let her accompany him, and went on into the wash house.

Chapter Twenty

The small tap-room of the Royal Oak at Crabbs Cross was, despite the comparative earliness of the hour, already well filled with Jonas Crowther and his associates. At the head of the single long table it contained, Jonas Crowther was carefully listening to the man seated at his left hand, and along that table the remainder of the 'Rippling Boys' also strained their ears to understand the hoarse whispers passing between their leader and his unexpected visitor.

Finally Crowther's porcelain false teeth grinned wolfishly and he fumbled in his pocket and handed what he found there to the visitor.

'Thank you kindly, Master Crowther. Thank you kindly.' The frowsty head bobbed in effusive gratitude.

Crowther jerked his head in dismissal and the visitor, still mumbling thanks, scurried through the door.

'What was all that about, Jonas?' Ben Fairfax demanded resentfully. 'You knows we doon't like to have any but ourselves in this room. Why d'you let a cunt like Will Smith join the company?'

Growling agreement rumbled along the table and the unshaven, ferocious features scowled at their leader. For the 'Rippling Boys' were not a docile, slavish crew, but more a pack of savage, mutinous rebels, whose loyalty was only loaned and could never be completely relied upon.

Crowther smiled easily, but his eyes were cold and hard. He was under no illusions about his followers' feelings regarding himself. He knew that his command over them was tenuous and uncertain at the best of times. But he also knew that they depended on his acute brain and his immense capacity for cunning shrewdness, because their only attributes were ferocity and gutter-devil, and no one of them was sufficiently intelligent or possessed enough education to plan and execute successful crime without his guidance.

'First things first, lads.' His tone was bantering. He nodded at Abel Chance and John Hancox. 'You two did a fine job o' Lambert's house. I'se had me reports on it and I'm pleased to say that theer's nobody down along theer who saw nor heard anything. Now, am you sure that you took nothing from theer?'

'Nuthin' at all, Master Crowther!' Abel Chance declared emphatically. 'Not a fuckin' penny piece's worth.' He sought confirmation from his friend. 'Anna that so, Johnno?'

The lantern jaw nodded positively. 'That's so, Master Crowther. That's true, that is.'

'Good, because iffen I was to find out that you had took summat that could be traced back to you then you'd be in a peck o' trouble, my buckoes, and that arn't no lie.' Crowther had his personal doubts as to the veracity of their denials, but accepted that there was little or nothing he could do to prove that doubt.

'We'em still waiting to hear about what Will Smith had to say, Jonas,' Joe Wright reminded surlily.

'I'm coming to it, Joe, have a bit o' patience 'ull you?' Crowther reproved huffily.

'Then for fuck's sake get on and tell it.' Ben Fairfax, like the rest of them, was feeling very snappish and hungover from the previous night's debauch.

'Well, lads, it's easy told.' Crowther realised that he had stretched their patience sufficiently for that morning. 'Daniel Lambert went to see Will Smith yesterday, and asked him to put faces to names this morning at the cock fight. From somebody or other Lambert's got a fair idea of who we be. He's got us marked down for "Rippling Boys".'

'Fuck me! Is that all!' Ben Fairfax snorted with

scathing disgust. 'I should reckon theer's bleedin' dozens in this parish who got a fair idea who the "Rippling Boys" am. The time we needs to worry is when any on 'um gets brave enough to lay information agen us in court.' He snorted again. 'And that day 'ull never dawn. They'm all too bleedin' feared on us to do that and well you knows it.' His expression became openly sneering. 'Does you mean to tell me, Jonas, that you paid that cunt good money just to be told that Lambert thinks he knows who we be? Youm getting yampy-yedded in your old age, you am.'

No trace of resentment showed in Crowther's voice or manner and still he smiled easily, although murder was in his thoughts.

'Well now, Ben, you might be right in what you say. But Daniel Lambert arn't the normal run of a man, is he? That bugger's a different kettle o' fish to most on 'um hereabouts. I reckon we'll needs do summat about him. Because he might be the one who'll upset the applecart.'

'What shall we do about him then, Jonas?' It was the young Will Fowkes who asked and Crowther smiled at him reassuringly.

'Ohh, I'll think of summat, Will, doon't you fret. I'll think of summat. And sooner nor later, that you may be sure on.'

He took a sip of his glass of ale, then remarked cheerfully, 'But for now, I reckon our best plan is to have summat to ate, and then goo and enjoy ourselves at the cock fight.'

Joseph Lewis' cock pit was set in a natural amphitheatre in a high-hedged field at the top of the Slough Hill. Almost the entire area of the flat bottom of the pit was taken up by the fighting stage, which was constructed of raised sods of turf covered with straw matting. In the centre of the matting two circles had been drawn with chalk, one inside the other, the outer circle a yard diameter, the inner only inches across. The fighting stage itself formed a further circle some twenty feet in diameter, bounded by big close-tied faggots of gorse. Beyond these faggots the spectators sat on the steep turf slopes of the amphitheatre.

By ten o'clock that morning the turf slopes were already crammed with more than six hundred noisy spectators, each of whom had paid a penny to gain admittance to the closely guarded field.

Daniel Lambert rode Saturn to Crabbs Cross. He paid a few pence to stable the horse at the ancient, crooked-roofed, Star and Garter public house, which was set back from the main roadway. Before he left the public house he bought a flask of French brandy and then went into the smelly privy at the rear of the stabling and carefully checked the priming and loads of a pair of short-barrelled pistols. Satisfied, he placed one in each of the concealed tail pockets in his wide-skirted blue riding coat, then began to walk the hundred odd yards to the cock pit field.

Both sides of the wide road were closely lined with the carriages and carts which had carried spectators there. For today's main had attracted wide interest in the district. It was a challenge match between, on one side, the game-cocks of Mr Robert Knight of Studley Priory and, on the other, the birds of the youthful Richard Hemming, son of the needle master, William Hemming.

Daniel Lambert had not been entirely truthful with Tildy when he had told her that the sole reason he was attending this match was to identify the 'Rippling Boys'. Although that was the main reason, he was also a great lover of cock fighting itself and now felt a keen anticipation of mingling some considerable pleasure with the grimmer business he was about. Daniel had also been a lifelong gambler and, priding himself on his knowledge of game-cocks, looked forward now to making a few wagers on the results of the contests.

Paying his penny at the gate he entered the field and circled the top of the amphitheatre seeking for sight of his cousin, William Smith. The air was quite still and warm and from the mainly male crowd rose a general odour of sweat and unwashed clothes and stale bodies, and plumes of rank tobacco smoke from clay pipes and cheroots wreathed most heads. As Daniel moved around above the pit his keen nostrils detected other smells. Oily swarf from the clothes of the male and female needlemakers, clay and scorched cloth from brickyard kilnworkers, the scented pomades and soaps and macassars of the dandies and their frilled and feathered ladies, farmyard manure and animal wastes from smock-clad countrymen, the appetizing tang of fried fish, the savoury reeks of black puddings, faggots, sausages and meat pies from the great baskets of the vendors crying their wares as they paraded through the close ranked crowd and, permeating all, the fumes of the ale and rum and gin and brandy being poured down throats made thirsty by the excitement of the morning.

Unconsciously that excitement was already infecting Daniel and he pulled out his flask of brandy and took a long swallow from it. He completed the circuit of the pit without sighting his cousin and he frowned and cursed the man's unreliability under his breath. Then he shrugged and told himself that it was early and there was plenty of time still for William Smith to put in an appearance.

Daniel moved a little way down the slope and seated himself on the springy turf just behind a trio of journeymen gardeners dressed in their traditional blue aprons, leather breeches and straw hats. Abandoning for the time being all thought of identifying the 'Rippling Boys', Daniel surrendered himself to the enjoyment of the scene before him and the colourfully varied spectacle the crowd presented to his eyes. At opposing sides of the fighting stage rough benches had been placed for the use of the main's protagonists and their guests. Knowing that Robert Knight had been the evictor of his aunt and Tildy, Daniel tapped one of the gardeners on the shoulder and asked him to point the man out.

'That's the barstard down theer, mate. Bad luck to him.'

Daniel smiled his thanks and studied Knight with close interest. He sat surrounded by a group of well-dressed, top-hatted gentlemen, whose clothing marked them out as gentry and whose general carriage and arrogant bearing reminded Daniel of the army officers he had served under. Daniel felt his resentment burgeoning as he saw Knight's aquiline features glancing about the crowd with openly displayed contempt and his own fingers moved to the heavy pouch he carried in his inside pocket. There was a great deal of money contained in its soft leather folds and Daniel's lips moved as he mouthed silently.

'Let's see if I can strip you of some of your money and pride this day, Master Knight.'

He switched his attention to the opposite side of the stage where the youthful Richard Hemming, slender and dashing with his white-plumed, gold-badged, black shako, his scarlet coat, tight-fitting black and red-striped overalls, massive silver epaulettes and white cross-belt of an officer of the Worcestershire Yeomanry Cavalry, laughed and joked with his friends and fellow officers all equally resplendent in scarlet, gold, white and black.

'My lords, ladies, and gentlemen, your attention please.' Joseph Lewis, proprietor of the cock pit and owner of hedgeside beer kens ana slumside gin shops, his massive belly and purple complexion tokening his devotion to his own sale goods, had taken centre stage.

'Cocking to be fought this day, between Mr Robert Knight, Esquire ...' Removing his tall black hat Joseph Lewis bowed as far as his belly would permit towards the Studley landowner, whose announced name was greeted with a storm of hisses and boos from the crowd. Knight's only reaction to this assault was a contemptuous curling of his thin lips and a sneering aside to his friends, who likewise displayed an utter indifference to the crowd's reaction.

'... of Studley Priory, and Mr Richard Hemming of Foxlydiate House.'

A bow towards the yeomanry contingent and a storm of cheering followed the latter part of the announcement.

When the noise abated Joseph Lewis went on. 'A main

of eleven battles, for ten guineas the battle and one hundred guineas the side. Rules and orders for cocking of the Cockpit Royal, Westminster, to apply. The birds have been weighed and matched according to those rules. The appointed masters of the match are Mr John Arnway, Esquire, of Alcester, and Captain Patrick Docherty of Bromsgrove. The setters-to are, for Mister Hemming, Master Henry Nash and, for Mr Knight, Master Joseph Gilliver.'

A rustle of appreciative comment ran through the crowd as the latter name was called. Joseph Gilliver was one of the most famous breeders and trainers of fighting cocks in the kingdom and bred and fed for more lords and gentry than any other of his profession.

'My lords, ladies and gentlemen, I declare the main begun!' Joseph Lewis bowed grandly, replaced his tall hat on his head and with a stately gait proceeded to his own chair at the side of the stage.

Two closed wagons were standing at opposite sides of the pit top and from the furthest away from Daniel a young man dressed in white shirt, kerseymere breeches and stockings, with gold-buckled shoes and a short-waisted blue jacket now emerged. He presented a raffish appearance with streamer ribbons tied about his knees and waist, and a garish-coloured kerchief around his throat. His fair hair was arranged over his forehead in the curl known as the Newgate Knocker, and his thin face was sun-tanned and gaminly appealing. This was Henry Nash, the rising star of the cockfighting world.

From the other wagon came old Joseph Gilliver, the acknowledged doyen of the sport, dressed similarly to his young rival, except that on his grizzled white head he sported a tall hat decorated with a huge plume of cock feathers. Both men were followed by an attendant carrying a large white linen bag and from both bags there sounded a furious clucking and rustling. Both parties descended through the crowd and onto the stage and, from the moment they stepped onto the straw matting, bets were shouted and accepted amongst the excited spectators.

'Three to one on Gilliver!'
'I'll take that, sir!'
'A crown on Nash!'
'Singles! Singles! Singles!'
'A guinea on Nash!'
'Five guineas to three on Gilliver!'
'That's covered, Cully!'

Nash's attendant produced a glossy russet feathered, red-rumped cock from the white bag and handed it to Gilliver, who examined the clucking, squawking bird carefully while a description of it was read out by one of the masters of the match. Satisfied of its identity Gilliver returned it to the attendant and then his own man repeated the action and it was Nash's turn to make careful examination of Gilliver's bird. Both men then paraded around the stage holding their birds high above their heads so that the crowd could see and admire the wickedly spiked two inch steel spurs attached to the birds' heels with thin bandages.

The betting rose to a crescendo and Daniel moved quietly down through the crowd until he was immediately behind the party of Robert Knight.

'Ten guineas to six on Nash!' he shouted loudly, and the head of Robert Knight swung round and their eyes met and locked.

'What's your wager, sir?' Knight questioned. 'I didn't hear clearly.'

'Ten guineas to six on Nash, sir,' Daniel answered, and the other man nodded curtly.

'Accepted, sir.'

The masters of the match took up their stations at opposing sides of the stage and Gilliver and Nash advanced to the edge of the larger white chalk circle. For a moment or two they provoked the birds to strike against each other, but did not allow the strikes to get home, then they knelt and set their birds down and quickly drew back. The crowd hushed instantly and the birds shook their clipped wings and arched their necks, their bright baleful eyes fixed upon each other. Like deadly dancers they weaved and feinted, seeking advantage, then with a sudden flourish of wings they rose and launched against each other striking with the murderous spurs, buffeting with their wings, razor-sharp beaks seeking to tear and rend, and the crowd vented a long drawnout howl of atavistic bloodlust.

Tildy's sense of foreboding did not lessen, but rather increased as the hours wore on, and old Esther watched her closely and understood what was in the younger woman's mind.

'You should ne'er ha' let Daniel goo up theer this day, Tildy.' She shook her head regretfully. 'I knows him too well.'

Tildy's anxiety caused her to challenge irritably. 'And how should I have stopped him?'

The old woman shrugged her frail shoulders, but made no other answer. 'Anyway, there'll not be any trouble with the "Rippling Boys". Daniel assured me he'd take care to avoid it.' Tildy was desperately seeking for crumbs of comfort.

'It arn't the "Rippling Boys" I'm worried about. It's his bloody gambling fever that's the trouble, my duck. He near broke his dad's heart the way he used to throw his money away betting on cards and horses and suchlike.'

'Surely he's gained sense as he's got older,' Tildy protested. 'He's not a wild young boy any longer, is he?'

'Gambling's a sickness wi' some men, Tildy.' The old woman laid down the stocking she was darning. 'Daniel's grandfeyther nigh on ruined hisself wi' it, and Daniel's like him. I'se known him to lose his week's earning on a turn of a card.'

'But that was years ago.' Tildy stubbornly refused to

accept what she was hearing. 'People change as they grow older, Esther.'

'How long has he bin gone?' the old woman demanded.

'Just a bit over five hours.'

'He said he'd be coming back directly, didn't he?'

Tildy vented a hiss of mingled worry and exasperation. 'What would you have me do, Esther? I'm not his keeper.'

She had been raised to the belief that the man was master in his house and did what he pleased and, although she did not agree with this, still the engrained teachings exerted some hold upon her. Nagging wives were customarily beaten by their menfolk and most people considered that beating to be perfectly justified. Some women who bore the name of shrews were even punished by being fitted with the brank or scold's bridle: a type of iron cage which was locked over the unfortunate woman's head and had fitted to it an iron plate covered with spikes which was forced into the woman's mouth so that if she attempted to speak her tongue would be torn and lacerated. With this brank over her head the victim would be led on a chain about the parish by the constables and sometimes left chained to a pillory or market cross so that all could mock and jeer at her. Tildy knew that Daniel Lambert would never beat her for nagging and would never even dream of complaining to the constables so that the brank could be used. But she also knew that should she begin to act the nag or shrew with him, then he would be subjected to merciless, contemptuous derision by the vast majority of the local people. Men whose womenfolk nagged them in public, or followed them about to see what they did, were objects of scorn, and Tildy loved Daniel Lambert too much to ever risk exposing him to such, no matter what he might do.

Old Esther softened as she saw the anxiety in her friend's eyes. 'It's sore hard to be a woman, arn't it, my duck? I'm wrong to badger you like this. We must just goo on wi' our work and hope the bugger arn't so daft as he used to be.'

The cock reeled like a drunken man, one of its eyes hung in bloody shreds and its once glossy feathers were torn and bloodied. Its opponent, scenting victory, came flurrying in once more and the wounded bird abruptly collapsed into a twitching mound of feathers. Again and again the victor's spurs struck and punctured the defenceless flesh, the razor-beak tore and slashed and shreds of flesh and feather and drops of blood sprayed through the air.

Captain Docherty's brightly-coloured handkerchief waved in the air and he bellowed, 'The battle to Gilliver!'

Both setters-to went to their birds and Gilliver licked and kissed his champion's red-stained head and held it high to receive the ovations of the crowd, his own mouth made scarlet by the dead bird's blood.

Daniel Lambert stifled a groan of despair and when Robert Knight turned to him, exerted all his self-control to smile pleasantly and bow.

'Your wager, sir. A fine cock, that one. A true champion.'

He mentally computed his losses, while Robert Knight entered the last sum in a small notebook, using a gold mounted charcoal pencil. Nine battles had been fought and Gilliver had won six of them, one had been adjudged a draw, and Nash had taken the other two. From the initial bet of ten guineas, each sum wagered between Knight and Daniel had risen sharply and Daniel's heart sank as he realised that he was now losing more than six-hundred guineas.

As the main had progressed Daniel's gambling fever combined with his desire to punish the other man for his cruel treatment of Tildy had synthesised with all his memories of past wrongs to produce within himself a lack of caution that was akin to madness. His knowledge of cockfighting and his judgement of the birds had been cast to the winds in his overwhelming lust to humble the other man. The wagers had developed into a personal battle between the two men and Daniel would sooner die than acknowledge defeat by withdrawing from the contest now.

'Do you wish to continue, sir?' Knight's aquiline features were impassive. 'I feel constrained to point out that you have already lost a considerable amount and my two remaining birds are probably the finest I own.'

Daniel did not reply immediately, there was an ambiguity in the other's words and tone and he could not decide whether Knight was acting in good sportsmanship by informing him of the quality of the remaining birds, or on the other hand was questioning his, Daniel's, ability to meet his losses and his will to continue their personal contest.

The setters-to and their attendants were bringing the white linen bags containing the fresh birds down from the wagons once more and Knight glanced at them and then looked back to Daniel and raised his eyebrows in silent query. The thin lips quirked in the slightest suggestion of a contemptuous sneer. Daniel's urge to shock that veiled sneer from those thin lips carried all remaining vestiges of rational thought irresistibly before it.

'Let's make the wager a worthwhile one this time, sir. What do you say to a thousand guineas?'

He exulted inwardly with a savage satisfaction as shock, followed almost instantly by apprehension, momentarily was visible on Knight's face.

The word of the proposed wager carried like wildfire through the crowd and people stood up and craned their necks to see the protagonists.

Jonas Crowther elbowed Ben Fairfax sharply. 'Tell me, is it Lambert?' He was short-sighted and could not clearly see the faces of Knight's group from his position midway up the opposite slope.

Fairfax nodded. 'It's him all right.' There was admiration in his voice. 'I know you hates his guts, Jonas, but you must gi' Lambert credit for being a cool bugger. For all the look on him, you'd reckon he warn't betting above a guinea. The other bastard's looking white about the fuckin' gills, so is he.'

Robert Knight had indeed been shocked out of complacency and his customary air of arrogant confidence was momentarily replaced by a nervous hesitancy. With a sense of exquisite satisfaction Daniel raised his own eyebrows in silent query and his lips curved in a smile.

'Well, sir?'

Knight's face flushed with embarrassment and anger, and he replied curtly, 'I accept the wager, sir.'

Although uncomfortably aware that he was the focus of all eyes, and able to hear many of the awed and admiring remarks being passed about his reckless daring in betting such a huge sum, Daniel would not allow even a flicker of expression to disturb his impassive features and kept his eyes firmly fixed on the preliminaries taking place on the stage. These completed, the setters-to met at the centre circle, provoked their birds, then set them down and stepped back. The cocks arched and challenged and the fight began.

Daniel drew a long deep breath, and silently prayed. 'Dear God, give me some luck. Give me some luck. Give me some luck ...'

Chapter Twenty-One

Full darkness had come and Daniel Lambert had still not returned home. Tildy tried to concentrate on her sewing, but her eyes continually went to the face of the grandfather clock, which by some miracle had escaped destruction by the vandals. Old Esther sat rocking herself on the opposite side of the kitchen hearth, her lips moving as she muttered sibilantly. At the kitchen table little Davy was drawing pictures of his pony with pencil and slate, his small face rapt and completely absorbed.

The candles which lit the room imparted a warm glow wherever their light touched and the shadows helped to hide the marks of damage still remaining. The two women had worked like demons to repair and restore what they could and Tildy had found to her relief that much of the damage inflicted by the vandals had been merely superficial in character. Their need for haste to avoid being caught had meant that the kitchen had only received a brief visitation.

A metallic whirring came from the clock innards and the chimes rang out sounding preternaturally loud in the quietness.

'One, two, three, four, five, six, seven, eight ...' Tildy counted softly.

'The bugger's going to bring grief back wi' him,' old Esther declared angrily. 'I know he is.'

Tildy's own sense of foreboding had returned in full measure as the hours had passed and she glanced at her companion with troubled eyes.

'I hope to God that you're wrong, Esther. Just because he's been away longer than he said he would be doesn't necessarily mean that he's in trouble. He's probably met with an old friend and that's what's delaying him.'

'The only old friend he's met with is the gambling fever,' the old woman stated with utter conviction.

Before Tildy could make any reply Davy looked up from his slate.

'I can hear Saturn, Mam.' He jumped up from his seat and ran to the back door. 'I'm going to help Daniel put him to bed.'

By now the sound of horses' hooves could be clearly heard from the stable yard, and Tildy said sharply, 'No Davy. Wait here. There's more than one horse out there.' Her heart was thudding painfully as her overstrained nerves caused her to visualise a dozen dire reasons for there being several men come to the house. She herself rose and went to open the door and the dark shapes of men loomed before her.

'Don't be alarmed, Tildy.'

It was Daniel's voice and Tildy breathed a sigh of relief that he was back safely.

'Please to step inside, sir,' Daniel invited, and Tildy's eyes widened in surprise when she recognised Robert Knight.

In the kitchen he lifted his tall hat and bowed curtly. 'Your servant, ma'am.' But he gave no indication that he recognised either Tildy or old Esther.

Daniel lifted a candle and asked the other man to follow him, then led the way along the passage and into the parlour.

There were two other men standing outside the back door, and Tildy invited politely, 'Will you step inside, sirs?'

One of them shook his head. 'No thank you, ma'am. We'll wait with the horses.'

'Then you'll permit me to close the door, it's grown chill.' Tildy closed the door and gave old Esther a warning frown, so that she would not speak out and maybe say something to alarm little Davy.

'Come honey, it's bedtime for you,' she told the child,

and disregarding his wail of protest she bustled him upstairs and very quickly put him to bed. As she passed the parlour door on her return downstairs Tildy could hear Robert Knight's clipped curt tones and she was tempted to press her ear against the door to listen, but fought down that temptation and went back in to old Esther. They sat in apprehensive silence and Tildy fidgeted restlessly, her hands enmeshed and nervously kneading on the table before her.

It seemed that hours had passed, but the clock showed that it was only minutes, when the two men came back into the kitchen, and Robert Knight bade them a curt good night and disappeared through the back door with a swirl of his riding cloak. Daniel Lambert stared at Tildy and his face was furrowed with deep worry lines.

'What ails you, Daniel? What's the matter?' Tildy beseeched him, and he gusted a long ragged sigh and slumped heavily down onto the bench across the table from her.

'I've been a damned fool, sweetheart,' he said hoarsely. 'I've brought ruination down upon us.'

'Theer now, what did I tell you?' old Esther screeched angrily. 'I knew this 'ud happen.' She rounded furiously on the dejected man. 'You'se bin gambling anna you, you bloody fool! You'se lost agen, anna you!'

'Be silent, Esther!' Tildy snapped forcefully. 'Let him tell us himself.'

The old woman subsided, muttering wrathfully, and sat rocking her body backwards and forwards, her black eyes glaring at her nephew.

'Have you been gambling, Daniel?' Tildy asked quietly, and her heart sank as he nodded.

'I've lost more than sixteen hundred guineas.' He seemed unable to look at her, but kept his eyes fixed on the table top. 'I'm sorry Tildy. I'm really sorry to have done this thing to us.'

Tildy gasped with shock. 'But that's a fortune!'

To her it really was. It was more than any working

woman and the majority of working men would earn in their lifetimes.

At the fireside old Esther's eyes widened and she snorted, 'Youm a bloody madman, Daniel Lambert, a bloody madman!'

Tildy felt half-dazed and for a while her brain could only keep reiterating the amount. 'Sixteen hundred guineas. One thousand and six hundred guineas. Sixteen hundred guineas ...'

Daniel Lambert forced himself to look at her and in halting tones told her, 'I shall understand it if you want to leave me now, sweetheart. I don't deserve a woman such as you. I've nothing to offer you now, except more poverty and hardship. I shall have to sell up everything I have to pay the debt, including this house and whatever's left of the furnishings that can be sold.'

'No, my lad, you doon't deserve a decent clean girl like Tildy,' old Esther spat at him. 'And iffen her's got any sense at all in her yed her 'ull leave you.'

'That's enough, Esther!' Tildy told her sharply. 'We'll have no more talk of leaving.' The daze of shock engendered by what had happened was fast receding and her fighting spirit was reasserting itself. Naturally she was greatly angered and upset by Daniel's foolishness, but she had committed herself to him both physically and emotionally and regarded him as her husband, and her loyalty once given was an absolute. She met his anxious eyes levelly, and told him firmly, 'And I'll not have you sitting here crying over spilled milk, Daniel. Instead you'd best be thinking of ways to repair the damage you've done. I want no weakling for husband, who gives up and cries surrender at the first sign of trouble. Especially when he's brought that trouble upon himself.'

His face mirrored sudden hope. 'Then you'll stay with me, Tildy, despite what I've done?'

She nodded, and he smiled with relief and his volatile spirits rekindled and rose sharply. 'I'll make this up to you, sweetheart, I swear I will. I'll get back all that I've lost, and more besides, you'll see if I won't.'

Old Esther snorted disgustedly. 'And pigs will fly, you'll see iffen they won't.'

Tildy ignored her old friend as her mind began to wrestle with the practicalities of the problems facing them. 'Listen Daniel, get pen and paper. We'll make a list of all your assets and see if there's to be anything left to us at all. How much time have you to pay Knight?'

Daniel's broad shoulders shrugged. 'Fair play to the man, he's not pushing overhard for the full sum to be paid at once. He's told me that he'll give me whatever time is needful.'

'Iffen it was left to me, then I'd be giving leg-bail, sooner than pay that cruel bastard anything,' old Esther hissed vindictively. 'He had my house pulled down and me and Tildy and the bairn chucked out into the bloody rain wi'out a second's thought, didn't he? He doon't deserve fair treatment.'

Daniel Lambert answered thoughtfully. 'There's justice in what you say, Aunt, I'll not deny that. But I wagered honourably, and I'm honour bound to pay my losses.'

'Honour?' The old woman spat out the word derisively and her eyes glittered with uncharacteristic cruelty. 'Honour? Am you forgetting, Nephew, that youm an ex-convict? Honour anna summat that ex-convicts am expected to know anything about.'

Daniel's face flushed deeply, and pain shadowed his eyes. 'I'll not argue on that score with you, Aunt.' His voice was husky. 'God knows I've brought only dishonour on my father's name up to this point in my life. But no matter what it might cost me, I'll not have the shame of welshing added to all the other shame I've brought down upon our family.' A note of fierce defiance entered his voice. 'Yes, I'm an ex-convict, and I've lived with some who were the scum of the earth, but not all of those who are transported are evil and vicious. I've known convicts who have more true honour in their little fingers than some of these self-styled gentlemen have in their entire bodies.'

'For pity's sake, will you both give over?' Tildy asked wearily. 'Quarrelling among ourselves will gain nothing. Go you and fetch pen and paper, Daniel, and let's see what can be done.'

He rose and went from the room and Tildy told old Esther in a whisper, 'Leave him be now, Esther, for all our sakes. You should remember that it's his own money he's lost. He's taken naught of ours.'

'Leave him be?' the old woman challenged furiously. 'How can I do that, arter he's bin such a damned fool?'

Tildy gave a wry smile. 'Have you ever known any man who wasn't? He's only behaved like all the rest of them.' She chuckled as unaccountably her mischievous sense of humour struck her. 'Just think, he'll be putty in our hands from this moment on, the poor benighted soul.'

For a moment or two the old woman's face continued to scowl, then her black eyes suddenly twinkled and she cackled with laughter. 'Oh yes, that's truth said indeed, my duck. That's truth said indeed. The poor bugger's going to be putty! Just bloody putty!'

Daniel came back into the kitchen carrying a small box, in which his father's papers were kept, an inkwell, pen and paper, and stared with amazement at the two giggling women, who at the sight of his bemused expression went into fresh paroxysms of laughter. They gradually calmed and Tildy found that the outpouring of emotion had acted as a catharsis, calming and clearing her thoughts. She was able to contemplate this reverse to her fortunes with some degree of equanimity. After all, her life had always been one of trouble and hardship, and she had survived worse things than this loss of a brief comparative affluence. Her main regret was that this present situation might mean that Davy could not now begin his education and that his beloved new pony might well have to be sold with the other possessions.

Their three heads bent closely together over the sheet of paper on the table and silence reigned as Daniel listed his assets and evaluated what he had. Finally he sighed and straightened his body, then took Tildy's hand in his own.

'It's not quite so bad as I feared, honey, thanks to my dad's prudence. He bought a deferred annuity some years ago, according to the papers here, and I can cash it in and use the money to help pay Knight. I'll still have to sell this house, but we can rent another place, can't we?'

Tildy nodded. 'We can make do with less space. So the rent should be cheap enough for a small house.'

He smiled his gratitude for her easy acceptance, and went on, 'I must find work straight away. I'm afraid that the partnership with Brandon Whittle is no longer a possibility now the money's gone. But I'll be able to earn a living for us at the soft work, I don't doubt.' Remorse clouded his eyes and throbbed in his voice. 'Oh Tildy, I can't tell you how sorry I am for bringing this upon our heads. I wanted to give you so much and like a bloody idiot I've thrown it all away.'

'Don't,' she told him softly. 'What's done is done, and 'tis no use your blaming yourself over and over again for it. We've got to look to the future now and put this behind us.'

He swallowed hard and tried to summon fresh confidence. 'We'll be alright, honey. I swear I'll make this up to you.'

'What about the bairn?' old Esther challenged her nephew with obvious resentment. 'What's to become of his schooling and his pony now? Has the poor little mite got to pay the price of your yampy-yed, you great mawkin?'

'Of course he shan't,' Daniel protested, with hurt in his tone. 'Do you think so ill of me, that you'd expect me to let the boy suffer through my fault? He shall go to school and he shall keep his pony. Naturally I must sell Saturn, but the pony stays, no matter what else must go.'

'I'm glad to hear it,' the old woman retorted scathingly. 'But truth to tell, Nephew, I anna got a deal o' faith left in you at this time. I'm wondering if you can keep off the drink and keep away from the gambling? That's

205

what I'm awondering.'

'Have done, Esther!' Tildy said sharply, but Daniel motioned her to silence.

'No, Tildy! Aunt Esther's got the right to speak her mind. God knows I deserve all she says and more besides.' He spoke directly to his aunt. 'All I ask of you, is to give me the chance to prove my words.'

The old woman nodded grudgingly. 'So be it, Nephew. I'll say no more, but it'll be God help you iffen you causes my wench here any more grief, you may be sure on that. It'll be God help you!'

For a moment he made no reply, then he gently squeezed Tildy's hand and said quietly, but very firmly, 'If I should ever cause this woman hurt again, then I'll not be wanting God to help me, Aunt Esther. For I'll take my own life first.'

Chapter Twenty-Two

'There now, let me look at you.' Tildy straightened the peaked floppy-topped cap on her son's unruly curls and gave a final brush to his new short blue jacket with its large brass buttons, and his cream pantaloons. She took the stiff new leather satchel and checked its contents of slate, slate pencils, and bread and cheese and a thick slice of ham were complete, before hanging it over his shoulder. Love and pride filled her as she smiled.

'Yes, I think you'll do. Now mind and be good and pay heed to what Mister James tells you.'

Davy was eager to depart on this new adventure and submitted impatiently to her embrace, then went off happily at Daniel's side. Standing at the front door with old Esther, watching her son trotting up the hill towards his first day at school, Tildy was near to tears and when old Esther abruptly started sniffling, her own eyes brimmed over, and they fell into each others' arms and sobbed noisily until man and boy were gone from their sight.

Other becapped and satchelled boys were making their way towards the Evesham Street and when Davy saw them he asked Daniel Lambert; 'Do they go to my school, Daniel?'

The man smiled and nodded. 'Some of them, I don't doubt. They'll be your new friends when you come to know them.'

The child reflected on this for a moment, then said wistfully, 'Then you and Zeke won't be my friends any more, when I've got new ones.'

Daniel laughed, and patted the child's shoulder. 'Don't

talk sarft. Zeke and me will always be your friends, but it's good for a boy to have friends of his own age. I want you to enjoy your schooldays, and I want you to try and make friends with the other boys.'

Within sight of Henry James' house, Daniel halted.

'Now Davy, you see where those boys have just gone into that gate, well that's where you must go. When you enter ask for Mister Henry James and present yourself to him. Now remember that you must always call him "Sir" and obey him without question. The reason I'm not taking you in myself, is because when I went to that school any boy whose mam and dad took him to the gates was considered a sissy by the other boys. Here, take this money.' He handed some coins to Davy. 'You must give it all to Mister James. Off you go now, I'll see you when school's over this afternoon. You must come straight home then.'

He patted the child's rosy cheek fondly and stood watching as the little figure entered the gates, surprised to feel something of a lump in his own throat. 'Jesus, I do believe I'm grown as fond of the boy as if he were my own.'

The four big boys lounging in the schoolyard nudged and winked at each other when Davy came through the gate.

'Twig the newcome.'

'He looks a real Johnny Raw, don't he?'

'Call him over,' one urged, and the largest of the four grinned, and shouted.

'Hey you? Johnny Raw? Come on over here.'

Davy looked and saw them beckoning him, and went trustingly over to them, not noticing the sly grins of the many smaller boys, who were giving the four a wide berth.

'What do you want here, Johnny Raw?'

Davy stared at his questioner, noting the ginger hair and red, pimply face, and not understanding why the bigger boy should speak to him in such a hostile manner, when Daniel Lambert had only just now told him that these boys at school were to be his new friends.

'If you please, I've come to begin my schooling here. Where is Mister Henry James? My dad says I'm to present myself to him.'

'Stand to attention, Johnny Raw, and say sir when I address you,' 'Ginger' Thomas shouted, and brandished his clenched fist threateningly beneath Davy's nose. 'Or you'll be feeling this a bit sharpish.'

Shocked and nervous, Davy's body stiffened involuntarily.

'Does you understand me, Johnny Raw?' 'Ginger' Thomas bawled, his face so close to Davy's that Davy could smell his foul breath and feel the flecking of spittle on his cheeks.

'Ye ... yes.' Davy stuttered, then cried out in pain as the big boy's fingers grabbed and savagely twisted his nose, causing tears to sting his eyes.

'Yes what? What do you have to call me? What did I tell you to call me?' 'Ginger' Thomas was thoroughly enjoying himself.

'S ... S ... S ... Sir!' Davy stammered out, and then staggered backwards as the bigger boy thrust his arm forwards and released Davy's nose.

The next instant Davy was propelled violently forwards as another of Thomas' cronies kicked his rear end. Before he could regain his balance, all four boys started to buffet him between them from one to another. His cap was snatched from his head and sent sailing over the gateway to fall onto the road, his satchel torn from his shoulder and its contents kicked all around the schoolyard. He fell heavily and was sent rolling over and over and over through the dirt, helpless to defend himself against a myriad of hands and feet all tearing at his clothes and kicking his body and legs. Sobs tore from his throat, but now they were more sobs of fury and frustration, than of fear and pain. Davy had been brought up to be a kind and gentle child, but he possessed all his mother's fierce courage and fighting spirit and had inherited some of the gutter-devil of his father, and now this dormant inheritance roused itself and flooded through his being and with blind instinct he began to fight back. A foot thudded into his stomach, winding him, but Davy grabbed it and sank his teeth deep into the calf of the leg. The leg's owner shrieked out and tried to pull free, but stumbled and fell against his cronies bringing two of them down to the ground with him in a struggling heap.

Davy came to his feet, and through a red haze saw the flushed sweaty face of 'Ginger' Thomas, and with a howl of rage threw himself at his chief tormentor. Although the other boy was much bigger and heavier the sheer fury of Davy's attack momentarily overwhelmed him and they fell together with Davy on top. Still howling like some ancient berserker Davy flailed his fists into Thomas' face and the bigger boy cringed and wailed as fear gripped him. Then there sounded a bull-like roaring and Davy felt iron-like fingers clamp onto the back of his neck and he was lifted bodily and shaken violently, while a long thin cane cut viciously and agonisingly into his buttocks and thighs until he shrieked and wriggled in fruitless effort to escape its white-hot stings.

Then he was dropped bodily to land on hands and knees and he lifted his head and blinked through his tears to see above him what looked to be a black colossus with sun-flashes instead of eyes.

'Now, sir, who may you be?' the bull-like voice bellowed, and Davy blinked again and his sight cleared and the colossus with sun-flashes metamorphosed into a black-garbed, white-haired man wearing bulbous lensed spectacles.

'Stand up, sir, and tell me your name.' The swarthy complexion of Henry James suffused to a purplish hue and all Davy's gutter-devil fled and, trembling with fear, he stood up and stiffened into a posture of attention, his dry lips forming words which his dry throat could not impart voice to.

The man's tongue clucked against his porcelain false

teeth. ''Pon my soul, but you're a pathetic young dog, are you not, boy?' His eyes hugely magnified by the thick lenses moved up and down the forlorn little figure before him, taking in the obviously new clothes, now torn and filthied, the bleeding nose, and the dirtied tear-stained face. Again tongue clucked against teeth. ''Pon my soul! What is the world coming to, when a ragamuffin like you can come to a school of this repute and behave like a demon out of hell? You'll be Davy Crawford, will you not?'

Davy tried to speak, but could not force out any words, and then he choked on a sob and nodded his head. With his eyes still on Davy, Henry James suddenly bellowed, 'Thomas, Pardoe, Powell and Conolly. Don't try skulking away, you miserable sinners.' The long whippy cane swished through the air and pointed. 'Line up there, you four. Stand two paces distant from each other, and bend over.'

Protesting whines sounded from the four boys and once again Henry James' swarthy face purpled and his thunderous roar erupted. 'Do as I say, this instant, you obdurate malignants! Do as I bid, or it will go sore hard with you this day, that I vow.'

The four lined up and one of them started to snivel loudly. Henry James bared his teeth in a savage grin. 'Behold, the sinner repents,' he declaimed sonorously, then swished his cane wickedly through the air. 'But your repentance shall not save you from the righteous chastisement you so richly deserve, you snivelling wretch!'

He stalked behind the boys as they bent over and gripped their ankles with their hands, then worked his way along the line of upraised buttocks and thrashed each pair of rounded globes of flesh thoroughly and mercilessly.

When his arm had finally tired, he told them, 'It is done, so stop snivelling like girls.' Then he addressed the crowd of pupils at large. 'I will tolerate no bullying in my school, you miserable sinners. If you have a quarrel with one of your fellows, then settle it like true Englishmen. Toe the mark and fight hard and fair, and let the best man win, that is the British way. I'll not have you behaving like a pack of cowardly foreign curs, with several of you ganging up against one. Remember this, and remember it well.'

He pointed his cane as Davy. 'Collect your cap and satchel, you miserable ragamuffin, and then go to the house and tell Mistress James that I want her to cleanse you. When you are so cleansed, then come to the school-room there.' He indicated a long low shed-like building that jutted out from the rear of the house.

While the other boys bunched up in a military style formation and marched into the schoolroom, Davy collected his cap and the contents of his satchel from the dirt. The bread, cheese and ham had been trampled and made filthy and Davy gave the ruined food to a half-starved dog that wolfed it gratefully down. Then he made his way to the back door of the house and timidly knocked.

Mistress James was as dour looking as her redoubtable husband and she scowled down at the child as she listened to his halting explanation. But her hands were gentle as they washed the dirt and blood from his hands and face and applied soothing ointments to his badly grazed knees and elbows. Then she sat him on a stool in her spotlessly clean kitchen and gave him a beaker of creamy milk to drink and fresh-baked bread with salt-butter to eat while she dextrously and neatly sewed the tears in his clothing. Before he left she cut and buttered another thick slice of bread and put it together with a big wedge of cheese into his satchel.

'That's for your dinner, boy. Now get you into the schoolroom.' The barest hint of a smile quirked her thin lips. 'And don't go attacking any more of the big boys, d'you hear me, you ferocious young rogue? Or I'll be taking the cane to you myself and dusting your pants with it.'

The long room contained lines of desks, each with attached backless seating for two pupils, and fixed to its walls were blackboards and brightly coloured cards with pictures and large words and letters on them. On a low dais at the far end of the room was the tall desk and stool of Henry James.

When Davy entered the room the boys were standing at their desks and Henry James, also standing, was reading from the huge bible on his desk:

'... This is a nation that obeyeth not the voice of the Lord their God, nor receiveth correction: truth is perished, and is cut off from their mouth.' He glanced around the classroom and frowned angrily, then thundered, 'Cut off thine hair, O Jerusalem, and cast it away, and take up a lamentation on high places; for the Lord hath rejected and forsaken the generation of his wrath.' In his right hand James clutched his long cane and now he raised his arm and brought the whippy bamboo slashing down against the side of the desk, and his roar could be heard even on the road outside. 'For the children of Judah have done evil in my sight, saith the Lord; they have set their abominations in the house which is called by my name, to pollute it.' Behind the thick lenses his eyes glared at his pupils as though they were the wicked children of Judah, and he was the wrathful Lord God.

Davy shivered nervously when the hugely magnified eyes fell upon him and the long cane lifted and pointed to a desk at the front of the classroom inhabited by a single small boy. He obeyed the summons and Henry James scowled fiercely and the long cane pointed at Davy's head. The child snatched off his cap and with considerable trepidation found that his appointed desk was within reach of the schoolteacher's cane.

The thunderous declamation continued and Davy felt the resonances echoing within his skull and time seemed to stretch endlessly onwards.

'... Then will I cause to cease from the cities of Judah, and from the streets of Jerusalem, the voice of mirth, and the voice of gladness, the voice of the bridegroom and the voice of the bride: for the land shall be desolate ...'

On this note of grim promise the roaring voice stilled and Davy felt actual physical relief. Henry James came down from his dais and stalked among the boys, now and again pausing to ask individual pupils questions, concerning the text he had just read to the class. A satisfactory answer was accepted with a curt nod, an unsatisfactory answer brought upon the unfortunate boy instant retribution in the painful form of the slashing cane

Eventually Henry James returned to the dais, and ordered, 'Monitors forward. Divide into your drafts for reading.'

While several of the eldest boys formed a line in front of the dais, the remainder hurriedly pushed and pulled their desks into formations around the separate blackboards on the walls, then seated themselves. Each monitor was given instructions by Henry James and was handed a book, then went to their appointed sections and commenced instructing.

Davy was seated with the youngest section and their monitor was a weedy bodied, bespectacled youth with a sallow face badly pitted by old smallpox scars, Samuel Crook by name. Instead of a book he had been given a pile of cards, each bearing letters of the alphabet and words and pictures.

Despite his un-prepossessing appearance Samuel Crook was a kindly boy and had a natural gift for teaching. Davy quickly became absorbed in this fascinating pastime and his mother's attempts to teach him how to read and write now bore fruit. By the time this first lesson was ended he had gained praise for his ability and Samuel Crook's promise that he would recommend to Henry James that he, Davy, be promoted to the more advanced sections.

A lesson in basic arithmetic followed, again in separate drafts, and again his mother's teachings bore fruit and gained praise for Davy and a further promise of advancement from Samuel Crook.

At midday the boys were dismissed for an hour and out in the schoolyard Davy found that his fight with the bullies had made him something of a hero among the younger boys and he was invited to join in their game of football. He threw himself into this new excitement, chasing the ball of rags, cheering and shouting at the top of his voice in concert with his fellow urchins and fearlessly thrusting into the thick of the fray.

The first part of the afternoon was spent in practising writing under the personal direction of Henry James himself. The entire body of pupils simultaneously engaged and the only division was that the more advanced pupils wrote on paper using pen and ink, while the less advanced used slate and slate pencils. Davy quickly tired of this and received a sharp cut from Henry James' cane for not applying himself diligently. The final lesson of the long day restored Davy's enthusiasm. It was the drill exercise, and as the pupils were marched about the schoolyard and instructed by the monitors in the intricacies of saluting and halting and turning about, Davy's vivid imagination took flight, and he visualised himself in all the glory of scarlet and gold, marching off to distant lands to fight the French.

At five o'clock in the afternoon the school bell was rung in dismissal and the horde of boys cheered their restored freedom and fought to be first out of the gate. Davy waved goodbye to his new-found friends and ran along the Evesham Street and across the green and down the Fish Hill, bursting with his eagerness to tell his mother and old Esther and Daniel of his adventures.

Tildy had awaited his return with an equal eagerness and the kitchen was the scene of excited, animated conversation. When she saw his damaged clothing and heard about his fight with the bullies Tildy's first reaction was to vow vengeance on them, but Daniel Lambert intervened.

'No, sweetheart. You must allow the boy to fight his own battles. If you interfere then it will only make it worse for him in the long run.'

She was reluctant to give way on this point, until Daniel promised, 'Listen, all boys get bullied at some time or another. If it should get too much for Davy to bear, then I'll go and see their fathers about it.'

'I'm not feared of them,' Davy insisted, his eyes shining. 'I can fight them all. Mistress James told me that I was a fero ... fero ...' He paused, unable to recall the long word. 'Besides, I've got some friends of my own there now.' He jumped up from his seat at the table. 'And now I must go and see Pony, and tell him all about today. I'll ride him over to Zeke's tomorrow and tell Zeke all about school as well.'

Tildy shook her head. 'No honey, you can't go to see Zeke tomorrow. You must go to school again.'

For the first time Davy's enthusiasm faltered. 'Must I go to school every day, Mam?'

She smiled. 'I'm afraid every day except Sunday, honey.'

Davy pondered this for a few moments, then his smile shone through again. 'Well, I suppose that will be all right. I can play football at school, can't I? Now I'm going to see Pony.'

He ran from the kitchen and a pang of acute sadness struck Tildy to the heart as she realised that she had lost her baby. He could never be solely her own ever again, because the world outside had claimed him.

Chapter Twenty-Three

Through the good offices of Brandon Whittle, his father's old friend, Daniel Lambert was able to rent rooms with an attached workshop in a tenement set in a dilapidated huddle of ancient buildings known as the Salters Yard which stood on the Alcester Street, midway between the lock-up and the Big Pool. The houses were the last remnants of a monastic grange attached to Bordesley Abbey, and for many years the Salters Yard had been considered a most desirable and respectable place to live, but now had fallen sadly low on the social scale and its dwellings were inhabited mainly by needle pointers, casual labourers and soft workers. Brandon Whittle's good offices did not end there. He also agreed to let Davy's pony be stabled at his own house in Bredon and subcontracted soft work to Daniel Lambert and Tildy.

Tildy adapted easily to the rough and raucous surroundings of the Salters Yard, as did Daniel and little Davy. But old Esther had spent too many years in the peace of the countryside to be able to make a similar easy adjustment. She complained constantly about the noise and the dirty habits of their new neighbours, and when those neighbours objected to her querulous strictures she threatened to cast spells and conjure demons against them. Many of the women and children in the yard feared her as a black witch and it was only Daniel Lambert's formidable reputation as a fighting man which saved the old woman from having violence done to her by the less superstitious relatives of those she had frightened.

Although Tildy kept herself to herself, she was always pleasant to her neighbours and willing to loan them a cup of sugar, a pinch of tea, a hunk of bread, or a shovelful of coal, and she was respected for her hard-working way of life and the cleanliness of her house and person. Davy became something of a favourite with the other children in the yard because he was always willing to give them rides on his pony.

To Tildy's relief Daniel seemed happy enough with his life as a soft worker. He evinced no desire to gamble and drank only the weak small beer and this only at meal-times. As the months passed and spring became summer and summer became autumn even old Esther ceased to complain so much and condescended to read the fortunes of some of the women, and her early unpopularity less-ened and many of the neighbours became secretly proud that such a noted wisewoman dwelt among them.

Winter came and went and Tildy and Daniel worked side by side for long hours making needles by hand in the small workshop at the rear of their tenement. The work was tedious and at first they lacked the dexterity and speed to earn more than the barest living at the trade. But slowly their joint skills improved and the initial uncertain clumsiness of their eyes and fingers metamorphosed into a speedy surety which improved their earning capacity and they were able to eat better and even to save a little money. The early passion of their relationship had mellowed into a deeply felt love and as their second summer in the Salters Yard drew upon them, Tildy was happy with her life and for the first time was beginning to tentatively believe that this happiness would continue.

True, there were fleeting shadows that crossed that happiness. There had still come no reply to Daniel's letters to the office of the commandant of Norfolk Island, and Daniel at times became angry at the continued delay to their wedding. Tildy herself wished that she could become pregnant and give Daniel a child of his own and sometimes worried secretly about her failure to do so. Old Esther's health periodically gave them all cause for concern. And there were occasions when the always simmering discontents among their neighbours erupted into savage violence which created uproar throughout the yard and brought them all from their own concerns to witness bloody brawls between cursing men and screeching women.

But there was also laughter to be heard in the Salters Yard and warmth and friendliness to be found and, although there were times when Tildy would close her eyes and wish that she was dwelling in isolation among sweet-scented, peaceful heath and woodland, there were also times when she would join in the laughter of her neighbours and feel a sense of comradeship with them. For despite their ignorance, their dirt, their violence, their drunkenness, they were still a tough and indomitable breed, who could be kind as well as cruel, who could laugh as well as curse, who could be gentle as well as violent, who could be generous as well as mean. That their lives were harsh and brutish was not entirely their own faults. They were born into poverty and almost from infancy ruthlessly exploited by monarch, Church and State, kept in subjection by repressive laws which denied them any real justice and mercilessly crushed by military might should they band together and attempt to gain justice for themselves. In a country which boasted of its freedom, and its democracy, these people of the lower orders in reality possessed neither.

During the months since Tildy had come to Salters Yard the 'Rippling Boys' had continued their depredations in the town and district, and still possessed their apparently miraculous immunity to capture. Opinion in the yard concerning their exploits was in general admiring. Most needle masters in the town were not loved by those who worked for them. The trade was a highly competitive one, and to sell their wares the masters needed to keep their prices as low as possible, which in turn necessitated keeping the costs of production, including wages, as low as they could be kept. Many masters also practised the 'truck' system whereby only part of their workers' wages were paid in true coin of the realm and the remainder paid in metal tokens. These tokens could only be exchanged for goods at shops and taverns designated by the masters, who in many cases owned those same shops and taverns themselves. The goods sold in the 'truck' shops were of poor quality, and the prices were high, which meant that the value of the already low wages was depressed still further, as was the unfortunate workers' standard of living.

So, when the 'Rippling Boys' plundered the warehouse, or shop premises, or the home of a needle master, there were a great number of local people who secretly applauded, regarding it as a case of a robber being robbed. Tildy was honest enough with herself to admit that if it had not been for the fact that the 'Rippling Boys' were declared enemies of her beloved Daniel, she would herself have regarded their assaults on the property of the needle masters with some degree of satisfaction. She had known near-starvation working in the needle mills and had no liking or sympathy with the masters. But, because of their threat to Daniel, Tildy longed to hear that the 'Rippling Boys' had been taken by the constables. As time passed however, and no further attempt to harm Daniel was made, the threat of the 'Rippling Boys' receded into the back of her mind, and she almost managed to convince herself that now he had lost his house and his money, they might consider he had been punished enough, and had lost interest in him.

Then, one day early in the month of September, the news spread through the Salters Yard that at long last the 'Rippling Boys' had been brought to book. Several of them had broken into one of the Milward's family warehouses and had stolen finished and unfinished needles. Unfortunately for them Joseph Cashmore, acting so it was rumoured on information received, had been waiting with the night patrol in ambush. The crafty constable had allowed the robbery to take place and then had followed the thieves to the house of Jonas Crowther.

Crowther himself, and the Wright brothers, with a couple of fringe members of the gang, had all been arrested, and now were in the Worcester Bridwell awaiting trial. Crowther's son-in-law, Ben Fairfax, had managed to fight free, but had been taken some days later and lodged in the Redditch lock-up. Some unknown helpers had helped him to escape from there and he had disappeared.

Now at last, Tildy could really begin to believe that her troubles were at an end.

Chapter Twenty-Four

It was the second Saturday in September 1830, and at midday Tildy and Daniel completed their week's work and with sighs of relief laid aside their hammers, punches and files, knowing that they would not take them up again until Monday morning. Daniel sorted through the piles of finished needles and selected the bent ones for straightening, a simple operation of rolling them out with a long curved iron against a flat stone until they had straightened themselves. While he did this, Tildy repacked the remainder in the canvas packets and tied the packets into a long roll of canvas so that Daniel could carry them easily to the mill.

Tildy hummed softly to herself as she worked and Daniel looked up from the straightening to smile fondly at her. With her hair hanging loose around her slightly flushed cheeks and her moist red lips parted slightly in concentration, she looked in his eyes breathtakingly beautiful and on impulse he put down his iron and, going to her side, took her in his arms and kissed her.

'I love you,' he told her, and she smiled, then jokingly pushed him away.

'And I love you, but kisses don't fill bellies do they? It's finished needles that do that. Will you get that straightening done so that I can finish the packing?'

'The straightening can wait.' He grinned, and would have kissed her again, but she laughed and ducked her head, then softened the apparent rejection by hugging him close and whispering, 'Save that 'til tonight, when we've more time to enjoy it.'

With assumed bad temper he returned to his work, but could not keep up the pretence, and sang out:

'When this night comes.
Then me and my true love,
Shall know paradise once morrrrree.'

He winked and caricatured a lascivious leer, and Tildy chuckled again and glowed with an inner happiness. Now that the threat of the 'Rippling Boys' had been removed, she was relaxed and contented as she had never been before in her life. The future, once something that stretched before her fraught with hidden menaces, now beckoned to her as a gleaming golden pathway which she would travel in company with this man she loved, in confident expectation that life would be good.

'When I've been paid I shall go to Jasper Davis and get that new bridle for Davy,' Daniel told her.

'You spoil him,' she rebuked gently. 'He's only got to mention that he'd like something and you get it for him. 'Tis not good for children to be given all they want.'

'Nonsense!' he countered banteringly. 'I was given all I ever wanted as a child, and it did me no harm did it? Look what a fine fellow I've turned out to be.'

'That's a moot point,' she retorted, then grinned mischievously. 'But then, I suppose if we don't count running off for a soldier and then being transported for poaching, well you haven't turned out all bad.'

'And well you know it, woman.' He laid down the iron. 'There, that's done.'

Together they packed the rest of the needles and then Daniel slung the heavy roll of canvas across his muscular back and kissed her goodbye.

'I'll not be long, sweetheart.'

'There's no hurry. Why don't you go and have a drink with the other men?' she suggested. 'It'll do you good to talk to someone else for a change. 'You've not been out of the house all week.'

'Maybe I will. I'll see how I feel after I've fetched the bridle.'

Tildy stood in the workshop listening to his footsteps

fade away and smiled fondly. Since they had lived together Daniel Lambert had never given her cause to regret the day she had met him. He had proved a doting lover and father to her and Davy, and she knew that as soon as the confirmation of Tom Crawford's death arrived from Norfolk Island, then she would marry Daniel without hesitation.

Using a besom broom she swept the workbench and floor, collecting the swarf and dirt into a neat pile to be thrown into the ash pit in the yard. Then she went through into the kitchen to join old Esther. Davy was out on his pony and Tildy looked forward to having a quiet period of rest before she must begin preparing their main meal of the day.

'I see hardship and great troubles acoming ...' Old Esther was sitting at the table, her eyes intent on a saucer full of oily black liquid which reflected her distorted image as if it were a dark mirror. Across from her two neighbour women sat with open mouths and awed eyes.

'... and it anna coming just to this yard.' The cracked old voice lowered ominously and the greasy black-grey hair hanging in long strands down her withered cheeks swung in concert as she slowly shook her head from side to side. 'This trouble is acoming to the whole o' this parish, and the next parish as well. It's acoming to the whole district, so it is. To every one o' the four parishes. And it's acoming soon ... Very very soon ...' Her voice died away and her two listeners visibly shuddered.

'Ohhh Esther, you doon't mean it?' one woman quavered nervously, and the old woman's black eyes flashed angrily, and she snorted.

'O' course I means it, Emma Duggins. What I sees when I'm scrying, is what's bound to be. The scrying ne'er lies.'

'But what sort o' trouble is it to be, Esther?' The other woman, younger and bolder, seemed inclined to challenge, but her face became fearful and her boldness fled when the old woman's hooked fingers pointed into her face and the cracked voice hissed, 'It's a trouble that none on us 'ull be able to avoid, my wench. But, you can take comfort that it anna death I sees in the scryer. It's trouble, sore and bitter trouble, but it anna death.'

The younger woman heaved a shuddering sigh of relief. 'Thank God for that, Esther. Thank God for that.'

Old Esther's toothless mouth grinned in fierce satisfaction that she had reasserted her control of her audience and she waved her scrawny, black clad arms in dismissal.

'You mun shooo now, girls. Here's my duck come to have a bit of a rest and a sup o' tay. Her doon't want you lot moithering her.'

Tildy smiled. 'Stay if you like, girls. Your company's never amiss.'

'No, my duck,' Emma Duggins answered with obvious regret. 'I'd love to stay and have a cank, but my man 'ull be home directly, and iffen I arn't got his grub waiting, then I'll be feeling the weight of his fist. You'd best come as well, Liza, and gi' me a hand wi' it. I'se bin here too long as it is, he'll bloody kill me iffen he finds out I'se bin sitting here instead o' doing me work.'

With a billowing of shawls and a clattering of clogs the two women scurried away and Tildy sat down thankfully and sipped at the dish of tea that old Esther bustled to place before her.

When the old woman rejoined her at the table, Tildy asked curiously, 'Could you see what sort of trouble it is that's coming, Esther?'

The lipless mouth pursed and the long hooked nose almost met the pointed chin. Then the old woman told her, 'It warn't clear to me, my duck. But I saw the black clouds agathering, just as clear as I can see you now. And I could hear the voices atelling all on us to beware.'

Much against her will, Tildy experienced an uncomfortable frisson of apprehension. Although her logic denied the existence of Esther's mysterious powers of perception, her emotions accepted that they existed, and in her own personal experience she had received confirmation that they did. If old Esther declared with such certainty that trouble was coming, then Tildy had perforce, however reluctantly, to accept that trouble would indeed come.

'But didn't the voices give any indication of what we must beware of, Esther?' she persisted.

'No, they didn't,' Esther declared flatly, then hesitated as if a sudden thought had occurred to her. 'But somehow I felt it 'ud be to do wi' the trade, my duck.'

'With the trade?' Tildy queried.

'Yes, wi' the trade ... Wi' the needles.'

'How bist, Daniel?' Brandon Whittle's long gnarled multi-coloured teeth grinned in welcome. Although elderly he was still an upright, muscular-bodied man, who had started in the needle trade as a pointer, and even now wore the distinctive pointer's rig, with the sleeveless leather jerkin, red shirt, knee breeches and thick ribbed stockings. His long wispy grey hair hung down from beneath his square brown-paper cap, framing his work-grimed, broken-nosed face.

'I'm well, Brandon, thank you.' Daniel smiled. He greatly liked this tough, hard-living, hard drinking, yet thoroughly decent man, and now could not resist teasing him a little. 'That was a bit o' good steel you gave me to work with this time, for a change. Hardly any wastage.'

'My steel's always good.' The old man scowled. 'I'll only use Hungarian, as well you knows, you young jacka-napes.' The scowl became a grin. 'Iffen you was any use at your trade, then it 'udden't matter a bugger what sort o' steel I give you. A good tradesman can mek a decent job wi' Brummagem tin, if needs be. But then, theer anna any good tradesmen about these days. Just bloody Johnny Newcomes, who reckons they knows it all arter they bin scarce a week or two at the business.'

The two men were in the room that Brandon Whittle used for his warehouse and weighing-room at the rear of his small workshop in Bredon, on the Tardebigge Parish side of the long road known as the Beoley Lane. From the front of the premises came the clinking and hammering of the few in-workers that Whittle employed. Although his was one of the smallest manufactories, the old man did a reasonable business, and was well respected in the trade for the quality, if not the volume, of his products.

With the speedy expertise of long practice he quickly checked and weighed Daniel's needles, and paid him. Then he said, 'I'm glad you'se come early, Daniel. It 'ull be a whiles afore any o' the other out-workers brings their stuff in, so it gives us chance to have a bit of a cank.'

Daniel smiled inwardly as he heard the word. Nowhere else in the world had he ever heard chatting described as 'having a bit of a cank'.

'What do you want to talk about, Brandon?'

The older man assumed an air of caution and glanced about him as if afraid that he would be overheard, then whispered hoarsely, 'I can't tell you here. Come on along o' me.'

He led the way outside across the cobbled yard, past the stables where he allowed Davy to keep his pony, and stopped at a small wooden shed, the door of which was heavily padlocked, and the solitary window covered with nailed-fast shuttering. He unlocked the padlock and jerked his head for Daniel to follow him inside.

Closing the door behind them, and barring it with a length of wood, the old man used tinder and steel to light a small oil lamp.

Daniel smiled at all these mysterious precautions, and asked jokingly, 'What is it you have in here, Brandon? The crown jewels?'

'This beauty 'ull turn out to be worth a sight more than the crown jewels in the long run, my buck.' Brandon Whittle pointed to the tall machine standing in the centre of the shed. 'It's my new "foot-stamp." This is agoing to make both our fortunes, Daniel.'

Daniel examined the contraption with great interest. Its base was a tall block of solid wood, some three feet high and fully two feet square, set on heavy flagstone. On top of the block was a thick iron slab with raised stanchions, transfixed by thick screw-bolts which could be tightened to hold an iron die firmly between them. Suspended on a chain above the die was a massive iron weight on the bottom of which was screwed another die. This second weight could be raised and let drop by means of an ingeniously geared footpedal and it was guided by two long runners bolted onto the rafters and into the metal slab.

'Just look at this.' Brandon Whittle took a dozen double needle lengths and ranged them in position on the bottom die, then operated the footpedal to drop the upper weight. It thudded down with an impact that caused the metal to ring and Whittle raised it again and picked up the thin metal slivers from the die-head. He crossed to a work-bench on which there stood another curious contraption, which Daniel could recognise as some sort of hand-operated press, weighted by a big iron ball at the top of its screwed vertical shaft. In rapid succession the old man passed the needle lengths beneath the press tool with his left hand while his right hand operated the lever that raised and lowered the screw shaft. Then he handed the needle lengths to Daniel.

'Theer now, what do you reckon to them?' He beamed with pride as Daniel's breath hissed out in surprise. In his hand he was holding a doubled bodkin needle, with a squared eye. Brandon Whittle took one of the needle lengths from him and holding it in the groove-fanged needle tongs rapidly used and discarded two small files, then broke the length in two, made a few more file strokes and handed the finished article to Daniel.

''Ull it serve, my buck?' His satisfaction at Daniel's reaction bubbled out in a wheezy laugh. 'Just imagine, one man at the stamp, arter he'd had enough practice to get his speed up, could keep two eye presses working and half a dozen good wenches going at the filing. I reckon I can up the soft work production thrice fold, wi' no sweat at all.'

Daniel's mind was racing. 'And you want me to work the stamp and press for you, is that it, Brandon?'

The old man laughed again and shook his head. 'No Daniel, I'se got better nor that in mind for you. Now you knows well that this idea of a foot stamp and eye press arn't all that new. Abel and Michael Morral bin experimenting wi' 'um down at Green Lane theer for more nor a year; and John Farr was trying it years back down at Coughton, and there's others trying as well. But they'se all bin on the wrong track to my mind, boy. They'se bin trying to stamp out of sheet iron. I'm told that the Morrals was hoping to stamp out fifty bodkins at a time. But what they'm producing be all 'eyes and limbs'. They'm trying to take too much of a short cut by using the sheet iron. Mind you, having said that, I'se also found out that theer's some on 'um ready to switch into full production o' stamped sharps and they'm readying the samples even now for their travellers to take round. So I must make my move straight away, or they'll catch me bloody napping, so they 'ull. I reckon that my way o' doing it is better, and my dies am far superior to their'n. I reckon that we can corner the market in the big 'uns like the pack and sail-needles and maybe the bodkins and suchlike iffen we moves fast.'

'We?' Daniel questioned. 'How can it be "we", Brandon? You know that I lost the money that I was going to use to buy into partnership with you.'

'Look Daniel, I'm agoing to be straight wi' you. Now you knows that I never had a son, only daughters. And they'm both on 'um married wi' husbands that I 'udden't give the time o' day to. Not if I was wearing two gold watches I 'udden't. But there's grand-childer that I does care for, and I wants to make sure that them little 'uns gets summat when I'm dead and gone. But I knows that iffen I doon't have somebody I can trust, then me bloody daughters' husbands 'ull get their soddin' greedy hands on the money that I wants my grandchilder to have.'

A sudden gust of fury shook him, and for a couple of

moments he swore beneath his breath, then went on. 'I truly hates them bastards, Daniel.'

And Daniel couldn't help but smile wryly. 'I can both see and hear that, Brandon.'

The old man grimaced humorously. 'Does it show so clear?' Then he sobered. 'I'll come to the point, Daniel. I thought the world o' your dad, and truth to tell, it's only thanks to him that I'se got this business. For all your wild ways in the past, I'se always known that you'm a chap that can be trusted, and I'se always liked you for yourself. That's why I offered you a partnership when you come back from Australia. I know that like a bloody fool you lost all your money. But I'se watched you real close since then, and it looks to me as if you'se learned your lesson this time. So, subject to certain conditions, I'm prepared to offer you that partnership now.'

Daniel was so astonished that he could make no immediate reply. The old man wheezed with laughter. 'Theer, that's took the bloody wind out o' your sails, arn't it? But ne'er mind that, you just keep quiet and hear me out ...'

He continued to talk, and Daniel continued to listen.

An hour later Daniel took his leave of the older man and hurried homewards, elated excitement bubbling through him. Tildy was peeling potatoes in the washhouse when Daniel came in and taking the knife from her hands picked her up bodily and swung her round and round before kissing her soundly.

'Remember me telling you that I'd make all the bad times up to you, sweetheart?' His eyes were dancing with delight. 'Well from this day on I'm starting to do just that. You're going to be a rich woman afore I'm done, sweetheart, with your own carriage and pair, and our Davy shall be educated for a gentleman.'

She stared at him in complete bemusement and he laughed long and loud and pulled her with him into the kitchen and sat her down on the bench, then made old Esther leave her work and sit down also.

'Now don't either of you say a word until I'm done,' he instructed, and began to tell them about the new foot stamp and eye press that Brandon Whittle had demonstrated to him and about the offer of a partnership. 'I shall buy my half of the business out of my share of the profits and I've agreed to become Brandon's sole trustee and executor of his will when he dies. I've got to ensure that all his money and goods go only to his grandchildren and until they come of age I am to be the sole trustee of whatever Brandon leaves to them. His grandsons are then to be given one half of the business to do as they will with it. Either to continue on as my partners, or to become a separate concern. We shall apprentice the grandsons to the trade and, if Brandon dies before they're of age to be apprenticed, then that responsibility shall fall to me.' He paused and demanded happily, 'What do you think to that then? Have our fortunes changed for the better, or not?'

Tildy could hardly believe what she had heard, afraid to credit that such good fortune was being showered on them. Daniel saw the doubt in her lucent eyes, and urged, 'You must believe it, honey. It's all true what I tell you.'

'It's wonderful news.' She shook her head dazedly. ''Tis just that it sounds too good to be true. I hardly dare let myself accept what you're telling me in case I suddenly wake up and find that 'tis only a dream.'

He laughed and told her, 'It's no dream, honey, that I do assure you. It's no dream. Tomorrow I'm going down to the factory and me and Brandon are going to start making up some batches of samples. Once we've enough, I shall be making the rounds of our buyers and looking for fresh buyers also.'

Tildy was a little disturbed by this information. 'Will you be gone long?'

His eyes were concerned as he told her softly, 'I'll not be gone a moment longer than I have to, sweetheart. But at this time I've no real choice in the matter if I'm to buy into this partnership. Brandon's too old now to be going on the road and also I have to meet and come to know those who buy from us. If we have the success we're hoping for, then it'll not be too long before we can afford to employ a traveller and then I'll be here all the time.'

Tildy thrust aside her doubts and smiled warmly at him. 'You must do whatever you think to be needful, and don't worry about us. We shall be here waiting for you, however long you might be away.'

Old Esther made no comment, but only sat in gloomy silence and when both Tildy and Daniel asked her what was the matter, would only shake her head and remain stubbornly silent. Daniel shrugged, and smiled ruefully at Tildy, and both of them decided that it was just another of the old woman's frequent bouts of crankiness.

Later, when Daniel had gone out once more to fetch the new bridle for Davy, Tildy again asked the old woman, 'What troubles you Esther? I thought you'd be happy at such good news. It means that you'll want for nothing for the rest of your days.'

The old woman's black eyes were full of foreboding, and she told Tildy sombrely, 'What's good news for us, my wench, might well turn out to be bad tidings for many folks hereabouts.'

Tildy frowned in puzzlement. 'I don't understand what you mean, Esther.'

'I means just what I says,' the old woman snapped pettishly. 'I knows what I saw in the scryer, and the scryer ne'er lies. You mark what I say, my wench. Our good fortune 'ull prove bad fortune to a lot o' folk hereabouts. You mark my words . . .'

Chapter Twenty-Five

October had come, bringing rain and high winds to Redditch. It had also brought a festering fear to the town's soft workers. Four of the local needle masters had switched the bulk of their large needle production to foot stamps and eye presses, and as a consequence most of the soft workers that those masters employed had lost their work and hunger and hardship stalked the alleys and courts of the town.

Early in the morning of the first Monday in the month several needle masters met together in the Fox and Goose Inn, in the market place, to discuss this new and disturbing trend in the town's staple trade. By virtue of his position as deputy to the Right Honourable and Reverend the Lord Aston, who stood second only to the great Earl of Plymouth himself in power and position in the district, the Reverend John Clayton took the chair.

The young clergyman's mood was very sombre as he declared the meeting open and his eyes travelled along the faces ranged around the big table: Charles Bartleet, William Hemming, Abel Morrall, Samuel Thomas, Henry English, Thomas Holyoake, Emmanuel Shrimpton, Henry Milward, William Boulton, James Smith, the men were numbered amongst the largest manufacturers and employers of labour in the entire needle district. They were tough minded, hardbitten, and ruthless where their own interests were concerned. John Clayton sighed inwardly as he looked at their hard-set faces, accepting that barring a virtual miracle, this present meeting could only end in acrimony and deadlock.

He briefly sketched in the reasons why he had

requested them to be present this morning:

'The introduction of the foot stamp and eye press here in Redditch has already caused considerable hardship to many of the soft workers, gentlemen, throwing many of them onto the parish. The select vestry has been forced to levy two extra poor rates already these last three weeks, to relieve the sufferings of those unfortunates who have been thrown out of their employment and, may I add, gentlemen, thrown out of that employment through no fault of their own. My fear is that with the onset of winter, and perhaps the further spread of these infernal engines throughout the various manufactories in the district, then we shall be facing a situation of increasing numbers of unemployed, which in its turn may lead to consequences of the very gravest nature.'

He paused, trying to evaluate what impression his words were making on his audience and glumly concluded that that impression appeared to be negligible. He decided to bring his big guns into action.

'I may tell you now, gentlemen, that Reverend the Lord Aston has been discussing the present disturbing train of events with the Earl himself and I speak on their behalf and at their behest. Both the Earl and my Lord Aston are cognisant of the fact that throughout the kingdom grave unrest and disorder are spreading through the masses of the lower orders. My Lord Aston in particular is most concerned that here in the needle district we do not contribute to this present unrest and disorder.' He paused again, then said, 'May I invite suggestions as to possible courses of action we might take in concern, gentlemen, to avoid such unpleasantness?'

Abel Morrall, big-bodied, his heavy florid features still bearing the brawl scars of his youthful pointing days, got ponderously to his feet. His clothing was curiously archaic and his hair was still tied in the long queued pigtail of earlier decades. But his physical presence was such that these peculiarities of dress only enhanced his air of masterful individuality. His voice was in keeping with his appearance: harsh and powerful. and unmistakably plebeian.

'We all knows, Clayton, that I'm the only one present who's brung stamps and presses into his mill. Apart from me, Tom Bayliss and Brandon Whittle has both begun working wi' 'um down at Bredon theer. And John Crook has set 'um up at Easemore Lane, just across the green theer.'

A rumbling of resentment sounded around the table and Morrall's blackened broken teeth snarled in contemptuous defiance.

'Oh you may all cuss and swear as much as you pleases, gennulmen. But I anna forgot how you was all on you laughing at me behind me back when I was spending good money on having them same stamps and presses made. I can remember some on you here atelling me that I was a bloody mawkin to throw away me money on such tomfoolery; atelling me that them engines 'ud be the ruination of me; atelling me that the only way good sharps could ever be made, was by the soft work.' His small bloodshot eyes went from one face to another, and again his teeth bared in a contemptuous snarling sneer. 'Well who's the bloody mawkin now, gennulmen? It anna me, is it? The proof o' the pudding is in the ateing of it, and I can tell you that mine is atasting real sweet to me.'

William Hemming rose to his feet. 'Your sweet tasting pudding, Abel Morrall, is being eaten at the expense of the soft workers. They are paying for it with their empty bellies, sir!'

A roar of approval greeted his angry words, and hands thumped on the table top in a resounding drumbeat of applause. Abel Morrall was completely unabashed by this demonstration. He waited for it to end, and then told them, 'I'm willing to wager, that it'll not be long afore every manjack o' you will have stamps and presses in your own factories. It's progress, gennulmen. Progress! And theer's naught that any on us can do to hold back progress. Either we goes forrards, or we puts up our shutters and goes out o' business. I'se bin to France and to Germany and to America, and theer's men in all them countries who'd dearly love to take the needle trade for themselves. To drive us here in Redditch to the bloody wall.'

He flung out one arm to point dramatically at the saturnine featured Emmanuel Shrimpton.

'That man setting theer knows what I'm on about, doon't you, Master Shrimpton? Theer's no need for you to tell us why you left Long Crendon and moved your works here. You did it because us Redditch men forced you to. You either had to come here and learn from us, or lose your business.'

He had his audience in his grip now and William Hemming discreetly seated himself once more and like the others gave his full attention to the crude, forceful speaker now dominating all of them.

'When I was a boy theer was a lot of rivals to the Redditch needle masters. Long Crendon, Chester, Limerick, London, Paris, Stuttgart, theer was needle makers in all o' them places. But they anna theer now! And for why? Because we beat 'um at their own game, gennulmen. We thought o' new methods and we made a better and cheaper product by using them methods. The day o' the soft worker has passed. The day o' the stamp and the press has come, and them who canna see that am so stupid blind that they doon't deserve to survive in this trade.'

His massive head swung towards John Clayton.

'I reckon you called this meeting to ask us to stop using stamps and presses, didn't you, parson? Well, for my part, you might just as well ask me to stop breathing. Iffen we doon't use 'um, then the bloody Yankees or the Frogs 'ull. And then it wun't be a case of the soft workers being thrown on the parish, but instead it 'ull be every manjack, 'ooman and child in the whole bloody needle district. So, gennulmen, you mun do what you will. But I'm agoing to goo on wi' stamps and presses. I bid you all a good day.'

He went stamping out of the room and John Clayton knew that any chance of being able to halt the spread of foot stamps and eye presses in the district went with him. The meeting ended shortly afterwards, and Clayton made his way to the Chapel where a little later that morning he and the overseers to the poor would deal with the applicants for parish relief.

The young clergyman felt very depressed. Although he was not a man who loved the poor for their own sakes, still he possessed a considerable degree of sympathy with those below his own station in life, and he knew now that inevitably the rest of the needle masters would follow the example of those others who had begun to use the stamps and presses. He also knew that the introduction of those machines would spread like wildfire and he dreaded to think what the plight of the soft workers would be within scant weeks.

He sighed heavily, and in his mind asked, 'Dear God, why do you allow this to happen?'

But no answer came from the master he worshipped.

Emmanuel Shrimpton was deep in thought when he left the Fox and Goose and returned to his factory which stood behind the old three-storeyed terraced houses known as the New End at the bottom of the Front Hill. He knew that what Abel Morrall had said at the meeting was nothing more than the truth: that eventually every needle master in the district would be forced to use stamps and presses. He also knew that the dies would be very expensive to have made, and at this time he was to all intents and purposes penniless. He was living on loans from the Birmingham moneylenders for which he paid crippling interest charges. The moving of his works to Redditch had brought about his precarious financial state and he hated these arrogant Redditch needle masters who had forced that move on him.

Now he was forced to acknowledge that once again some of those same men had stolen a march on him.

'Even if I had the plans drawn for the dies and could go to Sheffield and have them cast this very day, I could still be too late to regain the ground I've lost to those bastards,' he thought bitterly. 'I lost good customers when I had to make the move here, because all my production had ceased for so many weeks. And now I'm bound to lose more customers when Morrall and the others undercut my prices with their stamped sharps. The only way I can catch up with them now is if they all stopped production for a while, until I could get my own stamps and presses set up.'

An idea began to germinate in his mind and when he reached his premises he called one of his workmen into his office. The man was short statured and dark complexioned, a Silurian Welshman from the valleys of Glamorgan, named Idwal Griffin. Although Emmanuel Shrimpton knew him to be a thief and a liar, yet he continued to employ him, because Idwal Griffin could be relied upon to do practically anything for money, and Shrimpton had found him very useful in the past.

He wasted no time when the Welshman came into his office. 'Listen carefully, Idwal. I've got a job for you, which will put some extra money in your pockets. Are you interested?'

Griffin nodded. Unlike the majority of his volatile countrymen, he was not given to needless verbosity, another reason why Emmanuel Shrimpton entrusted him with tasks that did not adhere too strictly to legality.

'I thought you might be.' Shrimpton smiled bleakly, and began. 'Now listen well, Idwal, this is what I want you to do ...'

The clock on the wall of the small vestry room of Saint Stephen's Chapel had struck the hour three times before all the applicants had been heard and granted, or refused, their tokens for coals and groceries and in some cases for clothing or household necessities, and now the overseers to the poor were waiting for Joseph Cashmore, the constable, to claim his attendance expenses.

Ingram Monnox, grocer, and Josiah Cutler, coal merchant, sat on each side of the Reverend John Clayton, behind the battered old table used as their communal desk. To the side and slightly in advance of the table Joseph Davis, shoemaker and clerk to the select vestry, perched on a high stool behind his high desk, with the great leather bound relief accounts ledger open before him. His quill pen scratched across the heavy paper as he totalled the amounts granted in relief that day. He dusted the wet ink with drying powder from the wooden shaker on his desk, and brought the ledger to the table so that overseers might verify and countersign his estimates.

Monnox and Cutler wore satisfied expressions as they saw the totals. The issued tickets would be exchanged by them and their friends for the foodstuffs and fuel and other goods, and their profit on the transactions would be a high one. Paupers knew better than to challenge the quantity and quality of whatever they would receive in exchange for their tokens from the same men who had the power to give or withold the relief they sought.

John Clayton frowned as he signed the ledger. He was much opposed to the practice of issuing tokens, and would have preferred to give cash instead, which would have given the paupers the freedom to spend their money wherever they chose, and perhaps get full value for it, instead of being cheated by Monnox and Cutler and other unscrupulous shopkeepers. But he was powerless to put a stop to this corruption sanctified by centuries of usage.

He ran his forefinger down the list of names, and clucked his tongue in dismay.

'What's the matter, Parson Clayton? You seems a mite put out,' Ingram Monnox asked jovially.

'Yes, Master Monnox, I am a "mite put out", as you so term it. It dismays me to see the names here of good hard-working, respectable men forced onto the parish through no fault of their own, but because of the greed of local employers for ever larger profit.'

'I take it you means the soft workers, like George Paddock and Ezra Harman and the Boulton brothers.' The lean features of Josiah Cutler were dark with the engrained dust of the coal he dealt in.

'Exactly so, Master Cutler,' the young clergyman confirmed.

'Well I shouldn't get too aereated about 'um, if I was you, parson,' Ingram Monnox advised with a hint of mockery in his tone. 'Because afore this month is out I reckon we'em agoing to see a whole boiling of soft workers' names being writ in this ledger, and if you gets aereated by this number o' names, then it 'ull be God help you when the rest on 'um appears.'

Josiah Cutler spoke before Clayton could make any answer. 'I think Master Monnox is right, Parson Clayton. That meeting you attended this morning was concerning the new stamps and presses, warn't it? Well, I can tell you right now, that I knows for a fact that most on 'um that was theer this morn am already having dies cast and stamps built for their own use.'

'Are you sure of that?' John Clayton's hot temper instantly began to smoulder as he remembered how the meeting had applauded William Hemming's strictures against Abel Morrall. 'Because if that is the case, then those gentlemen who attended the meeting this morning are nothing less than blatant hypocrites.'

'Come now, parson, those are strong words to use against them,' Monnox protested. 'They've the right to have stamps and presses if they so desires.'

'If what Master Cutler says is the truth, then strong words are fully justified,' Clayton snapped curtly. 'And I shall stand by my words, Master Monnox, you may be sure on that score.'

'I'm speaking the truth, parson,' Josiah Cutler asserted confidently. 'Why, I saw the plans for the stamps that Henry Milward is having built with my own eyes. And I've heard him say as how he knows that most o' the other needle masters are having their own plans drawn.'

'That's what I'se heard as well,' Ingram Monnox supported. 'And like I said previous, they've a right to do so. Arter all, they'm men o' business, like me and Master Cutler here, and I'll tell you straight, Parson Clayton, I doon't let any other man tell me how I should conduct my business.'

Joseph Cashmore came into the vestry room and submitted his expenses for attending and keeping the crowd of paupers in good order.

'Tell me, Master Cashmore, what do you think is the mood of those soft workers who applied for relief today?' Clayton asked him.

The burly constable's heavy features were dour. 'I should say that their mood is bad, Parson Clayton.'

'Well it's bound to be, arn't it?' Ingram Monnox was derisive. 'Arter all, chaps like Paddock and Harman have never bin on the parish in their lives afore. They'm bound to be feeling upset about it, arn't they? It stands to reason, doon't it?'

'Please, Master Monnox, will you allow me to finish?' Clayton snapped curtly, and the grocer's drink-reddened face flushed hotly and he subsided with ill grace.

'In your opinion, Master Cashmore, could there be a violent outburst on their part?' the clergyman pressed.

The constable pondered the question for some moments, then shook his head doubtfully. 'I can't really venture any opinion on that score, Parson Clayton. Harman and Paddock arn't hotheads, nor be most o' the others. They'se always bin steady chaps. But, as you well knows, theer's plenty in this town who dearly loves a ruction. I reckon that if theer's many more thrown out o' work, then we might have trouble on our hands.'

Clayton nodded thoughtfully. 'I feel you may well be right, Master Cashmore, indeed you may.'

Chapter Twenty-Six

By mid-November the dire predictions of Ingram Monnox concerning the increase in the numbers of soft workers thrown out of their employment had been amply fulfilled. Henry Milward, and several other needle masters, had begun to use foot stamps and eye presses to produce the larger types of needles, and many of their soft workers had been forced onto the parish in consequence. November, the 'cruel' month, was living up to its reputation in the town and district of Redditch.

'Can you spare us a bit o' bread, Tildy? The kids arn't had a bite to ate since yesterday morn.' Emma Duggins had lost her plump rosiness and was now haggard and her pallid face bore livid fresh bruises inflicted by her husband's fists.

'Of course I can.' Tildy's heart welled with pity for the unfortunate woman, 'And you'll take this as well.'

She took a large chunk of cheese from her cupboard, and a big round cottage loaf, then went into the coolness of the scullery to re-emerge with a tin can of milk.

'Here, Emma, you can send the can back to me later.'

The woman's faded eyes filled with tears and she mumbled incoherently as she took the food and drink and shuffled away.

'Listen Tildy, you canna feed the whole yard, you know,' old Esther reproved. 'That's the third lot you'se give away this morning.'

'Would you see children starve, Esther?' Tildy challenged, and the old woman shook her head and snapped querulously, 'O' course I 'uddent'. But Charlie Duggins gets parish relief every Monday, don't he? So how is it that

242

on a Wednesday arternoon, Emma Duggins comes in here atelling you that her kids arn't had a bite to ate since Tuesday morn? What's happened to the food tickets the overseers gives him?'

'You well know what's happened to them,' Tildy said wearily. 'He's put them over the counter in some pub or other in exchange for drink.'

'Just so!' The old woman exclaimed triumphantly. 'So iffen the bugger chooses to drink his childers' grub, why should you have to feed 'um for him? It's him and Emma's fault iffen they'se got no grub in the house, not yourn.'

'You saw the state of Emma's face,' Tildy riposted. 'If she dares to open her mouth and take him to task for his drinking, then Charlie just goes mad and beats her. It's being out of work that makes him like he is, these days. He was a good enough provider when he was in work for Milward's.'

'It arn't your fault that Henry Milward's starting using stamps and presses,' the old woman pointed out reasonably enough.

'I'm not talking about whose fault it might be, Esther.' Tildy's patience was becoming a little strained. 'But I can't help feeling somehow guilty that we're making a good living because of the stamps and presses, while all about us a lot of people and their kids are suffering because of those same engines. I hear people cursing those masters who've got stamps and presses, and I cringe inside, knowing that my own man is one of those being cursed.'

'But nobody in this yard is blaming you for anything, my duck,' the old woman tried to soothe her. 'I only ever hears 'um blessing your name for the kindness you shows to them whom in need.'

Tildy chuckled ruefully. 'Oh Esther, you make me feel like one of those do-gooders who think that they're Lady Bountiful because they go round giving stale food and wornout clothes to the poor.'

'It arn't stale food you gives away, my wench, but good

243

fresh stuff,' old Esther asserted. 'You am good to the paupers, so don't deny it. And they only spakes true when they says that youm one o' the best.'

Tildy felt acute unease as the other woman praised her. She truly did not regard herself as being a particularly good or generous woman. She helped her neighbours certainly, but she did not have to make any real sacrifice of her own well being to give them food or a blanket, or some coals or clothing.

'If I were starving with hunger myself and someone gave me a piece of bread, and I gave half of that bread away in turn, then I would be a truly good person,' she thought now. 'But I only give what I can well afford to give. We're eating well, and there's always fuel for the fire, and candles for light, and we've money enough for rent, and clothes, and Davy's schooling. We're even saving a few shillings each week. No, what I do for others, is little enough and only what anyone else would do.'

Aloud, she said, 'I'll needs go down to the factory and collect our packets, Esther.'

Since Brandon Whittle had begun using the foot stamp and eye press he had concentrated solely on producing the large sail and pack needles, and bodkins, and no long employed any soft workers as such, only women and children to do the filing processes. Tildy and old Esther did their filing in the small workshop at the rear of their rooms and twice a week she would take the finished work to the factory and collect fresh packets to file.

She put her shawl around her shoulders and lifted the long canvas wrapped roll in which the packets were carried.

'Do you need anything fetching while I'm out, Esther?'

'No, my duck.'

'All right then, I'll not be long away.'

The air outside was dank and chill, and the skies heavily overcast with dark clouds. Tildy shivered slightly as she walked along the path towards the communal gate set in the long low brick wall that fronted the roadway.

'Hallooo, Missus Tildy!' The man who shouted was perched on the seat of a tall-sided cart drawn by a pair of horses.

She halted and waited for the cart to draw up at the gate. It was Pat O'Leary who had called her. He was an Irishman who lived in the Salters Yard and was a self-employed haulier who, among other contracts, collected the Royal Mail from Birmingham each week and brought it to the town. He had just returned from that city now and he grinned at Tildy and told her, 'There's a packet for you at the post office, Missus Tildy. Judging from the writing it 'ull be from your man. He's down in London, isn't he?'

Tildy smiled her thanks and confirmed, 'Yes, Master O'Leary, but hopefully he'll be home soon.'

The man's florid broad face beamed happily. 'Ach sure now, I'll bet that no one is hoping he'll be home soon more than himself. How he can ever drag himself away from a beautiful cratur like you, Missus Tildy, is more than I can fathom. 'Tis one o' the mysteries of the ages, so it is. If my own dear wife had half your looks, why sure I'd never stir a yard from her side.'

Tildy chuckled. 'It's easy to believe that you've kissed the blarney stone, Master O'Leary.'

She liked this genial man, notwithstanding his regular Saturday night custom of getting drunk in the alehouses, and then returning to the Salters yard to reel up and down its cobbles bawling out challenges to all and sundry to come out and fight him; an invitation invariably accepted by his massively fat wife and her swarm of equally large and fat sons, who would come boiling out of their house and batter their lord and master all about the yard until he cried surrender.

'O'Leary, get here this instant. I'se got a bone to pick wi' you,' Mrs O'Leary's clarion call sounded, and her husband winked at Tildy, and shouted, 'I'm coming, my jewel. I'm coming,' and hastened to obey the summons.

Smiling, Tildy decided to walk into the centre of the

town and collect her packet from the post office before delivering her needles.

The postal office was one of the front rooms of a house facing the chapel on the western side of the green. Miss Dulcinea Taylor, the middle-aged spinster daughter of the elderly Doctor Charles Taylor acted as post mistress. Unlike her younger brother, Doctor Hugh Taylor, who was generally considered to be the handsomest man in the parish, Dulcinea Taylor was woefully plain, with a stunted, stick-like body, pointed features and protruding front teeth which imparted to her face more than a passing resemblance to a squirrel. But she was a pleasant natured woman, who dearly loved to gossip, and her garnering of that commodity was thought to be the best in the district, a claim which Tildy took leave to doubt, since she considered that her own old friend, Mother Readman, was paramount in that field.

'It's Mistress Crawford, is it not?' Dulcinea Taylor's bright little eyes twinkled pleasurably, as she said archly, 'I've a packet for you. From Master Lambert, I'm sure. His handwriting is so fine, I can always recognise it.'

Miss Taylor possessed a romantic heart and she thrilled to be witness to love affairs. Particularly when they occurred between such attractive couples as Tildy Crawford and Daniel Lambert. She stared at Tildy avidly as she passed over the red sealed, flat oil-clothed packet, envying the younger woman's slender full-breasted body, the glossy hair beneath the shawl and the beauty of the oval face and the darkly lucent velvet-brown eyes.

'You've heard nothing from Norfolk Island yet, Mistress Crawford?' She grimaced sympathetically. 'Really, it's too bad of them, is it not? Keeping you from getting wed in this way.'

Tildy could not help flushing with embarrassment at this illustration of the public knowledge of her private life. But she knew the futility of harbouring any resentment that she should be gossiped about. In this town gossip was one of the main spices of life and she herself enjoyed hearing juicy titbits of scandal as much as the next woman.

She smiled non-committally and wished the other woman a polite goodbye but, before she could leave, Dulcinea Taylor came darting out from behind the tall grilled counter and held out a sheet of paper towards her.

'I think you should see this, Mistress Crawford, so that you may write and inform Master Lambert what's afoot here.'

Tildy scanned the sheet curiously. It was a crudely lettered poster and she silently mouthed its content:

'To all our brother workmen of the four parishes. We calls upon you to meet with us at the Big Pool at noontime on the second day in December, 1830. There to decide what's to be done to halt the spread of those accursed machines, known as the foot stamp and the eye press, which has took our work from us and the food from our children's bellies. Which being left to spread unchecked will prove the ruination of all the working men in the needle district. Act like freeborn Englishmen to save your wives and children from starvation and meet at the Big Pool on that day.'

A vague apprehension burgeoned within Tildy as she read the words, and she looked up into the small bright eyes before her with a questioning stare.

'It was pushed under the door here early this morning,' Miss Taylor told her excitedly. 'When I close the office I shall take it direct to Reverend Clayton. I think it to be most insolent and inflammatory in its tone. Do you not agree?'

A visual image of Emma Duggins' haggard, bruised face suddenly filled Tildy's mind. 'I don't think that you can justly term speaking the truth as being insolent and inflammatory, Miss Taylor.'

The spinster was visibly surprised. 'But do not Master Lambert and his partner Master Whittle have these machines in their own factory?'

Tildy slowly nodded, the awareness of her dichotomy

beginning to assail her with rapidly increasing force. Suddenly she was overwhelmed by the need to be alone and with a muttered farewell she hurried from the post office and with a bent head walked quickly across the green.

Chapter Twenty-Seven

The taproom of the White Hart Inn at Headless Cross was crowded with men wearing the white aprons rolled around their hips and the square paper caps of soft workers, but there was little drinking done. Most of these man had not got enough pennies to feed their wives and children with, let alone money to spare for ale and gin.

The middle-aged soft worker nicknamed 'Lawyer' Court was speaking. The sobriquet had been bestowed on him because in the local vernacular, he had 'the gift o' the gab', a loquaciousness which was admired by his friends and fellow workers, but viewed with suspicion by those who ranked above him in society. These latter regarded Lawyer Court as a dangerous radical and potential revolutionary, and their opinion was justified, because Lawyer Court could read and write and could think for himself, and could recognise and bitterly resent the injustices meted out to his class.

'. . . and last week Henry English sent off plans for a set o' dies to Sheffield.' Lawyer Court's bushy eyebrows drew down upon his deep-set eyes as he scowled angrily. 'I tell you all, brothers, that it won't be too long afore every manjack on us 'ull be out of work.'

'I canna see that, Lawyer,' an elderly white-haired man objected. 'No engine 'ull ever be able to take the place of a good tradesman. I'se sin some o' these new-fangled stamped sharps. They'm all eyes and limbs, so they be. Bloody rubbish!'

'I'll agree to that description, Edgar Smout.' Court spread his hands palm uppermost in an expansive gesture. 'Bloody rubbish! That's truly said. But you'm missing the point, Edgar, if I may say so.'

'I reckon we'em all missing the fucking point,' a young man shouted facetiously. 'We'em missing the points o' the bloody needles they'se took away from us.'

A rumble of laughter greeted his sally, but Lawyer Court resented any such interruption, and he scowled and shouted, ''Ull you hold your tongue, Charlie Powell, what we'em talking about here is a sight too serious to make a joke on it. Silly young buggers like you can always take the shilling and goo for a soldier if your belly gets too slack. But us married men wi' families canna goo off out on it. We has to stay put here and try to feed our women-folk and our kids. If you thinks it to be a joking matter, then you'd best bugger off out o' the room and leave us to talk serious about what's to be done.'

Many men were quick to side with Court, and young Charlie Powell slumped down low in his seat and looked suitably abashed in face of their indignant looks and loud reproofs. Magnanimous in victory, Lawyer Court softened his rebuke.

'Leave the lad be. He's young and unthinking, but he's all right at heart. Now, to continue wi' what I was saying afore. Edgar here is quite right in what he says. These stamped sharps are rubbish and no engine 'ull ever make as good a job on it as one of us skilled tradesmen. But what you must ask yourselves is ...' He paused for a moment to emphasise his next words. 'Do the bloody masters care whether or not the sharps they stamps out be as good as them we makes by hand? You must ask yourselves what comes first in their minds, a good product, or a bloody good profit?' He gave his audience no time to consider that question, but raised his arm high and declaimed, 'All the bloody masters cares about, lads, is to make their profit! And if they can make an even bigger profit, then they'll see us all starve, and not give a tinker's cuss for our sad plight!'

A roar of agreement greeted his words, and his sallow face flushed with his triumphant recognition that he had yet again taken an audience and by his eloquence swayed it in the direction he wished it to move.

'Tell us what we can do about it, Lawyer, bach,' a voice beseeched, and Court sighed theatrically, before lowering his tone to reply, 'At this time, theer arn't enough of us to do anything, Idwal Griffin'. His eyes momentarily locked on the Welshman's and it seemed that an unspoken message passed between them. Then Court switched his gaze and stared above their heads as if there was something he could see on the smoke-blackened ceiling of the room. 'We could always go cap in hand to the masters and beg 'um not to use these infernal engines.' He shook his head slowly. 'But we all knows the answer they'd give us.' He lowered his gaze and his eyes moved from man to man. 'We could all throw ourselves on the parish, and become yard-land men.'

A growl of angry rebuttal greeted that suggestion. These men, although un-educated and scholastically ignorant, were still skilled tradesmen, and took pride in their ability to earn their livings by utilising their skills. To become a parish pauper, a yard-land man, was anathema to them, and an insult to their pride and self-respect.

'Can I say summat, Lawyer?' A tall, sinewy bodied young man rose to his feet.

'By all means, Master Allcock.' Court invited with a wave of his arm, 'Come up alongside o' me, so that everybody can see and hear you easy.'

Richard Allcock flushed and shuffled self-consciously to join Lawyer Court in front of the crowd. He seemed flustered to find himself the focus of attention, and Court encouraged him. 'Come on, lad. Spake up. Youm among friends here.'

The young man drew a sudden quick breath, and blurted out, 'I just wants to say that I arn't got the book-larning like Lawyer's got, and I arn't got his gift o' the gab. But I got wed last year, and I'se got a babby, and another on the way, and I arn't agoing to stand by doing nothing, whiles they goes hungry. Sooner nor see them starving, I'll smash them soddin' engines!'

Several voices shouted approval and Lawyer Court's eyes flickered to meet the eyes of Idwal Griffin, and again it seemed that an unspoken message was passed and understood between them.

'Does you reckon that 'ud work though, Richard? Does you reckon that 'ud stop the masters bringing in the stamps and presses?' Although Court used Allcock's name, he addressed his questions to the crowd as a whole.

'It worked for the pointer lads when Robert Stafford tried to bring in safety masks, didn't it?' a man shouted, and applause greeted his words.

'That's truly said, George Paddock,' Court agreed. 'The pointers smashed the masks and the whole idea was let fall by the masters.' His voice became low-pitched, so that his audience were forced to listen hard to hear him. 'But if we was to smash the stamps and presses, we'd have the constables and the yeomanry coming agen us. Have you got the stomach to face them, my lads? To goo agen the law in that way?'

A hush followed his questions, and men looked at each other doubtfully. Although the soft workers were a tough and hardy breed, they lacked the recklessness and the savage uncaring brutality of the needle pointers. Most of the men in this room were married and had children. They were steady, respectable artisans who asked only to be left alone to earn their livings and raise their families as best as they could.

George Paddock rose to his feet. He was stocky and broad-shouldered and radiated an air of decent simplicity. Now he turned so that he faced the other men.

'You all knows me, lads, and you knows that I arn't a chap who seeks trouble and upset. I'm nigh on forty years old, and I arn't never in me life bin in trouble wi' the law. I'se worked as a soft worker for more nor thirty years and my sharps has always bin good 'uns.' His quiet intense manner of speech impressed his listeners far more than any ranting or raving could ever have done.

'Thomas Bayliss was my master for twenty years, until two weeks since. He turned me away from his gate like I was a thievin' beggar. Told me that now he'd got the stamps and presses he didn't need the likes o' me any more.'

Paddock's broad, clean-shaven face twisted into an expression of such bitterness that even his friends could hardly recognise him as the man they knew, and his voice hissed with venomous hatred.

'Thomas Bayliss and the other masters forgets that it was the likes o' me who earned their money for 'um. That it's through the hard toil o' the likes o' me, that Bayliss and his cronies has got their fine houses and lives on the fat o' the land.'

He paused, breathing harshly, and visibly struggling to regain control of his temper. When he had calmed sufficiently, he went on. 'I've no wish to goo agen the law o' this land. I'm an Englishman, and proud on it. Two o' my elder brothers died in Spain fighting for this country, and my family has always bin loyal subjects to the King. But a man can only stand so much. I'm no bloody cur dog to be chased away from any bloody needle master's gates, and told I'm not wanted no more, because some bloody engine has took my place. I agrees wi' Richard Allcock. Sooner nor see my childer starve, then I for one am ready to smash those soddin' stamps and presses.'

While Paddock spoke, Lawyer Court had been closely watching the crowd's reactions, and now he smiled inwardly with satisfaction. But some inner sense warned him not to attempt to drive these men into any wild actions at this moment in time. More physical numbers were needed before any direct attack on the stamps and presses could be made. And he knew that even now there were waverers in the room who were not yet quite ready to resort to violence. But he also knew that it would only take a little more provocation from the masters to cause an explosion. He intended to push the masters into just that provocation.

'Listen to me all on you,' he instructed. 'Go now, and try and persuade as many as you can to come to the meeting at the Big Pool on the Second of December. Go through all the four parishes, and spread the word. Tell 'um what you'se heard here this day, and tell 'um that unless we all acts together, and acts fast, then every manjack on 'um 'ull be thrown out of their work.'

He left the inn and made his way towards his cottage, which stood in a mean terrace some twenty yards from the White Hart. Before he reached his home, his name was called and he turned to see Idwal Griffin hurrying after him.

The Welshman came up to him, and grinned. 'You did well today, bach. My master will be pleased.'

Lawyer Court's bushy eyebrows came down in a scowl. 'Listen, Taffy, I'm doing what I'm doing for meself and me mates. Not for bloody Emmanuel Shrimpton.'

'Ohh I know that well enough, good boy,' Griffin mollified. 'But if I was to tell Shrimpton that, well then he'd not be inclined to pay, would he? He needs to think that you're doing it for him.'

'So that he can get his own bloody stamps and presses installed, and gain back some of the trade that he's lost,' Court declared angrily, and then jeered, 'You must think me some sort of a bloody mawkin, Taffy, to believe that I'd credit Shrimpton wi' paying me to get the engines smashed because he's worried for the poor bloody soft workers. The bastard only wants to catch up wi' them masters who's got the stamps working already. If and when we smashes their engines, why it 'ull probably take months for 'um to get new dies cast, won't it? And bloody Emmanuel Shrimpton 'ull already have had his delivered, won't he?'

The Welshman's foxy face showed a sly amusement. 'Shall I tell him that you don't want paying then, good boy?'

Court's sallow features darkened ominously, and for a moment he seemed ready to strike out at his companion.

Then he cursed beneath his breath, and gritted out, 'No, you'll tell him naught. Let the bugger pay me. I can always use the money to help those who'll be needing help most, when we'se done the business.'

'Now that's being sensible, that is Lawyer, bach.' Griffin's thin lips twisted in a sneer, and he walked off leaving Lawyer Court fuming impotently behind him.

Chapter Twenty-Eight

Tildy had replied almost immediately to Daniel Lambert's letter, and begged him to hurry back home. During the days that followed she became increasingly uneasy about the course events were taking in the town. Although no more stamps and presses had yet been put into operation, it was common knowledge that the majority of the needle masters were now having dies cast and engines constructed.

Of more immediate concern to Tildy however was, paradoxically, the very success Daniel Lambert and those others who already had the stamps working, were having with their sales of the new product. The large reduction in their prices was having immediate effect on the sales of the other manufacturers and these others were now rumoured to be meeting secretly in concert to discuss lowering the prices paid to their soft workers, so that they might compete with the stampers' sale prices. Although Tildy benefitted from Daniel's success, she could not suppress her feelings of guilt at the sufferings that that success was bringing upon the soft workers. No one had yet showed any overt hostility towards her personally, but she was uncomfortably aware of the resentments seething in the town regarding Daniel and the other stampers, and feared that it would only be a matter of time before those resentments exploded into violence.

She and old Esther were in the small workshop filing needles in the smoky guttering light of a couple of tallow candles. Emma Duggins was with them, because Tildy gave the woman some of her own packets to file, and so enabled her to earn a few pence. Emma was talking about

256

the latest rumour to spread through the town.

'They do say that Hemming and Bartleet am cutting the wages from Saturday next, and that John Clayton and William Hemming had high words about it. Clayton arn't a bad sort considering he's bloody parson.'

'No he's good-natured enough,' Tildy agreed. 'I think he truly does have concern for the poor.'

'Iffen he does, then he anna like the rest o' the bloody God-botherers hereabouts,' old Esther observed tartly. 'I can well remember when the nailers over at Bromsgrove was all out on strike years since. Bloody Parson Fessey said that he didn't gi' a toss for their empty bellies, all he was concerned for was their immortal souls.'

'That's true,' Tildy agreed. 'I was living there myself at that time. It went sore hard with all of us, I can tell you.' She looked out of the window at the deepening darkness outside. 'Davy should be home soon. I told him to come straight back here when he leaves school. I'm not happy to have him roaming about the town these days. Not with all this bad feeling against Daniel and the other stampers about.'

'But he's only a kid, Tildy,' Emma Duggins protested. 'Nobody in their right mind 'ud think to blame him for what Daniel's adoing.'

''Tis not the ones in their right mind that worry me, Emma,' Tildy told her. 'It's the others who when they get the drink in them don't stop to think about what's right or wrong.'

'He'll be all right, my duck,' old Esther assured her. 'Youm werritin' about naught.'

Tildy smiled ruefully. 'Yes, you're probably right.'

The school bell rang out freedom and in a hooting, excited pack the pupils boiled out of the school gates and split into their disparate groupings to make their ways homewards. Much to Davy's disappointment the snow that had fallen that afternoon had already melted, and now a cold murky drizzle fell upon the town's red-tiled roofs and turned the ground underfoot into a muddy slush.

'We won't be able to go sledging, Sammy,' he observed to his companion.

Although he was now fourteen years of age, Samuel Crook had not changed physically since Davy's first day at Henry James school. He was still stunted and weedy-bodied, his sallow face still badly pitted and his weak eyes still watering behind the thick lenses of his spectacles. Davy, at ten and a half years of age, was almost as tall as his companion, and stood straight and strong and even at this early age his face beneath the thick mop of black curls attracted bright-eyed glances from romantically-minded girls. But despite the disparity in their ages and physical capabilities, the two boys had become fast friends, and spent a great deal of time in each other's company.

Further along the Evesham Street towards the chapel crossroads was a huddled alley of houses known as the Red Cow Yard, which took its name from the public house at the far end of the alley. The house bore an unsavoury reputation and was the haunt of many of the town's riff-raff. As the bell of Henry James school signalled the end of its working day, a sudden brawl erupted among the drinkers in the Red Cow which ended in three of the combatants being summarily ejected by sheer weight of numbers from its sleazy taproom.

'And iffen you steps foot in here agen, I'll fetch the bloody constable to you,' the landlord bellowed, and then ran inside and barred the door when Abel Chance went back at him with raised fists.

'Fuck me, Abel, you put the fear o' Christ up that lousy bastard all right!' Johnno Hancox chortled delightedly, and the third young man, Charlie Powell, declared admiringly, 'And you left your mark on Hawky and his mates as well, Abel. By Christ, when you hit the bugger, I thought his yed was agoing to break clane off his bloody shoulders.'

Elated with combatative excitement, Abel Chance

briefly examined his bruised and bleeding knuckles, then used the back of his hand to wipe away the blood that trickled down his chin from a cut lip. He grinned with savage happiness.

'Ahrr, I bin awaiting to have that bugger, Hawkes, for more nor a few weeks. He wun't be able to ate for a month now that I'se smashed his chops for him. Cummon, let's goo to the Unicorn. I'se got a powerful thirst on me.'

Laughing and mock-sparring the three of them went out of the alley and into the Evesham Street. As they were about to turn towards the crossroads Charlie Powell came to an abrupt halt, and stared hard along the street in the direction of the New End.

'Hold hard a minute, lads, we can have a bit o' fun here,' he told the other two. 'Here's fuckin' Crook's son acoming.' Charlie Powell had been one of John Crook's soft workers, but had been dismissed from his employment when Crook had begun working with stamp and press.

The brawl in the Red Cow had only whetted Abel Chance's appetite for violence, and the normally more timid Johnno Hancox had drunk enough to want to see more blood spilt.

'That's it, Charlie.' Abel Chance growled in pleasurable anticipation. 'You give the bugger a leatherin' and me and Johnno 'ull make sure that you anna interrupted.'

Charlie Powell lacked the inherent viciousness of his companions, but his dismissal from employment had imbued him with a sullen resentment against John Crook, and he had brooded constantly about it, until a lust for revenge burgeoned within him. The three young men lounged against the wall of a house until the two boys came opposite, and then Charlie Powell ran across the roadway and halted them.

'Just a minute, Crook, I wants a word wi' you, you four-eyed little bastard.'

A sudden unexplainable impulse made Tildy lay down

her file and tongs, and rise to her feet.

'I'm going up the town to meet Davy,' she announced.

Old Esther clucked her tongue in surprise. 'Whatever drives you to want to goo out in this bloody weather, when you'se no need to, my duck?'

Tildy shook her head, and lifting her shawl from its hook on the wall draped it over her head and shoulders.

'I'll not be long,' she told them, and disappeared through the doorway.

Old Esther and Emma Duggins stared at each other, then shook their heads in mutual mystification and concentrated once more on their work.

Hurrying up the long gently sloping Ipsley Street towards the Big Pool, with the cold drizzling rain already beginning to soak into shawl and gown. Tildy was experiencing some degree of mystification herself. Why she had so abruptly had this irresistible impulse to go and meet Davy, she just didn't know. But she was a woman who trusted her instincts, and she forbore from questioning this present instinct any further, and only hurried onwards through the murk.

'What do you want with me?' Samuel Crook's watery eyes blinked nervously behind his thick spectacles. Beside him, Davy tensed warily as he saw the other two young men lounging against a wall across the roadway, both of them grinning expectantly.

Half drunk though he was, Charlie Powell experienced a momentary disquiet as he stared down at the weedy boy before him.

'Fuck me, but he's a pitiful cratur, arn't he? Iffen I hits him it 'ull make me look like a proper bully,' the young soft worker thought, and almost turned on his heel and walked away, but then Abel Chance's raucous shout came from across the roadway.

'What's up, Charlie? Be you fritted o' the little cunt?'

Stung by this gibe, Powell suddenly lashed out and Samuel Crook cried out in shock and pain and went reeling backwards, the blow sending his spectacles flying to fall into the slush and mud underfoot.

'Leave him be!' Davy shouted, and launched himself at Charlie Powell.

His flailing fists caught the soft worker a painful blow on the face and Powell's drunken fury erupted. With a howl of rage he gripped Davy by the lapels of his jacket and hurled him to the ground, then kicked savagely at the child's sprawling body. The heavy iron-shod clog thudded into Davy's stomach and he choked in agony as his spasming muscles bent his body into a foetal position and he fought desperately to draw breath into straining lungs.

Samuel Crook, weeping helplessly, was on hands and knees, his fingers scrabbling through the mud and slush desperately seeking the spectacles without which he was virtually blind.

Charlie Powell had now lost all powers of reason; lurching over to Samuel he kicked at the crouching boy's defenceless head. It was only Powell's drunkenness that saved Samuel Crook from terrible injury, because the wild kick was not on target and the iron-shod clog only grazed the side of his face. But still its force was enough to send him tumbling over and over on the ground.

'That's it, Charlie! Go it! Go it!' Abel Chance bawled encouragement, and Johnno Hancox laughed hysterically and screamed out, 'Give it 'um hot, Charlie! Give it to the bastards hot and strong!'

But by now the commotion had attracted the attention of passers-by, and people from the nearby houses and shops and a small crowd quickly gathered and, when they realised the unequalness of the fight, as quickly intervened to restrain Charlie Powell, and to lift the two boys to their feet.

'Bloody shame on you, you bullying sod!' a woman shrieked into Powell's drink-flushed face, and when he would have raised his hand against her, several men grabbed him and held him powerless against a wall.

'Cummon Johnno,' Abel Chance growled. 'Let's give Charlie a hand.'

He made as if to cross the roadway, but his friend suddenly gripped his arm and pulled him back.

'Hold hard, Abel. Look who's acoming theer.'

'What's you on about?' Chance tugged furiously to free himself. 'Cummon, Charlie needs a bit of help!'

But Johnno Hancox hung on grimly, and reiterated urgently.

'Wait, Abel. Just look who's acoming down the bloody street, 'ull you? Look at that bastard on the horse.'

As Daniel Lambert's mount trotted down the Evesham Street he saw the crowd near to the crossroads ahead, but paid it little attention. His thoughts were centred on the coming reunion with his beloved Tildy and at this moment in time nothing else was of any importance to him. Then, as he drew nearer to the noisy crowd he saw a woman come running from the crossroads towards it, and his heart leapt as he recognised Tildy. He shouted her name and urged his horse into a canter, but she disappeared into the clamour of people.

When he reached the crowd he dismounted. 'Here, boy. Hold my horse, I'll give you a penny.'

The urchin gladly assented and Daniel pushed through the packed bodies. Tildy was hugging Davy to her. The boy's face was pale, his clothing wet and muddied, and he held his hands tight against his stomach as though he were in pain. Daniel went to them and put his arms about them. 'I'm here now. Everything will be all right.'

Tildy almost wept with her glad happiness at seeing him, and he told her, 'We can talk later, honey. Tell me now, what's happened here?'

A dozen voices babbled out at once and Daniel's face grew grim as he listened. Then he told Tildy, 'Please honey, take care of Davy and his friend while I settle with the bastard who did this to them.'

Tildy did not argue. In her world men customarily fought with their fists to settle disputes, and every social class behaved similarly. Coal heaver, or peer of the realm, shopkeeper, labourer, or local squire, it made no odds. They resolved their quarrels with their fists.

Powell was still being held against the wall and Daniel confronted him. 'That was my boy you kicked, you bastard. Now you can try kicking me. Or haven't you got the stomach to face someone of your own size?'

The young soft worker was no coward and he snarled his willingness to fight.

'Let him go,' Daniel told the men holding Powell, and the cry was taken up.

'Form a ring! Form a ring!'

Abel Chance and Johnno Hancox pushed themselves forwards so that they could see clearly. Chance's drink-inflamed brain had cooled considerably by now, and he wanted to see how well this man Lambert could fight. He still lusted to revenge his brother, who was serving his prison sentence on crutches. But since the arrest of the leaders of the 'Rippling Boys', he and the other fringe members had been forced to tread very warily and try not to attract any undue attention to themselves.

Daniel Lambert shrugged off his coat and removed his low-crowned tophat and the two men stepped to face each other in the cleared space. Clouds of white breath smoked from the mouths of the excited crowd pressed tightly around the combatants and there were shouts of encouragement for both men. Because, although Daniel could be considered the injured party, yet the fact that he was one of the hated stamper masters impelled many of the crowd to hope to see him beaten.

Tildy had withdrawn a little way, but the two boys insisted on pushing through to the very front of the human ring to watch what happened. Tildy was both proud and afraid: proud that her man should have the courage to fight for his loved ones, yet afraid that he might be injured in doing so. She didn't want to look, but inevitably her eyes were drawn to do so.

The fight was brief. With a speed and ruthlessness that

was awesome to see, Daniel battered his opponent into bloody unconsciousness, and while the plaudits and shouts of the excited spectators were still ringing in the air he retrieved his coat, hat and horse and shepherded Tildy and the two boys homewards.

The fight left Abel Chance feeling very thoughtful. He was sufficiently honest with himself to accept that the intention he had previously had of giving Daniel Lambert a good hiding himself was best forgotten. He was experienced enough as a brawler to know that he would stand no chance against a man of Lambert's fearsome prowess.

'Fuck me, but he can fight, can't he?' Johnno Hancox observed with something akin to awe. 'I reckon he could get the better of any pug in this district, doon't you, Abel?'

Chance nodded disgustedly. 'He's a good 'un all right. Blast his fuckin' eyes!'

'I bet youm glad now that you didn't get the chance to take him on, arn't you, Abel?' Hancox's yellowed teeth bared in a snigger. 'Fuck me, iffen you had a done, then there'd be two Chances on bloody crutches, I reckon.'

In sudden fury Chance turned on his friend. 'If you doon't shut that big gob o' yourn, then I'll do it for you.'

'All right Abel, all right,' Hancox said aggrievedly. 'I was only joking, that's all. Only joking.'

The crowd was now beginning to disperse, many of them excitedly discussing the fight, and Charlie Powell still lay on his back, but was now twitching into consciousness. Abel Chance ran his fingers through his shaggy mass of greasy hair, his eyes fixed on the beaten bloodied man. Chance possessed a considerable degree of cunning and now his mind raced as he sought for some way of turning what had happened to his own advantage. He still lusted for revenge against Lambert and in the recesses of his mind an as yet vague idea was struggling to fruition. He instinctively knew that he could use Charlie Powell to gain that revenge.

'Listen Johnno,' he suddenly hissed. 'You look arter Charlie. Bring him up to my house and keep him theer until I comes.' With that he turned on his heel and trotted quickly away down the Evesham Street.

With a sour expression Johnno Hancox watched him go, and mouthed sibilantly, 'I'm getting good and tired o' you treating me as if I was a piece o' shit, Abel Chance. One o' these days youm agoing to push me too far, and then you'd better watch out for yourself, you bastard.'

But despite his inward defiance, Johnno Hancox still obeyed Chance's parting instructions, and took the dazed and loudly complaining Charlie Powell to Chance's home in the fetid slum of the Silver Street.

Chapter Twenty-Nine

Late that night, in the tender aftermath of their love-making, Tildy and Daniel talked for long hours. She told him of her disquiet at the situation in the town and expressed her sympathy with the soft workers.

He pulled her naked body tight against his own, and kissed her gently. 'I'm sorry for their plight also, honey. But I'm afraid that there's naught to be done about it. The stamp and the press are here to stay and we have to do whatever the other masters are doing in order to survive ourselves. It's progress, Tildy, and nothing will halt it.'

'Do you know that there's talk that the prices for the soft work are to be cut?' she asked him, and heard him sigh in the darkness.

'I think it's inevitable that those masters still without stamps will cut the prices for the bigger sharps. They'll lose all their trade otherwise. But mayhap the prices for the small sharps will stay the same. After all, there's no dies as yet that can produce decent small sharps. So the masters are still going to need good soft workers to make the small sizes.'

Tildy drew scant comfort from his words. 'You and I both know, Daniel, that there will soon be dies cast that will be cutting the smaller sizes of sharps. It's only a question of time.'

Again he sighed, made unhappy by her unhappiness. 'Listen, sweetheart, you're going to have to accept that there's nothing you or I can do about this situation. I have sympathy for those poor souls that are being harmed by it, but my first loyalty is to you, and to Davy and Aunt Esther. I'll do whatever I have to do, to ensure that you're all cared for. And if that means that I have to continue with stamping, then I'll so continue.'

She hugged him, and whispered lovingly, 'And my loyalty is to you, honey. Whatever you decide to do, then I'll stand at your side.'

They fell asleep, still locked in loving embrace, and Tildy's last waking thought was that she would also continue to try and help those unfortunates who were being made to suffer because of the new machinery.

Chapter Thirty

The Reverend John Clayton was a sorely troubled man as he rode out to the hamlet of Tardebigge late in the first afternoon of December. His destination was the home of the Right Honourable and Reverend Walter Hutchinson, the Lord Aston. The large house was close to the Tardebigge church, the tall slender spire of which could be seen on its hilltop from miles around. As always Clayton took pleasure from the grace and sheer beauty of that building, and could not help but contrast its elegant appearance with the decided inelegance of its present incumbent.

When he was ushered into the presence of his master, Clayton found to his surprise that he was not the only visitor this day. Two other clergymen were present with Lord Aston, both were also justices of the peace: the plump-faced, oily-complexioned Reverend Mark Pyndar, MA (Oxon), of Bromsgrove, and the small statured, birdlike-featured, Reverend Frederick Palmer from Alcester village in nearby Warwickshire.

'You know my curate, John Clayton, I believe, gentlemen.' Lord Aston seemed eager to dispense with any formalities. 'Be seated, Clayton and let's to business. We've little or no time to be wasting.'

'Your servant, sirs.' Clayton bowed curtly, and both men nodded acknowledgement as he took his seat at the table.

'Now, Clayton,' Lord Aston flourished a roll of parchment, tied with a blue ribbon. 'I have here the Lord Lieutenant's warrant empowering me to call out the Hewell Troop of the Yeomanry on active service: When you have done here I shall require you to go directly to

John Emmot and deliver it to him.'

Captain John Emmot was the adjutant to the Worcestershire Yeomanry Cavalry, and was at present also the officer commanding the Hewell Troop.

The younger man's ugly face frowned doubtfully. 'Do you really think it necessary to call out the yeomanry, my lord?'

'Indeed I do.' Lord Aston scowled petulantly and fingered his hanging jowls. 'I take it that you are aware of what transpired yesterday in Redditch?'

Clayton was well aware of what had transpired. It was that which was troubling him. William Hemming and Charles Bartleet had announced that they were cutting the prices for the soft work and they had been hooted and jeered at by their workers. But no violence had occurred.

'My lord, I am aware that some of the soft workers shouted insults at Messrs Hemming and Bartleet, but that was all that took place. No injury was done, or even offered to those gentlemen.'

'That is not the point, Clayton,' Lord Aston stated vehemently. 'The fact that no injury was done to them yesterday, does not mean that no injury will be done to them today or tomorrow or next week, does it? The country is in a state of grave unrest, as well you know, and it ill behoves us here in the needle district to be unprepared for whatever eventuality may occur.'

Clayton felt driven to protest. 'But my lord, with all respect, I fear that calling out the yeomanry can only worsen the situation. The soft workers may well be provoked into excesses when they see armed cavalry soldiers parading the streets.'

Lord Aston's always uncertain temper ignited instantly. 'Be damned to the soft workers! I'll not be dictated to by ignorant, unwashed rabble. I hope that they are provoked into excesses, because then, by God, we'll show them once and for always who are the masters here. You will do as I bid you, Clayton. Go directly to John Emmot with this warrant. Then at noon tomorrow meet

269

with me in Redditch at your house, and we shall begin the swearing in of special constables. My colleagues here will be swearing in the men at Feckenham and Studley.'

From the cluttered papers on the table top he lifted a sheet of coarse paper and held it high then threw it into Clayton's lap. 'Read this damned poster, Clayton. Calling the soft workers to a meeting at the Big Pool on the second day of December. Its tone is both insolent and inflammatory. These damned soft workers are challenging the very rule of law, and I can tell you, sir, that I am more than happy to meet that challenge. They will sorely rue the day, that I do assure you.'

'I have already seen this poster, my lord,' Clayton told him curtly. 'I think it to be desperation, not insolence, that has written it.'

The flabby features of Lord Aston suddenly contorted and he belched resoundingly. His dyspepsia was particularly bad this day and the sourness of his mood intensified commensurately.

'I care not a crooked farthing for your thoughts on this matter, Clayton,' he hissed viciously. 'I am the embodiment of the law in this parish and it is only my own thought that carries weight here. Get you gone to John Emmot's house this instant, or I may well find that I can dispense with your services permanently.'

For a brief instant John Clayton was sorely tempted to hurl the poster into that flabby pallid face before him. But in Derbyshire there was a widowed mother and three sisters absolutely dependent on his meagre earnings and he knew that if Lord Aston dismissed him from his curacy, then his career in the Church would be finished and his loved ones would face a bleak and hopeless future. He swallowed hard and rose to his feet, then bowed and, without another word, left the room.

John Emmot lived in the Webheath area midway between Tardebigge and Redditch Town, but when Clayton called at the house, the manservant informed him that Captain Emmot was away in Birmingham, and was not expected to return home until the following morning. The young clergyman was not unduly perturbed by this news. He thought that Lord Aston, yet again, was over-reacting to a situation, allowing his own paranoid fears of bloody rebellion to distort his judgement.

'There will be no real trouble tomorrow at that meeting,' he told himself now. 'The soft workers are not like the pointers. For the most part they are steady, respectable men, they're not the types to go on the rampage. I'll come back and see Emmot in the morning.'

Chapter Thirty-One

There had been a hard frost during the night and when dawn came with clear skies the white rime sparkled on hedges and rooftops in the early sunlight. A group of men stood outside Lawyer Court's house in Headless Cross; heavily muffled against the biting cold they stamped their feet and swung their arms trying to keep warm. Lawyer Court came from the house to join them, carrying in his hand an old cavalry trumpet. He seemed to be in high spirits as he greeted the other men.

'Halloo George, how bist Richard, Seth, Jason? Glad to see youm here, Ezra. Have you got your fife, Joe?'

Joe Dunsby produced the fife from under his coat and Seth Boulton beat a riffle on the side drum he carried slung from his shoulders.

Lawyer Court grinned happily. 'That's it, lads, a bit o' music 'ull encourage us all.'

His eyes flicked across the other men, and he nodded with satisfaction when he saw the long-helved sledge-hammers carried by George Paddock, Richard Allock and Ezra Harman.

'What's the reason for sending for us to come here so early, Lawyer?' the young muscular-bodied Jason Boulton wanted to know. 'I thought the meeting at the Big Pool was to be at noontime?'

Court pointed down the road towards an oncoming figure. 'Here's the man acoming who'll tell you that, Jason. He found out summat yesterday arternoon and come straight out to tell me of it.' He shouted to the oncoming man, 'How bist, Idwal?'

Idwal Griffin came up to the group. 'Now then, boys,

we've a fine morning to do the business in.'

'Tell the lads what happened yesterday, Idwal,' Court instructed. 'And tell 'um how you come to know on it.'

'They'se called out the Yeoman Cavalry, boys. And Lord Aston and the other beaks am agoing to be swearing in special constables from noon this day, down in Redditch, and at Studley and Feckenham as well.'

His audience exchanged concerned glances.

'How do you know this, Idwal Griffin?' George Paddock asked gruffly. He didn't like or trust this Welshman, and his manner clearly showed this fact.

'I was at work when the messenger from Lord Aston come to speak with Emmanuel Shrimpton. I kept me ear to a crack in the office door. I heard everything. Lord Aston wants the needle masters to send all their most loyal workers to be sworn in as specials, starting at about noon-time down at the Saint Stephen's Chapel.'

'And what about the yeomanry?' Ezra Harman queried.

'Parson Clayton was sent with the warrant to John Emmot's house yesterday afternoon.'

'Are they calling out the whole of the regiment?' Harman persisted, and the Welshman shook his head.

'I think not. I only heard mention of the Hewell Troop.'

'Right then, my lads, you knows it all now.' Lawyer Court's air of elation seemed to have intensified as the Welshman had been speaking. 'That old bastard Aston thought he could steal a march on us, but he'll need to get up a sight earlier in the morning to catch me out. What we'll do is to round up as many of the others as we can now, and we'll pay Thomas Bayliss and John Crook their visits afore the meeting at the Big Pool. Nobody 'ull be expecting us to start so early, 'ull they? We'll take 'um all by surprise.'

He paused expectantly, then frowned as no immediate chorus of enthusiastic agreement was voiced. A note of jeering entered his tone.

'What's this then? I canna believe that you've lost your stomachs for a fight? Surely you arn't afeared o' the

273

bloody yeomanry and the soddin' special constables am you? Have I got to do the business by meself?' He appeared to lose patience, and suddenly shouted, 'Give me that bloody sledgehammer, George. I'll goo by meself if needs be. I arn't agoing to turn me collar just because a few soddin' farmers on horseback and some bloody shopkeepers and arse-crawlers wi' Crown staves am coming agen me. You lot can do what you will, but I'm agoing to do as I swore I 'ud. I'm agoing to smash those bloody stamps and presses, though the Devil hisself should try to bar me way.'

He actually laid his hand on George Paddock's hammer and tried to take it from him, but the other man tugged the tool free and protested angrily.

'Leave it be, Lawyer. I'm feared o' no man and I stands true to me given word. I swore I'd smash those bloody engines, and smash them I 'ull. It's only that these tidings Taffy brought us took me back a bit, that's all. But now I knows all about it, well then, so be it. I'll not turn my collar neither.'

'That's the spirit, Cully!' Lawyer Court applauded loudly, and swung to ask the other men, 'How about you lot, are you still with George and me?'

Now they did shout in unison, 'Yes, we're with you,' and Seth Boulton's drumbeat pounded and Joe Dunsby's fife began to shrill out the rousing tune, 'Hearts of Oak'.

While the rest of the men began to roar out the words of the song at the tops of their voices, Lawyer Court stalked into the middle of the roadway and blew long blasts on his trumpet, until from the doors and window-casements of the nearby houses and cottages frowsty heads poked out and voices demanded to know what was happening.

'We'em off to Redditch, to smash the stamps and presses!' Lawyer Court bellowed. 'We'em agoing to stop the masters starving us all into our graves! Does you want to be one on us? Or 'ud you sooner be known as cowards for the rest o' your lives? And be mocked for being such by your own kids, because you arn't had the guts to fight alongside us to put food back into their empty bellies?'

Again and again the trumpet blast echoed through the still air, and again and again he roared challengingly at them, until many of the younger, more hot-headed of the men and women came hurrying to join him, and even the more cautious decided to follow on and see the fun. The crowd marshalled into a rough formation headed by drum, fife, trumpet and sledgehammers, and surrounded by swarms of yelling excited children and barking dogs, set out along the straight road towards Redditch Town.

Down Mount Pleasant they marched and on down the Front Hill into the Evesham Street, and the news of their coming spread like wildfire through the town, and from the slum courts and alleys, and from the respectable streets, the wild ones and the desperate ones came to swell their numbers.

Joseph Cashmore heard the shouting, and the thudding and shrilling of drum and fife, and came out from his cottage in the Evesham Street. He was a man of great physical courage, but alone he knew that he was powerless to do anything to halt this rampaging mob. He followed after them until they halted outside the Fox and Goose Inn in the market place.

Thomas Fowkes, the massively fat landlord, came to the door of his establishment, and his puce-complexioned face blanched when he saw their mood and numbers. His inn was a favoured meeting place and drink den of many of the needle masters and as such an object of resentment to the soft workers. He slammed his front door and bolted it just as the first clods of mud and stone smashed in his front windows. Panting and whimpering Fowkes scurried into his cellar and hid himself in its darkest corner, until the onslaught petered out, and the mob took up and obeyed Lawyer Court's shouted commands to move on.

'On to Bredon! On to Bayliss's! On to Bredon! On to Bayliss's!'

Roaring and screaming the mob marched on towards

its next target, leaving the Fox and Goose with all its windows smashed and its white-washed walls covered with the filth of the gutters.

As Cashmore hurried down the Fish Hill towards John Clayton's house, he met the young clergyman already on his way towards the town centre. Quickly he told him what was happening and John Clayton listened without interruption until he had heard the full story.

'Come with me and I'll lend you a horse, Master Cashmore. You must go down to Studley and alert Constable Shayler, tell him to send a messenger to the Reverend Palmer in Alcester. Then get back here as quickly as you can and get word to the masters to muster their loyal workers on the Chapel Green. I shall go direct to Captain Emmot's house and then on to Lord Aston's. I shall then return here.'

'Perhaps if you and me went down to Bredon together we could stop the mob ourselves, Parson Clayton?' Cashmore suggested.

The clergyman grinned mirthlessly. 'I'm in no mind to play at being King Canute, Master Cashmore. It will require a sight more strength than you and I alone can put forth to stop these fellows. The poor devils have been driven to such a degree of desperation that I fear only bloodshed will stop them now.'

He shook his head and sighed heavily. 'Between ourselves, Master Cashmore, I confess to feeling a deal of sympathy with them. I fear that if I were a soft worker, then I would be wielding a sledgehammer myself this day. Come now, let's get the horses.'

As the mob streamed past the Salters Yard its inhabitants gathered on the cobbles before their houses to watch. Charlie Duggins shouted, 'Am you going to smash Henry Milward's stamps?'

And some of the marchers invited him, 'Come and help us do it! Then you can make sure that we smashes 'um!'

'Doon't goo, Charlie! You'll only end up in trouble.

Doon't goo!' Emma Duggins begged him tearfully, but other women in the yard urged, 'Goo wi' 'um, Charlie. Get a bit o' your own back on the soddin' masters!'

'Doon't, Charlie! Doon't.' His wife clutched his arm, but he roughly tore himself free of her grip and clambered over the low brick wall to be swallowed up in the crowd. Emma Duggins threw her apron up over her face and slumped down onto her knees, sobbing helplessly, and Tildy went to her side and put her arms around the other woman's heaving shoulders.

'There now, Emma, don't upset yourself so. He'll come to no harm.' She lifted the woman to her feet and drew her into the house.

Old Esther was stood at the doorway, holding Davy tightly by the hand so that he could not break free and run with the swarms of shrieking children trailing after the mob.

'Mam, Mam, tell Nanny Esther to let me go. Tell her, Mam!' he begged his mother, but Tildy only frowned and told him sharply, 'You'll stay here! And I want no argument about it.'

The child stared at his mother's pale stern face, so unlike her normal pleasant expression, and wisely forbore to argue further.

'You set yourself down there, Emma.' Tildy lowered the other woman onto a chair, then she lifted her shawl from its hook and drew it around her head and shoulders.

'Wheer does you think youm agoing to?' old Esther demanded.

'I must go down and warn Daniel and Brandon,' Tildy told her.

The old woman's fear made her reply harshly, 'Doon't you be such a bloody fool, my wench! You'll not goo out o' this house!'

'Hold your tongue Esther!' Tildy's own fears were making her react with an unaccustomed irritability. 'I'll do as I please.'

'But it anna safe, my duck!' the old woman wailed.

'You could get your yed busted, or wuss even!'

'It's the stamps they're wanting to bust, Esther, not my head.' Tildy would brook no further hindrance, and told Davy, 'You stay here and look after Nanny Esther until I get back. Promise me that you will.'

His small face was very solemn as he nodded. 'I promise, Mam.'

She smiled and kissed him. 'Good boy.' Then she slipped from the house and ran to the rear of the Salters Yard and made her way towards a narrow footpath that wound through the fields towards Bredon.

'Let them stop at Milward's first, God,' she begged silently as she hurried along the winding track. 'Please let them stop at Milward's first, and give me the time to get to Daniel.'

When she reached Brandon Whittle's small factory she found that the word of the rioters' approach had preceded her, and Brandon Whittle was busily dismantling his stamp and eye press. He had already taken the precious dies and flung them into the deep cesspit of the privy to hide them.

He was alone in the factory, and when Tildy asked where the other workers were, the old man told her, 'I sent 'um all home just as soon as I heard that the soft workers was on the march. I didn't want any on 'um to see wheer I'se hid the dies, or wheer I'm agoing to hide this lot when I'se done wi' stripping it.'

'But where's Daniel?' she beseeched.

'Ohh, he went down to Alcester fust thing this morning to take a special order to the Stratford coach. He doon't know aught about what's going on here.' Brandon Whittle grinned ruefully. 'And I'll tell you summat, my duck, just as soon as I'se got this lot hid, then I'm off meself. I'm too bloody old to be fighting wi' a lot o' roughnecks at my age. Iffen they wants to burn this place down, then let 'um. But I'll not be inside on it.'

Tildy asked, 'Do you want me to help you here, Brandon?'

'Ahh, all right, then.' He nodded at the parts of the stripped down eye press. 'Take whatever you can lift o' them and chuck 'um into the privy. I don't reckon anybody 'ull be wanting to search among the shit and piss, does you?'

Tildy shook her head queasily, and could not help but smile wryly. 'The only trouble is, Brandon, who is going to get all these parts out of the privy when the trouble's over?'

The old man chuckled hoarsely. 'We'll argue about that when the time comes, my duck.'

The two of them worked feverishly, and in a surprisingly short space of time the metal machine parts were all hidden in the stinking hole in the privy.

'Do you know which way Daniel will be coming back from Alcester? The top road through the Crosses, or the bottom, by way of Green Lane?' Tildy asked.

'He said he was agoing to call in at Green Lane on his way back and have a word wi' Abel Morrall,' the old man told her.

'I'll go down and wait for him there then,' Tildy decided.

'All right, my duck. You take care though. I'm off home meself.'

The couple parted outside the wooden shed, and in the distance they could hear trumpet blasts and the rumble of many shouting voices.

'I reckon we was only just in time, girl.' Brandon Whittle winked. 'Let's hope they doon't burn the place down. See you later.'

Chapter Thirty-Two

Lord Aston faced the line of men outside the front doors of Saint Stephen's Chapel, and told them, 'I wish you all to raise your right arms and to repeat the following oath after me, giving your own names in the first sentence. Is that understood by all of you?'

His breath wheezed in his chest as the cold air struck into his lungs, and he scowled disagreeably as he waited for their murmurs of assent. Then he continued in a loud voice:

'I, give your own names, do swear that I will well and truly serve our sovereign lord, the King, in the office of special constable for the Parish of Tardebigge without favour or affection, malice or ill-will; and that I will, to the best of my power, cause the peace to be kept and preserved, and prevent all offences against the persons and properties of His Majesty's subjects; and that while I continue to hold the said office I will, to the best of my skill and knowledge, discharge all the duties thereof faithfully according to law. So help me God . . .'

At Lord Aston's side his fellow magistrate, the Reverend Mark Pyndar, MA, waited until the last mumbled repetitions had ceased and then shouted, 'File past Reverend Clayton and collect your staff of office.'

The line of men moved to where John Clayton was standing with a large wickerwork pannier before him, filled with blue-painted wooden truncheons, two feet long, and each one bearing a gold embossed numeral. At Clayton's side Joseph Davis, clerk to the vestry, noted each man's name and the number his truncheon bore in a small ledger.

Lord Aston squinted his eyes and stared around him, then muttered angrily beneath his breath. His colleague, the Reverend Pyndar smiled secretly at this display, and to add to his fellow magistrate's discomfiture, observed with apparent regret, 'It's a poor sort of loyalty the men of your parish are displaying towards you, my lord. There's not yet thirty sworn in as constables, and it's almost one of the clock.'

Aston's flabby face flushed with anger at this covert gibe, but before he could make any reply Joseph Cashmore came up to him and saluted by touching the crown of his long staff to the brim of his tricorn hat.

'Well, Cashmore, make your report, man,' Aston snapped.

'Theer's nigh on five or six hundred gathered at the Big Pool now, my lord, men, women and childer. Henry Milward's stamp and presses have been smashed, likewise Thomas Bayliss's. Brandon Whittle's workshop was deserted when the rioters got theer and no damage was done to anything theer, as far as I can make out.'

'Has anyone been injured?' Aston wanted to know.

Cashmore shook his head ponderously. 'No, my lord, not up to when I left, anyways. It seems that so long as they was let at the stamps and presses without hindrance, then the rioters didn't offer any harm to anything else. All they seems interested in is to smash them new machines, my lord.'

'What news from the other factories, Master Cashmore?' the Reverend Pyndar came in. 'Are the masters bringing their loyal workers down here to be sworn in as constables?'

'Well, sir, according to what my deputies tells me, it seems that the masters be more interested in putting their factories in a state o' defence. I canna spake for the outlying districts o' course, but here in the town that seems to be the state on it. I doon't reckon that we'll be having any more men come in to be sworn than we'se got here at present.'

281

'Any sign of the yeomanry?' Lord Aston questioned, and again the constable's heavy head shook ponderously in negation.

'No my lord, although one o' my chaps did catch a sight o' Captain Emmot agalloping towards Alvechurch an hour or two since.'

'Damn and blast it!' Aston's temper snapped. 'Here I stand doing my damnedest to find men enough to disperse these rioters, and the very people whose property I am trying to protect, will not budge an inch from their factories, but must cower behind their own walls preparing to be put under siege. It don't bear thinking of, do it! I'll take my oath it don't!'

He began to pace up and down, then came to a sudden halt and shouted at his coachman to bring his carriage up. Next he beckoned to John Clayton, Reverend Pyndar and Joseph Cashmore to come to him.

'Now, Clayton, you must remain here with Cashmore until I return. Myself and Reverend Pyndar will go direct to Feckenham and swear in the men who should be awaiting our arrival there. Hopefully when we return with the Feckenham men we should be of a sufficient number disperse the rioters and make an arrest of their ring-leaders.'

John Clayton's lips curled with contempt. 'Surely, my lord, we have sufficient numbers here already to make the attempt to disperse the crowd. Let us go in a body to the Big Pool now and read out the riot act, my lord, so that any misguided ones among the crowd may be brought to the realisation of the gravity of what they are about.'

Lord Aston's jowls quivered as he indignantly rebuffed that suggestion. 'Don't talk like a fool, man. I've had much experience of such matters. If we attempt to disperse them with insufficient strength and they overcome us, then this town could well be sacked and pillaged before troops could be brought in to restore order. Remember Clayton, that if you had done as I commanded you to do yesterday, if you had taken the warrant to Captain Emmot earlier than this morning, then we'd not be in such a predicament. We'd have the yeomanry at our backs, instead of them being the Lord only knows where.'

Clayton bit back the angry retort which sprang to his lips, accepting that there was some justification in what his employer said.

'Send a messenger to Studley,' Lord Aston went on. 'Inform the Reverend Palmer of the situation here and warn him that the rioters may well attack the Morrall's factory in Green Lane.'

'What do you wish me to do if the rioters should begin attacking the shops and taverns, my lord?' Clayton wanted to know.

Aston briefly pondered, then shrugged his meaty shoulders helplessly. 'You must do what you can to prevent it, Clayton. But I hope that, for the time being at least, they will content themselves with smashing only the stamps and presses.'

At the Big Pool Lawyer Court was using a heap of rubble as a makeshift podium from which to address the crowd. Personally he was well satisfied with the way things had gone up to now. The hated stamps and presses had been smashed to smithereens at Milward's and Bayliss's, and his spies had just come running to tell him of the scant numbers of special constables being sworn in at the chapel. The only yeoman cavalrymen seen had been tiny isolated groups apparently galloping frantically, seeking for their fellows.

Court called down a silent blessing for the fact that the needle district was split between so many parishes, and between two counties. This meant that the special constables being mustered by the magistrates just across the boundary of Warwickshire in Studley Village could not be invoked. Thus Lawyer Court's united forces were faced by divided forces. The yeomanry cavalry were similarly restricted by the law, and it was very unlikely that they would be allowed to pursue and take action against his men once they had crossed the county boundary to attack the needle mills in Studley and Ipsley.

'... so then, let's get down to Morrall's and finish what we've begun.' Court held up both his arms, 'But let's keep our discipline. We want only to smash the stamps and presses! We must not offer insult or harm to any innocent person, or to that person's property. Now, my lads, on to Morrall's!'

A roar of cheering greeted his final shouted words and once again the musicians and sledge-hammers led the procession from the Big Pool down the Ipsley Street towards Bredon and the Holloway Lane that led to Studley and the Morrall's factory.

Abel Chance, Johnno Hancox and Charlie Powell marched along with the rest. Much to their chagrin they had been still sleeping off the effects of the previous night's drunken debauch when the mob had smashed Milward's and Bayliss's stamps and presses, and Abel Chance in particular was seething at the missed opportunity to even his score with Daniel Lambert.

'I could ha' set fire to his and Brandon Whittle's factory,' he thought bitterly. 'Wi' a mob inside it, like there was, then nobody could ha' proved who'd started the flames agoing. Fuck my luck! Still, iffen I just boxes clever now, then I'm bound to get another chance at settling wi' Daniel Lambert afore this is all over.'

Cheered by this thought, he grinned and shouted lustily in concert with his fellows. 'On to Morrall's! On to Morrall's! On to Morrall's!'

Abel Morrall's factory at Green Lane stood on the outskirts of Studley Village on the road leading to Redditch. It was a long two-storeyed, red-brick structure consisting of a mélange of dwelling houses and workshops, and at each end it had a castellated tower. The local wags called the curious construction 'Abel's Castle'. Now its garrison of workmen and their families were fortifying that castle against attack. Shutters were being nailed across the windows, barricades constructed at its doors. Old sporting guns, and muskets and pistols were hurriedly cleaned and loaded, and lookouts stood on top of the two towers scanning the approaches for sign of the rioters. Under the formidable Abel Morrall's supervision, pits were being dug in the gardens of the dwelling houses and the dismantled stamps and presses buried in them.

Racked by indecision, Tildy stood outside the factory. Daniel had not arrived there, and now she wondered what her best course of action might be.

'Theer they be! Theer they be! Theer's bloody thousands on 'um!' the lookout screamed from the top of the tower, and his panic instantly infected those who heard him. Women shrieked and sobbed, children wailed, and men cursed and shouted. William Shayler, the Studley constable was with Abel Morrall watching the last clods of turf being replaced over the spots where the machinery was buried.

'You get your men posted, Abel,' Will Shayler told the needle master, 'and I'll goo and take a look outside.'

Three of his regular deputy constables were with him, and he instructed one of them, 'Run down to the Barley Mow, just as quick as you can, Reggie, and tell Reverend Palmer that the rioters be here.'

Outside in the roadway Tildy heard the screamed warnings of the lookout and bit her lips apprehensively as she stared up the Redditch Road. Its rutted, frosty surface ran almost straight for nearly a mile, and at first she could see no sign of life. She began to think that the man in the tower had allowed his fears to overcome him to the extent that he was hallucinating, but then, in the distance, the first ranks of the approaching rioters came into her view, and a new-sprung breeze carried the faint thudding of a drumbeat to her ears.

'What in hell's name be you adoing here, Tildy Crawford?'

Will Shayler came behind her and, startled, she cried

out and swung round to face him.

'Doon't be scared, my duck, 'tis only me,' he reassured, and asked again, 'but what be you adoing here?'

Quickly she explained that she had come in search of Daniel Lambert.

'Well he arn't here, is he? So the best thing you can do, my wench, is to get off away from this place afore the trouble starts. Now I must go and fetch my special constables up here.'

He turned on his heels and hurried back towards the village, and Tildy decided that she might just as well follow his advice, because if Daniel were not here, then he might be anywhere. She pulled her shawl up over her head and decided to take the quickest route back to her home. This meant that she would have to pass the approaching rioters, but they were much nearer now and she could see that crowds of women and children were following the ranks of men.

'I'll be safe enough,' she concluded. 'After all, it's only the machinery they've come for. Besides, if I keep well muffled, nobody will know me anyway.'

She went into the field bordering the road and began to make her way towards the oncoming crowd. Then a sudden desire to stay where she was and watch all these exciting events take place burgeoned within her. Although commonsense told her that this was foolishness, she found that the desire to see what was to happen abruptly gripped her with such force that she came to a standstill and swung around. The ground sloped sharply upwards to form a natural vantage point and Tildy climbed the few paces necessary to bring her onto this point from where, over the hedgerow, she had a clear view of the roadway and the factory.

At that moment Daniel Lambert was in fact only half a mile away from the Green Lane. He was passing the ancient half-timbered Barley Mow Inn in Studley village, in front of which the Reverend Frederick Palmer, and his fellow magistrate, the Reverend Francis Rufford, only a few minutes since had been swearing in special constables.

To one side of the square a group of gentlemen were sitting on horseback, laughing and joking and drinking glasses of ale and spirits brought out to them by the waiters of the Barley Mow. As Daniel Lambert came abreast of them, one of the group hailed him, 'How now, Master Lambert, have you heard what's happening in Redditch?'

It was Robert Knight, Daniel's old gambling adversary who had spoken, and Daniel reined in to answer him.

'Good afternoon to you, Master Knight. No, I don't know what's afoot. I've been in Alcester since early this morning.'

Although there was no shared liking between the two men, there was a mutual sense of respect. Daniel respected this man for the sportsmanship he had shown concerning his, Daniel's, gambling debt. Knight had accepted Daniel's word that he would eventually be paid in full, and had not pressured him in any way. In return Robert Knight respected the fact that Daniel had immediately paid that debt in full when his house had been sold.

'The soft workers have gone on the rampage, Lambert. They're smashing the stamps and presses,' Knight informed.

An immediate fear for his loved ones struck through Daniel. 'Has anyone been harmed by them?'

The other man shook his head. 'Not according to the tidings we've received. Strangely enough they appear to be well disciplined in their actions. Apparently they only attack the machines, and if no one attempts to bar them from that, then nothing else is touched.' He smiled grimly. 'I don't think that such restraint will continue however. Once the notion takes them to loot the alehouses then they'll behave like the brute beasts they are.'

'Not here they won't, Knight!' one of his companions blustered, and pulled a large pistol from his saddle holster

287

and brandished it threateningly. 'I'll blow their damned tripes out first.'

Although Daniel's overwhelming instinct was to put spurs to his mount and gallop off in search of Tildy, yet he knew that the more information he could gain now, the better. So restraining his impatience, he asked, 'Where are the rioters reported to be now?'

'On their way here.' Knight's thin lips curved in a smile of anticipation. 'But we are well prepared for them. See there.' He pointed to where a body of men were marching quickly away from the square.

'There go the last of the special constables under the command of our redoubtable Reverend Palmer,' he laughed sneeringly. 'We intend to let them get their heads broke and then we shall ride to their rescue and teach these damned soft workers not to annoy their betters. Do you wish to ride with us, Lambert?'

Daniel could not help but smile bleakly himself at the irony of the situation, that he, an ex-convict should be invited to aid the self-appointed upholders of law and order. He shook his head. 'I've a wife and loved ones in Redditch, Knight. I must go now and see to them.'

'Then you'd do well to take the top road through the Crosses, Lambert,' Knight advised. 'Because the rioters are already at Morrall's factory just along the bottom road there. It might well go hard with you if any one of them should recognise your face. I'm told that you have become one of those same stamping masters they hate so much.'

Daniel briefly considered that advice, but he knew that it would add length to his journey. 'My thanks for your concern, Knight, but time is pressing. I must take my chances on the bottom road. I bid you a good day, sir.'

He touched the peak of his riding cap and rode on.

The Studley special constables were drawn up in a body across the roadway some yards further towards Redditch from the Green Lane and the factory buildings. Twenty paces distant from them the crowd of rioters had come to a halt and the Reverend Frederick Palmer, dressed in his clerical garb, and a high top hat perched on top of his white tie-wig, looking incongruously tiny by the side of the bulky William Shayler, advanced steadily towards them.

In the front rank of the crowd Lawyer Court was flanked by his trusted henchmen, grim-faced and silent. The reverend and the constable came to a halt ten paces from Lawyer Court, and in his high-pitched, shrill voice Palmer began to read from the parchment he carried in his hands.

'Our sovereign lord the King chargeth and commandeth all persons, being assembled, immediately to disperse themselves, and peaceably to depart to their habitations, or to their lawful business, upon the pains contained in the act made in the first year of King George, for preventing tumults and riotous assemblies. GOD SAVE THE KING!'

As soon as he had finished reading, the clergyman and constable turned round and went back to the lines of special constables.

This reading of the riot act caused many of the more knowledgeable of the soft workers to reconsider their present course of action. They knew that if twelve or more rioters remained on the ground for one hour after the act had been read, then the penalties for those rioters were savage: transportation from fifteen years to life, or penal servitude from six years to life. Many of the more cautious and timid men began to sidle away from the main body of the mob, mingling with the crowds of spectators in the hedgerows and fields next to the roadway.

Standing directly behind Lawyer Court and the sledge-hammer men, Abel Chance suddenly spotted Daniel Lambert trotting up behind the lines of special constables. He nudged Charlie Powell.

'Theer's the barstard who gi' you a leathering, Charlie. He's looking mighty tall and proud, arn't he? Fuckin' stamping bastard that he is!'

Lawyer Court was shouting at the opposing ranks of

special constables. 'Youm only damaging yourselves by coming against us, brothers. Why should you defend the very men who'm agoing to throw you all out o' work? It's the Morralls who brought the bloody stamps and presses into this district and it's them who'll be putting you out o' work. You should be with us, not with them. Stand aside and let us through.'

Daniel reined in behind the constables, and Tildy saw him and waved in a vain attempt to attract his attention. In the mob Abel Chance bent and lifted some large stones from the roadway and handed them to his two companions.

'When I gives the word, let fly at that bastard Lambert,' he whispered, and Hancox and Powell nodded.

Lawyer Court knew that he must act quickly. He was well aware that the longer the mob remained at a standstill, then the less likelihood there would be of it being galvanised once more into violent action. He glanced at the men on each side of him, and ordered Seth Boulton, 'Rattle that bloody drum, Seth. The rest on you, stick close to me.' He bellowed at the top of his voice, 'Smash the stamps! Smash the stamps! Smash the stamps! Come on all o' you! Smash the stamps!'

The drumbeat pounded and he and his friends ran at the line of constables, and as they started forward Abel Chance shouted, 'Now boys!' and hurled the heavy stone at Daniel Lambert.

Tildy cried out as she saw the missiles striking Daniel's head and body and he reeled and fell from the saddle. His horse reared in fright and lashed out with its front hooves, catching the men in front of it and sending them staggering into the leading rank of constables. This totally unexpected impact caused the front rank to lose its cohesion, and Lawyer Court and his henchmen crashed through the resulting gap.

'Stand your ground! Stand and fight, damn you!' William Shayler bawled, and leapt into the forefront, his long staff cracking and breaking heads. Rallied by him the lines of constables reformed and succeeded in beating back the hotheads who tried to follow Court and his group. These latter, numbering a dozen men, ran on towards the Morrall factory. Tildy ran from the field and tried to force a way through the struggling, shouting, cursing mêlée to get to Daniel's side.

Up in the tower of his factory, Abel Morrall watched Lawyer Court's group and shouted to those men with him, 'Open fire, lads!' He aimed his old musket at Lawyer Court and pulled the trigger. The heavy slug tore into Court's shoulder and its impact spun the man completely around and dropped him. Other guns roared, and two others in the charging group screamed and dropped. The shock of this happening brought the remaining men to a standstill and, when Abel Morrall snatched up an old long barrelled pistol and fired a charge of heavy pellets at them, they broke and scattered.

Abel Chance, Charlie Powell and Johnno Hanncox were still battling with the special constables, trying to break through and get at Daniel Lambert, who was now painfully struggling to rise to his feet, still badly winded and dazed from the stones and fall. The gunfire kept most of the mob from advancing, and the constables were consequently only fighting with a small proportion of the more reckless and hotheaded. But that fighting was savage and ruthless, and men fell or were sent staggering with bloodied heads and broken bones.

Tildy herself was bleeding from a cut on her forehead where a stave had caught her a glancing blow and she was forced to give up her attempt to break through the mêlée. She ran back to the higher ground and anxiously peered for some sight of Daniel. Then from along the Redditch Road there sounded a trumpet call, and the crowd took up the cry:

'It's the cavalry come! It's the yeomanry!'

Tildy saw the scarlet coats and bell-topped shakoes of the advancing horsemen, and could have sobbed with relief.

Those of the mob who were still battling with the constables realised that they were caught between two forces, and most of them turned and ran. Abel Chance broke free and wildly stared about him. He ducked a blow from a constable's staff and kicked the unfortunate man between the legs, then broke through a hedgerow and ran across the rising field, threading his way between the excited shouting spectators. Then on a small hillock before him, he saw Tildy Crawford, and recognised her as Daniel Lambert's woman. Maddened as he was by the fight, he still lusted to wreck vengeance on Daniel Lambert.

'I'll have you, you fuckin' cow!' he panted out, and started up the hillock towards her.

Tildy saw him coming, and knew that she was facing death. She realised that she would stand no chance physically of fighting him off, so took refuge in flight. Gathering her skirts up in her hands she fled down the opposite slope and ran towards the roadway and the approaching yeomanry cavalry. Like a ravening predator Chance came after her, and his superior strength and fitness quickly told as he inexorably shortened the distance between them.

Tildy's lungs were straining and her muscles cramping agonisingly, but she forced herself on. Strangely it was not blind terror that was dominating her. She felt fear, but her mind was working even as she heard his hoarse panting breath coming closer and closer to her.

A young cavalryman suddenly sighted the fleeing woman and her pursuer, and realised instantly that she was in mortal peril. Without asking permission he wheeled his horse from the column and through a broken place in the hedgerow, then spurred it into a gallop towards the running pair. Tildy saw him and changed course to meet him. Chance cursed and redoubled his effort to catch her, he drew close enough to stretch out his hand and snatch at her long flying hair, and as he did so Tildy suddenly dropped to the ground and balled her body. Chance's flying feet collided with her and he went flying over her to sprawl helplessly face downwards on the ground. Before he could recover himself the yeoman had reached him, and his long curved sabre was hovering menacingly over Chance's head. Two more cavalrymen came galloping up, and dismounted to pinion Chance's body, and tie his arms behind him with a piece of rope.

Tildy could not draw breath enough to thank her rescuers and could only thank them with her eyes and hands as she struggled to breathe. She stood watching them drag the cursing, struggling Chance away, and then turned to go in search of Daniel.

All across the fields were running figures, and scarlet coated cavalrymen in hot pursuit of those who fled. Tildy walked slowly through the crowds that still noisily seethed along the road towards the Morralls factory, and then smiled in heartfelt relief as she saw Daniel limping towards her. He waved and called her name, and hobbled faster as she ran to meet him.

'I've lost my damned horse.' He grinned down at her and bent to kiss her lips.

'Never mind,' she smiled at him. 'You've found me ... let's go home.' She chuckled mischievously. 'You're going to have to fish our stamp and presses out from their hiding place, arn't you?'

<u>TILDY</u>

Sara Fraser

Set against the savage background of an 1820s Midlands
nailmaking community this is the powerful story of a
young woman of remarkable courage.

TILDY

She rises out of poverty to become domestic servant in a
squire's household only to be unfairly dismissed and so
find herself once again looking for work and a home in an
inhospitable land.

TILDY

Encumbered with a husband she doesn't want, heavy
with child and fearful of consignment to the poorhouse
she joins the badly exploited Bromsgrove nailers to put
food in their bellies.

TILDY

But never daunted, courageous, beautiful, determined she
becomes the spirited challenger of the nailers' oppressors
and with fist raised lays claim to a better future for herself
and her unborn child . . .

NURSING WOMAN

Sara Fraser

Autumn, 1821. Tildy's story continues amid poverty and violence in the Midlands, as she learns what cruelty can exist among the rich too.

TILDY

Freed from the Poorhouse, Tildy must earn a living as best she can. Her experience of caring for the sick in the Poorhouse will now, she hopes, stand her in good stead.

NURSING WOMAN

The job she lands as nurse to the invalid Mrs Dugdale means Tildy is forced to leave baby Davy in the dubious care of a child minder. When she suspects her master of ill-treating her helpless patient Tildy needs all her considerable courage to defy him, his sinister cronies and the dark doings she secretly witnesses. But further horrors await her . . .

POINTING WOMAN

Sara Fraser

In the autumn of 1822 Tildy has found employment as nurse to the aged mother of Charles Burke Bromley. Safe and sheltered with baby Davy, she nevertheless feels compelled to leave her haven after she turns down Bromley's offer of marriage. Back in the rough outside world, Tildy gets work in the needle trade – arduous and ill-paid.

POINTING WOMAN

Then her absent husband Tom Crawford erupts back into her life. Horrified, Tildy refuses to live with him again. But Crawford is a desperate man and will stop at nothing to force Tildy's hand – not even child-snatching . . . Searching for Davy, Tildy takes well-paid work as a 'pointer', grinding needles. But the male pointers will not let go of their supremacy without a struggle.

TILDY

Alone, she takes her stand against the might of law and order seemingly united against her as she determines to reclaim her child.

GANG WOMAN

Sara Fraser

By the summer of 1823, Tildy has been laid off from her
work at the needle mill and is relying on parish relief to
keep herself and little Davy. But the filthy conditions at
Tildy's lodgings threaten Davy's health; she is desperate
to take him somewhere more wholesome.

TILDY

Then the women and children paupers are rented out to
farmers as field gangs, slaving outdoors under the pitiless
eye of overseer Jeremiah Borth. This back-breaking
labour taxes even Tildy's courage to the limit; however
her luck changes when she starts work in the farmhouse
and Davy can join her. Arthur Winterton the owner is a
hard man, but his son Tobias, smitten with Tildy's
loveliness, seems determined to look after her.

GANG WOMAN

Life never stays settled for long where Tildy is concerned.
Sinister events at the Wintertons' farm compel her to take
refuge with Esther Smith the wisewoman – or, as some
claim, witch. Safe there, Tildy must nevertheless confront
danger once more before she can free herself from its
shadow.